DREAM HOUSE

DREAM HOUSE

ROCHELLE KRICH

BALLANTINE BOOKS • NEW YORK

In memory of my beloved father

Abraham Majer

*He taught us about peace and courage
and the sweet, uplifting magic of song.*

ACKNOWLEDGMENTS

Dream House wouldn't be standing without the nuts and bolts and other material graciously supplied by many people: Phil Bacerra, Los Angeles City Planning Department, and Officer Jack Richter, L.A.P.D. Media Relations. Susan Keirm enlightened me about home health care. Lee Barocas, County Inspector, Parks and Recreation, Capital Projects, and Shemaya Mandelbaum, Mirage Construction, explained building procedures and ordinances, and Meg Chittenden gave me concrete facts about concrete. John Chadbourne, equity title sales representative; Agavni Sandaldzhyan, full service banking specialist; and Benjamin Westreich, attorney at law, unraveled the nuances of real estate and title law and banking procedures. *Mi amiga* and former colleague Kathleen Gongosy told me the "truth," in Spanish; Maria Lima verified it. Paul Glasser, Associate Dean, Max Weinreich Center at the YIVO Institute, polished my Yiddish, and I hope he doesn't cringe too much at my regional spellings and pronunciations.

Detective Paul Bishop, West L.A., keeps my police procedure straight. Deputy District Attorney Mary Hanlon Stone keeps me legal. D. P. Lyle, M.D., author of the comprehensive and invaluable resource tool *Murder and Mayhem,* has all the answers to my forensics questions. For newspaper protocol I turned to Denise Hamilton, fellow mystery writer and journalist. Dr. Jonathan Hulkower, attending psychiatrist, Cedars-Sinai Medical Center, shared his medical and pharmacological knowledge. On a personal note, my brother and I are grateful for the tenderness and patience Dr. Hulkower showed our ailing father. My son, David, was my biblical consultant; and in what has become tradition, my daughter, Sabina, read the blueprints for *Dream House* and made suggestions that enhanced its framing.

I'm especially indebted to architect Michael Rosenberg. Michael was always available to answer my many questions about architecture and historical preservation in Los Angeles—its pros and cons. His passion about the subject fueled my interest, and his knowledge contributed to the background of the novel.

Many thanks to my wise and wonderful editors, Joe Blades and Patricia Peters; to my indefatigable agent, Sandra Dijkstra, and her staff, with special appreciation to Elisabeth James for "righting" my rights, and to Babette Sparr. Babette introduced Molly to Eileen Hutton (Brilliance Audio), who took Molly to a new audience, and to Liza Wachter, who took her to Hollywood. Thanks to Lisa Collins, who found several gaffes that would have kept *Dream House* from passing final inspection. To Ruth Blake and Margaret Winter and all the other Ballantine sales representatives who log thousands of miles to present my work to booksellers around the country. To Michelle Aielli, Marie Coolman, Kim Hovey, and Heather Smith for their creative efforts and the many long hours they spend to make sure I don't stay anonymous. To Carolyn Hessel of the Jewish Book Council, for taking me under her wing. To all the Jewish book fair chairpersons, booksellers, and readers who invite me to tell my stories.

I'm grateful to have people in my life who fill my days with meaning and joy. My Buds, my Monday night mah jonggs, my friends, and my extended family.

And finally, to my husband, Hershie, our children and their spouses, and our grandchildren: You are my foundation. Thank you for making our house a dream.

Rochelle Krich

A Note on Pronunciation

Yiddish has certain consonant sounds that have no English equivalent—in particular the guttural *ch* (achieved by clearing one's throat) that sounds like the *ch* in *Bach* or in the German *ach*.

Some Yiddish historians and linguists, including the Yiddish Scientific Institute (YIVO—Yidisher Visenshaftikhe Institut), spell this sound with a *kh* (*Khanukah, khalla*). Others use *ch* (*Chanukah, challa*). I've chosen to use *ch*.

To help the reader unfamiliar with Yiddish, I've also doubled some consonants (*chapp, gitte*).

> *Zh* is pronounced like the *s* in *treasure*.
> *Tsh* is pronounced like the *ch* in *lurch*.
> *Dzh* is pronounced like the *g* in *passage*.

Here are the YIVO guidelines for vowel pronunciation, which I've followed in most cases, except for those where regional pronunciations vary (*kliegeh* instead of *klugeh, gitte* instead of *gutte*):

> *a* as in *father* or *bother* (*a dank*—thanks)
> *ay* as in *try* (*shrayt*—yells)
> *e* as in *bed*, pronounced even when it's the final letter in the word (*naye*—new)
> *ey* as in *hay* (*beheyme*—animal)
> *i* as in *hid*, or in *me* (*Yid*—Jew)
> *o* as between *aw* in *pawn* and *u* in *lunch* (*hot*—has)
> *oy* as in *joy* (*loyfen*—to run)
> *u* as in *rule* (*hunt*—dog)

With a little practice, you'll sound just like Molly's Bubbie G.

—Rochelle Krich (*ch* as in *birch*, but that's another story)

For the pronunciation and definitions of Hebrew and Yiddish words used in *Dream House*, please see the glossary at the back. And while you're there, check out Bubbie G's recipe for challa.

CHAPTER ONE

IF YOU HAD ASKED ME BEFORE I HEARD OF MAGGIE Reston whether a house could be a magnet for murder, I would have automatically thought of The Dungeon, which is what we've always called the coal-gray house on Martel. As it turned out, I would have been wrong, but I would have been in good company. For as long as I can remember, everyone in the neighborhood has hated the three-story cube that hogs sky and sunlight and its gloomy facade, and has speculated about its reclusive owners.

The house has become the stuff of dark legend. As kids, my friends and I, intimidated by its brooding countenance, shivered as we whispered deliciously gruesome stories about occupants we never saw, men who kidnapped children and kept them in a

Chateau D'If–like basement. Years have passed. The flowers along the walk, beheaded regularly like Henry the Eighth's wives, have been replaced by threatening junglelike shrubs. But the house's charcoal walls are still decorated from time to time with bright-colored graffiti, probably by a new generation of kids who whisper about the bad guys inside.

I have learned that bad men have become brazen in the sunlight. I have learned that, as Tennyson says, "Woods have tongues /As walls have ears," and that dark houses are not necessarily those with dark secrets. But on that Monday morning I assumed the police report was about The Dungeon:

Friday, October 31. 9:37 P.M. 100 block of South Martel Avenue. A vandal threw a pumpkin through the front window of a house and several eggs at the front door.

It was probably another Halloween prank, I thought, all trick and no treat, a nasty, petty act. According to the police reports I'd read on my rounds of the stations, there had been Halloween vandalisms all over the city of angels—disheartening, but not surprising.

I copied the data from the Wilshire Division board for my weekly *Crime Sheet* column, the one that appears in the rubber-banded, sprinkler-soaked, sun-bleached independent tabloids you find on your lawn next to the Kmart and Target flyers. Several hours later, back in my apartment, I phoned my sister Mindy.

"It was The Dungeon, right?" I asked after I told her what I'd read. The house is across the street from hers.

"You'd think, huh?" Her sentence blossomed into a yawn. "No, it's the one-story taupe Tudor down the block. It looks awful, but they have someone repairing the damage right now." She yawned again.

Whoever said yawns are contagious was right. Mindy's

three-month-old son is the reason for hers. Mine are the result of another late-nighter with (Rabbi) Zack Abrams, the man in my life, although you'd think by now my body would have adjusted to sleep deprivation.

Not that I'm complaining. "Did you or Norm hear or see anything?"

Mindy laughed. "Are you serious, Molly? At nine-thirty on Friday Norm and the girls were sleeping, and I was trying to stay awake while nursing Yitz. We weren't exactly out trick-or-treating."

My family—my mom and dad and seven of us Blume kids (Mindy is second, I'm third)—is Orthodox Jewish and we observe the Sabbath. Even if Halloween hadn't fallen on Friday night, Mindy and Norm wouldn't have taken their two girls trick-or-treating (despite its commercialization and allure, the holiday has its origins in religious ritual), though they always stock up on Hershey's Kisses and Reese's Pieces for the children who come to their door. And for me.

Thinking of chocolate made me long for some, but I'd had my quota for the day. "Who lives in that house?"

"Walter Fennel. He thinks he owns the neighborhood."

Every neighborhood has a Walter Fennel. I scribbled his name on a pad, though the *Crime Sheet* doesn't identify victims. "I take it you don't like him."

"Walter's okay. He's kind of cute sometimes. But he's an eighty-year-old busybody with way too much time on his hands. He's Mister HARP. H-A-R-P? We call him Harpy."

I crinkled my nose at an image of the predatory bird. "Not a great name for an organization."

"They were thinking the musical instrument. That's their Web site logo. Community harmony and all that. Fennel headed our area board until a month ago. He still patrols the neighborhood daily looking for violators."

"One of whom may have lobbed the pumpkin and eggs?" I'd

heard Mindy and others complain about the Historic Architectural Restoration and Preservation board in their Miracle Mile North area. The members decide what you can do to your property's exterior—which, according to Mindy et al., isn't much.

"I'd hate to think it's a neighbor." There was a *but* in Mindy's voice. "Walter was harassing a homeowner on South Formosa about a new exterior light fixture, demanded to know whether he'd received HARP board approval. The homeowner, Ed Strom, told Walter to mind his own business."

"Strom?" I mentally scanned South Formosa and came up blank. Until five years ago, when I was twenty-four and left home to marry the philandering charmer who is now my ex, I'd grown up in the neighborhood, which has a large population of Orthodox Jews, many of whom I know.

"You wouldn't know him, Molly. He and his wife just moved here from New York. They bought the Gluckmans' house. Anyway, someone reported Strom to the board, and the city fined him. He refused to take down the fixture and swore he wouldn't pay the fine. Wednesday somebody ripped the fixture off the wall."

"Fennel."

"Fennel swears he doesn't know anything about it."

"I assume the police questioned Strom."

"He and his wife were with friends Friday night."

"He could've paid someone to do it," I said, pointing out the obvious. It's one of my failings.

"He *could* have. But a lot of the area homeowners are angry at HARP, Molly. They sympathize with Strom. Of course, Walter has his allies." Mindy sighed. "I'm all for preserving the neighborhood's character, but some HARP rulings are egregious, not to mention expensive. I don't think people realized how intrusive and controlling HARP could be. And it's all because of that damn house."

The Dungeon, I knew, had prompted area homeowners, anxious to prevent the construction of similarly oversize structures, to request HARP status. As my grandmother Bubbie G says, you have to be careful what you ask for.

"What's the makeup of the board?" I drained the last of my coffee and, with the cordless phone at my ear, padded barefoot to the kitchen for a refill.

"Five people, all appointed, so there's no neighborhood input. There's going to be an opening soon. I'm tempted to try to get on the board to add a little sanity, but until Yitz sleeps through the night, I'm too tired to commit to anything. I'm not even working full-time yet." She yawned again, as if to emphasize her point.

I yawned, too. Pavlov would have loved me. "When do they meet?"

"Once a month, seven P.M. on Thursdays. Unless there's an emergency. Why, are you planning on going?"

"Maybe. Sounds like good material for a feature."

In addition to penning my weekly *Crime Sheet* column, I'm a freelance reporter and I write books about true crime under my pseudonym, Morgan Blake. I also have income from a substantial divorce settlement I invested in property. I think I earned every penny, and if you met my ex-husband, Ron, you'd agree.

Right now I was between projects, as they say in Hollywood. I'd just pitched a piece to the L.A. *Times* on the latest outrage in the health care industry. This was prompted by my parents' insurer advising my mom that mammograms and ultrasounds are covered "in network" at the facilities she'd selected, those within reasonable driving distance of her home, but the radiologist's reading of the films isn't, if you can believe that.

I was also awaiting the galleys of my second book, *Sins of the Father*, and I'd completed the second draft of my newest true crime, *The Lady from Twentynine Palms*. I needed a few weeks to achieve objectivity and distance before I reread the manuscript, made changes, agonized about the book's worthiness, and FedExed it to my editor and agent. A HARP story sounded like the perfect filler.

"It's been done," Mindy said. "There was an article in the L.A. *Times* magazine a couple of years ago on another HARP. Whitley Heights, I think."

At least I hadn't spent hours on the piece. "I must have missed that."

"You can try a different angle. Some Hancock Park home-owners are pushing for HARP status. They got the city to commission a historical survey, which is a major step. Wednesday night they're presenting the survey and getting neighborhood reaction. Should be interesting."

"How do you know all this? From a client?" Mindy is a tax attorney, and many of her clients deal in real estate.

"From Edie. She's with the opposition."

Edie is the oldest Blume sibling. She's organized and determined and formidable once she's committed to a cause. "I see fireworks ahead."

"You see a story."

"Here's hoping," I said, ignoring Bubbie G's advice, and we both laughed.

CHAPTER TWO

AFTER GRABBING A HANDFUL OF KISSES FROM MY PANTRY (they're barricaded behind a pathetic first-line defense of cereal boxes and canned goods), I returned to my office and continued entering police data into my computer files.

If you've read my column or one like it, you're familiar with the kinds of crimes listed: car thefts, armed robbery, sexual and nonsexual assaults, DUIs, car thefts, stolen wallets, domestic violence, home burglaries, vandalized cars, shoplifting, car thefts, indecent exposure. And have I mentioned car thefts?

Until I started doing the column four years ago, I had no idea how often automobiles are stolen, which is all the time. So are personal items—purses, briefcases, wallets, cash, ID, checkbooks—that people leave in their jackets or on tables in restaurants or on their front porches or in their unlocked cars. A recent L.A. *Times* story told of an identity-theft ring that targeted Southern California and Vegas fitness clubs, many of whose members leave their wallets and purses in their cars while they're working up a sweat inside. Which raises the question: Why *do* people leave valuable personal property unattended?

Once in a while I'd love to write something like this:

> *A trusting soul who depended on the kindness of strangers left her purse on a nightclub chair while dancing and was shocked to find that her cell phone and wallet containing $210 had been stolen.*

In Arcata, a small town in Northern California's Humboldt County, there's a guy who writes a tongue-in-cheek and sometimes poetic police blotter, and I'm sure there are others like him around the country, but my editor, George, has excised all my attempts at creativity. Still, the *Crime Sheet* is quirky enough by virtue of the strange stuff that goes on in the city—the things people do and say to each other, most of it nasty, much of it bizarre. And you'd be amazed by the amount of mail we get. Some people love the column, some people hate it, but they sure do read it.

I finished entering the Wilshire Division data and found the item Mindy had told me about:

> *Wednesday, October 29, 10 P.M. 100 block of South Formosa Avenue. A vandal smashed an outside light fixture, then ripped it from the wall.*

I phoned Wilshire, asked for Burglary, and spoke to Detective Vince Porter, whom I'd seen just this morning. Which is what he said when he came on the line.

"What now, Blume? Didn't get enough for your column?"

Porter and I have a lukewarm relationship. He tolerates my questions and I try not to ask too many. Unspoken between us is the fact that my best friend, Aggie Lasher, was murdered five years ago, that the case has never been solved, and that I still phone Wilshire every few months, sometimes more often, to find out if any leads have surfaced. Although I direct those inquiries to Homicide, I'm sure all the detectives are aware of my nagging interest, and I suspect that's why they have me copy data from the big board instead of giving me sanitized photocopies of the police reports, the way some other division detectives do to make my job easier.

"About the light fixture ripped from the wall Wednesday night on South Formosa," I said. "Any idea who did it?"

"Not a clue. The homeowners were out, came back after eleven, and discovered the vandalism. Is that it?"

"What about Walter Fennel?"

"Walter who?"

I could tell he was playing with me. "The Walter on Martel whose house was vandalized Friday night, the Walter who was the reason Ed Strom was fined for violating a HARP ordinance. Obviously, there's a connection."

"For your information, Fennel and his wife were home watching TV at ten on Wednesday night."

"So they say."

"They're in their eighties, Blume."

"How hard is it to remove a light fixture?"

"Not hard if you can reach it. It was a stretch for me, and I'm five-eleven. Fennel is five-six. And before you ask, Strom's ladder was in his garage, which was locked."

"Maybe Fennel brought something along to stand on."

"Maybe *Mrs.* Fennel lifted him to do the deed." Porter snickered. "Give it up, Blume."

I tried picturing an eighty-year-old man dragging a stool four blocks and had to admit Porter was right. "What about the vandalism to Fennel's house?"

"Strom has a solid alibi. Friday was Halloween. It was probably kids."

"You don't find all this too coincidental?"

"Do you know something I don't?" he demanded.

"No." Even if I had information, I wouldn't have volunteered it. I don't respond well to snide.

"Thanks for your interest, Blume. It's good to know you're vigilant. We can all sleep better."

"If you find out anything—"

"You'll be the last to know," Porter said, enjoying his own sarcasm.

I accessed the L.A. *Times* online archives and found "The War of the Rosebushes." Great title. Great story, too, about the Hollywood Hills neighborhood, bisected by the Hollywood Freeway, that is home to some of the Industry's celebrities (Francis Coppola's family owns three houses there). It's also home to the garden that was the subject of the article, a garden one critic found "tacky and ridiculous" while supporters, including friends of the garden's creators (all in the Industry), called it "restorative," a "beautiful metaphor" for the "spiritual experience of an entire life."

The latter was a little de trop, I'll agree, and I suppose one man's Eden is another's Jurassic Park. But I was intrigued to read that tempers had flared among homeowners and threats had been exchanged because of the garden, because of paint colors and planter boxes.

Because of HARP? I thought about Fennel and Strom, wondered whether this was the beginning of another war, whether wars were being waged in other HARP neighborhoods.

I checked the *Times* site and found nineteen HARP articles

and a Web site with a list of all the HARPs. Twelve districts, and more under consideration. *Thirteen* soon, if the Hancock Park group had its way. Not a lucky number.

I did a search of last month's Wilshire Division *Crime Sheet* files. Almost every file had at least one case of vandalism, and most of them were car related.

Most, but not all:

Thursday, October 9. 1:00 A.M. 300 block of South Arden Boulevard. A vandal tore up a brick patio and damaged a wrought iron fence.

Saturday, October 11. 3:30 A.M. 200 block of South Larchmont Boulevard. A vandal threw frozen lemons at a house and then fled on foot.

Tuesday, October 14. 11:30 P.M. 100 block of North McCadden Place. A vandal struck the front window of a house with an unknown object.

Wednesday, October 22. 1:30 P.M. 100 block of South Highland Avenue. Vandals spray-painted graffiti on a gate, driveway, and signs.

The homes were in Hancock Park or the adjacent Larchmont Heights. Another HARP war? My mind raced with possibilities, and I forced myself to slow down. I tend to jump to conclusions.

My Zeidie Irving, Bubbie G's late husband, used to tell a bittersweet joke about two elderly friends, Shlomo and Moishe, talking on a park bench. (In Zeidie's version, they're on a boardwalk in Miami, but I got him to agree they could be anywhere.) It's a joke that should be acted out for maximum effect, but I think you'll get the picture:

Moishe, when the conversation reaches a lull: *Nu*.

Shlomo: So.

Moishe sighs. Inch by inch he straightens his hunched shoulders.

Shlomo watches.

With agonizing slowness and creaking knees, Moishe pushes himself up. A minute passes before he's standing, another before he takes a first, shuffling step.

Shlomo shakes his head: Moishe, where you're rushing?

I was probably rushing to get nowhere, too.

Chapter Three

Tuesday, November 4. 11:12 A.M. Corner of Hauser Boulevard and 3rd Street. A man became enraged at a woman over her driving and stopped his car in the middle of an intersection to yell at her. He then backed his car into her vehicle and drove off. (Wilshire)

HANCOCK PARK WAS ORIGINALLY RANCHO LA BREA, A Spanish land grant taken over in the 1860s by Major Henry Hancock, an oil prospector who found oil and dinosaur fossils, and an ancient skeleton of a Native American woman that you can see at the La Brea Tar Pits if you're so inclined.

Situated between downtown L.A. and the Pacific, Hancock Park is a rectangle bordered by Highland (west), Rossmore (east), Melrose (north), and Wilshire (south). The homes along the tree-lined streets, large and stately with lush foliage and velvet lawns, are a mix of two-story Tudor (brick-faced or stucco), Colonial Spanish, French, Mediterranean, and the occasional Moderne misfit that looks like it was air-dropped into the wrong neighborhood. The homes on Rossmore and Hudson and part of June have the added cachet of overlooking the rolling greens of the Wilshire Country Club.

The mayor's official residence is in Hancock Park (neighboring Windsor Square homeowners claim it's in Windsor), as is the Canadian consul general's English mansion. Nat King Cole lived here, and Muhammad Ali, and the neighborhood has among its residents contemporary Hollywood names like Antonio Banderas and Melanie Griffith, along with other actors and writers, producers, and directors who could live in Beverly Hills but may prefer the anonymity of Hancock Park, where celebrities' names and addresses aren't revealed on a Map to the Stars.

My dad says thirty-five years ago you could have purchased one of these mansions for $100,000. Today they run from $1 million to $6 million (the $1-million versions are fixer-uppers), and $100,000 won't buy you anything *anywhere* in L.A., except maybe a chimney. You can get the most for your Hancock Park dollar on Highland Avenue, especially on the east side of the street where the lots are deeper. It's a wide, elegant thoroughfare that loses some of its width and all of its elegance, along with the historically protected grass median showcasing a stately row of towering palm trees, when it exits Hancock Park at Melrose and runs north past the Hollywood Bowl to the 101 Freeway. The downside of Highland, which explains the slightly lower home prices, is the early-morning to late-night heavy traffic and the accompanying noise that most Highland homeowners mute with double-paned glass windows.

South Highland, the site of one of the vandalized homes, was my destination. I passed my sister Edie's house, crossed Second, and there it was on my right: a two-story taupe Tudor with scaf-folding on the sides and the framing of a large addition in the front. The black graffiti was stark and ugly against the ivory gates and the flagstone walkway, and a large *X* blackened the name of the construction company on a sign planted on a parched lawn.

After waiting several minutes in my parked Acura before a lull in traffic allowed me to open my door, I made a hasty exit and dashed to the sidewalk seconds before a car whizzed by. Many Highland homes have circular driveways. (Edie's does.) If you don't have a corner house, they're probably a must unless you're auditioning for *Fear Factor* or *Survivor: The Big City.*

Sometime during the drive from my house, the sun had burned away the marine layer that had painted the city a gloomy gray. Squinting in the sudden bright light, I stood at the front door, too warm in my red cowl-neck sweater and black pea coat, and rang the bell several times. No one was home. The home-owners had probably moved out during the construction.

I made out the contractor's name on the vandalized sign: ROGER MODINE, RM CONSTRUCTION. Another felled sign had been ripped in two. Bending down, I aligned the halves:

NO TO HARP!

Maybe I wasn't rushing after all.

Back in my car, I waited for a break in the endless stream of vehicles speeding along Highland. Finally it was safe. I pulled out and was headed toward First when the old man sprinted off the curb and darted in front of me.

I slammed my foot on the brake and gripped the steering wheel, my heart practically in my throat.

He had appeared out of nowhere, an apparition in a pale gray robe, with a full head of steel-gray hair fanning above his ears and sprouting from his unruly brows. His cheeks were sunken and blotched with color, his eyes an intense watery blue. He could have been sixty or eighty.

He rapped his cane on my windshield.

I lowered my window and leaned out. "Could you please move away from the car, sir?" I was trying to restrain my anger. My heart was still pumping madly.

"I have to get home." He had a child's voice, high and whiny. "Sir—"

"My leg hurts. My leg hurts and I have to pee."

I had no response for that. "Where do you live?"

"With Margaret," he said impatiently, as if I should have known. "Over there." He pointed to the west side of Highland with his cane, which shook along with his hand.

I put my car in park, got out, and approached him. He was wearing scuffed brown slippers and no socks on feet whose veins looked like mountain ridges.

"What street do you live on?" I've never given a ride to a stranger, but even with the cane, the man was hardly a threat, and I couldn't leave him here.

"Fuller. Like the brush." His head shook a little, too. He probably had a touch of Parkinson's.

Cars were lining up behind me. "Let me turn the corner to get out of traffic," I said.

He scowled. "If you don't want to help, just say so."

"I'll take you to Margaret. What's the house number?"

The driver of the BMW behind me honked. I motioned to him to pass my car as the cars behind him were doing, but he was too close to me, and traffic in the next lane was too heavy. I held up my hand in a wait gesture, and returned my attention to the old man.

"Don't you know Margaret?" he demanded with a flash of anger that sparked in his blue eyes. "She's my daughter."

The driver honked again and leaned out his window, a cell phone at his ear. "What the hell is this, a parking lot?" he yelled. "I have an appointment."

"Just a minute," I called. "I'm helping someone."

"Well, hurry up. I don't have all day."

"I can't remember the number." The old man sounded frustrated, angry. "I'll know the house when I see it."

"Okay. Let me help you to the car." I touched his elbow.

He jerked it away. "I can do it by myself."

I respect the independence of the aging. Bubbie G has ceded only a little of hers and has done so with great reluctance, refusing to grant victory to the macular degeneration that has stolen most of her central vision.

The driver sounded his horn again. It was a long, uninterrupted honk. I held up my hand, my index finger extended this time to indicate "one more minute," though I admit I was tempted to use another finger and suggest something less friendly and equally universal.

The old man was limping. I followed him to make sure he didn't fall and walked around him to open the car door. He tossed in his cane and, grabbing the inside handle, lowered himself sideways onto the seat. His robe fell open, and I caught a glimpse of green paisley boxer shorts ballooning over skinny thighs blotched with black-and-blue marks, doorknob knees, and bruised, bony shins, which he swung around so that he was facing the windshield.

"Do you need help with the seat belt?" I asked.

"I don't need a seat belt! I need to pee."

"I'll fasten it for you," I said, imitating the no-nonsense tone Edie uses successfully with her kids, and he didn't resist.

Back behind the wheel, I crossed First. The driver of the BMW stayed on my butt for half a block, swerved around my Acura, saluted me with a blare of his horn, and burned rubber as he sped up the street. Bubbie G has a wealth of great Yiddish curses, but I couldn't think of one.

"Which side of Beverly is your daughter's house on?" I asked, switching into the left lane. "North or south?"

"Which side? The same as the restaurant," he said with impatience. "The one with the animal's name."

"El Coyote?" I saw his nod. The south side. Just around the block from my sister. "What's your name?"

"What's *yours*?"

"Molly."

"Molly what?"

"Blume."

"Molly Bloom like in *Ulysses*." He frowned. "That's a ridiculous name. What were your parents thinking?"

I get that reaction often, though people are usually more diplomatic. My high school English teacher mother claims she was unprepared for a girl and didn't think about the repercussions of giving me the name of James Joyce's lusty heroine when she filled out the birth certificate. Sometimes I tell people it was the aftereffects of her epidural.

"I spell it B-L-U-M-E," I said.

The old man grunted.

I wasn't about to press the point. "What's *your* name?"

"Oscar Linney. *Professor* Linney."

"Professor of what?"

"Architecture. I taught at USC for twenty-two years," he said with pride. "I'm writing a book."

The University of Southern California is the rival of my alma mater, UCLA, though the rivalry matters mostly when you're talking football.

"I'm fascinated by architecture," I said. "What period are you writing about?"

"I don't want to talk anymore." He turned his head toward his window.

I've had worse rejections.

A few minutes later we neared Fuller. I turned left and drove slowly up the block.

"Stop here," he ordered when we were a little more than halfway up the second block.

After parking the car, I walked around and opened his door. His hand shook and he was having trouble releasing the seat belt, but I sensed that an offer of help would annoy him. Finally he was free. He grabbed his cane, transferred it to his right hand, swung his legs around so that he was sitting sideways, then scooted forward and pushed himself up.

I followed him about thirty feet to a beautifully maintained cream-colored two-story Spanish house with a red tile roof and black wrought iron balconies. A birch tree, its leaves stripped by autumn but no less stately, watched over a For Sale sign on a trim lawn bordered by a short hedge. In the flower bed against the front wall, a profusion of pansies preened in the sunlight. The driveway was empty.

Linney hurried along the concrete walkway and climbed the two steps to an oak front door that looked freshly varnished. He stuck his bony, shaking hand into his robe pocket and pulled it out, looking surprised to find it empty. He grunted. "Forgot my key."

He rang the bell. No one answered. He rang again.

"Damn bell is broken again!" he muttered, and pounded on the door. "Margaret! Let me in!"

The bell was fine. I'd heard its eight-part familiar chime. Maybe this was the wrong house. "Professor—"

"Margaret!" He lifted his cane and rapped on the door. "Margaret, this is your father! Open this door!"

"There's a For Sale sign on the lawn. Are you sure—"

"That's Hank's doing! Margaret would never sell this house. She *loves* this house!" He pounded on the door again.

A slim, brown-haired man walked over from the house next door. He was in his thirties, about six inches taller than my five-five, with a boyish face and friendly hazel eyes behind gold-tone wire-framed glasses. He was wearing khaki Dockers, a V-necked navy sweater, and brown moccasins.

"Professor Linney was walking near Highland and asked me to take him here," I told the neighbor when he was at my side. "His daughter's out. Or maybe this isn't her house?"

"It's her house." The man sighed. "He's done this several times. I'll talk to him."

He approached Linney and laid his hand gently on his shoulder. "Professor, it's Tim Bolt from next door."

The old man faced him. "Can you phone Margaret and ask her to open the door? Something's wrong with the bell."

"Margaret's not here, Professor."

"Of *course* she's here!" He turned back to the door. "Margaret, I insist that you open the door!"

"Why don't you come to my house? I can make you tea or coffee, and you can rest awhile. How does that sound?"

"My leg hurts!" Linney rapped on the door. "You know how much I love you, Margaret. Please, let me in!" He was crying as he hit the door with his cane.

It was a pitiful sight. Tim looked at me and shook his head, then faced Linney again. "Professor, Margaret had some errands to do."

Linney jerked his head around. "She said that?"

Tim nodded. "She probably forgot to tell you."

"She doesn't hate me?" He lowered the cane. "I did what I thought was best. I did it because I love her."

"She knows that."

Linney nodded. "When is she coming back?"

"Maybe Hank knows. Why don't we ask him, Professor?"

The old man's glare was ferocious. "Hank's a mean son of a bitch!" He stabbed the air with his cane. "I won't go back there!"

"All right," Tim soothed. "All right. Will you come with me, then?"

"Just until Margaret returns," Linney warned. "I have to pee. And I have to lie down. I'm tired."

"You can lie down in my house."

"I can't climb stairs. I'll fall and break my hip and die." He glowered. "Hank would love that."

"You can use the spare room downstairs, Professor."

Linney patted Tim's arm. "You're a good boy, Tim. I'll make sure Margaret knows."

Ignoring Tim Bolt's offered arm, the old man walked down the two steps and made his way slowly to the sidewalk. We followed a few feet behind him.

"What's with the daughter?" I asked in a low voice.

"It's a long, sad story," Tim Bolt whispered. "About five months ago she disappeared, and the police think—"

"Are you talking about me?" Linney whipped his head toward us, eyes glaring. "I know you're talking about me."

With an apologetic shrug and a brief smile, Tim hurried to the old man's side.

I tagged along to the neighbor's front door, hoping he'd invite me in and tell me the story once he'd settled Linney in the spare room. But after ushering the old man inside, Tim threw me a quick, over-the-shoulder "Thanks a lot" and shut the door behind him.

As Billy Crystal would say, I hate when that happens.

Chapter Four

Still thinking about the professor, I headed east on Third to the Larchmont address. It was the farthest of my proposed stops, but the vandalism was the most puzzling.

Why frozen lemons? Why not a rock or a brick? And if I were interested in making a mess rather than inflicting damage, I would have used raw eggs like Walter Fennel's vandals. Yolk beats out pulp any day, in my opinion.

Minutes later I parked at the end of a block lined with well-kept houses in a mix of Colonial American, Spanish, and Tudor styles. I'd never been on this block before. I *am* familiar with Larchmont two blocks north, where the street takes on a New England village atmosphere with Main Street–like storefronts that offer, among other things, clothing, antiques, cosmetics, hardware, and real estate and banking services. There's Chevalier's, an independent bookstore that I frequent, and there are bistros and coffee shops with outdoor seating, including a Coffee Bean & Tea Leaf where Zack and I have spent countless hours.

We've also spent many hours sitting on the glider on my landlord's porch and strolling along the beach and Santa Monica's Third Street Promenade. When the man who makes your heart race and various body parts tingle is a rabbi, and the way he looks at you says he feels the same way, but physical contact is verboten—well, unless you're into masochism, the privacy of an apartment is not a good idea.

Driving down the block, I'd seen no evidence of the Lemon Bandit's assault, though I'd seen several HARP signs—some pro, some anti. I spent fifteen minutes walking up the block and halfway down the other side. Most people weren't home. Three homeowners who *were* home knew nothing about the vandalism, and several Hispanic housekeepers hadn't understood my pathetic high school Spanish.

After a few pitying *¿Cómo?*s I made a mental note to look up the words *throw* and *vandalism* in my Spanish-English dictionary, if I could find it.

I walked to the end of the block, ready to cross the street to my car, but the Japanese bridge on the lawn of the corner house stopped me. It was a glossy, bright red bridge on a busy lawn bordered by a wood slat fence and crowded with groupings of shrubs and tiger lilies. The house had a wood plank exterior and a towering gabled entry, brightened by accents of that glossy red, where a statue of an Asian deity stood guard. A Shinto shrine.

To my right was a wishing well. Its side planks and rim were red lacquered, too. On a white rectangle on the side of the well, beside the words I'M WISHING printed in black Japanese-style characters, was Snow White.

"Adriana Caselotti lived here until she died in 1997," said a middle-aged, brown-haired woman who had come up next to me. She was wearing a black sweater over jeans that were a little baggy. "She left the property to a friend, but he doesn't live here. He keeps it just the way she left it, though." A heavenly yeasty aroma wafted from the shopping bag she was carrying.

I drew a blank. "Sorry. Should I know that name?"

"The voice in *Snow White*?" The woman eyed me with mild disapproval. "Disney chose her out of a hundred and fifty girls when she was nineteen. They owned the lifetime rights to her voice, and they kept Adriana's identity secret. She couldn't act in another movie without their permission."

I tried to imagine being controlled like that. "Did they let her act in anything else?"

"*The Wizard of Oz*. She was the voice of Juliet in the Tin Man scene. In her later interviews she doesn't *sound* unhappy." The woman shrugged. "They say that's why she put in the wishing well, so people would know who she was."

"Did her prince ever come? Adriana's, I mean."

The woman smiled. "Four times. She was widowed three times. I don't know what happened to the fourth husband. Are you visiting L.A.?"

I smiled back. "Actually, I'm a reporter. I read that one of the houses on this block was vandalized three weeks ago, but no one seems to know anything about it."

I handed her a business card. I never know how people will react when I tell them what I do—curiosity, anxiety, annoyance, contempt. Anger, even.

She glanced at the card. "The lemons," she said, her tone as sour as if she were sucking one. "It's the house at the end of the next block." She pointed north. "I live next door. You might think it's a silly prank, but they shattered the living room window."

"I don't think it's a silly prank. That's why I'm here." I'd obviously copied down the wrong block number from the Wilshire board. "Which house is it?"

"The yellow stucco. The owners replaced the window and had bars installed on all the windows. I put up bars a few months ago," she said with sadness. "You get used to them."

My parents put up bars last year, after they were burglarized. My mother still mourns the loss of the unhampered view of her garden through the family room's large picture window. "What are the homeowners' names?"

A look of unease replaced the open friendliness. "I'd rather not say. And they're both at work, if you're thinking of talking to them." She shifted her shopping bag to her other hand. "I have to go."

"One more question? Do the homeowners have any idea who the vandal was?"

The woman hesitated. "The police think it was kids."

"But you don't," I guessed.

"I didn't say that." The heightened color in her cheeks told me I was right. "I don't want my name in the paper. I don't want to get involved."

"I don't *know* your name." At least she hadn't walked off. I waited. Sometimes, I've learned, that's more effective than pushing.

"They received an anonymous note," she finally said. "They're with the homeowner's group that wants to make Larchmont Heights a HARP district. You know what that is?" When I nodded, she said, "Not everyone's for it."

I felt a prickling of excitement. "What's your opinion?" I hoped the question would make her open up.

"I think it's *wonderful*. Some of the people moving into the neighborhood don't care about its history. They just want to build bigger and bigger homes." She swept her free hand in a wide, tall arc. "A few years ago someone tore down a 1920s bungalow that was the home of one of the original Keystone Kops. He got a permit to put on a new roof and remodel the kitchen, and ended up building a seven-bedroom house." She pursed her lips in disapproval.

"But how often does that happen?"

"Not often," she admitted grudgingly. "But who's to say it won't happen more and more? Next time they'll tear down Adriana Caselotti's house and build some mansion that sticks out like a sore thumb."

Snow White's house was whimsical, but was it historically significant? And what about the Keystone Kop's bungalow? Who decides what constitutes history?

"Some people feel that no one has the right to tell them what they can and can't do with their homes," I said.

"No one's *dictating*." She squared her shoulders, prepared for battle. "HARP brings people together to maintain the beauty and integrity of the neighborhood. That's what it's done in other neighborhoods."

She sounded as though she'd memorized the brochure. "Do you know what the note said?" I asked.

" 'Bad neighbors make bad fences.' It's a twist on a line from a Robert Frost poem. 'The Mending Wall'? The writer called them Harpies. It's so *mean*."

The same lovely phrase Mindy had used. "Why the fence reference?"

"A couple on Arden put up a wrought iron fence around their property. It's handmade—exquisite craftsmanship. But it's higher than the city code allows, and the association wanted the owners to scale it down."

"I read about a house on Arden that was recently vandalized. A patio was torn up and a wrought iron fence was damaged?"

"That's the one. My friend lives next door. They pulled off

most of the brick and cracked the concrete. I don't think it's right, destroying people's property." She sounded defensive. "I don't like what's happening around here. It's getting ugly."

"So much for community harmony," I said, and earned a frown. "How much higher was the fence than the code?"

"Two inches. I thought that was ridiculous, myself," she added quickly, her face flushed, as if I'd accused her of making the ruling. "So did other people."

"You'd probably have to redo it." A handmade gate, I knew, was thousands of dollars. And a handmade fence?

"Probably," the woman agreed, unhappy. "It wasn't just about the fence. The fighting started over the patio. The homeowners wanted to cut down a beautiful lemon tree to build it. People from the neighborhood picketed and took turns for a few days forming a circle around the tree, but the police threatened to arrest them."

People are passionate about saving trees. Not long ago police with a warrant finally convinced a Pacific Palisades man to quit his weeks-long residence in a four-hundred-year-old oak tree that tree preservationists had named Old Glory.

"So what happened?" I asked.

"The homeowners cut down the tree and built the patio practically overnight, and a few weeks ago they cut down *another* lemon tree to build the fence."

That explained the lemons, though sour grapes would probably have been more fitting. "So someone damaged the fence and patio, and someone else retaliated and vandalized your neighbors' house. The fence owners?"

"Or one of their supporters. Or their contractor." She seemed to brighten at the idea. "I heard he lost several jobs because of the delays, and my friend told me he was *fuming* when they vandalized the patio. I can't blame him."

"Who's the contractor?"

"Roger Modine. He does a lot of work around here."

The same contractor whose sign I'd seen on Highland. "Were any other homeowner association members' homes vandalized?"

"Not as far as I know."

"Then why this house, do you think?"

Again, the woman hesitated. "The owner is the most outspoken proponent of making this a HARP district. In fact, she's on a HARP board in Angelino Heights."

I felt sorry for the homeowner, but I'll admit I was excited. I had a story. "Did they mention all this to the police?" I hadn't seen any details in the report.

"They decided not to. They didn't think the police would find out who did it, and they were afraid to start a war." She frowned. "I hope that's the end of it. I hope no one gets hurt."

After picking up a hot chocolate and a scone at the Coffee Bean, I headed for Arden. The house was easy to spot from the black wrought iron fence that was indeed exquisite, except for the damaged section. I found a NO TO HARP sign next to the RM Construction sign on a rising lawn, but no RM.

The gate was open, so I walked to the backyard, where two men were laying brick on a raised concrete slab that ran the width of the house. Three steps led from the patio to the garden.

Both men wore headsets, and I had to yell to make myself heard.

"Mr. Roger, he left a few minutes ago," the worker standing closer to me told me after he removed his earplugs. A red bandanna kept the sweat off his forehead, but his yellow T-shirt was plastered to his skin with perspiration.

"When will he be back?" I asked.

The man turned toward his coworker. *"¿Jorge, donde está Roger?"* he yelled.

There was a rapid exchange. I picked up the words *downtown* and what sounded like the Spanish for *permit*.

I thanked the men and left. My dad's a contractor, and I wondered if he knew Modine, or about him.

McCadden was next. I found the house, and a YES TO HARP sign, but the owners weren't home, and knocking on doors on both sides of the street elicited nothing other than the fact that most people are out during the day.

Porter wasn't in when I stopped at the Wilshire station, which was fine with me. I scanned the board where new crimes are listed and copied down two of interest:

Monday, November 3. 7:45 P.M. 100 block of North Hudson Avenue. A vandal, possibly with a pellet gun, shot at the victim's house and car windows. Broken glass injured the person inside the house.

Monday, November 3. 11:20 P.M. 900 block of Schumacher Drive. A vandal threw bricks through the front window of a house and injured a woman inside.

Wishing may have worked for Snow White and Adriana Caselotti, but it hadn't worked for my Larchmont tour guide: The vandalism was continuing, escalating in violence. And two people had been hurt.

The first house was in Hancock Park. The second was in Carthay Circle. I checked the pages I'd printed during my online research.

Carthay Circle was a HARP district.

CHAPTER FIVE

Wednesday, November 5. 9:32 A.M. 10700 block of Washington Boulevard. Officers responded to a possible bomb threat at an electronics store. "I'm going to place bomb chips all over your store," a caller said, then laughed and hung up. The victim said the caller's voice was very high, like a chipmunk's. (Culver City)

I DID FORTY MINUTES ON MY TREADMILL, HALF-ASLEEP because I'd stayed up way too late talking on the phone with Zack. My sister Edie, who set us up, says that given all the time we spend together, we may as well tie the knot. I tell her I'm not ready. After one failed marriage, I want to take things slow, and I'm not sure I'm cut out to be a rabbi's wife. And Zack hasn't asked.

After reciting my morning prayers, I did the *Times* crossword while eating my usual breakfast—an English muffin topped with tuna, tomato, and part-skim-milk mozzarella cheese. I figure that compensates for the chocolate. Then I phoned Hollywood Division and asked to speak to Andrew Connors. Connors is one of the detectives who make my data collecting easier and the experience more pleasant. I've known him four years, since I began doing the *Crime Sheet*. Though I know little about his personal life (he's mentioned an ex-wife in his native Boston but nothing else), I like to think we're friends.

"I'm crushed," he said in his flat accent when he came on the line. "You don't call, you don't write."

"I'll remind you of that the next time you complain that I call the station too often. How are you?"

"Overworked, underpaid, eating way too much junk food. You?"

"Ditto about the junk food, but I can't complain about the rest." Which was true.

"How are you *really,* Molly?" His voice was lower, quieter. "Still having nightmares?"

"Not as many," I lied. Three months ago I'd almost been murdered, and even after undergoing therapy, the scene plays in my head and shakes me awake more often than I admit to my family, or Zack. "I need information, Andy."

"Changing the subject, huh? Dial 911. Or try Google."

"Seriously."

"And here I thought you were calling to ask me out." He sighed. "Okay. You have five minutes."

I swiveled in my chair. "I'm writing a piece about home vandalism for the *Times.*" I didn't mention HARP, but the rest was true. The assistant editor at the "Calendar" desk—my contact—wanted to run the piece on Friday. I have data in my *Crime Sheet* files, but I don't enter every case I read about. The column can run just so long. I try to list crimes that are representative, and the bizarre ones.

"What about the DO sheets?" Connors asked, referring to the photocopies of the Daily Occurrence sheets he's kind enough to give me.

"I toss them after the respective *Crime Sheet* edition comes out. Otherwise, I'd be drowning in paper."

"So what do you need?"

"Any case of home vandalism that took place during the past two months. I need specifics. The nature of the vandalism. Whether there was an injury involved. The neighborhoods where the crimes took place, which homes."

"Why do you need to know which homes?"

I could picture his frown. "I want a sense of what type of homes are being targeted." In a way, that was true.

"Vandals are democratic, Molly. Of course, a run-down neighborhood is a tempting target. So what's your angle?"

"I'm curious to see if there are patterns. I noticed that some of the vandalism is more serious. Pellet guns, for instance."

"We're not living in Mayberry. Everybody's upping the ante. Drivers used to honk at each other. Now they're using AK-47s." He paused. "So that's your pitch? No offense, Molly, but the IRS manual is probably more exciting."

"I'm still fleshing it out." I wasn't about to tell Connors my theory, which was half-baked at best. "I checked out burglary crime statistics on the LAPD Web site, but there are no details. Vandalism is under Burglary, right?"

"Right. Unless we're talking gang graffiti. That's handled by S-E-U. Special Enforcement Unit. It used to be called CRASH. Community Resources Against Street Hoodlums. That's tracked pretty regularly."

"I'm more interested in home vandalism. Cases in Hollywood, Wilshire, Rampart, Northeast, West L.A., and South-west." All of which contained HARP districts.

"Vandalisms are low priority, although with Bratton as chief, that's changing. Unless there's a stalking or hate crime element—a swastika, for instance. Or if it's a church." There was a question in his voice.

"No, nothing like that."

"You're looking for a pattern. Any particular MO?"

Lemons, I thought. "Not that I know of."

"If a cop in Burglary noticed a trend in his area, he might write up a crime bulletin that would be distributed to all the divisions and surrounding jurisdictions. Other than that, you'll have to make nice to your pals at the different divisions."

"And ask them to photocopy sixty days of DOs? They'll never do it." If I were a detective, *I* wouldn't do it.

"They can try FASTRAC." He spelled it for me.

"It sounds liked a subway system."

"Focus Accounting Strategy Teamwork Resources Commitment." He repeated it, slowly, while I wrote down the words. "It's a monthly crime control meeting at the bureau level that examines crime statistics. The statistics are derived from a computerized database managed by CADs at each division. Crime Analysis Detail."

"CADs? Who comes up with these acronyms?"

"So if someone were inclined," Connors continued, ignoring my comment as I'd known he would, "he could ask CAD to do a search for home vandalisms that occurred within the past two months in that division or bureau. Shouldn't take long."

"Do they have street addresses?"

"Sure."

"How often is FASTRAC updated?"

"Every day. I just finished looking at eighteen pages of printouts from last night."

I was loving FASTRAC. If I could buy stock in it, I would. "So if someone were inclined, could he get information from *all* the division CADs?"

"Is that a subtle request?"

"Can you get it for me, Andy? Plus crime bulletins about vandalism, if there are any."

"What about your dry cleaning? Do you want me to pick that up? Walk your dog?"

"I don't have a dog, but it's nice of you to offer. I really appreciate this, Andy."

"I'm a homicide detective, in case you forgot."

"One of the best."

"*One* of the best?"

"If I said the best, you'd think I was flattering you just to get my way."

"Which you'd *never* do." He laughed. "I'll check into it."

"When should I stop by to get the report?"

"I'll phone you. It'll be a while."

"You said yourself it shouldn't take long."

"You're nagging, Molly."

"Sorry." I call it persistence, but others disagree.

"The minute we hang up I'm leaving to interview two witnesses. After that I testify downtown. If that's okay with you?"

I ignored his sarcasm. "It's fine. *Thank* you."

"If I come back to the station today, I'll try to get to it then. If not, tomorrow morning."

"If you *do* get back today, can you fax me the report?"

Connors groaned. "God, you're relentless! Why the urgency, Molly?"

"No urgency. W-I-P."

"What?"

"Waiting Is the Pits."

"Cut the crap. Are you onto something the department should know about?" The banter had left his voice.

"It's probably nothing."

"Then why are you pursuing it?"

"Curiosity. And I have time to kill."

"A dangerous combination. Ask George."

"If I find out there's a pattern, I'll tell you."

"Damn right you will," Connors said.

CHAPTER SIX

FEDEX DELIVERED THE PAGE PROOFS OF *SINS OF THE Father* as I was loading the washing machine. I'd contemplated visiting the Hudson and Schumacher houses vandalized on Monday, but they would have to wait. I was eager to read the typeset pages—one small step away from a book.

I was nervous, too. I suppose it's like seeing your dream house after the drywall has been covered and the exterior walls stuccoed. It's a real house, and you plan to love everything about it because it's your design, after all. But some things aren't exactly what you imagined from the blueprints and framing, and it's too late to change them without great expense.

This was a real book. I wanted to love every word and hoped there weren't any "walls" that would have to come down or be moved, because, as the accompanying letter from the production department warned, "This isn't the time to make major changes."

With a cup of coffee on my nightstand next to a pad of the smallest yellow Post-its and two freshly sharpened pencils, I settled myself on my full-size bed with the page proofs and the manuscript. It's my ritual. I do all my writing and revisions on the computer in my office, but I always read completed manuscripts or large chunks of them in my bedroom. I can't explain why, but the energy is different here, quieter, and it's not just the absence of the computer's hum. (My mom, who has published one romance novel under the pseudonym Charlotte D'Anjou and is working on another, does her best writing with Beethoven playing in the background.) I also can't explain why words and sentences and paragraphs that had seemed so right three months ago when I reviewed the copy-edited manuscript seemed so glaringly wrong now. I winced more than a few times, but at least there were no "walls" to relocate.

By late afternoon I had finished the pages, many of them now flagged with Post-its. I would read the galleys at least once more before FedExing the pages with corrections to my editor, and I knew that, careful as I was, I'd overlook something. A typo. A missing word. I often see what's in my mind, not on the page. I hoped more objective eyes would catch the errors before the presses rolled.

On the whole I was satisfied. I was saddened, too. It was a grim story. So was my first book, and the one I'd just finished.

I often wonder why I'm drawn to write about true crime. I suppose with each book I'm hoping that if I understand the *why* of that act of violence, I'll be closer to understanding why someone would murder my best friend, Aggie. After five years and three books, I still have no answers—not to Aggie's murder, not to what makes people do the terrible things they do to one another. A part of me knows I never will.

I phoned the Hollywood station and asked for Connors. He wasn't in, and I didn't leave a message.

CHAPTER SEVEN

"WE ARE *SO* LATE," I ANNOUNCED AS ZACK PARKED HIS Honda two blocks from the school where the HARP meeting was taking place. Judging by the number of cars, the attendance was high. "We probably missed the good stuff."

"No comment," Zack said, more pleasant than I would have been if he'd had me drive around for over fifteen minutes in the wrong neighborhood.

"I'm *really* sorry. I thought Edie said John Burroughs." I didn't volunteer that I'd cut her off as she was about to give me the address. "If Edie asks, tell her you were delayed, okay?"

He looked at me. "Is this a sibling rivalry thing?"

"Kind of." I unbuckled my seat belt. "Of course, if you'd picked me up *earlier* . . ."

Zack raised a brow in a way I find extremely sexy, like everything else about him. "Shifting the blame?"

"I figured it was worth a try."

He laughed. "Fuggedaboutit."

"Not a very rabbinic response."

"I'm off duty."

I waited for him to open my door and got out of the car, tugging down my short black wool skirt, which had slid up during the ride and exposed an expanse of black-tights-covered thigh. When I looked up, he was gazing at me intently with those killer smoky gray-blue eyes.

"Why are we here again?" he said, his low, gravelly voice making my heart beat faster.

If you had told me four months ago that I'd be dating a rabbi, or Zack Abrams, I would have asked you what medication you were on. But here I was, in a three-months-and-going-strong relationship with the high school heartthrob who had dumped me and had reappeared twelve years later—a newer, improved version. Life was good.

"*Kenehoreh*," I said in an undertone (the compacted form of *keyn ayin horeh*—"Let there be no evil eye"), in case Satan was tempted to screw things up. Which he usually was.

Zack looked puzzled. "What?"

"I said, 'Can we hurry?'" The dark November night hid my pinked cheeks.

Inside the lobby I picked up a packet of HARP literature and entered a cavernous auditorium chillier than outdoors. I scanned the crowd at the front of the room, huddled around posters on easels. I didn't see Edie. With Zack at my side, I took geisha steps down a sloped aisle in new stiletto-heeled boots that pinched my toes and had felt steadier and more comfortable in the store. When it comes to shoes, I'm like Othello, loving "not wisely but too well."

"You wanna see chutzpah?" asked a forty-something man

with close-cropped silver hair, his voice echoing in the high-ceilinged room. He took a flyer from the pocket of his black parka and thrust it into my hand. "This is chutzpah."

I glanced at the house on the flyer. Nice house.

"The homeowner's pushing for HARP in Hancock Park, but look at that addition!" The man stabbed at the page. "He's trying to do everything before the area goes HARP. Hypocrite!" He swiveled sharply and tackled someone else.

People were clustered in threes and fours. I recognized my Larchmont tour guide, talking to a tall, stocky man wearing a brown corduroy jacket. I spotted several yarmulkes and was trying to identify the faces belonging to them when I saw my sister approaching.

Edie is thirty-four, five years older than I am and four inches shorter. Aside from our brown eyes and highlighted blond hair, originally medium brown (I wear mine long and curly because there's less upkeep; hers is a chin-length bob that she has trimmed once a month), we look nothing alike.

"You were so late, I thought you weren't coming," Edie told me after she greeted us and kissed my cheek.

"My fault," Zack said.

Is the guy wonderful, or what?

"Molly didn't mention that you were interested in HARP," Edie said, craning her neck to look up at Zack, who at six feet towers over her.

"I'm not, really. I figured I'd keep Molly company."

Edie smiled. "You two seem to be doing lots of that."

All that was missing was the wink. "Who are the main players here, Edie?" I asked, to change the subject.

"Molly says you're living with your parents, Zack. I'm sure you're eager to find a place of your own."

"I've seen a few possibilities," he said. "But I don't want to rush into anything."

"You're very wise. And you'll want something large enough

for a family." Edie has a single-mindedness befitting an Iraq arms inspector and is as subtle as TNT.

"Zack has a Realtor. I'm sure he'll find something." I darted a glance at him. He looked amused. "Who's the guy holding court?" I pointed at a ruggedly handsome thirty-something with longish dark blond hair. He was wearing a cropped brown suede jacket, camel turtleneck, and tweed fawn-colored slacks. And a large bandage at his temple. "Very Ralph Lauren. What did he do, fall off a horse?"

"That's Jeremy Dorn, an architect. Someone shot at his house on Monday with a pellet gun. I heard he's okay, but he's playing it up. He's spearheading the HARP drive and chairs the Miracle Mile North board but lives in Hancock Park."

He could have been seriously hurt, I thought, regretting my flip comment. Was this the Hudson house I'd read about? I definitely wanted to talk to Dorn for the story I'd promised Amy Brod, my *Times* contact.

"What about Man in Gray?" I asked. Gray sports coat, gray shirt, gray tie. The only things not gray were his short brown hair and the small tortoiseshell glasses that were very in, according to my optometrist. He looked more *GQ* than Ralph Lauren, more professorial than rugged.

"Ned Vaughan. Another architect." Edie made it sound like a four-letter word. "He's with the company the city hired to do the historical survey. And the skinny redhead is Linda Cobern from Councilman Harrington's office." Edie put her mouth near my ear. "She's a witch."

Bruce Harrington, Edie had told me, was pro-HARP, playing to the longtime area residents who had put him in office.

"What are the numbers tonight?" I asked.

"We're well represented, but so are they." She frowned. "I made hundreds of calls. So did Roger. Modine," she added. "But a lot of people haven't showed yet."

"The contractor?" That was a surprise.

"He lives in the area. The HARP rules are affecting his business. That's him over there." Edie pointed to the man talking to the Larchmont woman. They both looked edgy.

"Don't the proponents need a certain percentage of area homeowners who want HARP status?" Zack asked.

Edie sniffed. "We think they fudged the numbers. Also, according to the survey, seventy-five percent of the houses contribute to the neighborhood's historical identity. That's *ridiculous*."

A couple I recognized from Zack's synagogue walked over. He introduced them to Edie. "And you know Molly."

"Of course," the husband said.

The wife smiled. "We've met."

Was their greeting stilted, or was it my imagination? And did Zack seem suddenly awkward? I'm still self-conscious around his congregants, auditioning for a role I'm not sure I want. It doesn't help that my ex and his parents attend this same synagogue, and that many of the congregants were at our wedding.

"I'm going to play reporter," I told Zack. "Want to come along?" I'd do better alone but hesitated leaving him with Edie. She'd probably have him sign a prenup by the time I returned.

"Go do your thing. Don't worry about me."

I wondered if he was relieved. Zack has never said, but I imagine he's uncomfortable when we're in public with the way I dress—sleeves and skirts falling short of strict Orthodox rules, necklines a little too low. Nothing risqué, but not appropriate for a rabbi's girlfriend. (I wear pants, too, though not when we're out.) Edie, whose skirts end just above the knee, says I should be sensitive to Zack's position. ("Is a couple of inches such a big deal if you love someone?") I remind her that I hadn't wanted to go out with a rabbi, that Zack knew what I was like from the first date.

Bubbie G says, *"Az es iz nisht vi ich vill, vill ich vi es iz."* If it's not as I want it, I want it as it is.

The question was, did I want it?

Roger Modine had moved off. I scanned the room but couldn't find him. Instead I flitted from cluster to cluster, a bee looking for pollen.

". . . philistines tore down a lovely Craftsman and replaced it with a cookie-cutter nouveau Beverly Hills."

". . . didn't pay over two million dollars so that someone can tell me what kind of landscaping I can have."

"Well, that's the point. I wouldn't want a purple house next to mine, or aluminum windows."

". . . can't argue that every house with Spanish tile is a contributing structure!"

". . . it's the *religious* people who need big houses for their large families. Let them go elsewhere."

". . . property values will go down because people won't want to buy with HARP breathing down their backs."

Half an hour later I was ready to report that it was a draw. Edie wouldn't be happy, and I didn't have a zinger for my story. So much for the fireworks I'd expected.

I was crossing the room, looking for Roger Modine, when I heard an auburn-haired woman say the name Linney.

The Professor.

She was talking to a tall, large-framed man in his late thirties or early forties with a broad face and wide nose. His outfit—a black leather jacket over a loose, oversize camel sweater and tan slacks—looked almost shabby next to her expensive black wool suit.

". . . a shame he couldn't be here tonight," the woman said. "He's so passionate about historical preservation."

"He didn't have a good day, so I promised I'd come here and give him a full report."

Was the man Linney's son? I wondered.

The woman *tsk*ed. "Is he still working on his book? I know he was excited about it, before everything happened."

"Most of the time, between the Alzheimer's and the Parkinson's, he's too confused. Yesterday he wandered out of the house. Again." The man sighed. "I'm worried he'll get hurt one of these days."

The woman arched a penciled brow. "He was *alone*?"

The man's ruddy complexion deepened. "The caregiver says he was taking a nap. When she checked on him, he was gone. I'm not sure she was all that attentive. It doesn't matter now. She quit."

"Who's with him now?"

"A caregiver from a different agency. First Aid. She won't last the week. The Professor can be mean. He yells at them, accuses them of stealing from him, orders them to leave. I'm running out of caregivers and agencies."

"I admire you, Hank. I'm sure this isn't easy."

Nice sentiments, but her tone was mocking and I wondered why. Hank didn't seem to notice.

"I keep telling myself he's more frustrated than I am," he said. "And he's lonely. He doesn't see much of anyone. Well, Ned Vaughan comes over, of course. So does the former neighbor, Tim Bolt. But the Professor yells at Ned and Tim, too, so I don't know how long that'll last. The last time they came by, he refused to see them."

"You may have to place him in a home," she said, not mocking now.

Hank tightened his lips. "I can't do that. Maggie would never— I just can't."

Maggie was Margaret, I assumed.

"I'm sure you know best," the woman said. "I should go see Jeremy and rescue him from that awful Linda Cobern. Do you want to come with me?"

"I don't think so." His cheek twitched.

"Oh, of course. I'm sorry." Her satisfied smile said she wasn't sorry at all. "Well, it's nice that you're getting out, Hank. I'm sure we'll be seeing more of you."

He watched her as she walked over to Dorn. There was anger in his cold brown eyes and the set of his wide jaw, in the flare of his nostrils. I wondered at whom the anger was directed. Dorn or the woman? Or both.

It wasn't the best time to introduce myself, but I grabbed the opportunity and stepped closer. "Excuse me? I couldn't help overhearing you talk about Professor Linney."

He turned and stared at me, the anger replaced with a guarded expression.

"I drove him to the Fuller house yesterday," I said. "I'm Molly Blume."

"Hank Reston." The tension left his face. "Thanks. I hope he didn't put you out too much. He can be a handful." He tried a smile but looked weary, as if the weight of the world were lying on his broad shoulders.

"A little stubborn, but he wasn't a problem." I smiled back. "I was happy to help. It was so sad, though. He was agitated about not being able to see his daughter. At least the neighbor was able to calm him down."

Hank nodded. "Tim has known the family for years. He called me on my cell phone, and I came right over."

"Professor Linney is your father?"

"Father-in-law." His eyes were focused over my head. "Would you excuse me? There's someone I have to talk to. Thanks again for your help." And he was gone.

I was consumed with curiosity, but I couldn't run after him and force him to tell all. Turning, I watched him walk up to Roger Modine, of all people. Two birds, I thought, and not one stone. Modine was in a heated conversation with Ned Vaughan, glowering at him as though he wanted to throttle him. Reston placed a hand on Modine's shoulder and apparently defused whatever had been going on, because the contractor calmed down and Vaughan laughed, though he still looked nervous.

Several roads led to Jeremy Dorn. I walked over to him, passing the black-suited woman, who had joined another cluster. Dorn had the glazed smile of a *Jeopardy* contestant who hasn't buzzed once. A tense Linda Cobern was listening to the silver-haired man who had thrust the flyer at me.

"Nothing's decided, Mr. Seltzer," Linda said.

"It's un-American! If Harrington thinks he'll get my vote next time . . ."

I waited until he stormed off. "A lot of people seem unhappy with the regulation that comes with HARP," I said.

"That's because they don't understand how it works." Linda Cobern studied me. "Do you live in the area?"

I had the feeling that if I lied, she'd demand to see a picture ID. "No, but I'm interested in the subject."

"You're a reporter." She cocked her head. "I don't remember seeing you before. Are you with the *Chronicle*?"

The local paper. "I freelance. Apparently, there's real friction between the two sides."

"I wouldn't call it *friction*." Her smile was tight, as though she were afraid to crack a facial mask. "People have opinions. That's healthy."

"According to police reports, a number of homes in the area have been vandalized lately. The victims seem to be on one side of the HARP issue or the other." I turned to Dorn. "I understand *your* home was vandalized this week."

A woman screamed. Something crashed. I turned to my right. One of the easels had been toppled.

"You put that there!" the woman yelled at the silver-haired Seltzer. She pointed to the floor.

"It wasn't me!"

Linda Cobern tightened her lips. "Excuse me." She headed toward the easel, Dorn at her heels. Whatever had prompted the scream was making people keep their distance.

I followed them. Lying on the floor next to the fallen easel was a dead bird.

Chapter Eight

Thursday, November 6. 7:53 A.M. 1300 block of South Curson Avenue. "I'm gonna kill you. I wanna see blood. Red is my favorite color," a man yelled across the street at a neighbor. (Wilshire)

"A DEAD BIRD," CONNORS SAID. "VERY HITCHCOCK."

"I think it's a symbol for a Harpy. A plundering bird. That's what some people call the HARP board members."

"I know what a Harpy is, Molly. In mythology, an ugly, filthy creature with the head of a woman and the body of a bird. More loosely, any rapacious person or animal."

"I'm impressed."

"I got a thirteen forty on my SATs. Okay." He clasped his

hands behind his head. "'Splain it to me, Lucy. From the beginning."

Connors had borrowed a chair for me and pushed back his own, propping his tan cowboy boots on his desk ("table" in cop talk). Even sitting, he gives a tall appearance, and though his face is unremarkable, and he has a significant bald spot on the crown of his thinning brown hair, there's something enormously appealing about him. Sexy, too.

I started with Fennel and Strom, then told him about the other vandalized homes. "Highland, Larchmont, Arden, Hudson, McCadden, Schumacher. There seems to be a war going on between HARP proponents and opponents."

"Homes are vandalized all the time, Molly."

"True." I nodded. "But three of them belong to people who are on HARP boards. Or in Fennel's case, *used* to be. But he's still involved. There may be a fourth, in Carthay Circle. I haven't checked that one yet."

I was encouraged by the interest in Connors's hazel eyes. One boot came down. "Go on."

"That's it. Well, except for the bird, which raises the creepiness level. Obviously, someone's targeting HARP board members, and from the escalating violence, it looks like his anger is growing. One of the victims needed stitches. Next time it could be worse."

"Any idea who's doing this?"

Roger Modine's name popped into my head. "Not really."

"Ennhhhh." Connors imitated a buzzer. "Try again. You've spent three days on this. You must have something."

I wanted to talk to Modine first, but Connors is generous with information. "There's a contractor who's lost projects thanks to delays imposed by the homeowners groups. Some of his remodels have been vandalized. But there were a lot of anti-HARP people at last night's meeting, Andy. Any one of them could have brought in the dead bird."

"Who's the contractor?"

"Roger Modine. RM Construction."

Connors wrote that down. "You could have told me all this over the phone, Molly. Why the visit? Not that it isn't a treat to see you."

I handed him a list of names. "I got this off the Internet last night. These are the members of all the HARP boards in the city. I'm hoping you can find out if any of their homes have been vandalized lately. I need it ASAP."

"For your pattern," Connors said.

"And my story. My deadline is in four hours." I'd worked on the story until three in the morning. If Amy had it by noon, it would run in Friday's morning edition.

He scanned the list. "A lot of names."

"Sixty. Five members on each board."

"Do you know any of them?"

"Jeremy Dorn. I met him at the meeting. He's on the Miracle Mile HARP board. And Rita Benton." The Lemon Bandit's victim. I'd spoken to her and her husband. "She chairs the Angelino Heights board."

Connors tapped the list against his fingertips. "I'll check into this."

"FASTRAC?"

"D-C-T-S."

I smiled. "I'm not even going to ask."

"Detective Case Tracking System. But there are two conditions." He fixed me with his I'm-not-kidding look. "One, you don't talk to Modine until I say so."

I had enough sources without him: Jeremy Dorn, Linda Cobern. Rita and Hal Benton had insisted on anonymity, but a dozen other neighborhood residents hadn't.

"What's the second condition?" I asked.

"You don't mention the dead bird."

"Why not?" I needed the bird. The bird gave the story edge.

"Because it's a detail that may be valuable if we find this guy. And we don't want to encourage copycats."

"There were over a hundred people at the meeting last night, Andy. They all know about the bird. Believe me, the bird has flown the nest."

CHAPTER NINE

I'M NOT A GOOD WAITER, AS YOU MAY HAVE NOTICED. And my deadline was looming like the *Titanic*'s iceberg. I finished my *Crime Sheet* column, checked the data against my notes and the police reports, and e-mailed the file to my editor.

Zack had phoned when I was out. I returned his call and learned he was visiting a congregant at the hospital. I didn't like the way last night had ended—my fault. I'd been preoccupied with the dead bird, and though he'd said he understood that I couldn't do our nightly phone marathon because of my deadline, he'd seemed distant. Maybe he was annoyed. Maybe he welcomed the reprieve.

Maybe my imagination was working overtime. Zack had dumped me in high school. My ex-husband had cheated on me.

So, yes, I'm insecure when it comes to men. Zack was different now, and I trusted him. But *I* was pondering our relationship. He probably was, too. Did he want me "as is"?

With the soundtrack of *Mamma Mia* to keep me company (I love everything ABBA), I dusted and vacuumed and folded the laundry I'd washed yesterday. Then I resumed work on the galleys. I'd reread thirty pages when Connors phoned.

"Four homes in the past three weeks, not counting Fennel, Dorn, and Benton." He sounded tense. "One of them late last night."

"Four more?" That was more than I'd expected.

"I thought you'd be thrilled. Not enough for your story?"

Connors likes to kid around, but he was touching some of my buttons. "I'm not thrilled that homes are being vandalized and people are traumatized and injured. But, yes, I'm gratified that I'm right. Now that we know, maybe we can put a stop to it."

"We?"

"You. The men in blue." His attitude was really annoying. "You should be thanking me. What's your *problem*?"

"Vince Porter."

I frowned. "What?"

"I called him about the vandalism, since a lot of it's in his backyard. He's pissed you didn't go to him. He thinks you're trying to make him look bad."

I rolled my eyes. "You *told* him I asked you to check this out?"

"He guessed. You asked a lot of questions about vandalism on Monday, he said. You mentioned HARP. It doesn't take a genius to put two and two together. And, yeah, I forgot. *Thank you*. Nice work. I mean that."

"Thanks." I didn't relish a confrontation with Porter. "Seven homes isn't a coincidence, is it, Andy?"

"I don't think so." He was glum now.

"What kind of vandalism?"

"What you saw, for the most part. Graffiti, shattered windows, smashed concrete. One woman had stitches. No dead birds, in case you're wondering."

I ignored that. "Which HARP areas were involved?"

"Angelino Heights, Carthay Circle, Whitley Heights, Spaulding Square."

"The Carthay Circle house is the one on Schumacher?"

Connors didn't answer right away. "Yes."

"What's the homeowner's name?"

"Sorry."

I had the address in my police report. I could find out. "Can you tell me which other homes were vandalized?"

"Again, sorry."

Sometimes I can push. I could tell this wasn't one of those times. I wondered why. "What about those FASTRAC pages? When do you think you'll have those for me?"

"It'll take some time. I've been busy running these names and following up."

Something told me he was holding back. Maybe Porter had pressured him to shut me out. "Following up?"

"We've issued a crime bulletin to all the divisions with the names and addresses of all HARP board members. We're talking to Burglary in all divisions with HARP districts. I already talked to Porter. Carthay is his. So is Harvard Heights. Rampart covers Angelino Heights."

"What jurisdiction is Spaulding Square?"

"Ours. So are Whitley Heights and Melrose Hill. We're increasing patrols and alerting board members. I assume the other divisions will be doing much the same thing. It's a hard line, warning people without frightening them. Which brings me to your story. What are you writing?"

"What I said. That not everyone's happy with HARP, that there's been a suspicious amount of home vandalism, that it all seems to be connected."

"You didn't talk to Modine, did you?"

"I promised I wouldn't. Have I ever lied to you?"

"Not that I know of. That doesn't mean you haven't. Don't mention that the victims are board members, Molly."

"Are you writing this, or am I?"

"This is serious, Molly."

"Exactly. I'm a reporter. I report news. This is news. You said yourself it's not a coincidence."

"I said I don't *think* it is. What if we're wrong? You print that, you could be panicking people for nothing."

"What's the downside, Andy? People are more careful? Neighbors look out for each other? Ooh, how *horrible.*"

"I don't want our guy to know that we know. Okay, Lois Lane? It gives us an advantage. If he knows we're watching board members' homes, where does he go then?"

"You're going to stake out sixty houses?" I said, ignoring Connors's question. I had to admit he had a point. Still . . . "I'll have to see how it plays out."

I returned to my computer and my story, but Connors had bothered me. It wasn't what he didn't want me to write. It was what he hadn't told me—the names, the addresses. His hedging about FASTRAC. I'd attributed his attitude to pressure from Porter, but maybe it was something else. And maybe the police weren't planning on watching sixty houses.

"Walter Fennel's house was vandalized," I told my computer screen. "So were Jeremy Dorn's and Rita Benton's. Rita and Dorn head HARP boards. And Fennel . . ." I tried to remember what Mindy had said.

I checked my notes. Fennel had chaired his HARP board until a month ago. I phoned Hollywood, asked for Connors, and played computer mah jongg while I waited.

"Did I mention I'm busy?" he said when he came on the line.

"The four other homeowners who were vandalized," I said. "They were heads of their HARP boards, right?"

"No comment."

"That's a yes."

"You print that, and don't ever ask me for help again," he warned.

"Andy—"

"The vandalism last night? Someone threw a torch through the front window."

I shut my eyes for a second and sighed. "Was anyone—"

"*Luckily,* the owners had moved out. They're doing extensive restorations. *Luckily,* there wasn't much damage. There are five other HARP board chairs. We plan to watch every one of their houses. We want to get this guy, Molly. But if you print this, he won't show, will he? And next time we might not be so lucky."

I can tell you it wasn't an easy decision. I agonized for some time, inserting the fact that six of the victims (seven, if you counted Fennel) were heads of HARP boards. Deleting it. Inserting it again. One little sentence, but it made a huge difference.

I asked myself what Woodward or Bernstein would do. What would Ellen Goodman do? Wasn't it my responsibility to tell my readers the complete truth? Or was that ego masquerading as righteousness?

And what about the public's safety? What if all board members were being targeted? Shouldn't they all be warned?

I saved three versions of my story on the computer. "HARPs—Sweet Chords or Discord?" At 11:47 I addressed an e-mail to Amy Brod at the *Times* and attached the version that speculated about HARP board members being targeted, but didn't narrow it down to the board chairpersons. A compromise. I kept the bird.

I tapped the computer mouse, deliberating. I won't tell you it was a portentous moment. It wasn't. And while I'm not a fan of the if-only-I'd-known school of writing, I do sometimes wonder whether things would have turned out differently if I'd never pressed SEND. Connors says no, but I think he's being kind.

CHAPTER TEN

Friday, November 7. 7:28 P.M. 11100 block of Venice Boulevard. A woman reported that she went to her car in the morning and found a note on the windshield. "Nice car, hope it stays that way? Still buying lots of beer. Loser." (Culver City)

My family and i had finished the *BIRKAT HAMAZON* (grace after meals) when we smelled the smoke. It curled into the dining room through the inch of open window, and we realized why the fire engines we'd heard earlier, their sirens a shrill accompaniment to the Sabbath *zemirot* we'd been singing, had seemed so close. Only three blocks away, we soon learned.

My dad and my brothers—Noah is twenty-four, Joey is two

years younger—pushed their chairs away from the table and stood in unison, their movements choreographed by curiosity.

"We'll be back soon, Celia," my dad told my mom.

He slipped on the suit jacket he'd draped over the back of his chair. My brothers did the same.

"You and the boys should take coats, Steven," she called as they hurried out of the room, her smile a half reproach. She removed the cream-colored lace mantilla from her shoulder-length chestnut brown hair and folded it.

"Where are they going?" Bubbie G asked, searching my face with her once-bright blue eyes.

"To see where the fire is."

Bubbie harrumphed. *"Nahrishkeit."* Silliness.

She pushed herself out of her chair and, using her cane, walked toward the family room. My nineteen-year-old sister, Liora, followed at a discreet distance to make sure she was all right. Bubbie doesn't like us to hover.

My dad is fifty-six, but when it comes to sirens and fire engines in particular, he's as much of a kid as my brothers. So is my ex, Ron. I guess it's a guy thing. Norm, Mindy's husband, would probably be there. Zack's parents live on Poinsettia near Oakwood, seven blocks away from my parents. Maybe he'd heard the sirens, too, and followed them. I suppose that's why they call them sirens.

Taking a napkin, I brushed challa crumbs off the white tablecloth into my cupped palm.

"He's cute, isn't he?" my mom said, stacking plates.

"Zack?"

"Your dad. Zack, too." A smile deepened the fine lines around her brown eyes. Even with the lines, she looks younger than her fifty-five years.

I blushed. "Very cute. You picked a good one."

"I think so. Is Zack coming later?"

"He didn't say."

Zack usually walks over Friday nights when I stay at my parents' home on Gardner (my Blackburn apartment is about a mile and a half away). We'd talked yesterday for over an hour. This morning he'd called to congratulate me on my story but had to hang up to prepare his Sabbath *drash*—his sermon. Fridays are *his* deadlines. Maybe making plans about walking over tonight had slipped his mind.

"Could be he's tired, Molly. I wouldn't read into it."

"I'm not," I lied.

After clearing the table, I went into the family room. Bubbie G was sitting next to Liora, her thinning, short silvery hair a sharp contrast to Liora's thick, glossy dark brown mane; their ankle-length, A-line navy velour zip-up Sabbath robes striking against the tan leather of the sectional sofa. My mom and I were in robes, too. (My mom's was a sable brown; mine was black velour, part of my trousseau, but I didn't hold that against it.) It's always been our Friday night garb, and if you peek into Orthodox homes across the country, you'll probably find a number of women and girls similarly clothed, some of them in robes so elegant you could wear them to a banquet.

Bubbie was listening raptly as Liora read aloud the week's Torah portion and commentary. Even large-print editions don't compensate for her failing vision. I sat at the end of the sofa's *L* and was engrossed in the local Jewish newspaper when the men returned.

"It's a small one," my brother Joey said, taking off his jacket and tossing it onto the couch. "Two trucks."

"Don't leave that there," my mother chided gently. She's been asking Joey not to leave his clothes around for most of his twenty-two years. I would've given up by now. She turned to my dad. "Was anyone hurt, Steven?"

He shook his head. "Norm said the place has been vacant for months."

"Thank God," my mom said.

"*Baruch Hashem*," Liora echoed. She's the most pious in the family, and since her return in May from a post-high-school year at a Jerusalem girls' seminary, she's been sprinkling more of her conversation with Hebrew phrases.

"I talked to some of the firemen," Noah said. "They wouldn't say, but I think it was arson."

I put down the newspaper. "What makes you think that?" I asked, my tone sharper than I'd intended.

"The living room window was shattered. And I heard a fireman say something about lighter fluid." Noah is a third-year law student at UCLA and shares my interest in crime, though our reasons are different. "You're thinking this ties in with the other vandalisms in your story, huh?"

It wasn't my first *Times* byline, but my dad had bought extra copies of the paper, and we'd talked about the HARP conflict after kiddush. My parents are anti-HARP, in case you're wondering.

"Maybe you're prophetic," Joey said.

I scowled at him. "Don't say that!"

He raised his hands in mock defense. "Hey, I was joking. Chill."

He was right. I was overreacting. "How do you know the house was vacant?" I asked my dad.

"According to the neighbors, it's been for sale for some time. I don't know why it hasn't sold. It's a nice house, and Fuller is a great block."

Fuller. Fuller like the brush. I felt a knot in my stomach, the kind I get when I'm in a roller coaster a second before it begins its descent. "A two-story on the west side between First and Second?"

"How did you know?" My dad was frowning.

I told them about Professor Linney. "It doesn't fit the pattern," I said, brooding aloud. "And the vandal already struck in Miracle Mile."

"Your pattern could be wrong," Noah said, tentative. I could tell he didn't want to hurt my feelings.

"Maybe." I wondered how Amy Brod would react if my story was punched full of holes. But the pattern was *there*. Connors had seen it, too.

I stood. "I'm going over there."

"What can you do tonight?" Liora said. "It's *Shabbos*."

I caught the brief eye contact between my parents and knew they were wondering the same thing. Since my return a few years ago to Orthodox Judaism, they've been tiptoeing around my religious observance, which is basically the same as theirs. But there are nuances, like this one.

"I won't be long," I said, not answering Liora's question, ignoring the inner voice that said she was right. I headed for the hall closet and my coat.

"Go with Molly, Noah," my dad said. "I don't want her walking alone at night."

"How come you didn't ask *me*?" Joey said.

It was Margaret Reston's house.

I'd never witnessed a fire. I'd written a book about a torched church and interviewed the surviving victims—some disfigured, all emotionally scarred. I'd seen news coverage of fires and their devastation and had found the scenes frightening. But news coverage doesn't transmit the awesome, mesmerizing power of the fire that had engulfed the Fuller house, or the ominous, crackling sounds, or the acrid smoke that made my throat burn and my eyes water. I raised the collar of my jacket over my nose and mouth.

Neighbors were in the street, on the sidewalk. Some, like me, wore coats over their robes. I saw a few yarmulkes, a few women with scarves covering their heads. I looked around and found Tim Bolt. He was wearing a heavy black sweater and had covered his mouth with a black shawl.

I left Noah talking to someone he knew and walked over to Tim. "Do they know what happened?"

For a second he didn't recognize me. Then he did. "You drove Professor Linney here."

I nodded. "Molly Blume."

He returned his attention to the house. "A neighbor on the other side called it in. They think it may be arson. How did the bastard know no one was inside? Or that the fire wouldn't spread?" The glow of the fire illuminated his fierce glare and created a halo around his head.

Fire has its own drama. We watched and listened in silence as firefighters directed wide arcs of water at the burning house. After half an hour the blaze seemed under control, although fugitive flames leapt here and there. *Catch me if you can.* Night made it hard to see the damage.

"I'd better go," Tim said with reluctance. "I told my wife I'd be a few minutes, and I've been here two hours."

Minutes later—it could have been ten, it could have been twenty—a fireman entered the house. A while later he emerged from the front entrance. He walked over to another fireman and pointed toward the house.

The second fireman accompanied him back inside. A few minutes later they returned. The second man walked over to a firefighter standing near the fire engine cab. Now *he* pointed to the house and shook his head.

I made my way to the fire engine.

The man near the cab had a phone at his ear.

I moved closer.

". . . told by all the neighbors that the house was empty, and there was no sign anyone was inside," he said into the phone. He paused, listening. "An old man."

CHAPTER ELEVEN

Saturday, November 8. 5:53 P.M. 1800 block of Edgecliffe Drive. Two assailants approached the victim on foot. "Don't be a chump," one of them said. "I know where you live. I'm gonna burn down your house." (Northeast)

THE TWIN FLAMES OF THE BRAIDED LAVENDER-AND-white havdalah candle became one and leapt to life. My dad handed me the candle, and raising a footed silver cup, he recited the blessing that separates the Sabbath from the rest of the week—"between the holy and the secular."

On a scale of "holy" I'd scored a five out of ten this Shabbat at best. Probably a four. Yes, I'd observed all the rules. Even when I'd bolted from Orthodox Judaism, I'd observed the rules at my parents' home out of respect for them. Yes, I'd prayed next to Liora this morning at shul, and I'd participated in the family discussion of the weekly Torah portion at lunch. But my mind had turned again and again to Oscar Linney and his death.

My dad finished reciting the final havdalah blessing. I handed him the candle, and while Joey shut off the overhead kitchen light, my dad poured Glenlivet onto a plate and touched the candle to the liquor. Crowding near the counter, we watched tiny hot blue ghostly acrobats dance and leap along the alcohol trail, sometimes in pairs, sometimes alone, until the alcohol was consumed and all the acrobats took their final bows and disappeared.

Today's Torah portion, in fact, had reminded me of the professor. *Lech lecha.* "Leave your country," God had instructed Abraham. Abraham, who, the commentaries say, was thrown into a fiery furnace when he wouldn't bow down to idols. Abraham had survived a furnace. Oscar Linney hadn't.

As a child I thought my dad was a magician, making fire dance on liquid. Sometimes he uses wine instead of liquor. When he does, he presses the torch into the shallow pool that has spilled onto the chalice's tray, and the flame sputters and hisses as it dies. I was grateful that tonight he'd used the Glenlivet. I'd had a restless night, imagining the old man trapped, hearing in my mind the sounds of his fiery death.

Thinking about Oscar Linney wasn't the problem. The problem was that my preoccupation with Linney had marred the beauty and repose of Shabbat that I treasure. If I'd listened to Liora and stayed home, Linney would still be dead, but I wouldn't have been itching all day for the "holy" to end so that I could rush into the "secular" to find out the what and how of what had happened, the why.

I'd been tempted to ask questions at the scene. I'd like to think I would have gone home with my questions unasked if Noah hadn't been there, but I'm not sure. And I envy people like my sister who are never tempted.

My dad began singing "HaMavdil" in Hebrew, and I joined the others. Then Bubbie G, her voice thin and wavery but still beautiful, led us in the Yiddish "Gut voch." A good week. A week filled with *mazel,* luck. I hoped so. I tried to stay in the moment, but my mind was on Fuller and the questions that had troubled me all day.

"I still can't believe the Professor is dead," Tim Bolt said. "I keep thinking, what if I'd told the firemen Linney might be inside? But I didn't see him arrive. None of us did. And there were no lights on in the house."

Bolt had been startled and a little uncomfortable to see me on his doorstep. After a slight hesitation he'd invited me into a living room done in tones of ocher and sand livened by a startling splash of blues and reds in the oil painting of a woman above the stone fireplace. The room was heavy with the smell of a floral air freshener—to cover the smoke, Tim had explained before I'd asked.

I made myself comfortable on a taupe chenille sofa. "Did the police say what happened?"

Friday night, prompted by my brother and my conscience, I'd left after overhearing the news. I still hadn't phoned Connors. Even if I'd dared bother him on a Saturday night, he wouldn't have information about a case outside his jurisdiction. Porter would know, but the odds of his talking to me were slimmer than Calista Flockhart.

"The fire department is handling the investigation," Tim said. "Hank told me they're pretty sure it's arson."

"He didn't know his father-in-law was missing?"

"He was on an overnight business trip. The caregiver didn't show that morning, and Hank couldn't cancel, so he asked the housekeeper to stay until he returned Saturday. She claims the Professor told her Hank had phoned and said he was returning

Friday afternoon. He'd seemed fine and insisted he'd be okay for the hour or so he'd be alone."

I wouldn't want to be in the housekeeper's shoes. "You seem close to the family."

"We've been neighbors since I was a kid. This was my parents' home." He waved his hand around the room. "Peggy and I moved in after my parents died. When I was a teenager I mowed the Linneys' lawn, and the Professor helped me with my history papers. Mostly, he told me how terrible they were." Tim's smile turned into a sigh.

"Was Linney's daughter on the local HARP board?"

Bolt gazed at me, curious. "I don't think so, no. The Professor was. He was quite involved. Why?"

"An unusual number of homes have been vandalized lately in HARP districts, and the targeted homes seem to belong to HARP board members."

Tim frowned. "Really?"

The first time one of my pieces ran in the *Times,* I'd been dismayed to find out that the entire world hadn't read it. I've learned better. "There was an article about it in yesterday's L.A. *Times.*"

"I haven't read yesterday's paper yet. My wife hasn't been feeling well, and I've been playing nurse. Not very well, I'm afraid." He smiled ruefully. "I'll go get it. What section is it in?"

"'Calendar.'" A while back it would have been in a separate section called "Southern California Living," but the *Times* is always changing things around; don't ask me why.

While he was gone, I stretched my legs and took a closer look at the lithograph and framed photos, one of a younger Tim with a pretty brown-haired woman, another of a little girl and boy who looked just like the couple.

Tim came back into the room, paging through the newspaper as he walked.

"Your children?" I pointed to the photos.

"None yet," he said with some sadness. "But we're hoping. That's me and Peggy. My wife. We were childhood sweethearts."

He sat on an oversize armchair and read the article. I returned to the couch and waited until he was done.

"Molly Blume," he said, and looked up. "That's you, right?" He scanned my article again. "So this guy is targeting HARP board members?"

"I thought so. I guess I was wrong." I tried again to console myself with the fact that Connors had made the same assumption. "If Margaret Reston—"

"Linney," Tim corrected. "Reston's her married name, but she kept her maiden name for most things."

Whatever. "If Margaret Linney was never on a HARP board, I don't understand why she was targeted."

"Maybe it was the Professor who was targeted," Tim said. "It was his house."

I frowned. "He told me it was his daughter's house."

"It was, as of around six months ago. The Professor signed the house over to Margaret when he was diagnosed with Alzheimer's. He wanted to put his affairs in order while he still had the mental sharpness to do it. He *loved* that house. So did Margaret. I don't think she wanted to move. Even if the new house *is* in Hancock Park."

What Linney had said, plus a measure of disdain. "Mr. Reston put the house up for sale?"

"Three months ago, a month before the Muirfield house was finished. The Professor was devastated. He didn't want strangers living in his house. But of course, Hank couldn't let him live there alone, even with a caretaker. I promised the Professor I'd screen the buyers carefully. It's in my best interests. I want nice neighbors." Bolt smiled.

"You're with Central Realty?" That was the name I'd seen on the For Sale sign.

He nodded. "It's a beautiful house— Well, it was, before the fire. I've been keeping an eye on it, making sure the gardener does a good job, letting the housekeeper in to clean the place every week. It was in immaculate condition and everything was the original work—the tile, the fireplace, the hardware, the moldings. But it's a hard sell, because of Margaret's disappearance."

This was the sad story. I vaguely recalled reading about a woman's disappearance in a police report a while back, but the reports I get are sanitized and don't have names. And in a large city like L.A., people often disappear, often voluntarily. "I don't remember seeing media coverage about it."

"There were a few write-ups in the papers, and something on the local TV news. There would have been more, but a little girl went missing, so that took over. But by law we're required to tell potential buyers something like that, especially since it looks like Margaret was kidnapped from the house. At the first two open houses, most of the people who stopped by were from the neighborhood. They weren't interested in buying. They just wanted to snoop. Vultures." Tim sniffed.

"What happened to Margaret?"

"One day I saw her working in her garden. The next morning she was gone. Just like that." He was looking somewhere else, not at me, probably lost in the memory. "There were signs of a struggle in her bedroom. And the police found her car at a mall, and her blood."

"Did she seem different that day?"

"I didn't think so at the time. That morning she dropped off a book I'd asked to borrow, and then I showed her a lithograph I just bought. She paints, so I value her opinion. She couldn't stay, though, because she had a busy day ahead of her. Later, when the police asked me, I realized she was tense. But I have no idea why."

"When did she disappear, exactly?"

"It'll be five months this Wednesday, November twelfth. The

police think she's dead, but her husband hired a detective. He told me he won't give up till he finds her. Dead *or* alive," Tim added.

"Where was he when Margaret disappeared?"

"Out of town, on business."

A flicker of disapproval flitted across his face so quickly that I almost missed it. Reston had been out of town Friday night, too. I wondered if the police would find that as interesting as I did. I flashed to Scott Peterson, who had beseeched the public to help him find his missing eight-months-pregnant wife, Laci, and was now awaiting trial for her murder.

"What about Professor Linney?"

"He was asleep for the night, and in the morning, Margaret was gone. He blamed himself." Tim sighed. "I kept telling him he couldn't have saved her. And if he'd tried, he probably would've been killed."

And now he was dead anyway. When trouble comes, Bubbie G says, it often doesn't come alone. "Who reported her missing?"

"I did," Bolt said, somber. "The Professor pounded on my door at six in the morning. He couldn't find Margaret, her room was a mess, he was afraid something had happened to her. He wasn't making sense, and I thought she'd run to the market or something. But then I saw the bedroom." He grimaced, as though he were reliving the discovery.

"No one on the block heard anything? No one saw any strange people or cars that didn't belong?"

Tim shook his head. "It happened in the middle of the night. Margaret kept her car at the end of the driveway, near the garage. So if she was kidnapped, the kidnapper could have taken her out the back door and no one would have seen."

Bolt's choice of words interested me. "You're not sure she was kidnapped?"

"I guess she was. They were waiting for a ransom demand— Hank has money—but it never came."

I sensed he was holding back. Reporter's intuition. That and his earlier disapproval; his slight, uneasy hesitation; the fact that he wasn't making eye contact. I thought about the mocking tone of the woman I'd heard talking to Reston, about Reston's anger directed at her and possibly the architect. What was his name? Dorn. Jeremy Dorn.

"I heard people talking about this case just the other night," I lied. "I didn't realize they were talking about Margaret Linney. They seemed to think the husband was a suspect in the disappearance."

Tim shrugged. "You'd have to ask the police."

Not exactly a denial. "What about Jeremy Dorn? Was there something going on between him and Margaret Reston?"

He stiffened. "I've known Margaret all my life. She was a beautiful person, inside and out. People like to say nasty things, but that doesn't make them true." His face was flushed with anger.

So there *had* been talk. "Did she know Jeremy Dorn?"

"They both did. Hank and Margaret were building their dream house. Dorn was the architect."

"The other day Professor Linney asked you if Margaret still hated him. What was that all about?"

"I really can't say." Bolt glanced toward the stairs visible through the arched doorway and stood. "I'd better check on Peggy."

Couldn't say, or wouldn't? I stood, too. "I appreciate your talking to me, Tim. One more question? Was Professor Linney the head of the HARP board when he served on it?"

Tim looked at me with curiosity. "I don't think so. What's the difference? Either way, he's dead," he said quietly. "That sad old man is dead."

CHAPTER TWELVE

ZACK WAS ROCKING ON MY PORCH GLIDER, HIS HANDS IN
the pockets of his black leather jacket, when I pulled into my
driveway.

He met me at the trunk of my car.

"Another five minutes, and I would've been the first cryon-
ically preserved rabbi. Who said L.A. doesn't get cold?" He
smiled. "*Shavua tov,* Molly." Have a good week.

"*Shavua tov.* Why didn't you call first?"

"I did. You weren't home, and your cell phone wasn't on.
Your mom said you left right after havdalah, so I figured I'd pick
you up at seven."

He lifted out my roll-aboard overnighter and wheeled it
along the pavement and up the steps to the porch.

I checked my watch. It was five after. "Did we have a date?" I took out a bag with the quart of Baskin-Robbins Pralines 'n Cream I'd bought after leaving Tim Bolt's.

Zack turned and gave me a quizzical look. "We always go out Saturday night. Why would tonight be different?"

I shut the trunk and joined him on the porch. "You didn't mention it on Friday. And you didn't walk over last night, or this afternoon. So I wasn't sure."

"My cousins are visiting from New York. Remember?"

"Not really." Now that he said it, I *did* remember something about relatives coming. All that worry . . .

The apartment smelled musty. I opened a window in the breakfast nook, where I left Zack while I wheeled my luggage to my bedroom and took off my jacket. When I returned he was in my tiny kitchen, rearranging frozen vegetables in my freezer to find a spot for the ice cream.

"I need five minutes," I said. "Where are we going?"

"There's an eight-thirty showing of the new Tom Hanks film at The Grove. How does that sound?" He removed his jacket and slipped it around a dinette chair.

"Fine."

I'm a big fan of Tom's, though not of war movies, which this was. But it was "kosher"—no steamy sex, no nudity, little or no profanity. Aside from animated films, action flicks, selected thrillers, and romantic comedies (my favorite), there's not much out there for a Modern Orthodox rabbi to see.

"Where were you, by the way?" he asked. "Aside from Baskin-Robbins."

"Interviewing someone about the death of an old man who died in a fire last night on Fuller. I happened to give him a ride a few days ago." I told him what had happened, my heart heavy with sadness for Oscar Linney.

"That poor old man." Zack shook his head. "People were

talking about the fire in shul. According to the news, the police suspect arson. So what was he like?"

"Cranky, confused. Lonely, sad. Looking for a daughter who's missing and is probably dead." I repeated what Tim Bolt had told me, felt another twinge of pity for the old man.

Zack sighed. "Not knowing is worse than knowing, isn't it? The pain must be unbearable. You hear about people with missing spouses, kids. Look at Yakov and Yosef." Jacob and Joseph. "Yakov spent twenty-two years mourning for his son, not wanting to accept that he was dead even though he'd seen the blood on Yosef's coat."

I still have trouble believing that this man who slips so naturally into talk of Judaism and Jewish ancestors was the jock I'd necked with in high school. Zack had made a 180-degree turn. If anything, I'd turned a few degrees in the opposite direction.

He was studying me. "You're frowning. Is something wrong, Molly?"

This is why I can't bluff at poker. "It's my *Times* story." Not really a lie. "The house that was torched, where the old man died? It was his house, and he was on the HARP board. But I don't think he *chaired* the board."

Zack looked puzzled. "And that's a problem because . . . ?"

I told him what I'd left out of my piece. "So if Oscar Linney's house was targeted, that doesn't fit the pattern."

"So maybe the pattern's a little different. It's still a HARP connection, right? And you didn't mention this other pattern in your story, so there's nothing to retract."

Thanks to Connors. He'd never let me forget. "There *was* a pattern, Zack. Seven out of twelve chairpersons targeted in a two-month period can't be a coincidence."

"You're right." Zack rubbed his chin. He does that when he's thinking hard.

"We're not going to solve it tonight. I'm going to change."

I took a step toward the hall and turned around. "Okay if I wear pants?" I could see that the question surprised him. I'd surprised myself.

"You don't need my permission."

"But would it *bother* you?"

He cocked his head. "Is this a test?"

"It's a question." I was beginning to be sorry I'd asked. I sat down at the dinette table.

"Well, if you're asking, I'd be more comfortable if you didn't."

"You were uncomfortable at the HARP meeting when the Hammers saw us together, weren't you?"

"Not in the least."

He was making me nervous, standing there. "Aren't you going to sit down?"

"Do I need an attorney?"

I felt myself blush. "Sorry."

He took the seat across from me. "Is that why you were so distant on the way home, and the next night, when we talked on the phone?"

"*I* wasn't distant. *You* were distant."

"I was trying not to get in your way, Molly. You were think-ing about a dead bird. You had a deadline."

I had to admit that was true. "I told you on our first date that I wasn't right for you."

"And *I* said, 'Let's get to know each other, see what happens.' Unless I'm totally clueless, things are great between us." He gazed at me intently. "Aren't they?"

"Yes." *God,* yes. My face felt warm. "That first date, were you figuring that if we hit it off, I'd change the way I dress?"

"I wasn't figuring anything. I felt incredibly lucky that we'd reconnected, and then you made it clear you weren't interested. But I couldn't stop thinking about you, and then I saw you in shul. And, well, here we are."

"And my skirts and sleeves are still too short." I smiled to lighten the moment.

He smiled, too. "You're hardly Jennifer Lopez in short shorts or a sheer Versace. But you're right," he said, suddenly serious. "As a rabbi, I'm expected to follow the rules, and people look at who I'm with. Human nature."

"So what are you saying?"

"I'm saying I believe in the rules. I live my life by them." He leaned toward me, his arms folded on the table. "I'm saying you're the best thing that's happened to me, Molly, and I can't imagine not having you in my life, and I hope we can work it all out. What are *you* saying?"

He was so close that I could smell the musk of his aftershave. I had an urge to trace the contours of his face with my finger, to lean closer and press my lips against his. What would that feel like after twelve years?

"I'm saying you're the best thing that's happened to me, and I can't imagine not having you in my life," I repeated softly. My face was tingling. "But I'm not good with having rules forced on me. That's what pushed me away before. And I don't want to give up my individuality."

"And your individuality is defined by your hemline?"

"Among other things."

"Orthodox Judaism has a lot of rules, Molly, most of which you have no problem following." He leaned back against the chair. "Is this going to be a problem?"

"I don't want it to be."

He nodded. "Maybe this isn't about hemlines."

Maybe it wasn't. Maybe it was about not knowing whether I could trust my feelings. I'd been wrong before. I'd thought Ron and I would last forever, but our marriage had expired before the warranty on our large-screen TV.

"I guess I need some time," I said.

CHAPTER THIRTEEN

Monday, November 10. 9:24 A.M. 100 block of North Croft Avenue. A woman reported that a man called her six times and hung up without saying anything, then called back and said, "I will kill you and eat your heart with mushrooms." (Wilshire)

VINCE PORTER SHOWED UP AT MY DOOR WITH ENRICO Hernandez, a Wilshire detective I'd seen at the station. I had just stepped out of the shower after a long date with my treadmill—penance for the weekend. A jumbo bucket of popcorn during Tom's movie, followed by hot dogs and fries at The Grove's kosher kiosk; Sunday dinner with Zack at an Italian restaurant that makes irresistible olive bread with a garlic spread and great veal scallopini. And tonight was mah jongg at Mindy's—more nosh.

I threw on a sweater and jeans that felt tighter than they had three days ago and towel-dried my hair. I almost felt sorry for Porter and Hernandez, who were probably being grilled by Isaac, my thrice-widowed, seventy-seven-year-old landlord. He'd been engaged in his favorite pastime when they arrived—people-watching while drinking coffee and rocking on the front porch glider. I heard him clack his dentures with excitement as I invited the detectives inside, and he'd probably have given me a month's free rent to be in on the conversation so that he could report it to his "boys" at their weekly poker game.

Porter is tall and muscular with surfer wavy blond hair and swimming-pool blue eyes that have probably taken in a lot of suspects, especially of the female gender. The eyes, not surprisingly, weren't all that friendly this morning. Hernandez is a few inches shorter and leaner and has thick straight black hair and eyes the color of dark chocolate.

They sat on the taupe sofa in my sparsely furnished living room, and I sank into the cushy chintz armchair facing them. I'd been expecting a visit from Porter. I wasn't exactly nervous, but there is something unsettling about having police detectives in your home. The last time had been five years ago in a different apartment, when detectives had questioned me about the murder of my best friend Aggie.

Hernandez began. "As you may know, Miss Blume, Friday night a man died in a fire. We're assisting the fire department in the investigation of his death."

"Has arson been determined?" I asked.

Porter gave me a we're-asking-the-questions scowl, but Hernandez didn't seem perturbed.

"They found traces of an accelerant," he said.

I'm a sucker for accents and I loved his—Hispanic, soft and musical. "Where was Professor Linney found?"

"I'm afraid I can't answer that. I *can* tell you he was on the local HARP board, which suggests that this incident is connected to the recent vandalisms you so kindly brought to the department's attention." A hint of a smile played around his lips.

Porter, I saw, was not amused. "Did Linney chair the board?"

"As a matter of fact, he did, a year ago."

That fit the pattern, then. But would the vandal have known that? And why would he strike twice in the same area?

Hernandez took out a small spiral notepad. "We have a few questions about the HARP meeting Wednesday night."

"The one you wrote about in your piece in the *Times.*" Porter's sneer and grating chalk-on-a-blackboard tone indicated what he thought of my journalistic efforts.

There went my Pulitzer. "What would you like to know?" I asked Hernandez.

"Let's begin with the bird."

I was sick of the damn bird. "There's not much to tell. It was a medium-size bird." I held up my hands about eight inches apart. "Kind of a grayish brown. A woman found it hanging on the ledge of an easel holding up a poster. She knocked down the easel and screamed."

"What time was that?" Porter asked.

I considered. "Around eight-fifteen." I was hungry and craved coffee, but it would be rude to drink alone, and I wasn't inclined to play hostess to Porter.

"Any idea who placed it there?" Hernandez asked.

I shook my head. "I must have passed the easel half a dozen times during the evening, but I only looked at it when I first arrived. That was around seven-twenty. I was across the room talking to people when the woman screamed."

"Which people?"

They were eliminating suspects. "Linda Cobern. She's with Councilman Harrington's office. And Jeremy Dorn. He's spearheading the Hancock Park HARP drive."

Hernandez wrote down the names. "Anyone else?"

"There was a gray-haired man talking to Cobern and Dorn. He left after I walked over and was near the easel when the woman screamed. He was furious about HARP."

"What's his name?" Porter was a tiger pouncing on his prey.

I blanked for a second, then remembered. "Arnold Seltzer. I quoted him in the *Times* article."

"Who else had access to the easel?" Hernandez asked.

"Everyone. And the room was cold, so a lot of people were wearing jackets or coats. It wouldn't have been hard for someone to hide the bird and put it on the easel's ledge when no one was looking. I think that's why the organizers decided not to call the police." And because they didn't want the negative publicity.

"What about Roger Modine? Was he there?" Porter asked.

Connors must have given him the contractor's name. "Yes." I'd asked my dad. He'd never met Modine, but had heard of him: decent work, but something of a hothead. I decided to keep that to myself.

"Was he wearing a jacket?"

"I think so." I tried to visualize the contractor. "Brown corduroy, bulky. Seltzer was wearing a black parka." I hoped Roger Modine had a solid alibi for Friday night.

"You're very observant, Miss Blume." Hernandez smiled. "We're fortunate that you were there."

He was the "good" cop. He was flattering me, and I knew it, but what the hell? I smiled back.

"What about your sister?" Porter asked. "Edie Borman," he prompted when I didn't respond.

"I know my sister's name," I said before my better judgment kicked in. There was no advantage in being snippy with Porter. "What about her?"

"We understand that she was at the meeting, and that she's very involved with the Hancock Park anti-HARP drive. She could have put the dead bird on the easel."

Edie won't open a carton of cottage cheese that's a day past its expiration date, let alone touch a dead bird. But that wouldn't impress Porter. "So could half the people in the room," I said. "I could have, too."

"Did you?"

Forget better judgment. "Sure, I always carry a dead bird in my purse. You never know when you're going to need one to liven up a party."

"Or a story. Maybe you figured it would punch up your ending." Porter smirked.

I decided not to dignify that with a response.

Hernandez frowned at Porter, probably for my benefit. "Timothy Bolt told us you gave Professor Linney a ride to the Fuller house," he said. "When was that?"

"Tuesday morning, around eleven-thirty." I described the circumstances. "Apparently, Professor Linney had wandered out of his son-in-law's house several times before, looking for his daughter's house."

"How do you know that?" Porter demanded.

I was tempted to say I'd used a crystal ball. "Tim Bolt said so. So did the son-in-law, Hank Reston. I overheard him at the HARP meeting talking about Linney. Reston was very concerned." I faced Hernandez, knowing it would annoy Porter. "Why all these questions, Detective?"

"We're trying to establish how Professor Linney happened to be at the Fuller house. So what you're telling us is helpful. It corroborates a pattern."

"Miss Blume *loves* patterns," Porter said.

I smiled at him and silently invoked a Yiddish curse: May you grow like an onion, with your head in the ground. Maybe that's what the Mona Lisa was thinking, too.

"Did Professor Linney tell you why he wanted to go to his daughter's house?" Hernandez asked.

"No. But when he was pounding on the door, trying to get in, he said that he hoped she didn't hate him, that he'd done what he had because he loved her. He was crying." I felt a wave of sadness for the old man.

"What do you think he meant?"

"I have no idea." I wondered again whether Bolt knew. I debated telling the detectives that Linney hadn't wanted to return to his son-in-law's house but decided not to sic Porter on Reston.

"You told us Linney was pounding on the door," Porter said. "He didn't have a key?"

"He said he forgot it."

"Did he seem lucid, Miss Blume?" Hernandez asked.

"Lucid, but confused. He thought his daughter still lived in the house. And as I said, he was agitated."

"Did he say anything else?" Porter asked in that same grating tone that made me grit my teeth.

Hank's a mean son of a bitch. I shook my head. Partly because Porter was getting on my nerves. Partly because I suspected there was more to Hernandez's questions than he'd admitted. Intuition, a sixth sense. It's worked for me before. Other times, of course, it's led me nowhere.

"You mentioned that Mr. Reston was at the HARP meeting," Hernandez said. "Was he pro or anti?"

"I don't know. I didn't have a chance to ask him. I overheard him telling a woman that he'd come to the meeting because he'd promised to give Linney a report."

"Was he wearing a jacket, by the way?"

I pictured Reston. "He had a black leather jacket and an oversize sweater. I remember thinking it made him look larger than he was."

Hernandez flipped a page of his notepad. "You interviewed many people for your article. Did any of them speculate as to who was responsible for the vandalisms?"

I shook my head. "Are you assuming that the person who placed the bird started the fire in the Fuller house?"

"It's a strong possibility. You probably didn't use all your interview material in your *Times* article, correct? Something in your notes might give us a lead."

I didn't like where this was heading. "I don't think so, but I'll check them again."

"If we could take a look . . . I'm sure you want to help us apprehend the person responsible for Professor Linney's death."

"Absolutely." I nodded. "But I'm not comfortable handing over my notes." I had nothing to hide and no one to protect, but my notes were as private as my underwear.

Hernandez looked disappointed but not angry, unlike Porter, who was glaring. "At some point, Miss Blume, we may have to insist," Hernandez said, a pleasant but unapologetic warning in his musical voice. "So please take good care of your notes. Thanks for your time." He stood. "If we have more questions—"

"About Professor Linney," I said. "Tim Bolt told me Margaret Reston disappeared several months ago. What's happening with that case?" I'd accessed the *Times* archives yesterday but had found only a few small paragraphs in the "California" section stating the bare facts and asking anyone who had information about the missing woman to contact the police.

"After five months, the trail is cold. But of course, if we get any leads, we follow up."

"Do you think she's dead, Detective?"

"Probably. But without a body, we can't be certain."

"Is her husband a suspect?"

"I can't discuss the Reston case, just as you can't share your notes." Hernandez smiled. "I'm sure you understand."

Chapter Fourteen

"IF YOU HAVE ANY MORE *PATTERNS*, YOU SHOULD CON-sider taking up knitting," Connors said when I finally reached him on the phone a little after two.

I hadn't talked to him since Thursday morning. He hadn't been at the station today when I'd stopped by on my rounds for my column, and he hadn't returned any of my calls. I knew he was pissed.

"I didn't mention that the chairpersons were being targeted, Andy." I filled a glass with tap water and downed half. My fourth glass of the day—I was trying to be good but felt like an inflated flotation device.

"I asked you not to mention the bird, Molly. I asked you not to mention the board members *at all*."

"I did what I thought was right." There was no point in beating a dead horse—or bird, in this case. And that wasn't why I'd phoned. "I had a visit from Vince Porter and Enrico Hernandez this morning. Do you know Hernandez?"

"I know Rico. He's a good man."

"They wanted to know all about the HARP meeting. And they asked me about the man who died, Oscar Linney."

"Why would they ask you?"

"Porter didn't tell you? I gave Linney a ride to his daughter's house the other day." I sighed. "I can't get the old man out of my mind, Andy."

"You see dead people," Connors said in a droll monotone. "How'd you know Linney?" he asked, more serious.

"I didn't *know* him. We met in front of my car." I gave Connors the details. "Bolt told me it wasn't the first time Linney showed up looking for his daughter. I imagine he told Porter the same thing. So I'm wondering why he and Hernandez are asking so many questions."

"Ask *them*."

"I did. Hernandez said they're trying to establish how Linney got to Fuller from his son-in-law's house Friday."

"There you go, Molly. Mystery's solved. We return you to our regularly scheduled program."

"I had the feeling there was more to it. Did Porter tell you what's going on, Andy?"

"He's Wilshire, I'm Hollywood. Believe me, I have enough on my own plate."

Not really an answer. "But the vandalisms crossed divisions, Andy. Are you telling me you haven't talked to Porter since the fire?"

Connors hesitated. "I've talked to him."

"I heard that the accelerant was lighter fluid. Is that true?"

"No, it's not."

That surprised me. "It's not? What was it?"

"You really should talk to Porter, Molly. It's his case. The fire department's, actually. But Porter and Hernandez are helping."

I frowned. "Why are you shutting me out, Andy?"

"Maybe because I don't want to read about it in tomorrow's *Times.* Maybe I like my job and being able to pay the bills."

"I won't write anything until you say I can. You have my word." I paused to give my promise weight. "What was the accelerant?" I downed the rest of the water. "Andy?"

"Paint thinner."

Interesting. "Where was Linney when they found him?"

"At the bottom of the staircase. His cane was in an upstairs bedroom. From the impression on the bed, they're guessing he was asleep when the fire started."

"I wonder why he didn't call the fire department."

"You said he had Alzheimer's, right? He was probably confused. He panicked and fell trying to get downstairs. If he'd stayed up there, he probably would've been okay. There was very little damage to the second story."

That made his death even sadder. "How do they know he wasn't hurrying up the stairs to get away from the flames?"

"From the position of the body and the injuries. Possible broken neck. They found contusions on his face and bruises on his legs. The M.E. is doing the autopsy, probably tomorrow morning. Until they get the results, they won't know what killed him, the fall or the fire."

I pictured the old man as he got into my car. I saw the robe open, the exposed bony knees. "The bruises were there when I met him." I told Connors what I'd seen.

"Tell Porter or Hernandez, not me."

With my ironing board set up in my bedroom and Elton John belting out "Rocket Man," I tackled the first of half a dozen blouses I'd laundered the other day. My sisters think I'm crazy,

but I'm one of those people who find ironing relaxing. I also—
don't laugh—derive pleasure from turning something wrinkled
into something lovely, if only temporarily so. Plus I do some of
my best thinking when my mind wanders and my only concern
is not burning my fingers.

I ran the hot Rowenta over a striped sleeve (if you're going
to spend quality time with an iron, use a good one) and reviewed
my session with Porter and Hernandez. The more I thought
about it, the more convinced I was that they hadn't come to ask
me about the HARP meeting. It was Linney they were interested in.

I finished the blouse and phoned Connors.

"All the questions Hernandez and Porter asked me?" I said
when he came on the line. "'What did Linney say? What was he
like?' They're wondering whether Linney happened to be at the
house when it was torched, or whether the house was torched
because he was there."

"Molly." Connors sighed.

"It's because Margaret Reston disappeared, isn't it? Linney's
daughter, but I assume you know that. She's gone, presumed
dead. Now *he's* dead, too."

"The two incidents aren't necessarily connected."

"Linney doesn't fit the pattern, Andy. Why would the vandal strike the Miracle Mile area a second time?"

"Why *wouldn't* he? Porter told me Linney headed the HARP
board, so he definitely fits the pattern."

"Linney chaired the board a *year* ago. How would the vandal have known that?"

"The information's not hard to get. He could've found it online. *You* did. Or he could've asked a HARP member."

"And waited a year to strike?" I flipped another blouse onto
the board and ran the iron across the collar. "Excluding Linney,
six chairpersons' homes were vandalized. Plus Fennel, who was

chair until his term was up a month ago. The first chairperson was vandalized a month ago, too," I continued, thinking it through as I spoke, "so when the vandal made his target list, Fennel was on it."

"And Linney wasn't." Connors sounded thoughtful.

"No, but someone tried to make it look like he was part of the pattern. Whoever torched the house took advantage of the fact that someone was targeting HARP board members, but he didn't know that the vandal was targeting the chairpersons." The significance of what I'd said hit me. *A copycat. My fault.* I think the knowledge was there from the moment I'd watched Linney's house burn. I just hadn't wanted to face it.

Connors was silent. The iron hissed steam.

"I know what you're thinking," I said. "If I hadn't written the article, if I hadn't mentioned the board members . . . Linney might be alive." Tears smarted my eyes. I bit my lips.

"You're being hard on yourself, Molly," Connors said quietly, his kindness worse than an I-told-you-so. "You're assuming he was the target. This *could* be the work of the same guy who vandalized the other places. Maybe Linney just happened to be there."

"A man's daughter disappears, and five months later he dies in a fire started by arson? Porter and Hernandez are suspicious. I would be, too. So are you."

"I've heard of stranger coincidences, Molly."

"He didn't want to go up the stairs," I said.

"What?"

"I just remembered. The day I drove Linney to his daughter's house? The neighbor invited him to rest at his place, and Linney said he didn't want to climb the stairs because he was afraid he'd fall and break his hip. So what was he doing in an upstairs bedroom Friday night?"

CHAPTER FIFTEEN

WALTER FENNEL EYED ME THROUGH THE PRIVACY WIN-
dow of his front door. "What did you say your name was?" he
asked again in a squeaky voice that needed oiling.

"Molly Blume." I said it louder this time.

"I know that name. Have we met?"

He was either a James Joyce fan or he'd read my article. I
hoped it was the former. "I don't think so. I'd like to ask you a
few questions about Professor Linney."

"Are you a police detective? I talked to two of them today.
A tall blond fellow and a Latino."

"No, I'm a writer." So Porter and Hernandez had been here.
Porter may be annoying, but he's no slouch.

"I'll bet they're sorry they didn't take the vandalism to my house more seriously." He grunted with satisfaction. "Let me see some ID. Slide it under the door, would you? It's hard to see anything through this damn window."

I took a business card from my wallet and did as he asked. A few seconds later the door opened and I had my first look at the neighborhood watchdog.

Hangdog was more like it. He had a thin, bony face with folds of loose skin that disappeared into the wattles of his scrawny neck. He was mostly bald, except for a yellow-white fringe at the back of his pink scalp that looked like dandelion fur. Porter had said the old man was five-six, but his hunched posture sliced off a few inches.

"I've seen you before." His pale brown eyes studied me through gold-tone bifocals lowered on his long, sharp nose.

"My sister lives across the street," I said, speaking a little louder than normal. "Mindy Wollensky?"

"You don't have to yell, young lady. That's what these are for." He pointed to his hearing aids. "Sometimes I turn the damn things off and pretend they're not working well. Don't tell my wife." He winked at me. "Your sister just had a baby. A boy after two girls, right? How's the little guy doing?" His tongue made a sweep of his thin upper lip.

The FBI had nothing over him. I bit the inside of my cheek to keep from smiling. "Fine."

"Who are you talking to, Walter?" a woman called. A moment later she was standing beside him, wearing a navy velour sweat suit that strained across her chest and hips.

She was a large woman with a full face and a set of chins that looked like nesting tables. The fullness, along with her tinted brown hair and a touch of pink lipstick and blusher, made her look years younger than Fennel.

"Her name is Molly Blume," he practically yelled. "She's a writer." He did that tongue-sweeping thing again.

"Are you selling magazines?" she asked. "We have too many as it is."

"She's here about Linney. She's Mrs. Wollensky's sister." He faced me. "I see your sister pushing the carriage sometimes. She's a lawyer, right?"

"You're the reporter!" The wife pointed an accusing finger. "You wrote that article in Friday's *Times*."

Fennel pushed his glasses high up against the bridge of his nose and frowned. "You called us Harpies."

I was blushing as though he'd caught me buck naked. "I reported what some people are saying, Mr. Fennel. I didn't mean to offend you."

"Well, they can say what they want. I won't apologize for trying to keep this neighborhood from being destroyed. I'll bet you thought that was funny, someone throwing a pumpkin and eggs at our house." He scowled at me.

"I thought it was nasty. Who do you think did it?"

Another sweep of the lip. It was something he did every few seconds, like a metronome. He studied my face, as if trying to determine whether I was telling the truth.

"I thought I knew," he said. "Now I'm not sure. Why do you want to know about Oscar Linney?"

"She's going to write about him, Walter."

"Let the girl talk, Winnie. Well, *are* you?" he asked me.

"I don't know. I drove Professor Linney to his daughter's house last week. I feel terrible about what happened and want to know more about him. I'm hoping you can help me." I didn't add that I was tormented by the possibility that I'd contributed to his death, that I hadn't been able to think of much else since talking to Connors.

"Well, Molly Blume. I was about to take my daily walk. You can come with me if you want."

Apparently, I'd passed some sort of test. He put on a heavy

gray wool jacket and, at Winnie's insistence, wrapped a red shawl around his neck.

"How long will you be gone?" she asked him.

"Planning to sneak your lover into the house?"

"Two of them. Go on, now!"

She gave him a playful shove that almost knocked him over, pecked at his wrinkled cheek, and stood in the doorway watching us. Fennel was using a cane, but he scurried down the walkway, and I had to hurry to keep up.

"I walk two miles a day," he told me as we headed toward Second. "I'm probably in better shape than you are."

No contest. He *could* have ripped the light fixture off of Strom's wall and used his cane, with its three-pronged base, to do it. I wondered if Porter had seen the cane.

"Have you lived in the neighborhood long?" I asked.

"Only fifty years." He smiled proudly and flashed me a look. "I take it you're Orthodox like your sister, but you're not wearing anything on your head. So I guess you're not married. Most of the married Orthodox women around here cover their hair."

Most, but not all. Something else to factor into the Zack equation. "I'm divorced."

"How long were you married?"

"A year and a half." I sensed his disapproval and fought the temptation to tell him I'd had good cause.

"Young people today don't work at marriage. Winnie and I had our fifty-fifth anniversary in September. We went on a cruise to Alaska. Any children?"

"No." I'd been eager, but Ron had wanted to wait. He was probably too exhausted conducting his romantic trysts and keeping his lies straight. At the time I'd been disappointed, but I believe God was watching over me.

"You're lucky." Fennel grunted. "One of our granddaughters

is divorced, with a two-year-old boy. She moved back in with her parents until she can afford to get a place of her own."

We were heading toward Second when he stopped suddenly and glared at The Dungeon.

"They ought to take a wrecking ball and knock the damn thing down," he muttered. "Looks like a prison."

I had to admit he was right. Huge oak trees with gnarled trunks and sharp branches that reminded me of witches' finger-nails stood in front of three hulking stories of unrelenting dark gray. The trees cast shadows on a lawn overgrown with untrimmed shrubs that shrouded the exterior walls. It was the perfect setting for a Gothic novel.

"Who lives there?" I asked.

Funny, but all those years I'd never really known. To tell you the truth, I hadn't *cared* to know. Knowledge would have stripped the house of its mystery, reducing it to an ugly but or-dinary structure and depriving my friends and me of hours of shivery fun.

"Charlene and Glen Coulter built it," Fennel said. "I don't know why they needed three stories. They had one boy, and then it was the two of them. Glen died years ago, so now it's just Charlene in that monstrosity. Winnie took over a casserole when Glen died and invited Charlene over, but she wouldn't come. She didn't even invite Winnie in, just took the casserole and said thank you, although she did send a note. She almost never leaves the house."

Like the Stick Lady, I thought. She lives on the other side of Beverly in a black house surrounded by a black stone fence. She walks on stilts and wears her hair so that it stands straight up on top of her head. We had invented stories about her, too.

"The whole family's always kept to themselves," Fennel said. "I never knew what Glen did for a living. I tried talking to him a few times but finally gave up."

A black mark on Fennel's report card. I wondered whether

the Coulters would have been more neighborly if the neighborhood had opened their arms and been less *up* in arms, though I had to agree the house was overpowering and ugly.

Fennel slowed to a stroll and started pointing out houses and the features that made them historically "contributing." Windows, doors, gables, arches, roofs. He stopped in front of a deep yellow Tudor.

"See those aluminum side windows? Those are pre-HARP. The owners would never get away with that now. Or with that color. Mustard is for a hot dog. But for a house?"

"Professor Linney was involved with HARP. Is that how you knew him?" Normally I do more journalistic foreplay, but at this rate, I'd never get to first base.

"We were both with the homeowners association. Now, look at *this* place." Fennel pointed to the one-story Spanish on my right. "They had an open house a few months ago. The original ceramic tile in the bathrooms is in excellent condition, but the owners plan to rip it out and put in Formica. Formica!" he repeated with disgust. "They can do it, too, because we have no say over the interior."

For the next hour Fennel gave me an architectural walking tour of the neighborhood: the type of home, what work had been done and when, what family lived there now, who had lived there before. I made one more attempt to steer the conversation to Linney, then gave up. Fennel was determined to show me the beauty he was trying to preserve, and barring an earthquake, nothing would divert him.

An hour wasted, I thought as we headed back to Martel, but we turned the corner and found ourselves on Fuller. A minute later we were in front of Oscar Linney's house. A half sheet of plywood covered the shattered bottom of the front window. The remnant of a yellow crime-scene ribbon on the charred front door fluttered gaily, a streamer inviting party guests.

I think Linney's house was Fennel's destination all along. He had fallen silent and was staring at the devastation, which was greater in the fading daylight, especially the downstairs, where whole sections had been blackened. I tried not to picture the professor lying unconscious on the landing, inhaling the fumes that would kill him. I still smelled smoke, but that was probably my imagination. For a second I thought I detected movement through one of the upstairs windows, but then it was gone. That was obviously my imagination, too, aided by the reflected sunlight bouncing against the windowpane.

A moment later the curtain moved aside, and closed. Less than an inch. Just for a second. If I hadn't been staring at the window, I wouldn't have seen it.

CHAPTER SIXTEEN

SOMEONE WAS UPSTAIRS. PORTER OR HERNANDEZ? THE
dark maroon Chevy I'd seen them enter this morning after they
left my apartment wasn't here. Hank Reston? It was his wife's
house. But there was no car in the driveway.

"Rotten shame," Fennel said, his voice hoarse.

I wasn't certain whether he was referring to the burned
house or Linney. I stole a glance and saw tears in Fennel's eyes.
He found a handkerchief in his jacket pocket, wiped his eyes,
and trumpeted his nose.

"I guess the only good thing is that he died in the house he
loved," Fennel said in a low voice.

"The two of you must have been close," I said, my eyes fixed
on the upstairs window.

"We were, until he moved with his son-in-law into that new house." Fennel sniffed. "I didn't see Oscar much after that."

"You don't like Mr. Reston?"

"I don't like or *dis*like him. I hardly know the man."

"But Professor Linney didn't like him?"

Fennel didn't answer. He swiveled with military precision and hurried down Fuller. I wanted to stay, to talk to Reston if he was inside, or find out who was there. But I couldn't, not with Fennel around.

His lips were set in a tight line when I caught up with him, and he didn't say a word all the way back to Martel. I figured the interview was over and was surprised when he invited me into his house.

Fennel sat me at an oak pedestal table in a yellow breakfast nook with a lead glass window looking out on a deep yard. Winnie was probably taking a nap, he told me while he poured two cups of coffee in a cozy country kitchen with a blue and white tile counter. He lifted the lid of a stockpot on the stove and stirred—"Minestrone," he said—releasing steam perfumed with sautéed onions, tomatoes, and other vegetables I couldn't identify that fogged the window and made my stomach grumble.

"The detectives asked about Hank, too," Fennel said a few minutes later as he brought the coffee to the table, along with white plates with a blue willow design and a matching platter piled high with brownies. "Did Oscar and Hank fight. I'm not sure I should be talking about Oscar, especially to a writer." He picked up a brownie and took a bite. He made wet, smacking sounds as he chewed.

I sensed he was playing coy, eager to tell, or why would he have invited me here? "The day we met, Professor Linney called Hank a son of a bitch. So it's no secret that he didn't like his son-in-law."

That was green light enough for Fennel. He nodded. "Oscar

thought Hank was a boor. To him, that was worse than being poor. Which Hank isn't. He's loaded. He built up a floor covering business and used the profit to buy houses and flip them or tear them down."

Everything Linney was against, I thought.

Fennel pointed to the brownies. "Aren't you going to try one? They're homemade."

I smiled. "No, thanks."

"You're not on a diet, are you?" He scowled at me. "You look fine to me. You young people are always dieting."

"I keep kosher."

He frowned. "What's not kosher about brownies?"

"It could be the ingredients or the utensils." I hoped he wasn't offended. "They look great. Winnie baked them?"

"*I* did. Winnie can't bake worth a damn. Can't cook, either. She's great at canasta and bridge, though. A great kisser, too." He chuckled and ate the rest of the brownie.

I felt a pang of longing for Zeidie Irving, who died nine years ago. (Mindy's baby Yitz is named after him.) I used to love walking behind him and Bubbie G on the way to shul and seeing their locked hands, their heads leaning in toward each other. Zeidie was a great kisser, too. He'd place his hands on the sides of my face and touch his soft lips to my forehead and cheeks.

Fennel was still chewing. I sipped the hot coffee while he finished swallowing. I wasn't eager to test my as yet untried Heimlich maneuver skills.

"How did Margaret Linney meet Hank Reston?" I asked.

"Through Ned Vaughan. He and Hank were high school pals."

The name sounded familiar. Then I remembered: He was the architect at the HARP meeting who'd been engaged in an unpleasant conversation with Roger Modine until Reston had joined them. He'd left before I had a chance to interview him.

"Ned Vaughan is with the company that did the Hancock Park historical survey, right?" I said.

Fennel nodded. "He was also in Oscar's department at USC. Oscar would invite him to the house for dinner, and the three of them—Oscar, Margaret, and Ned—would talk architecture and history. I joined them once, when Winnie was out with the gals. I was bored silly." Fennel took another brownie.

"What about Mrs. Linney?"

"Roberta died when Margaret was fourteen. Cancer," he said, with sad solemnity. "Terrible thing. She went pretty quick, and I guess that's a blessing, because she didn't suffer. After she died it was just Oscar and Margaret. I think that's why he was so attached to her. *Too* attached, in my opinion." He nibbled on the brownie, smacking his lips, sweeping the crumbs with his tongue like a cat.

I waited again until he'd finished. "Professor Linney didn't want her to marry?"

"Probably not. But he was forty-seven when Margaret was born. When his health started to go, I figure he wanted to make sure she'd have security."

"How did Hank enter the picture?"

"Oscar was recarpeting the house. Ned mentioned that his friend was in the business and could give Oscar a good deal. The next thing you know, Margaret and Hank eloped. I guess she was more interested in Karastan rugs than the countries that made 'em."

Fennel's chuckle turned into a laugh. He laughed so hard that his face turned cherry red and tears streamed out of his eyes. I was afraid he would choke, but the laughter trailed off into hiccups. He wiped his eyes.

I gave him a moment to calm down. "Was Margaret attracted to Reston's money?"

Fennel shook his head, serious again. "Roberta came from

money and left a nice sum. Oscar couldn't figure the attraction. Margaret was a concert pianist. She played at Carnegie and all over the world. She was writing her own music, too. And she painted. Hank has a high school education. His idea of high culture, Oscar told me, is *The Lion King*."

I was intrigued. "So what *did* Margaret see in him?"

"Have you met Hank?"

I nodded.

"Big guy, isn't he? Determined, too. He started with one small floor covering store. Now he has stores all over the state. Residential and commercial. And there's his real estate business, too. Hank sees something he wants, he won't stop till he gets it."

"And he wanted Margaret," I said. "Was she beautiful?"

"I don't know that I'd call her beautiful, but you'd notice her. Dark hair, pretty face. A little skinny for my taste. Oscar said Hank wanted to buy a classy wife the way he buys art. He wanted someone who'd pick out his clothes and fix up his house, someone who'd make him look good."

Reston wouldn't be the first person to seek a trophy wife, especially in L.A. "How did Ned Vaughan react to the marriage?"

"He was thrilled, toasted them at the reception Oscar threw when they came back. Ned knew about the elopement but kept their secret. Oscar was mad as hell."

Not what I'd expected. I felt a twinge of disappointment. "Ned didn't feel jilted?"

Fennel gave a harrumph almost as good as Bubbie G's. "Relieved is more like it. See, Oscar picked Ned for Margaret. I can see why. Oscar was my friend, but he was full of himself. Ned is, too. But there was no chemistry between Ned and Margaret. Zip. Architecture and history, yes."

Fennel chuckled again. I was prepared for another coughing paroxysm, but it didn't happen.

"But Ned was over at the house all the time," I said.

"Oscar was his mentor. Maybe Ned didn't want to disappoint him. Plus remember, he was in Oscar's department, so he wanted to stay on his good side. It wouldn't surprise me if he brought Hank around hoping he and Margaret would hit it off and he'd be off the hook." Fennel cleared his throat. "He's seeing someone now. Diane, I think her name is. Ned is, I mean. Hank isn't seeing anyone. Well, not that I know. If he is, he's keeping it quiet. He wouldn't want Oscar to know."

"Were Hank and Margaret happy?"

"To hear Oscar tell it, Margaret knew she'd made a mistake. About the marriage, about giving up her concert career, the composing. That was Hank's doing, according to Oscar. I thought he was going to cry when he told me about it. All those years of lessons, all those dreams—down the toilet. I guess she had other dreams. The couple of times I saw her with Hank they looked fine. But who knows?" Fennel shrugged.

Anyone who had seen Ron and me together toward the end of our marriage would have thought we were fine, too. "How long were Hank and Margaret married before she disappeared?"

"About a year. They were renting a place while they were building their dream house on Muirfield. Then Oscar was diagnosed with Alzheimer's, so Margaret and Hank moved in with him. Not the best idea. Oscar didn't like the way Hank treated Margaret, like he owned her. Oscar didn't say, but I'm sure there were fights. Oscar was outspoken."

"Do you think that was true? That Hank thought he owned Margaret?"

Fennel considered for a moment, his tongue doing an extra few sweeps of his lip. "Oscar gave a party for his department and some other folks a couple of weeks before Margaret disappeared. She played hostess. She knew all the guests, of course. Hank hardly knew a soul. He was watching her all night. A couple of times when she was gabbing with the men, he looked ready to punch their lights out."

"*There* you are." Winnie stood in the doorway. She'd traded the sweats for an ankle-length, zebra-print velour robe. Not the best choice. "I thought I heard voices."

"I'm telling Molly about Margaret and Hank."

Winnie came to the table and frowned at the brownies. "How many of these did you eat, Walter?"

"Just one." He waited until she turned to me. Then he winked at me.

"His sugar is borderline, but he doesn't give a hoot," she told me, sitting down. "Don't go filling her head with nonsense, Walter."

"I'm just saying what Oscar told me."

"Well, you don't know that everything he told you is true. He was ill, remember." She tapped her finger against her temple.

"When did you last see him?" I asked Fennel.

"The Thursday before he died." Saying the words saddened him. His face sagged. "Winnie drove me to Hank's house. I'm not supposed to drive." He scowled at his wife, but I could see that his heart wasn't in it. "I hadn't seen Oscar in over a month. He looked like he'd aged ten years."

"Because of Margaret." Winnie clucked. "Grief did him in, not the Alzheimer's. It broke his heart and his spirit."

I could believe that. Bubbie G is resilient and a fighter, but some of her spirit died along with Zeidie Irving. "Did he talk about his daughter?"

"He talked about Hank." Fennel glanced at his wife defiantly. "He said Hank hit him."

"He said that about the caregivers, too. It's the Alzheimer's."

"He had all his marbles," Fennel insisted.

I thought about the bruises I'd seen. "The day we met he thought Margaret was still living in the Fuller house."

"Did he?" Fennel frowned. "When I visited on Thursday, he knew she'd disappeared."

"He said that Margaret hated him, that he'd acted out of love. Do you know what he meant?"

"No, I don't." Fennel sounded disappointed. "Maybe he meant because he was always saying nasty things about Hank." He reached for another brownie. Winnie moved the plate. "Maybe he thought he drove her away."

"She didn't run away," Winnie said. "She was kidnapped, and killed. There was blood in the house, blood in the car, which the police found in some mall lot." It was a dry, impatient recital of the facts, and I sensed that she and Walter had gone over this before.

"Maybe she left it there, with some of her own blood, to make it look like someone kidnapped her," Fennel said. "That's what Oscar told me Thursday."

Winnie snorted. "You're watching too many movies."

I thought about Joseph's coat, smeared with animal's blood by his brothers to convince their father he was dead.

Fennel reached past Winnie and grabbed a brownie.

"You want to kill yourself, go ahead," she said. "I'll have a good time with the life insurance. There's lots of places I haven't been to."

"What's the point of old age if you can't enjoy it?"

"Paris. Italy. Scandinavia." She counted off the names on her pudgy ringed fingers.

"Don't forget China. You always wanted to go to China."

With *Matrix* speed she lunged, wrested the brownie from his hand, and moved the plate to the white tile counter. "I'm doing this because I love you."

"Love me a little less," he grumbled into his coffee.

I bit my lip to keep from smiling. "I understand that Hank was out of town when Margaret disappeared."

"He's out of town a lot on business," Walter said. "That's hard on a marriage. And like I told you, Oscar said Margaret knew she'd made a mistake marrying Hank."

"Do you think she was having an affair?"

Winnie and Walter looked at each other.

"Oscar thought she liked the architect," Walter said. "I don't know if they were having an affair, but she was spending a *whole* lot of time with him."

Winnie crossed her arms. "And maybe Hank found out, and paid someone to kill her. Or maybe he came back early and did it himself."

"Is that what Professor Linney thought?" I asked.

"I *told* you, he thought she was alive," Fennel said, impatient. "She *is* alive."

Winnie rolled her eyes. "You're as crazy as he was."

Fennel clamped his lips together.

"How do you know she's alive?" I asked him.

"I just know."

"She came to Oscar in a dream," Winnie said. She turned to her husband. "First he tells you he dreams about her screaming for help. Now he tells you she's alive."

"You want to make fun, go ahead." He glared at her. "That's why I don't tell you things."

I wished Winnie would shut up. "How do you know?"

"He doesn't," she said. "He wants to sound important. Tell her the truth, Walter, and don't waste her time."

"You don't know everything." His face was mottled with patches of red.

She placed her hands on her hips. "Really, like what?"

"Like Oscar told me he was going to see Margaret at the Fuller house on Friday." He was breathing hard and looked like a puppy waiting for a pat on the head after having performed well.

I hid my disappointment. "He went to the Fuller house several times to see his daughter. He was confused."

"This was different. He said Margaret told him she had to see him. She said it was important."

Winnie snorted. "And you *believed* him?"

"Why wouldn't I believe him, Miss Know-It-All? I was in the room with him when she phoned."

Winnie stared at him, her mouth open, her hand pressed against her heaving bosom that sent ripples along the robe's zebra stripes. I was staring, too.

"Where was she all this time?" she demanded. "Why didn't she let Oscar know she was all right? Imagine letting him worry like that!"

"She didn't say." Fennel sounded nervous. He probably regretted what he'd revealed. "She was afraid to talk on the phone. Maybe that's why she didn't show up on Friday."

"Who was she afraid of?" I asked.

"She didn't say that, either."

"I can't believe you didn't tell me," Winnie said.

"He was so happy, Winnie. After she hung up, he kept saying, 'You came back, Margaret, you came back.' He was crying like a baby." Fennel's lips trembled.

Winnie narrowed her eyes. "How did he know it was her? He was confused so much of the time. How did he know the person who phoned wasn't working with the kidnapper?"

I'd been wondering the same thing. "Did the housekeeper take the call?" If so, maybe she could identify Margaret's voice.

"No, Oscar did, in his room. He has his own line. He took me there because he wanted privacy. He didn't like the new Filipino gal Hank hired to take care of him. He said she spied on him."

"What's her name?" I asked.

"Maria something. A long last name." He turned to his wife. "Oscar was sure it was Margaret."

Winnie snorted. "As if he'd know."

"It was Margaret's voice," Fennel insisted. "I heard it."

"You talked to her?" I asked before Winnie could.

Fennel shook his head. "But I *heard* her. See, by the time Oscar got to the phone, the answering machine went on. So I heard the first few words."

"What did she say?" Winnie demanded.

"'This is Margaret.' Or something like that. Then Oscar picked up the receiver, so I didn't hear anything else. She didn't stay on long. Just a few seconds. It was *her*," he said again, quietly this time.

"You should have told me," Winnie said. "You should have told Hank."

"Don't you think I know that?" Fennel's face was contorted in pain. "If I'd told Hank, maybe Oscar would still be alive. But Oscar made me swear I wouldn't tell anyone, not even you."

I wanted to put my arms around Walter Fennel and give him a hug. I wanted to kiss his parchment-paper cheek and tell him I understood.

"Oh, Walter." Winnie sighed. "Did you tell the detectives?"

He bowed his head. "I told them Oscar was planning to meet her at the house. I didn't tell them about the phone call. I *wanted* to. But they'd tell Hank, and Hank would be angry with me. Everyone would think it was my fault that Oscar died. My fault."

Fennel started to cry. Winnie walked over and put her arms around his shaking shoulders. She patted his bald head and rocked with him. It was time for me to leave.

I stood. "You have to tell the detectives, Mr. Fennel. But don't tell anyone else you were with Professor Linney when he received the phone call."

"Why not?" The fear in Winnie's eyes told me she knew.

"The killer might think Professor Linney told your husband something that could lead the police to him."

"That house is bad luck," Winnie said. "First Margaret, and now Oscar."

I couldn't argue with that.

CHAPTER SEVENTEEN

THE BIT OF CRIME-SCENE RIBBON WAS GONE.

The driveway was still empty, and there were no cars in front of the house. I doubted that anyone was inside, but I rang the bell and knocked when I didn't hear the chime that had played the other day. The fire had probably burned out the wiring.

I turned the doorknob and was surprised to find the door locked. Firemen had axed it to gain access to the house, so it was hardly a deterrent to anyone who wanted to get inside. Like the someone I'd spotted half an hour ago?

Careful to avoid splinters, I slipped my hand through a gaping hole, felt around for the knob, and twisted it. Although the breaking had already been done by others, if Reston or Detectives Porter or Hernandez came by, I'd have some 'splaining to do. But I was determined to find out who had lured Oscar Linney to his death and had used my story to make the death—the *murder*—look like a tragic coincidence. Along with the sadness and the guilt that were my constant companions, I was beginning to feel anger.

The house reeked of smoke and mildew. In the fading afternoon light I viewed the scorched remains in the dining and living rooms—the mahogany baby grand, its ivories stained like an old man's decaying teeth; the tattered drapes; the disemboweled sofas and chairs, their stuffing bloated with water from the firemen's hoses. Here and there I found hints of beauty that intensified the poignance of loss. Chenilles and stiff cotton brocades in maroon, cream, a touch of green. The singed ends of a gold tassel. A patch of dark burled veneer on a mahogany table that had escaped the conflagration. I tried to imagine the rooms before the fire had blackened the walls and consumed the furnishings, before firemen's boots had tracked mud on the sodden, half-eaten rugs.

The entry was darker than the living and dining rooms. That was one reason I'd avoided it till now. The other reason was that Linney's body had been found at the foot of the stairs. There was no chalked outline. Connors told me that's a Hollywood cliché, and a violation of the crime scene. But in my mind I saw the old man lying there, heard the *thump, thump, thump* as his frail body hit the wood steps, heard his pained, frightened cry.

Had he yelled for help when he'd smelled the smoke? For Margaret? Had the fall killed him, or had he been alive, gasping for air, when the smoke smothered his lungs?

My hand went to the light switch at the foot of the staircase, but I pulled it back. I didn't want to advertise my presence. Even without full light I could see that the bottom two steps of the oak staircase were gone. The rest looked seared but intact, like grilled steaks.

Holding on to the wood banister with both hands, I stretched my right leg to the third step, then pulled myself up and gingerly rested my weight on the step. It held. The stairs creaked as I climbed—normal house sounds—but with each step I braced myself for disaster, and I expelled a relieved breath when I reached the landing.

The ceilings were blackened, but the smoke was less noticeable here, blown away by a strong current coming from the two open doors to my left. I walked into the first room and sucked in the cold air from the open French window facing the backyard.

It was Linney's office. When you're selling a house, Realtors recommend showing it furnished and giving it an inviting lived-in look. That's probably why Reston had left touches of the old man. On the wall were photos of Linney posing with other men and the occasional woman, probably university colleagues. Linney standing in front of various buildings. There were squares and rectangles of lighter paint where other framed items had hung. Phone books were stacked on a black metal filing cabinet near a love seat upholstered in a navy and taupe plaid, and the bookcases on both sides of a handsome dark wood desk held a few novels and nonfiction works. Linney had probably insisted on taking his architecture texts to the Muirfield house.

The next room had twin beds and a dresser with a framed wedding photo of Linney and his dark-haired bride. One bed was covered with a navy-and-tan spread with a geometric print. The other bedspread was gone, along with the bedding—no surprise, since the police believed Linney had been lying on the bed. They'd no doubt wanted to check the spread and bedding for hair and other evidence.

They'd left the white mattress pad—stark, clinical, final, as though Linney had never existed, as though his essence had been bundled up with the bedding and whisked away from this house that he'd never wanted to leave. I was surprised at how sad I felt over a man I hardly knew. But maybe it wasn't just about Linney. Maybe it was about going with my mother to Zeidie and Bubbie G's apartment after Zeidie died in the hospital nine years ago, about helping her strip Zeidie's bed and put on the bedspread and pretend that everything would be the same.

Had Linney lain down while he waited for Margaret to arrive? Had he been half-asleep when the fire started? Had he smelled the smoke and, in a panic, rushed to the landing and lost his footing on the stairs?

But if his leg hurt and he was afraid of falling, why hadn't he waited downstairs?

The police had dusted for fingerprints. I recognized the telltale black powder residue on the cream-colored door and window frames and sash, the silver residue on the bedroom dresser, on the desk and filing cabinet in the office. In the desk drawers I found a red leather coin pouch, a compass and ruler, a handful of rubber bands. The file cabinet was empty, its contents no doubt moved to the new house along with Linney's other possessions. My fingers were sooty from the layer of ash that had settled on everything like a shroud, and would probably continue to settle over the next few days.

Maybe the person pretending to be Margaret had lured Linney upstairs. *"I'm up here, Dad!"* Or did she call him Daddy? Did he hurry up the steps, bad leg and all?

And then what?

Across the hall was the bedroom where half an hour ago someone had parted lace curtains.

It was a woman's room, with pale mauve walls and off-white trim and hardwood floors. It smelled of lavender and jasmine and was dominated by a mahogany four-poster queen-size bed covered with a scallop-edged, white matelassé spread. A mahogany secretary with Queen Anne legs stood against one wall.

The desk chair had a needlepoint seat with a forest motif that was repeated in the pillows on the olive green velvet window bench. Framed watercolors—still lifes and florals—hung on the walls. I glanced at the signatures. Margaret Linney. Margaret Reston.

Margaret and Hank had slept in this room, on this bed. Had they made careful love, aware of her father just across the hall? If Winnie and Walter were right, and Margaret had a lover, had she brought him here, too?

From the moment I stepped into the room I'd sensed that something was off, and now I realized why: Someone had removed the mist of ash. The same person, probably, who had scented the room to camouflage the smoke. I sniffed the air. Perfume, I decided, not freshener.

Someone had perfumed the adjoining bath, too, and wiped away whatever ash had fallen there. The bath was large and all white—tub, pedestal sink, commode, tiled shower and floor, cabinets, throw rugs. The fixtures and hardware were satin chrome, the towels shades of burgundy and mauve, the scented miniature soaps a pearl gray. Feeling very much like the intruder that I was, I opened the medicine cabinet. Aspirin, hand lotion, a plastic box with hairpins, hair spray, birth control pills, a depilatory cream, nail polish remover.

Between the bath and bedroom was a dressing room with a two-door wardrobe on one side, a vanity table and ornately framed mirror on the other. On an antique silver tray, lipsticks lined up like soldiers formed a protective circle around a brush, comb, and mirror with mother-of-pearl handles, and perfume—a bottle of yellow Bulgari, a frosted bottle of Quel Que Violet. The crime ribbon was gone, so the police were done here. I picked up the brush and pulled out one of the black strands of Margaret Linney's hair entwined among the boar bristles.

The housekeeper. *That's* whom I'd seen at the window. Tim Bolt had said she came every week. She'd probably been here today, dusting the vanity tray, arranging the lipsticks, freshening the air. It was odd, given the damaged condition of the rest of the house, but Reston had probably asked her to do what she could in the upstairs rooms, and she'd paid particular attention to Margaret's bedroom and bath. Maybe Reston had asked her to. Or maybe she was a Mrs. Danvers, keeping the lady of the house alive by preserving her possessions.

In any case the mystery of the person at the window was solved. I smiled and shook my head, grateful that I hadn't run to Connors with my suspicions. I could practically hear his snicker. *"Seeing ghosts, Molly?"*

Wrapping the strand around my finger, I sat on Margaret's olive green velvet stool and closed my eyes. According to Tim and Winnie, the police had found signs of a struggle in her bedroom. Had she been sitting on this stool, brushing her hair, when the intruder attacked? Or had she hurried downstairs to answer the door, possibly for someone she knew?

Her lover?

Her husband?

Maybe she *was* alive. Maybe Fennel was right. Maybe she'd staged her kidnapping and called her father last week and asked him to meet her here.

I didn't think so. In spite of the sweet smell of lavender and jasmine in the air, there was death in this house, and not just Linney's. I felt it.

Her clothes were still in the wardrobe, a pastel rainbow of dresses, skirts, blouses, slacks. All fine quality, classic, nothing trendy. They'd need airing to get rid of the faint smoky odor. Neatly lined up on the bottom were designer shoes I recognized and, under different circumstances, would have coveted. I told myself I was looking through Margaret Linney's things because I needed to find out what she was all about if I had any hope of understanding what had happened to her and to her father, but I still felt like a voyeur.

Maybe Linney had never lain on the stripped bed. Maybe

the impression on the bed had been made by the person who had lured the old man to the house and up the stairs. Everyone knew Linney was confused. He'd often wandered here to look for his daughter. So he'd come here again, and rested awhile. So sad, who could have known he'd be there?

It was only five o'clock, and night was creeping in like a cat. Another few minutes and it would be dark. I miss daylight saving time. I suppose some people appreciate the extra morning hour of daylight, but there's something oppressive about the shortened day, something that makes me want to turn on all the lights and the radio or TV. I wasn't going to turn on the lights here, so if I was going to search Margaret's room, I had to hurry.

From the mahogany armoire in the corner I learned that she had exquisite taste in lingerie, that she liked Victoria's Secret bras and low-cut panties and sexy, lacy nightgowns, and Banana Republic and Ann Taylor cashmere sweaters. In the desk drawers I found art supply catalogs, a box of oil pastels, blank music composition sheets, other sheets with penciled musical notations.

Walking to the nightstand, I spotted a pair of white satin mules under the bed. The slippers bothered me more than the perfectly arranged towels and the spotless chrome faucets, more than Margaret Linney's monogrammed cream-colored stationery on the desk, or the magazines on the mahogany nightstand. *Town and Country, Architectural Digest, Vogue,* all dated June of this year. Five months ago, when Margaret Linney disappeared.

The slippers spoke of hope. They told me that time had stood still in this room, that someone had been waiting for Margaret to return.

Her husband? Her father?

This was where she'd struggled with her kidnapper. Had she invited him up here, unsuspecting, or had he followed when she'd tried to escape? Or had he let himself in?

I knew so little about Margaret Linney and the circumstances surrounding her disappearance. Porter would die before he told me anything, and I didn't think Hernandez would be much better. That left Connors.

It was dark in the room, and the only light came from the pale moon peeking through the lace curtains. There was a slim drawer in the nightstand. I opened it and found a burgundy leather-bound daily planner with an address book. I always carry a small pen-size flashlight with me. I sat at Margaret Linney's desk, flipped through the planner until I reached June 12, and beamed the thin point of light on the penciled entries.

Cyndi's.
Granite.
Kitchen flooring.
M/Drop off info re HARP.
Golden Vista!!

It seemed a mundane way to spend the last day of your life. *If* she was dead, I reminded myself. I looked at the entries again. I'm no expert, but the handwriting of the first four appeared uniformly even, unlike the fifth, which took up several lines.

I turned back a page, to Wednesday.

Bath fixtures.
Marble/entry/bath.
Beverly Wilshire.
Call V.
Mtg w/ Dr. E.
D.?

The last two items had been underlined twice, and the handwriting again seemed bolder. Tuesday was dedicated to more house stuff. Monday's entries were more interesting:

Lighting.
Pool tile.
Call pb?!
Tiler!!

Over the weekend, Margaret and Hank had gone to dinner and a movie with friends. Friday had been another Muirfield house day, with some additional entries:

Kohler showroom.
Wood flooring.
D/MS??
Bank? HELC?

A door slammed. For a few seconds I didn't breathe, and I could feel my heart pounding. I noticed sudden light coming from the hall. A stair creaked.

I shut my penlight, slipped the planner into my purse, and tiptoed to the dressing room.

Another stair creak, and another.

I opened the wardrobe doors and cringed at their squeak. Parting Margaret's clothes, I stepped inside, swallowed by the silky folds of fabric. It was pitch-black when I pulled the doors shut, and I felt choked by the cloying smell of moth repellant tinged with smoke. I covered my mouth to stifle a cough.

The sound of my heartbeat was loud in my ears, and I had to strain to hear the footsteps.

In the hall.

In Margaret's room. Light seeped into the dressing room.

There was no place to move, but instinctively I took a step back, away from the wardrobe doors. I was jolted when I felt resistance, and realized with rising panic that the hem of my black skirt was stuck between the white doors.

The footsteps were coming closer. I flashed to the games my siblings and I would play Shabbat afternoons while our parents tried to sleep.

Where are you?

I'm hiding.

Am I warm?

You're cold.

I tugged at the skirt.

How about now?

Warmer.

Even warmer.

For a moment I thought the fabric moved, but it was just my sweaty fingers sliding along the rayon.

And now?

Cooler.

The floor creaked. Heavy footsteps were coming closer.

What about now?

Warmer.

A click, and the dressing room was flooded with light.

Hot.

My heart thudding in my chest, I pressed my right eye against the hairline slit between the two doors. I couldn't see much, just a hand holding the pearl-handled mirror. A second later the mirror clattered to the floor, followed by the tinkle of glass breaking.

"Shit!" A male voice.

I flinched. My heart was pounding so hard I was amazed he didn't hear it. If he bent down, if he saw the bit of cloth poking out . . .

With my eye against the slit of the door, I saw jean-covered knees bending. I heard a few clunks. He was probably tossing the mirror fragments into the trash can.

His black shoes swiveled toward the wardrobe.

I held my breath for what seemed like an eternity. If I yelled, would Tim Bolt hear me? Would he get here in time?

The knees straightened. The light went out as suddenly as it had gone on and I was plunged back into darkness again. I loved the darkness.

I heard footsteps walking away. Then silence.

I let out my breath.

The wardrobe door was jerked open. A hand grabbed my arm, yanked me out, and twisted my arm behind my back.

I screamed.

CHAPTER EIGHTEEN

IN THE DARK, ROGER MODINE LOOKED FORMIDABLE.

I recognized him in that split second before he twisted my arm and forced me to turn. I screamed again at the top of my lungs, praying a neighbor would hear.

"Shut up!"

He grabbed my other hand and held both behind my back, his fingers locked around my wrists like a vise. With his free hand he flipped up the light switch, then rummaged in the closet for a belt. He tied my wrists together so tightly that I winced.

Fear had temporarily frozen my thoughts. Now they were bombarding me, like ammunition in an electronic game. Had Modine torched the house because he was pissed with HARP and its board members? Had he come here to make sure he hadn't left any evidence? But that meant Linney's death hadn't been planned.

Grabbing my shoulder, Modine spun me around so that I was facing him. Up close he was a few inches taller than he'd appeared when I'd seen him across the room at the HARP meeting. He had a flat pug nose, thinning reddish-brown hair on the sides of his head, and a high forehead that blended into the large bald oval of his crown. His wide chest and muscular arms bulged under a black knit sweater, and his large hands were reddened and calloused with knuckles the size of bolts, and fingernails that were bitten off. They were the hands and body of a man who was used to lifting heavy sheets of lumber. Someone strong.

"What the hell are you doing here?" The veins in his neck stood out like wood cording.

I opened my mouth, but the words were stuck in my throat. It's hard to speak when you're about to vomit.

"I want some answers, lady!"

His bared teeth were yellowed with nicotine, and his breath and clothes stank of cigarettes. His eyes, brown streaked with yellow, reminded me of the tigereye necklace my ex-husband had given me and that I rarely wore. I loved the necklace, but not the history.

I leaned my head back to put distance between my nose and Modine's rancid breath, and cleared my throat. What to say? "I met Professor Linney last week, and I felt bad when I heard that he died. I was curious about how it happened. What are *you* doing here?" I asked, struggling for cool.

Modine glared at me. "I'm asking the questions."

"Which I answered." Beneath the bluster I heard defensiveness. That reassured me. "Now it's my turn. You don't live here, Roger. Why are you here?"

That startled him. I'd read in a woman's magazine that it's a good idea to take the offensive in situations like this, not to show fear. Plus I told myself that if he'd intended to harm me, he would have done so by now. And maybe he was worried that a neighbor had heard me scream.

"How do you know my name?" He stared at me.

So far, aggressive seemed to be working. "I've heard about you and your work. Which I understand is excellent. It would be a good idea if you untied me now, Roger."

"It would be a *better* idea if I called the cops."

My luck, Porter would show. He'd love that. But at least Modine wasn't threatening violence. "Fine. Then you can explain why you tied me up. I think that's kidnapping. It's a felony, Roger."

"You have chutzpah, lady." He grunted. "You're the one who broke into this house. That's a felony, too."

"Actually, I think it's a misdemeanor. But untie my hands and we'll call it even, okay? I won't press charges."

He pulled a key out of his pocket and dangled it in front of me. "The owner asked me to stop by and assess the damage from the fire. Where's *your* key?" He was smirking.

I didn't blame him.

He cocked his head. "So what are you, one of those nosy parkers without a life? You hear someone got killed, you have to find out all the gory details?"

"Yup, that's me. It's a bad habit, but I can't seem to stop."

He glowered at me. "You have some mouth, lady."

"I get like that when I'm tied up. Look, I'm sorry," I said in my most conciliatory voice. "Untie me and I'll leave. I shouldn't have come here. I won't do it again."

"What's your name?"

"Untie my hands and I'll tell you."

"I don't think so." He reached behind me and yanked on the belt, sending shooting pain up my arms.

I let out a small yelp. Apparently, taking the offensive doesn't work all the time. Maybe I'd read that advice in the same issue that talked about how to wax your legs like a professional, which I've never been able to do.

He gave another tug. "What's your name?"

I winced. "Molly Blume."

"I want to see some ID."

My name didn't seem to ring any bells, which was more than fine with me. "My wallet is in my purse on the floor of the closet."

"I'll get it. Make a funny move, and you'll be sorry."

I decided to take his word for it.

He was still holding on to my leash, so when he bent his legs, I did, too. He felt around on the bottom of the closet until he found my purse, then straightened up. I did the same. When I'm nervous—and believe me, I was nervous—I tend to get sassy and try to fill voids with conversation. I considered making a quip about synchronized bending as a possible Olympic event, but he didn't strike me as the kind of guy who would appreciate the humor.

He dropped the belt. Moving to the doorway of the dressing room, his feet spread apart, his wide frame blocking any attempt at escape, he unzipped my red Coach bag and fished out my wallet. He flipped it open, looked at me, at my driver's license, back at me. He frowned.

"I have more highlights in my hair now," I said, "and I was five pounds thinner then." He was still frowning. "Okay, seven."

He dumped the contents of my purse on the vanity table. Lipstick, receipts, a tampon. Margaret's daily planner. He picked it up. In the light I noticed the initials *M R* embossed on the leather cover.

"You stole this," he said.

I flushed. "I was looking at it when I heard someone coming into the house. I panicked and put it into my purse. I don't know why I did it."

"You were afraid you'd be caught."

"I thought I was in danger. I wasn't thinking clearly." Humiliation, I found, could be harder to swallow than fear. I considered telling him I was Edie's sister, hoping that would give me some points, but decided it wouldn't make a difference. And why involve Edie?

He hefted the planner in one large hand, as if weighing it would tell him the truth.

"I have to call Mr. Reston," he said.

CHAPTER NINETEEN

WE SAT IN LINNEY'S OFFICE WHILE WE WAITED FOR
Reston. Modine appropriated the desk chair, which he'd pushed
into the doorway. I was on the love seat. He'd untied my hands,
but had held on to my purse, into which he'd stuffed all my be-
longings, minus Margaret's planner.

I'd been hoping to talk to Modine, but not under these circumstances. He wasn't much of a conversationalist. I tried safe
topics—what he thought of HARP, did he enjoy his work, was
he a sports fan. I gave up after a few minutes of watching him
study his abused fingernails. At one point Modine jerked his
head toward the door. After warning me with a glare, he stepped
around the chair into the hallway. A few minutes later he was
back.

"The wind," he said.

It was another ten minutes before Reston arrived, but the itchy silence made it seem like a year. Time is relative. It's like the routine from the Yiddish comedy team, Dzigan and Shumacher, whose tapes I'd listened to several times with Zeidie Irving: Sit naked on the lap of a beautiful young woman, and time goes by like a flash. Sit naked on a hot stove . . . Yiddish, by the way, has a wealth of ribald jokes that they never taught us in school.

The front door slammed shut.

"Roger? Where are you?"

"Up here," Modine called. "Watch out for the bottom two steps."

He moved the chair back to the desk and smirked at me again—the teacher dragging a student to the principal's office. I stared him down. My fear had subsided, and I was more embarrassed than nervous. I doubted that Reston would file charges, and I wanted to talk to him.

Judging from the rapid creaking, Reston was bounding up the stairs. No hesitation for him. A moment later he was in the doorway, his eyes widened with surprise. Modine had given him my name over the phone, but apparently Reston hadn't connected the name with the woman who had accosted him at the HARP meeting.

I stood, trying to muster a semblance of dignity. "I want to apologize, Mr. Reston. I had no business coming into your home without your permission. I meant no harm."

"She stole your wife's planner," Modine said with the glee of an adolescent tattler. "If I hadn't showed up, Hank, there's no telling what else she would have taken."

"Where's the planner?" In the auditorium, Reston's voice had been muted by the crowd, and I'd missed the slight drawl. Even with the drawl, he sounded deliberate, confident, a man who took charge.

Modine handed him the planner. Reston ran his finger over the embossed monogram, then flipped to the back.

"It's Maggie's," he said with anguish and a touch of wonder that puzzled me. He looked at me. "Where was it?"

Was he testing me? "In her nightstand."

"She had it in her purse," Modine offered.

"He broke your wife's mirror," I retaliated like a three-year-old.

Modine's face was instantly red. "That was an accident. I'll buy a new one."

Reston gave him a look that would freeze water. "What were you doing with Maggie's mirror?"

"I just picked it up. Come on, Hank. It's a mirror."

"I asked you to check the downstairs. That was it."

"I wanted to make sure nothing up here needed fixing. Why don't you ask *her* what she was doing up here?" He pointed to me. "I found her hiding in your wife's closet."

Reston returned his attention to me.

"Can we talk alone?" I asked him.

He eyed me, assessing me as if I were one of his carpets and he was checking for a problem with the nap. "Why don't you come back tomorrow, Roger." Still gazing at me. "Take a look and give me an estimate."

"Sorry about the mirror, Hank. I can probably find one just like it, or have the glass replaced."

"I'll take care of it."

It was a dismissal, and a cold one at that. Modine made a hasty exit. I sat down on the love seat and Reston settled his large frame on the chair.

"You're the one gave my father-in-law a ride the other day," he said. "You talked to me at that meeting."

"I'm terribly sorry about Professor Linney's death, Mr. Reston. I felt bad for him that day we met, and I feel responsible for what happened. That's why I came here."

"Call me Hank. Why are you responsible, Molly? You didn't start the fire, did you?" He smiled grimly.

There's a subtle change when people are on a first-name basis. It's something I try to establish in every interview, and now he was doing it. I wondered if he was trying to show me what a sincere, open person he was. Generous, too, considering that I'd trespassed in his home.

"I'm a reporter," I said. "I wrote an article for the *Times* about the HARP meeting and all the vandalisms that seem connected to HARP."

"I read it," he said, his tone noncommittal.

"Then you know I mentioned that houses of HARP board members were being targeted. And that night Professor Linney's house was torched, and he died in it. So I feel there's a connection, and I needed to see where he died."

"You're lying, Molly," Hank said calmly, as though he were commenting on the price of paper towels at Kmart.

Sure, I was lying. I wasn't about to tell him I suspected that someone had lured Linney to his death, especially when that someone could be Reston. Who had conveniently been out of town the night his wife disappeared and the night his father-in-law died.

"My father-in-law didn't die in Maggie's room," Hank said. "So what were you doing in there?"

"Okay." I sighed with exaggerated chagrin. "I heard about your wife's disappearance. I figured as long as I was here, I'd look around. I'm sorry. I realize I caused you pain."

He was studying me. "You want to know all the details, don't you? What she had for breakfast that day. What she was wearing. When was the last time I saw her, what was the last thing she said to me. Where did they find her blood. What did I do when I found out she was gone. Do I think about her often."

His voice was filled with pain and contempt, and I found I couldn't answer.

"There's not a day goes by, not an hour, that I'm not think-ing about Maggie, wondering where she is, is she alive. Did they tell you I hired a detective?"

I nodded.

"The best in the business. I also offered a reward for infor-mation. The detective couldn't find out a damn thing. He thinks she's dead. So do the police, but nobody knows where her body is." He leaned forward. "You want to know what I think, right?" he asked quietly.

"If you want to tell me."

"I think she's dead." Hank sagged against the chair. "I don't want to believe it, but I'm not a stupid man. At first the cops thought it was a home invasion that turned into a kidnapping. I said to myself, 'Okay, we can handle this. It's only money.' I have buckets of money, and I'd have given every cent to get Maggie back. But he never called. The son of a bitch never called." His voice broke, and he pinched his lips together.

He sounded convincing, and his face was scrunched in pain. But killers have wept convincingly while proclaiming their in-nocence to me. "Sometimes people are unhappy and run away," I said, dipping my toe into unknown waters.

"Who told you that?" He glowered at me. "That's bullshit. Maggie and I—" He stopped, brought his face and voice under control. "Maggie and I had something special. You've probably been talking to people, so you know I'm not as educated as she is, or cultured. So what? So *effing* what? I made her happy. I may not know much about art, or who wrote what symphony, but I made her laugh. And you don't need a Ph.D. to appreciate the colors in the sunset."

You certainly don't. "What about Professor Linney?"

"I don't think he ever looked at a sunset. Too busy with his books."

"Did he approve of your marrying his daughter?"

Hank wagged a finger at me. "You know he didn't, so why the games, Molly? Oscar didn't think the man existed who was good enough for *Margaret*." He pronounced the name with sarcasm and a poor attempt at a British accent. "He certainly didn't think it was me. You know what? He was right. But I sure had every intention of trying to be that man. Look, it's not like I forced Maggie to marry me. She was thirty-two. She loved her father, she respected him, but she wanted to live *her* life, not one he chose for her."

I thought about Adriana Caselotti, bound to Disney all those years, forced to keep her identity a secret. Maybe Margaret Linney had felt bound, too, by a possessive father. Maybe like Snow White, she'd wished that the one she loved would find her and free her.

Or had she been bound by Reston? Had she been infatuated with him and realized she'd made a huge mistake? That's what Linney had told Walter Fennel.

"As long as we're being candid, Mr. Reston?" I said.

He nodded. "Go ahead. I have nothing to hide. The police grilled me for days when Maggie disappeared, so this is a piece of cake."

"Professor Linney told people you were rough on him. The day I drove him here he called you a son of a bitch."

"Plus a few other choice names." Reston's laugh boomed through the small room. "You spent what, twenty minutes with him? He was a handful, right? I lived with the old man twenty-four/seven. Listen," he said, serious. "I felt sorry as hell for him. A man whose whole life is learning and books, it probably drove him crazy knowing that down the road—a year or two, maybe less, maybe more—he might not even recognize the people around him. And naturally, things were worse after Maggie disappeared. He was devastated. We all were. But he was a pain in the ass. Not just to me. He drove the caretakers crazy. He'd hit them with his cane. He'd bite them, call them names, accuse them of hitting him. Why do you think the caregiver didn't show Friday? 'Cause she wasn't getting paid enough to take the crap he was dishing out. Why do you think the housekeeper skipped?"

"The day I drove him here, I noticed that Professor Linney's legs were all bruised."

Reston frowned. "So you're saying what? That the caregivers *were* hitting him?"

"Or someone else was."

"Like who?" Recognition dawned. He cocked his head and stared at me. "You think *I* was hitting him? I never laid a hand on the old man, Molly. Anyone who says otherwise is lying. Oscar had Parkinson's. His balance wasn't great, but he insisted on doing things himself. So he fell a lot."

It was plausible. And it could be a pack of lies. I recently read that 4 percent of people sixty-five-and-over in this country are victims of elder abuse or neglect, mostly by family members, and experts believe that only one out of five cases is reported. I pictured Oscar Linney's frail, shrunken frame. From what I'd seen myself and heard from others, he'd been irascible, demanding, a daily pain in the neck to the mountain of a son-in-law he made no pretense of liking. Which didn't prove anything.

"It must have been tense," I said. "The three of you living under one roof."

"Ya think?" Reston smiled again. "He wasn't happy with me, and he let me know it. He'd make fun of me. Hank the Tank, he called me. Most of the time I'd take it, for Maggie's sake. She'd tell him to stop, and he'd get defensive. Sometimes I'd lose my cool. Then Maggie would get upset with me. It was rough for her, being stuck in the middle like that, but we had no choice."

"Did you consider placing Professor Linney in an assisted care facility?"

"*I* considered it. Maggie didn't. So I didn't push it." He

shrugged. "It was her father, her call. And I knew she'd be miserable if I talked her into doing it."

"But after she disappeared?"

"I felt I had to do what Maggie would've wanted, hard as it was. And believe me, it was no picnic."

"You said your wife was stuck in the middle. Maybe she ran away because she couldn't handle it?"

"And leave her father?" Reston shook his head. "Never. And whatever people have told you, she loved me. We were finishing our dream house. Why would she run away?"

"I understand that she didn't really *want* to move."

"*Oscar* didn't want to move. Maggie did. She didn't want to live in her father's house. She was having a great time working on the new place. She designed it, along with the architect."

"Jeremy Dorn. I saw him the other night at the HARP meeting. Very good-looking. They must have spent a lot of time together, working on the house."

Reston gazed at me with quiet menace. "Maggie would never cheat on me, and I don't take kindly to people who hint that she did."

"You were away a lot on business," I said, leaving the intimation unspoken.

"That's what businessmen do. That doesn't mean I liked it. Where'd you find the planner, Molly?"

The question, out of left field, took me by surprise. "In your wife's nightstand, like I told you. Why?"

"Because it disappeared when Maggie did. It was her bible. She didn't make a move without it. It's one of the things that had me thinking she was still alive."

I was speechless, which for me is unusual, as you may have noticed.

"I saw it the morning before she disappeared," Hank said. "I was getting ready to leave. She was in bed, but not asleep, because we'd just . . ." He was blushing. "Anyway, she asked me when I'd be back, and I said, 'Friday afternoon, why don't you pencil me in for Friday night and all day Saturday?' Joking around, like we did." He smiled, as if remembering. "So she took the planner and flipped to Friday, and she wrote in what she had in mind for us, and I said, 'God, what if your dad sees this, he'll have a coronary, or we'll be arrested,' and she ripped out the page. We were both laughing."

He had a vulnerable look on his face—part wistfulness, part heartbreak. It was an intensely private look, and I felt more like a trespasser than before.

"I searched all over for the planner after Maggie disappeared," he said. "The police searched, too. It wasn't anywhere in the house. And now it's back."

I thought about the person at the window but decided not to say anything. I needed to think things through. Like the possibility that Reston had taken the planner and returned it. And if so, why had he taken it, and why had he returned it now. True, he'd looked surprised when Modine had handed him the planner. But surprise can be rehearsed.

"Whoever put the planner back in the nightstand had it all along." Hank was clenching and unclenching his fist, the way you do when a nurse is taking your blood. "I want you to find out who he is."

"I'm not a detective," I said.

"You're a reporter. You can find out stuff from people who don't want to talk to the cops. I'll pay whatever you want. I need to know what happened to Maggie."

"I thought you said you believe she's dead."

"I know it here," he said, tapping his temple. "But until I see her body, I won't know it here." He thumped his chest. "I need to get on with my life. Right now part of me is waiting for her to walk up these stairs. I guess that's why I haven't touched her things. You probably think it's dumb." His dark brown eyes dared me to agree.

In my mind I saw the white satin slippers at the side of Maggie's bed. "It's hard to let go," I said, thinking of my friend Aggie. I still dream about her, and waking brings with it the sharp pain of renewed loss. I can't begin to imagine how her parents cope.

"The police will want to see the planner," I said. "It may give them new leads."

Hank grunted. "The police have given up looking for the kidnapper. They think I killed Maggie. I figure they're watching me and tapping my phone like they did with Scott Peterson. They usually suspect the husband. Doesn't seem to matter that I have a solid alibi for the night she disappeared." He shrugged and flashed a half smile, inviting me onto his team.

"And for the night your father-in-law died?"

That erased the smile. I tried to read his expression. Surprise, mostly. Some irritation, a hint of amusement, a little grudging respect. If there was fear, I didn't see it. But Reston didn't strike me as the kind of man who would *show* fear, even if he felt it.

"You're not one for subtle, are you?" He nodded. "Yeah, I have a solid alibi. I didn't think I needed one. I thought the fire—" He stopped. His forehead was creased in bewilderment—real or feigned, I couldn't tell. "Are you saying someone torched the house to kill the Professor?"

"Not necessarily." Porter or Hernandez would be pissed if they found out I'd suggested the possibility to someone who was, after all, a prime suspect. They'd probably want to witness his unrehearsed reaction. "But you have to admit it's a little odd, your being away both times."

"Only if someone murdered Linney," he said slowly, thinking it through. "But why would someone kill him?"

I shrugged.

"I didn't kill him," Reston said. "I didn't kill Maggie. I loved her. We were going to live happily ever after. Isn't that how the story goes?"

CHAPTER TWENTY

EDIE TOOK THREE MAH JONGG TILES FROM MINDY, WHO was sitting to her left, and placed them on her rack. "You're actually considering *working* for this guy?" she asked me.

We had finished the first game, and while setting up for the next, I'd told everyone about Reston and his request. Maybe that hadn't been such a good idea.

"I'm not *working* for him. I'm investigating his wife's disappearance. As a journalist, not a detective. Which I know I'm not."

She frowned at her tiles. "He's giving you a photocopy of her planner. He's letting you look through her stuff, and her father's. He'll expect something in return, Molly."

"He's not my type. Which is too bad, 'cause I haven't had sex in two years, and it ain't gonna happen anytime soon with Rabbi Zack."

Mindy laughed. For a moment she looked less tired, the bags under her brown eyes less pronounced. My sister-in-law Gitty giggled shyly and cast an anxious glance at the doorway. She has blue eyes and the most gorgeous red hair, most of it covered now by her navy snood in case Norm, Mindy's husband, came into the room.

Edie scowled. "Don't encourage her, Mindy."

"To have sex?" she said with a straight face.

We often tease Edie. As the oldest sibling, she can come across as patronizing and annoyingly motherly, but she does everything out of love.

I reassured her. "I made it clear to Reston that I don't owe him a first look, and that I can't promise I won't share what I find with the police."

I exchanged three tiles with Gitty, who was sitting across from me, and scooped a cup of popcorn still warm from the microwave.

Edie said, "I'll bet he calls you nonstop. At least he doesn't know where you live."

I wasn't so sure, and I wasn't about to volunteer that Modine had spent a long time studying my driver's license, maybe memorizing my address, which he could pass on to Hank Reston should Reston inquire.

"So how *are* things with Zack?" Edie asked.

I sighed. " 'Inching' along."

Mindy flashed me a smile.

Edie said, "If you love someone—"

"Are you planning on keeping those tiles, Edie, or are you passing them?" Mindy asked.

Edie shot her an annoyed look. Which is ironic, because she's the one who usually complains that talking slows down the game. "I'm thinking."

"Well, don't think too long. Yitz will be up soon."

We generally take turns hosting the game, but since Yitz was born we've been coming to Mindy's. We did the same for Gitty when her now eleven-month-old son Yechiel was a newborn (accent on the second syllable, a guttural *ch* as in Bach). Gitty has become as committed as we are to mah jongg (the American version), which my sisters and I learned almost twenty years ago from our mom, and has replaced Liora, who never really caught the bug and has been busy of late with her Santa Monica College courses and a succession of dates that move through her life with the speed and single-minded determination of commuters passing through a New York subway turnstile.

I love mah jongg. There's something inexplicably gratifying and soothing about handling the ivory tiles with their exotic characters, arranging them into double-tiered "walls," hearing their *click, click, click.* Many times it's the highlight of my week, and for a dark few months after my marriage died, Monday night was my only respite from the pained, troubled thoughts that dogged me all day and kept me awake nights. It was better than therapy. Cheaper, too.

"I'm concerned about Molly's safety," Edie said now to Mindy. "Aren't you? Reston could be a killer."

"So could your friend Roger Modine." I had given an edited version of my encounter with the contractor, leaving out my panic and bound wrists. "I still don't know why he was snooping around in Maggie Reston's bedroom."

"For the same reason you were," Edie said. "Nosiness."

I bristled at that. I'm often guilty of being nosy, but not this time. "I'm trying to figure out what happened to Maggie, and Professor Linney. I feel responsible."

"Whatever." Edie passed Mindy three tiles. "And Modine isn't my *friend.* We just happen to be working together on the anti-HARP drive. I've always found him to be pleasant."

"If he's not treating you to his smoker's breath," I said. Or tying you up. I refilled my popcorn cup.

Mindy said, "I don't know if he torched the Fuller place, but all those construction delays cost serious money, and he's probably losing business from homeowners who don't want to go through the hassle of remodeling with the Harpies on their backs."

"Maybe the vandal wasn't out to do damage," Gitty said. "Maybe he wanted to scare off the pro-HARP people."

"Well, if that was the plan, it backfired," Edie said, glum. "I heard they're more determined than ever. They're pressuring Harrington to push the HARP status through."

Mindy said, "And *I* heard that a few other HARP areas are considering repealing their HARP status."

"Can they do that?" I asked.

"Apparently if you get enough signatures from the area residents. It's not easy, though."

"Is HARP such a bad thing?" Gitty asked, tentative. She's twenty-three years old, married two years to my brother Judah, and it's taken her a while to find her "voice" in the family. We Blumes can be overpowering.

"Not if you live in an apartment," Edie said, matter-of-fact. "If you and Judah owned a house, would you want people telling you what you could or couldn't do to it?"

"Probably not. But I'd hate to see historic buildings destroyed. Like the Ambassador Hotel. Or the Hollywood Bowl. I read they're remodeling it, and maybe getting rid of the amphitheater shell."

"They want to improve the acoustics," Mindy said. "But it would be weird not to see the shell. And L.A. Unified can probably incorporate the Ambassador into the school campus they're planning. If they want to."

You've probably heard of the Ambassador. It's on Wilshire

near Vermont. Though it's been vacant for years, it was one of the two most prestigious L.A. hotels (the downtown Biltmore is the second) and was host to the Oscars and to every U.S. president from Hoover to Nixon. It was also the home of the famed Cocoanut Grove nightclub, and, tragically, the site of Robert Kennedy's assassination.

"It would be a shame if they tore down the Ambassador," Edie said. "Mom and Dad were married there."

"So if it doesn't touch your neighborhood, you're *for* historical preservation?" I teased.

Edie didn't look amused. "You can't compare tearing down the Ambassador or the Hollywood Bowl with remodeling a house that looks just like a hundred others."

"But some people build homes that really don't fit the neighborhood," Gitty said.

"Which is probably what they said about Frank Lloyd Wright," Edie responded. She studied her tiles.

I looked at the three Gitty had passed me. One of them, a one Bam, had a green bird painted onto it. Which reminded me of another bird . . .

"Is Reston pro-HARP?" I asked Edie.

"I have no idea. He's never come to a meeting. I didn't know he lived in Hancock Park. I never even *heard* of him until I read his name in today's write-up of the fire."

The *Times* had run a small article about Linney's death, and had mentioned Margaret's disappearance. A few inches that stated the bare facts and didn't speculate about any possible connection between the two events. I wondered if the omission was Porter's doing.

In my mind's eye I saw Reston and Modine talking at the meeting—*before* the fire made Modine's construction services necessary. And Walter Fennel had told me that Reston bought homes, fixed them up, and flipped them.

"Do you know if Reston and Modine have business dealings?" I asked Mindy. As I mentioned, many of her clients are in-volved with real estate, so I figured she might know.

"I don't," she said. "I can ask around."

"Okay, no more talking," Edie said, ignoring Mindy's raised brow and my snort.

We played the next seven games without much conversa-tion. Tossing tiles, naming them, taking them to complete a group. The only other sounds in the domed-ceilinged room were the *click, click, click* of the tiles and the crunching of pop-corn and the potato chips and trail mix Mindy had set out for us and was studiously avoiding all night. She complains that she's having a hard time losing the last ten pounds from her preg-nancy. I can't see them, but she's following a diet that Gitty, a nu-tritionist, tailored for her so that she can fit into her lawyer suits. Mindy's willpower is stronger than mine under most circum-stances, and tonight I was munching absentmindedly, my mind on Reston and Modine and Margaret's planner. Which is why I tossed a tile that I could have used to redeem a joker that would have given me mah jongg.

I was still grumbling when Norm came in with Yitz.

"Right on schedule." He handed the blanket-swaddled baby to Mindy after she pushed herself away from the table.

Norm is three years older than Mindy, an inch taller than her five-eight, and several inches wider. He has blond hair to her dark brown, which she wears shoulder length and covers with a wig or hat when she's in public, and blue eyes that their two daughters have inherited, and maybe Yitz, too, although it's too early to tell.

"Take over my hand, okay, honey?" Mindy said.

Norm has learned the game, and we call on him once in a while to fill in as a fourth. He sat in Mindy's seat and a few min-utes later called "Mah jongg" and collected Mindy's winnings, fifty cents from each of us.

It was the last game of the evening. Edie and Gitty left after putting the tiles back in Mindy's case. I stayed to talk to Norm. He's in health care (he recently took over the lease for the nursing home where he was the administrator for several years), and I thought he might know something about Golden Vista, which sounded like a retirement home. Being related to a variety of experts is one of the perks of having a large family—or *mishpacha,* if you want to use the Hebrew/Yiddish term.

"Golden Vista is assisted living," Norm told me when I asked. "There's also Golden View, Golden Hills, and Golden Valley. Those are retirement facilities. Golden Valley is for convalescent care, like my place."

A lot of gold in them hills, I thought. "I'm interested in Golden Vista."

"For Bubbie?" A frown puckered his high forehead. "The macular degeneration's getting to her, huh?"

"Bubbie's managing fine," I assured him, hoping it was true. I wondered, not for the first time, whether my grandmother was really coping or whether she was pretending to, for our sakes. "Do you know the owner?"

"Everybody knows everyone in this business. Walter Ochs." He looked at me with curiosity, but he didn't press.

It's one of the things I like about my brother-in-law. "Can I use your name?"

"Not on a charge slip." He smiled. "Sure, go ahead."

"What's the place like?"

"Nice wallpaper."

It was my turn to frown. "Nice wallpaper? Is that supposed to be an important quality in a facility?"

He smiled again. "Exactly."

From down the block I saw a white paper tucked under my windshield wipers. Like an increasing number of neighborhood streets, Martel has permit-parking-only after six P.M. My first thought, accompanied by an expletive, was that a parking enforcement commando had ignored the permit hanging from my rearview mirror. It's happened before.

It was a flyer. Probably advertising the services of a handyman or gardener, I thought as I unfolded the paper and read the large words handwritten in thick black marker:

HE THAT TROUBLETH HIS OWN HOUSE
SHALL INHERIT THE WIND.

BE CAREFUL.
THE NIGHT HAS A THOUSAND EYES.

Someone peddling salvation, I thought, crumpling the paper.

CHAPTER TWENTY-ONE

Tuesday, November 11. 7:18 A.M. 4900 Cromwell Avenue.
During the day, a thief entered a gated property and took nude
statues from the front yard, valued at $6,800 in all. (Northeast)

THE MORNING FOG HID THE SUN, AND I HOPED IT WOULD
do the same to the bags under my eyes, the result of my staying
up late watching *French Kiss* with Meg Ryan and Kevin Kline,
whom I adore. I'd shaved ten minutes off my treadmill workout,
made tolerable by the *French Kiss* soundtrack, downed a power
bar with a glass of milk instead of my usual muffin, and with "La
Vie en Rose" still in my head, wondered why I'd agreed to meet
Hank Reston at his Hancock Park house at seven-thirty.

Fog thinned and turned into drizzle just as I got into my car.

I drove east on Third and joined the slowing queue of automobiles heading downtown. Parisians or tourists may love Paris when it drizzles, but we Angelinos overreact to even a few drops of precipitation, and it must have been a slow news day, judging by the "You give us twenty-two minutes, we'll give you the world" KFWB radio reporter, who talked about the rain as though it were the precursor to Noah's flood. ("We'll bring you updates as they occur," he promised somberly.)

Minutes later I neared Muirfield, and making a left turn on the corner, I cast a quick, automatic glance to my right at the infamous Norwood Young house. I've seen it countless times, yet I always find myself looking. Most people look, which I understand is the point.

It's stark white—the exterior, the roof, the wrought iron gate that gives the property a fortress feel. So are the nineteen pedestals, replacing the original pine trees, that form an arc on the lawn, and the eighteen anatomically correct marble copies of Michelangelo's *David* that grace them. The nineteenth statue, placed in the arc's center, is an armless nymph whose bored expression says she's seen it all before, or has seen better.

The neighbors aren't bored. If The Dungeon on South Martel precipitated HARP status in Miracle Mile North, I suspect it's this white house that makes many pro-HARP Hancock Park residents see red.

I wasn't particularly offended, but I didn't live next door. Last night at mah jongg, Edie told me a prospective homeowner had opted not to buy in Hancock Park because of "the *David*s." He'd probably be less inclined today. With the drizzle, I imagined that certain body parts on the statues would appear to be leaking.

I wondered again who decided what was historically significant, and what happened when the rights of the individual clashed with the sensibilities of others. And how far would people go to protect those rights? Was it possible that Linney's death was, after all, a tragic unforeseen event and not premeditated?

But what about the phone call from Margaret?

Reston's house, half a block away from "the *Davids*," was a stately two-story brick-faced Tudor with lead glass windows, a roof with multiple gables, and a sloped lawn the size of a small park. It was the kind of setting where a uniformed butler wouldn't seem out of place, and I was almost disappointed when Hank opened the door himself. He was wearing another baggy sweater—forest green this time—and black Dockers.

After waiting while I inaugurated a woven hemp mat, he invited me into a vaulting entry that faced a wide, curving stairway and a living room you could bowl in. My eyes were drawn to the huge, ornately framed portrait hanging above the black marble fireplace of a dark-haired woman in a burgundy velvet gown.

"That's Maggie," Reston said in the reverential tone of a curator unveiling a work from an Old Master. "But I guess you figured that out."

He walked into the living room and I followed, our footsteps echoing in the bare, high-ceilinged room. He stopped in front of the portrait and studied it as if he were seeing it for the first time.

"Oscar wouldn't give me the satisfaction of saying so, but I could tell he liked it," Hank said. "It shows her a little more stiff than she was, but the artist was going for regal. She's something, isn't she?"

"She's beautiful," I said, keenly aware that we were both talking as though she were still alive.

To be honest, she was more interesting and vibrant than beautiful. The face was too narrow, the nose a little too sharp and too long, the lips too wide. But my words gave Hank pleasure and cost me nothing, and the warmth in her large dark brown eyes and the smile that played around those lips lit her face and more than made up for any flaws. It was a smile that spoke of contentment and joy and made you want to smile right back. It was a smile that, given what had happened, seemed terribly poignant.

The artist had gotten the regal part down. I didn't know if it was his suggestion or Margaret's (or Reston's?) but she'd pulled her hair into a tight, gleaming chignon, revealing a shapely skull and patrician forehead and an elongated neck around which lay a circlet of diamonds. Each stone was larger than my one-and-a-half carat engagement ring, and the center teardrop could have held its own on a chandelier. More diamonds sparkled in her ears and on her wrist and on her finger. If diamonds are a girl's best friend, Margaret had had a sorority.

She wore the jewels well, as if they belonged on her, but I could see what Hank meant about her stiffness. It was in the set of her shoulders, in the posed hands folded on her lap. They looked restless and gave the impression that she wanted to gather her velvet skirts and get on with the business of enjoying life.

And now she was missing, presumed dead.

There was no other artwork on the sand-colored walls, no drapes or shutters on the many large windows, no rugs on parquet floors lacquered to a mirrorlike gloss. A black grand piano sat imperiously alone in the otherwise empty room as though it were on a concert stage, waiting for someone who would elicit magic from its keys.

Reston's gaze followed mine. "Maggie ordered it a few weeks before she disappeared," he said. "I forgot all about it until they delivered it."

"It's magnificent," I told him, not knowing what else to say.

"Yeah." There was a world of sadness in the word. "I don't know if I'll keep it. I don't know if I'll stay in the house. I don't need anything this big, this fancy. But if there's the smallest chance she's alive . . ."

He stood a moment longer staring at the piano, or past it, I couldn't tell. Then he glanced at the portrait again, turned sharply on his heel, and left the room. I did the same.

CHAPTER TWENTY-TWO

"MOST OF THE STUFF HASN'T COME YET," HANK TOLD ME as he led me into a library lined with empty built-in bookshelves. "The decorator ordered couches and tables and rugs and all that stuff, but it's taking forever. Maggie chose her, so I know she's good. *I* sure as hell wouldn't know what to do."

I figured the books were on order, too. Literature by the pound, I thought, recalling a fan who'd asked a sales clerk at one of my book signings for a hundred dollars' worth of *Out of the Ashes*. He'd left with four hardcover copies of *Ashes*, an Ann Rule paperback, and a magazine. If he'd waited for the *Ashes* paperback . . .

I decided I was being a snoot. For all I knew, Hank was an avid reader. I'd been colored by Linney's prejudice, a prejudice I'd heard secondhand.

Hank walked to a rosewood desk cluttered with papers and handed me a stack of stapled sheets. "A copy of Maggie's planner. I read it last night but didn't find anything helpful. Maybe you'll see something I didn't."

That was unlikely. Reston would be familiar with names and abbreviations that would make no sense to me. "Was there anything different about your wife in the days before she disappeared?"

"Why don't we talk in the kitchen, Molly." A good idea, since the massive black leather studded desk chair provided the only seating in the room. "You'll have to excuse the mess. The housekeeper had to go to the dentist."

I'm a lover of kitchens, and this one was Cordon Bleu worthy. It was enormous—I'd expected no less—but the designer had managed to create a cozy feeling by using warm lacquered woods for the cabinets and flooring, and the walls were painted a soft buttercup. The granite counters looked black, but on closer inspection were a dark green, and decorative tiles accented the beige ceramic ones on the backsplash. There were two Sub-Zero refrigerators, Hank showed me proudly, and two freezers, two Thermador double ovens, and a Viking range top with six burners under a stainless steel hood large enough to suck up a small city.

"Maggie and I loved to cook together," he told me, the wistfulness in his voice just short of a sigh.

I love to cook, too, although since my divorce I haven't been doing much of it, unless you call broiling chicken or fish or heating pizza or take-out Chinese "cooking." And my kitchen is about the size of Reston's center island. Since I keep kosher, if it were my kitchen I'd add a second dishwasher and sink (one for meat, one for dairy). But that's quibbling. I would *chalesh* to have a kitchen like this. That's Yiddish for *swoon*, but it means to crave intensely. Which I did.

The "mess," by the way, was a plate, silverware, and two tumblers stacked in the stainless steel sink. My brother Joey does more damage preparing a snack.

Adjoining the kitchen was a breakfast room painted in that same soft yellow. The rain partially obscured the view through the French doors, but I could see the rectangular swimming pool at the end of a beautifully landscaped garden.

Hank brought two crackled yellow mugs to a glass-topped table with a wrought iron base. We sat across from each other on chairs upholstered in a polished cotton print whose blues and yellows were echoed in ceramic bowls and knickknacks around the room. Some of the "stuff" the decorator had ordered had obviously arrived.

The coffee smelled wonderful. I added creamer and a packet of sweetener, then took a sip. It tasted wonderful, too, rich with a hint of cinnamon.

"You asked about Maggie," he said, his large hands cupping the mug. "She seemed tense, but I figured it was the house. It's exciting building from scratch, but even with a decorator and an architect, there's so many decisions, and things never go the way you planned. Plus she was worried about her dad."

From what I could remember, several of Maggie's notations had been house related. Granite, flooring, bath fixtures. "Was she more tense the last few days?"

"I don't know." Reston shifted his gaze to the bare-branched trees visible through the windows. "I keep going over it, wondering if there was something I missed. And I was doin' a lot of business travel. I keep thinking about that, too. If I'd been home that night . . ."

I'd been down that road myself. The night Aggie was murdered, she'd wanted me to accompany her to a prayer vigil for a young woman stricken with cancer, but laziness had made me turn her down.

I pushed the thought back into a recess of my mind. "You mentioned a home invasion. Was anything taken?"

"The diamonds Maggie had on in the portrait. A necklace, bracelet, ring, earrings. She wore them to a black-tie dinner Wednesday night and was going to put them back in the bank vault Thursday. I guess she didn't get around to it."

That added an interesting dimension, and an excellent motive. "How much was everything worth?" I asked, because it was relevant and I was curious.

"The good stuff was appraised at a million three," Hank said. "Another five or ten thousand for some pieces Maggie kept at home. And, yes, it was all insured. That was the first thing the cops asked. They'd be idiots not to. But the insurance won't pay till they know for sure Maggie didn't skip with the diamonds. I told the cops, if I killed her for the insurance, why would I hide the body? They didn't have an answer for that." Hank sounded bitter.

I admired his candor but cautioned myself not to be taken in by it. "Who knew about the jewelry?"

"The cops had me make a list. My friends, some business associates. Maggie's friends. One of them told her she'd kill to have a necklace like that, but I think she was joking, don't you?" Hank flashed a faint smile. "Everyone who saw Maggie at the Beverly Wilshire Wednesday night. I told the detective maybe it was a waiter or valet. Or maybe it was one of those follow-home burglaries, but they waited a day to pull the job. The detective said they'd check into it. Did they?" Hank shrugged.

"What about the housekeeper?"

Hank shook his head. "Not Louisa. She's been with the family since Maggie was a little girl. She helped raise her after Maggie's mom died. Anyway, the cops talked to her."

"Maybe Louisa mentioned the jewelry to someone, not meaning anything, and that someone mentioned it to someone else." I could see that Hank wasn't buying it. "What about the artist who did Maggie's portrait?"

"The police checked. He was in Taos when it happened."

I took another sip of coffee. "Suppose it was a burglar. Why would he kidnap your wife? Why not just take the jewelry and run?"

"The cops asked that, too. The way I see it, the bastard saw the jewelry and realized he was dealing with big money, figured there was more where that came from. Or, he planned the kidnapping, and the jewelry was a bonus."

Both scenarios were possible. Kidnapping will earn a person a much stiffer sentence than burglary, but from talking to criminals I've learned that many of them are more greedy than smart. Which is why they're often caught.

"But no one ever contacted you for a ransom," I said.

"That's what makes me think Maggie's dead." He stared into his coffee mug. "They found her blood in the house. Maybe she was hurt worse than the guy realized. Or maybe she tried to escape later."

"She didn't mention that she was worried about anyone? *Afraid* of anyone?" I asked.

He shook his head. "Maggie got along with everyone. I can't think of anyone who'd want to hurt her."

"Who knew you were going to be away Thursday night?"

"This wasn't someone we knew," Hank insisted with a flash of exasperation. "This was a stranger."

"Were there any signs of forced entry?"

"No." His tone was grudging. "But when I talked to her she was planning to paint. Her studio's in the garage, and there's an intercom to the house, but she checks on her dad 'cause sometimes he gets up in the middle of the night. So she doesn't always lock the house side door. I think the guy sneaked in and was waiting for her upstairs."

It was possible. In collecting data for my *Crime Sheet* column, I've read about similar occurrences. It was also possible that the assailant was someone who had a key. Someone like Margaret Linney's husband.

From what Winnie and Tim Bolt had said, the police had found evidence of an assault. I asked Hank about it.

"The desk chair was knocked down, the phone was off the hook. They found blood on the corner of the desk and on a drawer pull." Hank's mouth was grim. "A porcelain clock was on the floor, broken. That's how they figured when it happened, from the time on the clock. Ten minutes after one in the morning."

"Whose prints were on the receiver?"

"What you'd expect. Hers, mine, Oscar's, the housekeeper's. I figure Maggie was trying to phone the police when the son of a bitch hit her." Hank had laced his fingers into a tight, knuckled ball that he brought to his mouth. His eyes were filled with pain.

I pictured Margaret running to the desk, grabbing the receiver. Her assailant clamps his fingers around her wrist. She drops the receiver. Did he smack her? Shove her? Did his hands lock around her neck the way my assailant's had locked around mine? For a second I was back in that dark room and I couldn't breathe. I realized that my hand was at my throat and dropped it to my side.

"She must have struggled," Hank said. "But see, if she opened the door for the guy, or if he'd followed her in, why didn't they find signs of struggling downstairs?"

It was a good point. I could see the muscles working in Hank's face. I gave him a moment, wishing there were a better, gentler way to ask the next question. "Was she raped, Hank?"

He glared at me, as if I were the offender. "There's nothing to say she was. They didn't find anybody else's . . . fluids. They found mine, on the sheets, but why wouldn't they?" His face was flushed with discomfort, and there was challenge in his voice. "I told you, we were together that morning, before I left."

With an abrupt movement he shoved back his chair and walked to the window. He stood there with his broad back to me, hands stuffed into the pockets of his Dockers.

"I try not to think about how scared she must've been," he said, his words muffled by the rain. "I try not to hear her screams, but they wake me up." When he removed his hands from his pockets, they had formed fists. "I fantasize about what I'd do if I found the bastard. It's what keeps me going, but it's not enough."

The rain was stronger, slapping the window, demanding entry. I flipped through the stapled sheets Reston had given me and found the page with Maggie's last entries. *Cyndi's. Granite. Kitchen flooring. Check out Sub-Zero. Golden Vista!!*

"Who's Cyndi?" I asked.

Hank turned around. "Who?"

I held up the page. He came back to the table and looked at the name.

"I don't— Oh, *Cyndi.* I think that's her hairdresser. I don't remember where she works, but you can check the pages at the back of the planner. I photocopied the index with names, addresses, and phone numbers."

"What about Golden Vista?" I pointed to the entry.

"Yeah, I saw that last night. I figure it's a resort. We were talking about getting away for a few days, and Maggie was checking into a couple of places."

I debated telling him that it was the name of an assisted living facility and decided not to, though I'm not sure why. "Did Maggie have close friends?"

He slumped into the chair—a risky movement for a man of his girth, but the chair held. "Not really. I guess you could say her father was her best friend, until I came along."

A shy smile softened the planes of his rugged face, and I could see why Margaret had found him attractive.

"Well, she had a couple of women she'd go to concerts with, or operas or museums," Hank said. "Stuff I tried to like but couldn't get into, and Maggie finally gave up asking me to come along." Another wry smile flitted across his face. "I wouldn't call them friends, though," he said, all seriousness now. "Maggie and I liked spending time together, just the two of us. We didn't need friends."

When Ron and I were newlyweds, we'd done the nesting thing, too. But the nest had become crowded. "Do you know if the police talked to these women?"

Hank shrugged. "I gave the cops their names. I don't think Maggie saw them the day she disappeared, though. There's nothing in her planner that said she did."

"She may have talked to them."

"Maybe." He nodded. "But they weren't people she'd confide in. And even if she did, how would that help unless the guy who kidnapped her knew her?"

Which was a strong possibility, one Reston seemed to have trouble accepting. "Did she quarrel with anyone in the days before she disappeared?"

"Not that I know of, and she would've told me." He took a long sip of coffee. "Everybody loved Maggie. She was interested in what you had to say and was easy to get along with. And she was real soft-spoken. Me, I'm the yeller."

His expression was almost mischievous, disarming. I wondered again if what I was seeing was the real Hank Reston or the person he wanted to portray.

"You mentioned headaches with the construction," I said. "Did Maggie have arguments with a subcontractor or worker?"

"You're asking everything the cops did." There was approval in his voice and his nod. "She had a problem with one of the tile setters. Karl Linz. A Czech guy. Maggie didn't like his work, and he got angry and rude when she told him, so she fired him."

"When was that?"

"When?" Hank squinted, concentrating. "Around two weeks before Maggie disappeared. He made some noise about making her sorry, but we thought he was just mouthing off. The cops checked him out. His sister says he was home with her that night. But she could be trying to protect him."

"I'd like to talk to him. Who did the construction on the house, by the way? Roger Modine?"

"That's right." He gave me a warning look that said, What of it? "Roger's a little rough around the edges. I hope he didn't hurt you. He was just protecting the house from snoopers."

"No scars," I said, making light of the incident. "Did he and Maggie get along?"

Reston frowned. "You're barking up the wrong tree. Roger wouldn't lay a finger on Maggie. He knows I'd kill anyone who hurt her," he said simply, as though he were talking about swatting a fly.

He hadn't really answered my question. I asked Hank to get me Linz's phone number and paged backwards through the photocopied pages while he was out of the room. Maggie had written *Tiler* on the next-to-last page. With two exclamation points.

Something about that bothered me, but I couldn't figure it out. Something bothered me about the other pages, too, but Reston was back before I could mull it through.

"Who's the last person Maggie spoke to before she disappeared?" I asked.

"Aside from her dad, you mean." He handed me a slip of paper with Linz's phone number. "I called her around ten, but she was getting Oscar to bed. He had a rough day, so of course, Maggie did, too. She said she'd call back, and when I didn't hear from her, I figured she was painting. She does that when she wants to relax. I didn't want to bother her, so I went to the casino and played the tables and found out later she'd called. By then it was late and I didn't want to wake her."

"You were in Vegas?"

"On business. I was in San Bernardino earlier in the day."

The cops had checked the phone records, he told me. Except for a 10:30 call to the hotel, Maggie hadn't made any long-distance calls that night—not on the house phone, not on her cell phone.

I looked at the page again. "Maggie wrote about a meeting with Dr. E, and on the same page, *V* and *D*."

"*D* is the Professor. *V* would be Ned Vaughan. He's a family friend and very close to Oscar, although I would have thought she'd write *Ned*. The doc is his internist. El-something." Hank remained standing, his hands locked on the scrolled iron back of his chair.

"She didn't have any friends or colleagues with a first or last name that starts with *D*?"

He shook his head. He was shifting his weight from one foot to another, a sprinter waiting for the starting shot. His restlessness was making me nervous.

I thumbed back a page. "What about *pb?* Would that be *plumber?*"

"Sounds right." He picked up his mug, took a sip, and made a face. "This is cold. You want a refill?"

I covered the top of my mug with my hand. "I'm good, thanks."

He dumped the coffee into the sink. I flipped back several pages and waited for him to return with his refilled mug. "A week before Maggie disappeared, she wrote something about bank and help. Any idea what that is?"

"Banking is hell, everyone needs help," he said, unsmiling. "I don't know. Sorry."

I showed him the notation about the MS, but he had no idea

whether or not Linney had been diagnosed with multiple sclerosis. "Maggie took care of all that," he told me.

I looked at the following page again. *Lighting. Pool tile. Call
pb?! Tiler!!* I must have been frowning because he asked me what
was wrong.

"Just thinking," I said. "When are the police coming to pick
up the planner?"

"I haven't told them about it yet." The color in his face
deepened. "To tell you the truth, I hate the thought of giving it
up. When I hold it or read it, I can see Maggie sitting on the bed
writing in it, her legs crossed under her. Or in the car." He
paused. "I guess I'll call the detective this morning."

CHAPTER TWENTY-THREE

I ASKED TO SEE PROFESSOR LINNEY'S ROOM. I WAS PRE-pared to answer Reston's "Why?" with some vague explanation that would avoid any intimation that the old man had been killed (I didn't want to piss off Porter or Hernandez more than I already had by seeing the planner and Linney's room before they did), but Reston didn't ask.

The old man's ground-floor bedroom, carpeted in taupe, its walls painted ecru, was larger than his room in the Fuller house. Someone had filled it with the basics. A maple sleigh bed, nightstand, dresser, a desk with a book-filled hutch. His Columbia undergraduate degree hung next to a plaque from the University of Southern California. On the desk were a black ceramic cup with pens and pencils, a pad of lined paper, and a tape recorder.

"The Professor used it for department meetings, and to record notes for his book," Hank said when I asked him about the recorder. "He wasn't into computers." He looked around the room and sighed. "I haven't been in here since the old guy died. It's strange, not seeing him."

"When did you last talk to him?"

"Friday morning, just before I left. He asked me when I'd be back. He didn't usually give a damn, but at the time I didn't give it any thought."

"I understand that the housekeeper left him alone in the house."

Hank frowned. "He told Louisa I said it was okay 'cause I'd be home within the hour. He seemed real clearheaded that morning, so I can see how she'd buy it." His tone indicated otherwise.

"I'd like to talk to her."

"She'll be back tomorrow. But like I told you, the police talked to her. She didn't know anything about Maggie's disappearance."

The housekeeper had probably been nervous talking to police and might be more open with me. I also wanted to ask her what Linney had been like in the days before he died.

"And the caregiver?" I asked. "She didn't show?"

"Can you believe it?" He rolled his eyes. "I have half a mind to sue."

I'd heard Reston mention the agency's name when he was talking to the black-suited woman at the meeting and dug it out of my memory bank. First Aid. "What's the caregiver's name?" Maria something, Fennel had said.

Reston hesitated. "I don't want you talking to her just yet. In case I *do* decide to sue. I want to check with the lawyers. Anyway, she wasn't with the Professor when Maggie disappeared."

But Linney might have said something to her about Margaret. "Can I take a look at Professor Linney's papers? He may have made some reference to your wife's plans, written down something she said." I wondered if my explanation sounded as lame to him as it did to me.

"The police asked. Oscar didn't hear anything that night, didn't know anything. But go ahead and look, if you want. Knock yourself out." Hank checked his watch. "I have a few calls to make. I'll be in my office if you need me."

That was fine with me. I'd assumed that Reston would oversee my search, and I wondered if he'd left me alone to show that he trusted me or that he had nothing to hide. Or, my suspicious self suggested, because he'd already removed anything incriminating.

Sitting at Linney's desk, I pressed the EJECT button on the tape recorder, but there was no cassette inside. The desk's center drawer was filled with odds and ends: paper clips, pens, a gold bookmark. No address book, which was disappointing.

In the bottom of the two drawers on the right I found his USC material—class roll books, curriculum sheets for various architectural courses, typed minutes of department meetings, an assortment of cassettes labeled with the day and date of department meetings. The second drawer yielded several accordion folders: two with architectural sketches, one with photos of homes (many black-and-white, some full color), and the last with two loose pages filled with tiny, cramped handwriting and a cassette labeled TREASURES. I played the tape and heard his whiny voice announce the date, February of this year, and the title. Then nothing.

I glanced at the top page, dated almost a year ago. *Treasures of Yesterday and Tomorrow: Preserving the Architectural History of Los Angeles.* Linney's book—or what would have *been* his book if the Alzheimer's hadn't aborted the project. The photos were filed into pockets of the folder labeled with neighborhood names, arranged in alphabetical order: Angelino Heights, Carthay Circle, Melrose Hill, Miracle Mile . . . all the HARP areas I'd been reading about.

At the back of the drawer I found a manila folder with bank statements and correspondence from Skoll Investment, Incorporated, based in Denver. I thumbed through the pages and noted that Linney had invested over forty thousand dollars with them in property. Not a small sum. I checked the dates. April of this year. Around the time he'd been diagnosed with Alzheimer's, according to Tim Bolt. I copied down the names listed on the correspondence and the company's address and phone number.

Thinking of phone numbers reminded me about the call Fennel had overheard. I walked to the answering machine on Linney's nightstand, pressed REWIND, then PLAY.

Nothing but the whirr of a blank tape. Either Linney had erased Margaret's message, or someone else had.

I checked the old man's dresser but found nothing of interest. On top of the dresser were photos. A duplicate of the formal wedding portrait I'd seen in Linney's Fuller bedroom. Linney with Margaret, from infancy through chubby-cheeked childhood. The professor and an adolescent Margaret with braces on her teeth, her face slimmer, his gaunt; both subdued, presumably by the loss of wife and mother. A smiling Margaret in black cap and gown, clasping a rolled diploma. Margaret seated in front of a grand piano, her slender hands poised on the ivories.

There were no photos of Margaret as bride, none of her groom. That was telling, I thought, but not surprising.

Returning to the desk, I checked the drawers again, not knowing what I was looking for. Then I took down Linney's books, and behind a biography of Frank Lloyd Wright I found an unlabeled tape cassette.

"Expect nothing," Alice Walker tells us in a poem of the

same name, so I tried not to but of course I did, because why would Linney have hidden the tape if it weren't important, at least to him?

I was tempted to slip the cassette into my purse, but that would be theft, and possibly obstruction of justice. So I inserted it into the recorder and pressed PLAY.

A few seconds of lead, then, "Professor, it's Ned. Sorry you couldn't make the meeting last night. Hank said you weren't up to it, and I guess he told you about the excitement. Hope you're feeling better. I'll call again."

The HARP meeting, I thought.

"This is Dr. Elbogen's office reminding you that you have an appointment . . ."

". . . come by tomorrow, if that's okay, Oscar." Fennel's squeaky voice. "Want to make sure you're not getting into too much trouble."

"What's that you're listening to?"

I stopped the tape and turned toward the doorway and Hank. "I found this behind Professor Linney's books," I told him. "I thought maybe he'd recorded something about Margaret," I lied. "But it's just messages."

"Go on," he instructed, approaching the desk. "Play the rest."

So I did. I rewound a second or so and pressed PLAY.

". . . make sure you're not getting into too much trouble."

"Fennel," Hank said. "The Professor's friend."

"Mr. Linney, this is Joan Eggers returning your call. I'll be here till five today."

"Professor, Tim Bolt. Just checking to see if you're feeling better. I wanted you to know that the gardener added seed and fertilizer and trimmed the bushes, so everything's looking fine, just the way you like it."

There was a caller who left no message. We listened to a long stretch of taped silence, and then another beep.

Hank sighed. "I guess that's—"

"This is Margaret. Meet me at the house Friday at four. I'm afraid. Don't tell anyone."

A soft moan escaped Reston's lips. He grabbed the edge of the desk to steady himself, a giant oak about to be felled by a storm.

"Play it again," he ordered.

I rewound the tape and did as he asked.

"Again," he said.

I think we listened to it about five times before he told me he'd heard enough.

"It's Maggie's voice," he said, his voice hushed with wonder and anguish and a strangled joy. "I can't—" He stopped, and I watched hurt and bewilderment cross his face. "But why didn't she call *me*?"

CHAPTER TWENTY-FOUR

"SO WHAT BRINGS YOU TO WILSHIRE, ASIDE FROM YOUR column?" Rico Hernandez asked.

Several other detectives were in the large room—some standing and talking to each other; some at their desks, writing or on the phone. A few had seemed to follow me with their eyes as I'd made my way to Hernandez's desk. Maybe it was my hair. The rain had stopped, but the air was still full of moisture that had given my natural curls a wild voluminous look much like Madeleine Kahn's electrified "do" after she's done the deed with the monster in *Young Frankenstein*. Or maybe I'm just self-conscious at Wilshire where, as I mentioned, my questions about my best friend Aggie's unsolved murder make me as welcome as herpes.

I usually do my *Crime Sheet* data collection on Mondays, but yesterday I'd been otherwise occupied. Today I'd made Wilshire my first stop. It's the division closest to Reston's Muirfield house. More important, I wanted to talk to Hernandez without Porter around. Lucky for me, Hernandez was in and willing to see me. Luckier still, Porter was out. Well, not luck. I'd listened while Hank phoned Porter, who had promised he'd be right over to pick up the answering machine tape and planner. So I was feeling a little pleased with myself.

"I was hoping you could tell me what you've learned about Professor Linney's death," I said, eyeing the "blue books" on Hernandez's dauntingly neat desk. I didn't recognize the names on the labeled spines of the three books standing upright, and the spines of two others were facing away from me. I wondered if one of the latter held reports and photos from the Linney case. If in fact there *was* a case, I cautioned myself.

"And *I* was hoping you'd had a change of heart about your notes." The corners of Hernandez's mouth were turned up in amusement. "What's your interest in Professor Linney's death, Miss Blume?"

I took that as encouragement and settled onto my chair. "Please call me Molly. The truth? I feel somewhat connected. First of all, I gave Professor Linney a ride the other day. And I think someone lured him to the Fuller house and made the arson look like another one of the HARP-related vandalisms I wrote about in my *Times* piece."

"So you're feeling used."

"*And* somewhat responsible." The way he said it made me sound self-centered, which I guess was partly true. "So naturally, I'd like to find out how he died."

"I see."

No further comment from Hernandez. I suppose I'd been hoping for a comforting statement like the one Connors had offered. "Do you have the autopsy results, Detective?"

"Yes."

"Was Professor Linney murdered?"

"Unfortunately, I can't discuss the results at this time," the detective said, pleasant but official.

I'd expected a stock answer. "But you think his death and his daughter's disappearance are connected?"

"Again, I can't comment at this time."

"His death is obviously suspicious, or the fire department would be handling the case, not you." I turned my head and nodded at the blue books, hoping Hernandez would instinctively look their way and confirm my guess.

He tugged on a snow-white monogrammed cuff peeking out of the sleeve of his navy blazer.

The Rosetta Stone was probably easier to read. Maybe I would have done better with Porter. "According to one of Professor Linney's close friends, Margaret phoned her father last Thursday." I repeated what Fennel had told me. "I advised Mr. Fennel to contact you," I continued, hoping to earn points and information. "Did he?"

Hernandez nodded, a noncommittal go-on expression in those chocolate brown eyes.

"I found the tape this morning in Professor Linney's bedroom in his son-in-law's new house. Mr. Reston asked me to help find out what happened to his wife," I added when I saw Hernandez's raised brow. "I urged him to give you the tape, along with his wife's daily planner, which I found in her bedroom last night. Mr. Reston told me it had been missing from the time his wife disappeared."

Hernandez studied me for what was probably less than a minute but felt longer. "You seem to have a knack for finding things," he finally said.

His tone and gaze made me shift on my seat even though he had no way of knowing I'd been trespassing when I'd come across the planner. It was the kind of penetrating look my dad does well, the kind that probably had suspects spilling all for Hernandez.

My cheeks tingled. "My point is, Detective, I'm trying to help your investigation, not hinder it. I'm hoping you'll share information with me, and I promise not to print anything until you give me the green light."

Hernandez treated me to another amused smile that on Porter would have looked snide. "Thank you, Molly, but I have a partner. I'm not looking for a replacement."

"You can check with Detective Connors. He'll vouch for me." After my *Times* article, I hoped that was still true.

"Where was Margaret Reston's planner?"

"In her nightstand." I told him about the movement I'd noticed at the window, about the perfumed and dusted room. "Whoever was there could have replaced the planner."

"Perhaps it was Margaret Reston," Hernandez said.

"Margaret Reston?" I repeated stupidly. I hadn't considered that, though of course, I should have.

"If she made that phone call, she may still be alive. From what you tell me, her father and Mr. Fennel recognized her voice. So did her husband."

"I guess they'd know."

Hernandez cocked his head. "But you're not convinced. I take it you've talked to Margaret Reston?"

"No. I've never even met her."

"Then why the skepticism?"

"What about the autopsy results?" I countered.

Hernandez wagged his finger at me. "We're not bartering here, Miss Blume." Along with the return to formality, a flinty note had deepened his musical voice.

Nothing ventured . . . "Her voice was stiff. You'll hear it when you listen to the tape."

"Tension or anxiety can do that," Hernandez said, but he looked thoughtful.

"And her message was abrupt. 'This is Margaret. I'm afraid. Meet me at the house. Don't tell anyone.' It's strange, don't you think, considering she'd disappeared and hadn't talked to her father in five months?"

"Maybe she was afraid someone would overhear, or trace her call."

"Maybe." I had to admit that was a possibility.

"Mr. Reston didn't comment about the message?"

"He wants desperately to believe his wife is alive. I think he noticed something was off but didn't want to admit it. Why else would he listen to the tape five times?"

Rico Hernandez drummed his fingers on his desk while he contemplated what I'd told him.

"If Margaret Reston is alive," I said when the drumming stopped, "why hasn't she come forward? Doesn't she care that her father burned to death? And why didn't she let the poor man know all those months he was grieving for her? Why didn't she leave a note?"

"Fear," Hernandez said with quiet certainty. "The same fear that drove her away in the first place."

"What about the blood on the desk and in her car? And the missing jewelry?" I frowned. "Unless she staged the kidnapping and skipped with the jewelry so she could sell it and live off it," I said, answering my own question. And if that were the case, why? "Was it her blood?"

"It was, yes. And before you ask, we didn't find anyone else's."

Finally, an answer. "What about the jewelry? Has any of it turned up?"

"Not yet." Hernandez's face showed a flicker of disappointment. "For all we know, the stones could be in several different countries by now. If Margaret Linney died, I imagine her kidnapper would be extremely nervous about being found through her jewels."

I felt a beat of excitement. "So you *do* think she's dead?"

"On the other hand, if she staged her kidnapping, she'd be nervous about being traced through her jewelry."

I mulled that over, then thought again about the tape. I shook my head. "I can't believe she'd phone her father and set him up like that."

"Maybe she planned to meet him but was prevented from doing so. Maybe she was killed."

Hernandez's seesawing was driving me crazy. "Is that what you believe?"

"I'm reserving judgment until I hear the tape. About the planner, Molly. We'll need your fingerprints since you handled it. I take it you've examined it?" He spoke with the resignation of a parent who's been asked to meet with his child's principal, again.

"Only the last few entries." I didn't volunteer that the photocopied pages were in the Coach bag at my feet. "I *did* find something interesting," I said, in my best dangling-carrot voice.

"Bartering again?" Hernandez asked when I didn't continue.

"Trying to." This time he didn't sound annoyed. That and the fact that he was using my first name renewed my hope. "Mr. Reston told me his wife had quarreled with Karl Linz, the tile setter, but Linz's sister alibied him."

Hernandez nodded. "The quarrel took place weeks before the disappearance."

"But there's a notation in the planner on the day before Margaret disappeared about the tiler. With two exclamation points. Why would she be upset about Linz two weeks *after* the quarrel, unless they had another one?"

"As a writer, you're clearly attuned to the significance of punctuation," Hernandez said dryly. "But you're right. It's an excellent question, Molly, and a fine observation." He jotted something on the small notepad in front of him.

I have to admit his approval pleased me. "And then there's Professor Linney's bruises. The day we met, his legs were black and blue."

"Did he mention how he obtained the bruises?"

I shook my head. "Not to me. Apparently Professor Linney accused several people of hitting him. The caregiver, the house-keeper, his son-in-law."

Hernandez wrote that down, too, but didn't look impressed. "Linney suffered from Alzheimer's, so he may have imagined the abuse. The fact that he accused several people makes that more likely, don't you think? But thank you for telling me. Anything else?"

Time to play my ace. "Linney told me he didn't want to climb stairs because he was terrified of falling and breaking his hip." I paused. "So what was he doing in an upstairs bedroom in the Fuller house?"

"You didn't mention this yesterday."

I had the detective's interest now. I could hear it in the F-sharpness of his melodious voice. I could see it in the stiffen-ing of his posture. And in his scowl. It wasn't the response I'd hoped for.

"I remembered after you left." I spoke with sincerity born of truth, but I had that squirmy feeling again. "Anyway, I thought you should know. That's why I'm here."

"And because you want information."

"That, too," I agreed. "I'd be grateful for details about Mar-garet Linney's disappearance. Whom you suspect. I don't suppose you'd let me take a look at her file?" I probably had a better chance at winning the lottery.

"I wish I could help you, Miss Blume." We'd gone from for-mal to friendly and back to formal. "I appreciate the information you've shared."

"Was Professor Linney murdered? Just tell me that."

"I believe this is where you came in." Hernandez braced his hands on his desk and stood. "If there's something I can tell you that won't compromise our investigation, I will."

"Like the Lakers' score?" I picked up my purse and slung the strap over my shoulder.

Hernandez smiled. "I'll give your regards to Detective Porter. He'll be sorry he missed you."

Chapter Twenty-five

Back in my parked car I made several calls on my cell phone, then spent the rest of the morning and a good chunk of the afternoon collecting *Crime Sheet* data at police divisions in the other areas the paper covers: Northwest, Pacific, West L.A., Culver City, West Hollywood. I left Hollywood for last, hoping I'd catch Connors, but he wasn't in.

I did have plenty of material for my column. There were the usual suspects—car thieves and street muggers—and, apparently, a rash of males flashing their privates, no doubt inspired by last week's warm weather. There *is* something to be said for arctic temperatures, although Manhattan's Naked Cowboy apparently struts his stuff even in the snow. Well, not *all* his stuff. He does wear briefs.

I'd noted only one new home vandalism, and that was in West L.A. in a non-HARP neighborhood. My guess was that the HARP vandal had been frightened into inactivity by the torching of the Fuller house and Linney's death. Unless, of course, the person who had vandalized the other residences was responsible for the Fuller arson. I didn't believe that for one minute. I didn't think Rico Hernandez did, either.

The small waiting room of Dr. Bernard Elbogen, practitioner of internal medicine, was overheated and furnished with a crackled brown Naugahyde sofa and four ugly turquoise vinyl chairs permanently indented from too many rumps. I fit mine onto a chair across from an elderly man whose shoulders and torso seemed to have shrunk inside his plaid sports jacket. Next to him was a middle-aged man with almost identical features—probably a son—who, in between entering data into his laptop, kept checking his watch and clearing his throat loudly for the benefit of the platinum blond receptionist at whom he darted annoyed looks. When that didn't get her attention, he walked over to her.

"We've been waiting a half hour," he told her in a voice straining for politeness.

"We'll call your father as soon as there's a room."

Judging from her bored tone, she'd said the same thing to a thousand-plus patients or family members thereof. I was pretty sure she was the woman I'd talked to this morning on my cell phone, though she'd sounded friendlier then, telling me how lucky I was someone had canceled. After my disappointing meeting with Hernandez, I wasn't feeling all that lucky, but I took her word for it.

I thumbed through an issue of *Newsweek,* smiled at some of the cartoons and quotes, read about another Democrat throwing his hat into the presidential ring, then about the latest attack in Israel. Sixteen killed and forty-three injured, some critically, on a bus blown up by two Palestinian Al Fatah terrorists who drove a car packed with explosives into the bus, turning it into an inferno of crumpled metal and charred bodies. I closed my eyes and sighed deeply.

"My lips are dry," the old man announced in an Eastern European accent that reminded me of my Zeidie Irving's. Grabbing the cane at his side, he pushed himself up and walked to the receptionist's window.

"Can I have a little bit water, please?" he asked.

She rolled her eyes, stood, and disappeared from view. A moment later she returned and handed the old man a small white cup.

"Thank you." He took a sip, wet his lips with his tongue, and shuffled back to his seat.

Fifteen minutes passed. I finished the magazine and picked up a copy of *Health*. I was reading about the danger of fad diets when the old man stood and made his way back to the receptionist.

"My lips are dry," he told her again, his voice soft with apology. "It's the medicine. Could I maybe have a little more water, please?"

He handed her the cup and thanked her a moment later when she returned it, filled.

"If you have a problem, you should bring a water bottle with you next time, Mr. Abramson," she said sternly. "I can't keep giving you water every few minutes."

His lined face turned red, as though she'd slapped him. "I'm sorry. It's the medicine."

You should be sorry, I thought, glaring at her. For keeping an old man waiting so long, for begrudging him a little water, a little kindness. She was oblivious to my stare, and she probably wouldn't have understood if she'd seen it. Wait till you're old, I wanted to tell her.

I watched the son. He'd looked up from his laptop at the

receptionist's rebuke, and I saw anger pinch his lips. He made a motion as though he was about to stand, and I tensed in anticipation. *Tell her off,* I cheered silently. But indecision crept into his eyes, and then a sort of embarrassment because he saw me looking at him. He sat back, his face flushed, his eyes avoiding mine, and returned his attention and fingers to the laptop.

I supposed he didn't want to create a scene. I supposed that in those few seconds he'd decided that the repercussions of an outburst would outweigh any momentary satisfaction. Maybe the office would give his father a hard time scheduling appointments or filling out insurance forms. Worse, maybe they'd ask him to find another doctor. I understood. But, damn, I'd wanted him to put the woman in her place. I wondered what I would have done if it were Bubbie G who'd been yelled at. To be honest, I didn't know.

And then it occurred to me that maybe I had it all wrong. Maybe the son was upset not with the receptionist, but with his father, who had annoyed her and was a source of embarrassment, like a whiny child. I thought about Oscar Linney and the people he might have annoyed. I thought about his bruises.

Twenty minutes passed before I was ushered into Dr. Elbogen's wood-paneled office. He was a portly man with Pillsbury Doughboy cheeks, dark hair, and a handlebar mustache that would have made Hercule Poirot jealous.

"I understand you're here for a consultation," he said when we were both seated. "How can I help you, Miss Blume?"

"I'm a reporter," I said, watching a frown eclipse his smile. I seem to have that effect on people. I handed him a business card. "I wanted to ask you a few questions about Professor Linney."

The doctor dropped the card onto his desk as if it were contaminated. "I can't discuss a patient with you."

"Of course not. I'm not here to ask about Professor Linney's physical condition. I wanted to know if he said anything about his daughter's disappearance."

Elbogen sighed and relaxed against the black leather of his armchair. "He talked about it all the time. He was devastated. She was everything to him, his whole world."

"Did he tell you what he thought had happened to her?"

The doctor shook his head. "All he knew was what the police told him, that Margaret was apparently kidnapped. He didn't want to believe she was dead."

"Did he express any fears about his own safety?"

"No." Elbogen looked at me appraisingly. "I thought you were interested in Margaret."

"I'm doing a story about the father and daughter. When I talked with Professor Linney a few days before he died, he said people were hitting him. Do you think he could have been imagining that?"

"A detective phoned earlier and asked the same question." Elbogen shrugged, uncomfortable again. "I'll tell you what I told him: I'm not a psychologist."

I was pleased that, for all his professed lack of interest, Hernandez had followed up on my information. "I understand. Let me ask you another question, Doctor. Can Alzheimer's make a person paranoid?" This time I was careful to keep the question general.

"A third of Alzheimer's patients present with paranoia. So the answer is yes. But it depends on the individual, and on the stage of the illness. Some Alzheimer's patients can also become physically violent if they're agitated, because they think they're protecting themselves."

I thought for a moment. "Are there medications that can make a person paranoid?"

Elbogen gave me a look that was part approval, part reluctance: I was playing Go Fish, I'd made a match, and he had to relinquish a card.

He nodded. "Parkinson's patients lack sufficient dopamine, a neurotransmitter in the brain, so we prescribe medications that *increase* the dopamine."

"For example?"

"Levodopa and Carbidopa are some of the classic medications. There are newer ones, like Mirapex. Most of the medications that increase dopamine can potentially cause psychosis, and one of the symptoms of psychosis is paranoia. By the way, if a schizophrenic receives too much of an antipsychotic, he may present with Parkinsonian features, including tremors."

Linney had suffered from Parkinson's. And possibly from MS, according to Margaret's planner. I wondered if that had been confirmed, but knew better than to ask Elbogen. "So if someone has Alzheimer's and is taking medication for Parkinson's, would that make him more susceptible to paranoia?"

Elbogen nodded. "Quite possibly."

"Was Professor Linney taking medication for Parkinson's?"

Elbogen smiled in answer. "A for effort, Miss Blume."

I'd noticed only a mild form of the tremors typical of Parkinson's in Linney, but no facial rigidity, which is another symptom. So I assumed he'd been taking something. I wished I'd checked his medicine cabinet when I was at the house. I'd have to come up with a reason to go back.

"Dr. Elbogen, did Professor Linney ever tell you he was being abused?"

"I told you I won't discuss a patient with you."

"Okay, but do you *think* he was being abused?"

"If I'd thought so, I would have done something about it, wouldn't I? Is that all?" He sounded indignant, and defensive.

Which made me wonder. "One more question? According to Margaret Linney's planner, she met with you two days before she disappeared. Can you tell me what that was about?"

Elbogen flinched as though I'd thrown freezing water at him. Obviously, I'd touched a nerve. But which one?

"Was it about herself or her father?" I pressed when he didn't answer.

"Have a nice day, Miss Blume. Please pay the receptionist on your way out. A personal check will be fine."

"The police will be looking at the planner," I said. "They'll be asking the same questions."

"You can't leave things alone, can you?" His puffed reddened cheeks looked like ripe tomatoes. "You don't care how many lives you ruin. It's all about the story."

I like to think I'm ethical, and I'd never deliberately hurt anyone, but in my profession I often trespass on people's privacy. So I'll admit his comment stung, especially in light of Linney's death.

It would have stung more if I hadn't heard the fear that quivered behind the indignation in the doctor's voice.

CHAPTER TWENTY-SIX

IT WAS AFTER FIVE BY THE TIME I CAME HOME, AND THE ominous charcoal sky promised more rain. My landlord, Isaac, was out of his apartment before I shut my car door. He must have heard me pull into the driveway.

He looked like Big Bird. He'd tightened the hood of his bright yellow slicker around his face, hiding his forehead and throwing his beaklike nose into prominence.

"Your mail was getting wet, so I took it inside," he informed me as I climbed the steps to the porch.

I was tired and hungry. Though I like Isaac, he can be chatty, so I hoped he'd hand me my mail. But he invited me in and I couldn't say no. The price of postage has gone up, I thought, and was immediately ashamed of myself.

I'd been in Isaac's apartment, and it's always something of a jolt seeing the hodgepodge of sofas, chairs, bureaus, and other pieces he's accumulated from marriages to three women with tastes ranging from Danish Modern to French Provincial to lacquered Chinese. It's like walking into one of those discount stores on Western Avenue so crowded with furniture and accessories that you can't really notice anything, and you're afraid you'll either bump into something and bruise your shin or break something ugly and have to pay for it.

I followed Isaac through the living and dining rooms into the kitchen, where he'd put my mail. I wanted to go home, peel off my boots, and curl up on my sofa with a cup of hot chocolate while I skimmed Margaret's planner. But Isaac offered me coffee, and I hesitated only a second or two before I said fine. He seemed lonely, probably because he hadn't been able to sit on the porch, watching people the way he does every day. Maybe he was always lonely, and I'd never really noticed. Maybe I was more attuned because of Linney and the old man in Elbogen's office.

So we sat at his yellow Formica breakfast room table, where he was working on a decoupage of a rose. We had fresh brewed coffee and polished off half a loaf of Entenmann's pound cake (Isaac always stocks up on kosher nosh for me), and I admired recent photos of his Chicago grandchildren and listened while he told me about the cute things they'd said when he last talked to them and how he was thinking of maybe going to see them for Chanukah next month if he could get a cheap ticket on Priceline.

Back in my apartment I checked my phone messages: Zack, canceling our date tonight because of last-minute shul business. He was sorry and would phone me later. My mom, reminding me that I'd offered to take Bubbie G for a haircut on Thursday. Linda Cobern, asking me to call. Who was Linda Cobern? I wondered, and then I remembered: the witchy woman who worked for Councilman Harrington. Served me right for giving her my card.

It was six-thirty. I pride myself on returning calls promptly, and Linda Cobern might still be at the office, but I wasn't in the mood to be harangued about my *Times* piece. Even the thought made me grumpy, or maybe it was the relentless rain that was fogging my windows and chilling the apartment, and Elbogen's parting jab, and the fact that I'd be spending the evening alone.

I understood about tonight. I really did. I admired Zack's sensitivity and dedication to his congregants. But I couldn't help wondering whether this was an example of what life would be like if I married a rabbi, and whether I was suited to be a rabbi's wife.

Or even a rabbi's girlfriend. At mah jongg I'd joked about being sexually frustrated, but though my clothes may skirt Orthodox standards, the prohibition against extramarital sex is one rule I'm not about to break. Even when I'd come dangerously close, telling myself that sanctifying intimacy was quaint but irrelevant, something had always kept me back. God, from whom I couldn't seem to run away; my conscience; the values my parents had instilled in me; an image of Zeidie Irving watching me from Heaven, his kind face filled with disappointment. So Ron had been my first lover, and so far, my last, and I wasn't sorry.

But Orthodoxy prohibits *any* physical contact between men and women outside of marriage. While I have bent that rule, and so had Zack (maybe he'd done more than bend it; he'd never said, and I'd never asked), he definitely wouldn't break it now. I respected that, too, but I missed being touched, being kissed.

Which is one of the reasons, I reminded myself, that strictly observant men and women have short courtships—like my brother Judah and sister-in-law Gitty, whose first embrace was in a private room after the wedding ceremony.

And I was the one who'd asked for more time, as if another month or three or eight would give me a certainty I knew didn't exist. Sometimes you have to take a leap of faith.

I phoned my mom, thanked her for reminding me about Bubbie G, and listened to her vent about a woman who had berated her last night at parent-teacher conferences for giving her daughter a "demoralizing" A-minus on an essay that would probably "scar her for life."

You could laugh or cry, we both agreed.

Then I phoned Bubbie G and confirmed that I'd pick her up on Thursday at eleven.

"You sound not yourself, *sheyfele*," she said. "Everything is all right?"

The endearment (it's Yiddish for *little sheep*) and the concern in her gentle, accented voice were an instant balm. If I closed my eyes, I could practically feel her satin-soft hand stroking my cheek.

"I'm fine, Bubbie. Just a little tired."

"Have a *gleyzele* hot tea, and then a bath," she advised. As far as Bubbie is concerned, a glass of hot tea and a bath solve most problems. "You're writing about the man who died in the fire, yes? And his daughter? This is making you sad, no?"

"Very sad. And I'm having a hard time learning what really happened."

"*Der emess iz a kricher*, Molly."

Truth is a slowpoke.

I'd have to remember that.

Over a spartan dinner of broiled trout and a salad—compensation for the pound cake—I read Margaret's planner. I learned that she'd practiced piano three hours a day, that she'd played doubles tennis Tuesdays and Thursdays, that she had a standing monthly hairdresser appointment. I learned—no surprise here— that in the past months she'd spent most of her time meeting with Jeremy Dorn and the contractor and the decorator who had been helping her with the Muirfield house. On May twenty-eighth she'd written *Talk to Linz*. The tile setter.

She'd also been busy with her father. In January she'd taken Linney to a lab for X rays. In February she'd taken him to Elbogen, and again in March, after he'd had a second set of X rays. In mid-May she and Linney had met with an attorney to transfer ownership of the Fuller house to her. X rays, again. Later that month, three weeks before she'd disappeared, there had been a flurry of activity.

"Dad's party," she'd written. A birthday? His retirement as chair of his USC department? Margaret had made all the arrangements: table, chairs, and linen rentals; florist; caterer.

He must have been more alert six months ago, I thought. I couldn't begin to imagine his bitterness and his fear, the knowledge that every day might bring with it more confusion, another fact or face or memory lost forever, a silent, treacherous slipping away from the world he knew into a dark, lonely place.

The page for June thirteenth and fourteenth was missing. I checked to see if Hank had stapled the pages out of order, then remembered: Margaret had torn that page out.

I scanned the planner again. Three sets of X rays in four months. I thought about that as I reread the last few pages and pondered the cryptic entries, brooded about Linz. Why had Margaret written *Tiler* if she'd fired the man two weeks earlier? And why, come to think of it, hadn't she written his name, the way she had in the May entry? Maybe she was referring to a different tile setter.

Something else niggled at me. I was in the tub with my eyes closed, inhaling the sweet jasmine of my bath oil and hoping the warm, soothing water would jiggle free from my unconscious the little puzzle piece that was eluding me, when my ex-husband Ron phoned. I saw his number on my portable phone's caller ID. A moment later I heard his voice on the answering machine.

"Something I have to tell you, babe. It's important."

CHAPTER TWENTY-SEVEN

Wednesday, November 12. 10:30 A.M. 6000 block of Cadillac Avenue. A man became angry with a woman at a hospital while waiting for service and threw a cup of urine at her, striking the victim in the chest. (Wilshire)

I MUST HAVE DRIVEN BY GOLDEN VISTA A THOUSAND times before, but I'd never noticed it, which is probably what the owners intended. It was a pineapple yellow, two-story stucco structure near the corner of Orange and Fairfax, a block north of Wilshire and in the heart of Miracle Mile, which was originally named for eighteen acres of empty land along the stretch of Wilshire between La Brea and Fairfax that A. W. Ross developed in the 1920s and turned into a prestigious business and shopping district. The "miracle" of Wilshire was later extended to Beverly Hills, where you'll find Neiman's and Saks Fifth Avenue and Rodeo Drive. Until I learned otherwise, I thought it was named for the medical offices that filled most of the tall buildings along Wilshire and have been moved to the twin Third Street medical towers connected to Cedars-Sinai Hospital or to buildings on Rexford and Bedford in the heart of Beverly Hills. But that's a different kind of miracle.

Golden Vista was across the street from a 99¢ Only Store and kitty-corner to the historic 1939 Streamline Moderne May Company building with its distinctive four-story gold mosaic quarter cylinder at one corner. (The building now belongs to the Los Angeles County Museum of Art.) It's also a block away from Johnie's Coffee Shop Restaurant (run-down and defunct but available for film locations) and the Petersen Automotive Museum that organizations use to host events and where Edie's friend's son just had his bar mitzvah reception. A great neighborhood for bargains, cheap nosh, art, and nostalgia, depending on your fancy.

The facility was half a mile from my apartment on Blackburn and would have made for a brisk walk if I were so inclined and if the skies weren't dumping sheets of water. After finding a parking spot, I hurried down the block and entered through glass doors into a lobby filled with sofas, a table, a tall potted plant, and a Rockettes-like chorus line of wheelchaired residents, most of them elderly women. They returned my smile with glum stares, probably dejected by the downpour that was keeping them indoors.

Norm had been right about the wallpaper, a pebbled gray with a gray, yellow, and blue paisley ceiling border that spiffed up the carpeted lobby and linoleum-covered corridors. Through partially open doors I caught glimpses of a coordinating paper and matching bedspreads in the residents' rooms as Walter Ochs, his arm on my elbow, whisked me to his office. Along with the vinyl-and-paste smell of new wallpaper, I was accosted by the acrid odor of urine and something else that made my nose twitch and that I was content not to identify.

I caught glimpses of the residents, too. Many were lying on their beds, staring at those pretty paisley borders or a TV screen; some with their bare legs uncovered; some flashing a hint of blue diaper. One woman was moaning. A man was yelling for an attendant. Two female nurses were chatting ten feet away, but neither rushed to the man's side until a red-faced Ochs prompted them.

"We're short staffed today, so it's been hectic," Ochs said when he was seated behind a utilitarian wood-tone desk. He smoothed what was left of his graying hair against the sides of his head. "If you weren't Norman's sister-in-law, I'd ask you to come back another time." He was smiling, but clearly annoyed.

Norm had advised me to stop by unannounced—"If you want to see what a place is *really* like, Molly." I wasn't scouting for a facility, but I'd been curious.

"I really appreciate your seeing me," I said.

"You didn't say exactly what you needed to know. Something about a resident?"

"Professor Oscar Linney."

"The old man who died in that fire." Ochs sighed. "Terrible thing, terrible. I read about it in the paper, and I recognized the name. But he wasn't a resident."

"No, but I understand that his daughter came to see you in June of this year."

"That's right." Ochs sounded wary, probably wondering where I was headed.

"Was she planning to have him admitted?"

Ochs hesitated. "I'm not sure I should be discussing this, Miss Blume."

"Call me Molly." I smiled. "As you said, he wasn't a resident, so you wouldn't be violating his privacy."

Ochs straightened one of the photos on his desk. "What's your interest in Professor Linney?"

"I'm writing about what happened to him, and I'd like to get as much background as possible. I know he had Parkinson's and Alzheimer's. I don't know much else. I'm trying to fill in the blanks, and I'm hoping you'll help me."

He took a few seconds before answering. "I guess there's no harm. Yes, the daughter talked about having him admitted. We have a dementia unit, so that fit his needs."

"Did she say why? I'm curious, because her husband said she was against placing her father in a facility. So I'm wondering what happened to change her mind." And why she didn't tell her husband about it.

"Miss Blume—"

"Molly." I smiled again.

"Molly." This time he smiled back. "Most children resist placing a parent in a facility. They feel guilty. They want to take care of the parent themselves, to do the right thing. But at some point—and it's different for everyone—many children come to realize that doing the right thing isn't always achieved by keeping the parent at home. Dealing with an ailing parent can wreak havoc on the rest of the family, and it isn't always medically sound. So they search for a place that will provide their parent with the highest standard of care in a secure environment. That's what we pride ourselves on at Golden Vista."

It was his spiel, and he'd delivered it with sincerity. It would have been more effective if I hadn't smelled the urine and witnessed the indifference of two of his staff. But that wasn't why I was here.

"I'm still not clear why she changed her mind so suddenly. Did something happen?" Something that would explain the two exclamation points next to the entry—unless, of course, Margaret was fond of exclamation points, the way some people draw little hearts instead of dots over their lowercase *i*s.

"I don't think it was anything dramatic. She told me Professor Linney was deteriorating, physically and mentally. He was becoming increasingly combative with the caregiver and everyone in the house."

"With her husband?"

Ochs shrugged. "She didn't say. A major factor was Professor Linney's refusal to move to the new house she and her husband were building. Basically, she realized she could no longer keep him with her."

I didn't believe it. Something had happened. Another altercation between Linney and Hank? Had Margaret tired of playing referee and peacemaker? Had she chosen her husband over her father? Reston hadn't mentioned quarreling with his father-in-law the day before his wife disappeared, but why would he? And I had only his word for his wife's romantic mood before he left for his business trip.

"I'll tell you one thing," Ochs said. "This was a tough decision for her. She was extremely agitated, had a hard time holding herself back from crying."

"Do you know if she'd decided to place him here?"

"Oh, sure." Ochs nodded. "She filled out all the admission papers. To be honest, I was kind of surprised."

"What do you mean?"

"Most people ask a thousand questions. They want to know everything: schedules, menus, activities, staff, therapy, visiting hours, home visits. I showed her around, she liked what she saw, asked me a few things, and that was it." Ochs shrugged. "She was desperate. She wanted us to take him that day. I told her we didn't have a bed, and she got this look in her eyes, like she was going to lose it."

Why the urgency? I wondered.

"People are like that," Ochs said, as if reading my mind. "Once they make up their minds, they want to get it over with. I phoned her later that day to tell her we'd have a bed on Monday. She wasn't home, so I left a message. I never heard back from her. Then I read that she'd gone missing and was probably dead. And now the father is dead, too. It makes you stop and think, doesn't it?"

CHAPTER TWENTY-EIGHT

ANGELINO HEIGHTS IS A TWENTY-MINUTE DRIVE FROM my apartment if there's no traffic. At four-thirty this evening it was more like fifty minutes because of a rush-hour snarl compounded by the on-and-off rain that made the streets slippery and drivers brake-happy and prone to blaring their horns, which pissed off more drivers and incurred more blaring of horns. At one point I realized I was one of the blarers. Reflex, I guess, or the call of the wild.

Bounded by Sunset Boulevard on the north, the Hollywood Freeway on the south, Boylston Street on the east, and Echo Park Lake on the west, Angelino Heights is one of the oldest neighborhoods in Los Angeles and has been called its first suburb. It's an ethnic mix—primarily Asian, white, and Latino—and an economic one, too: It's not unusual to find new immigrants living next door to a wealthy businessman. The neighborhood is also well located. It's five minutes from downtown, practically in spitting range of the nexus of three overlapping freeways, and within walking distance of Elysian Park and Dodger Stadium.

I learned all that in my HARP research. I also learned that Angelino Heights was one of the first areas to be designated a HARP. Even in the fading gray light I could see why. It's charming and old-world, and the city and the area residents would naturally want to preserve the homes—Mission Revival, Craftsman-California Bungalow, and, most significantly, the Queen Annes and Victorians.

Ned Vaughan lived on "the hill," as residents refer to the neighborhood, on the 1300 block of Carroll Avenue in a gray two-story wedding-cake Victorian with turrets and gables, a white wraparound porch, and frostinglike medallions and other intricate architectural details.

He stood in the doorway in gray tweed slacks and a black cashmere sweater, looking more casual than he had at the HARP meeting. He looked taller, too, now that I was wearing flat boots instead of those high-heeled ones that looked divine but had blistered my toes.

"Molly Blume, huh?" He looked at my card, then up at me, a hint of patronizing amusement in his blue eyes. "I wondered about your name when you phoned me this morning. I'll bet you get teased."

"All the time." I smiled and gritted my teeth. At this rate I'd need them capped before long. Though if Vaughan didn't invite me in soon, I'd probably freeze to death first. The wind, wet and blustery, made me shiver right on cue. "Thanks for agreeing to talk to me," I prompted.

"Hank said you're helping him." Vaughan opened the door wide and stepped aside to let me enter, but he sounded only a little less reluctant than when I'd reached him at his USC office, and his "Come on in" had forced enthusiasm, as if he suspected I carried the Ebola virus.

In the entry he set my umbrella in a brass stand, divested me of my raincoat, which he folded in half so that it wouldn't drip on the heavily veined black marble floor, and invited me to wipe my shoes on an old mat.

"I don't mean to be a fusspot, but I just found this lovely antique and I'd hate to get it dirty," he said, indicating a fringed round burgundy area rug.

I wiped my shoes well. Twice. Reassured, he disappeared somewhere with my raincoat—probably the laundry room or bathroom. The house was toasty, and by the time he returned I had warmed up.

Vaughan warmed up, too, after I told him how much I admired the exterior of his home.

"You should have seen it when I bought the place. It was covered with asphalt shingles." He grimaced. "Taking them down was a bitch, and then we had to putty thousands of nail holes and sand the walls before we could paint. Four coats," he added.

"But it was obviously worth it," I said, laying on a thick coat myself.

"Absolutely. I was lucky to buy this beauty a year ago, just before housing prices skyrocketed. By the way, this block is listed in the National Register of Historic Places," he told me, and beamed when I made the appropriate admiring response.

He took me on a tour of the living and dining rooms and three bedrooms ("Victorian houses typically have small rooms," he explained), pointing out the hardwood flooring that had been hidden by "nasty" carpeting, ceiling and base moldings that had been stripped of generations of paint and refinished, light fixtures that had been repaired, hardware restored and polished to a burnished luster.

"Everything you see is architecturally authentic," he told me with a lover's pride, caressing a large brass doorknob as if it were a woman's breast.

He led me to the rear window of the unfurnished bedroom where we were standing and pulled aside the drape. "In the daylight you can look out across Elysian Park to the San Gabriel Mountains. It's quite a view."

From my bedroom window I can see the neighbor's bathroom, about six feet away. Sometimes I can hear him, too, and the program is more *South Park* than PBS. So I was duly impressed and envious and said so.

The tour over, Vaughan walked me back to the living room, where he turned on Tiffany lamps on both ends of a dark green brocade sofa with a wood frame, ornate carved legs, and a seamless bench seat that looked punishing but was actually comfortable. The light from the lamps cast a subdued jewel-toned glow on the ecru moiré papered walls and on a parquet floor Vaughan had stripped and restained.

He sniffed the air. "You can still smell the protective finish. I hope it doesn't bother you."

I had the feeling that to Vaughan, the scent was as heady as an expensive perfume. "You've done a wonderful job with the house."

"It's coming along." He looked pleased. "I haven't touched the kitchen or either bathroom. Restoring is much more expensive than remodeling. More time-consuming, too. But it's worth it, and I'm in no rush."

"Professor Linney loved his home, too," I said, grabbing the opening. "I understand that you were in his department at USC."

"Oscar was my mentor. More than that, he was a good friend." Vaughan's eyes filled with tears, which he blinked away. He clamped his lips together, fighting for control. "I still can't believe he's dead. Did you meet him?"

"Once, a week ago."

"Then you didn't know him. He was a brilliant architectural historian before the Alzheimer's took its toll. It was frustrating and terrifying for him. He was aware he was deteriorating. Seeing it broke my heart."

I tried to imagine being in Linney's situation and felt fresh pity for the old man. "Did his personality change? I know that can happen with Alzheimer's."

"Are you asking if he was crabby *before*? Yes, he was. Sometimes I thought he was proud of it." A smile softened the architect's angular face. "The disease made him worse, but he was always demanding of himself and others. He didn't brook mediocrity or ignorance."

"How did he feel about his son-in-law?" I asked, jumping right in.

Vaughan frowned and opened his mouth to say something. Then he laughed. "Hank warned me that you're direct. He made his first million when he was twenty-four, by the way, so I wouldn't sell him short. But no, he and Oscar weren't a match made in heaven."

"I understand you and Hank have been close for years."

"Since high school. I helped him with his papers. He kept the bullies from picking on me." Vaughan smiled.

"I'm surprised he didn't hire you to design the Muirfield house."

"Between USC and my consulting job, I'm way too busy. And mixing business with friendship is never a good idea."

"So they say. By the way, who took over as department chair after Professor Linney became ill?"

"Robert Langhorn is acting chair. I don't envy him. Being chair is no picnic. Endless politics." Vaughan crossed one leg over the other. "Hank says you're helping him find out what happened to Margaret. No offense, but do you really think you can do more than the police?"

I didn't blame him for being skeptical. I was, too. "I doubt it. But sometimes a fresh pair of eyes is helpful. When did you last see Margaret?"

"I spoke to her that Wednesday. She called to confirm that I would keep Oscar company while she and Hank went to a dinner. I saw her about a week before that. Hank was out of town, and I had dinner at the house with her and Oscar."

"Just like old times," I said.

He threw me a sharp, reproving look. "Margaret and I were friends, nothing more. Sure, Oscar was dying for us to be together. I'm a great guy." Vaughan smiled. "But we didn't click. And I wouldn't have wanted to be Oscar's son-in-law. I loved the man, but dealing with him at USC was enough. I didn't need him controlling my life. Don't get me wrong," he added quickly. "I owe Oscar everything. He groomed me. He got me on the tenure track. His recommendation got me a consulting job with a large firm."

"Anderson, Finch, and Mulganey. Your firm did the Hancock Park historical survey, right?"

"Right." Vaughan's eyes showed surprise.

"I covered the HARP meeting last week for the *Times*," I told him. "Someone pointed you out."

"I thought you looked familiar." He studied me as though he were seeing me for the first time. "A lot of angry people at that meeting, on *both* sides of the issue."

"Like Roger Modine. You and he were going at it."

Vaughan seemed taken aback. Then he laughed again—a little nervously, I thought. "You *are* observant. Modine is a sore loser. He didn't like the results of the survey." He shrugged. "We didn't invent the statistics. And we don't benefit one way or the other."

"Aside from the fee. How much did the city pay your firm? Two hundred fifty thousand, wasn't it?" I'd checked the details for last week's story.

"Something like that. There's a great deal of research involved, Molly, and if you calculate the cost per hour, it's not high at all." He managed to sound patronizing and defensive at the same time. "I didn't set the fee. I certainly didn't see much of it."

"I was just curious." I'd succeeded in annoying him, which didn't bode well for eliciting information. "What's your view about HARP?"

He tugged on an exposed inch of patterned maroon sock. "Obviously, I'm all for preserving the beauty of L.A. Take this area, for example. The homes in the 1300 and 1400 blocks of Carroll Avenue represent the highest concentration and best collection of Queen Annes and Victorians in the city. And it has a rich history." The architect was in his element now, relaxed, expansive. "Mary Pickford and Gloria Swanson had homes here, and they filmed the Keystone Kops chase scenes on these streets. But if developers had their way, they'd tear down some of the older structures and build high-rise apartment buildings."

"Professor Linney was for HARP, too, correct?"

Vaughan nodded. "Preservation was his passion. He talked about writing a book on the subject, before the Alzheimer's. He even wrote down some notes and came up with a title, but that's as far as he got. It's a shame."

"Why don't you write it?"

"Oscar was pushing me to do just that. About a month before he died, I said okay." Vaughan sighed. "A few weeks before that I'd surprised him with photos I'd taken of structures in the different HARP areas. I thought he'd be pleased, but he barked at me. 'What the hell do I need these for?'" Vaughan had imitated Linney's high, whiny voice well. "Seeing them probably made him realize he'd never write the book."

He was silent, no doubt thinking about Linney, and my thoughts went to Bubbie G. She's been stoic about not being able to drive her car anymore, but I know she misses reading and doing the needlepoint that used to keep her company most evenings, and my heart aches for her when she can't make out the faces of her family and friends. So I understand better than I did before why, in our daily prayers for the sick, we ask God to grant them "a healing of the soul and a healing of the body."

Vaughan stood abruptly. "Excuse me a minute."

He left the room and returned with a pack of cigarettes and a cut crystal ashtray that he set on the mahogany coffee table. "I stopped smoking three weeks ago," he said, sitting down, "but Oscar's death kind of ended that. Do you mind?"

I shrugged. I hate cigarettes—what they do and how they smell. But this was his house, his lungs. His teeth, too, although unlike Modine's, they weren't discolored, and his breath didn't reek. I was surprised that he wasn't concerned about the effects of the smoke on the expensive upholstery and drapes and rugs he'd chosen with such care. I also wondered if lacquer is easily combustible.

Vaughan lit up and dropped the match into the ashtray. He took a luxurious puff and exhaled slowly, sending a mini-tornado-like plume into the air inches from my face.

"I imagine that Professor Linney and Hank didn't agree about HARP," I said, moving my head back and resisting the urge to fan away the smoke.

Vaughan smiled. "Among other things."

"That must have been rough on Margaret, playing referee."

"It made life hell for her. Sometimes I think I should never have—" He stopped. "It was hard on everyone."

"You should never have what? Introduced Hank to her?"

"Maybe." He took another, longer puff. "Because things turned out so tragically. You know what I mean."

I didn't know, and I didn't think that's what he'd meant. "But not because Hank and Margaret met," I said, a question in my voice. "He's not responsible for her death, or Professor Linney's."

Vaughan stared at me. "Of course not."

"Do you think she ran away and faked the kidnapping?"

He attacked the cigarette again. "The idea crossed my mind," he finally said. "Because sometimes it was awful in that house. You could feel the tension. She loved Oscar. She loved Hank. What was she supposed to do? But not to leave a note?" He took another puff. "Hank told me she phoned Oscar on Thursday, so I guess she did. Run away, I mean. But where the hell is she now?" he demanded with a flash of anger. "Where has she been all this time? How could she put her father and husband through this?" Leaning forward, he mashed the butt against the hapless ashtray.

"Some people I've talked to said Hank was possessive."

"He was crazy in love with her. He'd waited a long time to find someone like her."

"He made her give up her career."

"Who told you that?" Vaughan scowled. "That was Margaret's idea. She didn't want to travel all over the country. She wanted to be with Hank. They were newlyweds, for God's sake. And after they moved in with Oscar, they didn't have much privacy."

"So he *wasn't* possessive?"

Vaughan reached for another cigarette, tapped it on the table. "I thought you're trying to find out what happened to Margaret. Why the third degree about Hank?"

"Maybe she ran away because he was possessive. Maybe she was afraid of him."

"That's ridiculous! Hank would never hurt her! And he'd kill anyone who did." Vaughan was glaring at me now.

"I'm trying to understand her motivation, Ned."

He lit the cigarette and puffed. That seemed to calm him. "Okay, Hank can be possessive," he allowed. "Margaret was his whole world, and he wanted her to feel the same way about him. The thing is, aside from me and one or two others, he doesn't have many friends. Margaret—well, she knows everybody."

"What about her male friends? Was Hank jealous of them?"

"So we're back to Hank?" he asked in a warning tone.

"Again, motivation. If Margaret *thought* he was jealous . . ." I let him fill in the rest.

Vaughan sighed. "He didn't like the way men looked at her or talked to her. Margaret is outgoing, friendly. She played hostess at all of Oscar's parties. Hank had a hard time sharing her. But he trusted her one hundred percent. One hundred percent," he repeated.

The architect was protesting a bit too much, it seemed to me. Protecting his best friend? "Was Margaret a flirt?"

He frowned. "I wouldn't say a *flirt*. She liked men and was comfortable with them. I don't think she realized the effect she had on them."

"Men like who?" Jeremy Dorn, I thought.

He hesitated. "If I tell you, you'll tell Hank."

"Not necessarily. I'm not in his employ."

"I thought you're doing this for him."

"I'm doing this because I write about true crimes, and because I met Professor Linney, and I want to know what happened to Margaret. Men like who?" I repeated.

"Roger Modine."

That was a surprise. "Margaret liked him?" I couldn't picture the concert pianist with the crude, oxlike Modine. Bubbie G would have called him a *bulvan*.

"Not particularly. Hank may not have a college degree, but he's a gentleman. Modine is vulgar and he's a brute. Hank doesn't like him much, but they're partners in some real estate deals, so Margaret had to make nice. Modine obviously thought there was more to it."

"How do you know?"

Vaughan hesitated again. "She told me. Oscar threw a party a few weeks before she disappeared. Modine was doing work at the Fuller house and saw the preparations. He got Hank to invite him." The architect crinkled his nose as if he'd sniffed something offensive. "Modine had a few drinks too many and cornered Margaret when Hank wasn't around, said some pretty suggestive things."

I raised a brow. "To his partner's wife?"

"I told you, he's a pig." Vaughan grunted. "He'd sell his mother for the right price."

I wasn't surprised by Vaughan's assessment. My encounter with Modine had left me unimpressed. "So what did Margaret do?"

"That's the thing. There were people nearby, and she didn't want to make a scene. So she laughed it off."

And maybe Modine thought she liked the attention. "She didn't tell Hank later?"

Vaughan shook his head. "Bad timing. Hank and Modine were having problems with some of their properties."

I sensed from his tone that there was something else, and that he was deciding whether or not to tell me. "And?"

He studied the fiery tip of his cigarette. "He'd told Margaret a few times that she was too friendly, that guys could get the wrong idea. She told him he was being silly."

Now I was confused. "Too friendly with Modine?"

"Too friendly with *everyone*. But you can see why she didn't tell him about Modine. And she was afraid Hank would over-react if she did."

I decided to think about that later. "What about Jeremy Dorn?"

"What about him?"

I could tell Vaughan was being coy. "Did Hank think Margaret was too friendly with him?"

"If he did, he didn't tell me about it."

I wasn't sure if I believed him. "You mentioned that Hank

and Modine were having problems with some properties. What kind of problems?"

"You know, I think you'd better ask Hank." He flicked cigarette ash into the ashtray. "I really don't see how any of this will help you find out what happened to Margaret." He sounded unhappy and nervous.

"It may not," I agreed. "So what do *you* think happened, Ned?"

He frowned. "If you'd asked me yesterday, before the tape with Margaret's phone call, I would've said someone killed her. Maybe for the jewelry, maybe it was about something else."

"Like what?"

Vaughan shrugged.

"Maybe someone did it to shut her up," I said, speculating aloud. "Like Modine."

Vaughan had turned pale. He licked his lips. "Listen, you can't tell Hank what I told you about Modine. Modine will know it came from me, and I don't need him breaking down my door." His fingers shook.

"Didn't you tell all this to the police?"

"There's nothing to tell. Hank thought it was a kidnapper. I thought so, too, because of the jewelry. That's what I told the police. Just because Modine came on to Margaret doesn't mean he killed her. Why would he do that?"

Vaughan put out his cigarette and stood, sending a mist of ash onto his newly finished floors. Interview over.

I considered his question while he retrieved my raincoat. Suppose Modine had dropped by the Fuller house that night. Suppose he'd taken advantage of the fact that Hank wasn't home and made a move on Margaret.

Suppose Margaret had threatened to tell Hank.

Her husband.

His partner.

CHAPTER TWENTY-NINE

ZACK BROUGHT ME CALLA LILIES. "TO MAKE UP FOR LAST night," he said as I arranged the flowers in a vase and set them on my breakfast room table.

"Did you resolve the shul crisis?" I asked.

"It wasn't a crisis. How's your investigation going?"

Obviously, he was changing the subject. He sounded uncomfortable and I wondered why but didn't press. On the way to the restaurant he asked me about Linney, and I started filling him in on what I'd learned. I told him the rest over steamy butternut squash soup, a perfect antidote for the chilly air that blew in every time someone opened the main door and made me shiver in my just-above-the-knees Burberry skirt and long-sleeved, V-necked camel cashmere sweater.

On a modesty scale I was about a seven and a half (points for the sleeves; deductions for the neck and hemlines; the sweater's snug fit; my hair, which I'd left curly and mussed into what I hoped was sexy disarray; and general attitude). It was a compromise, prompted by the weather and my reflection before falling asleep last night that maybe Edie was right and I was making a mountain out of inches. The *maybe* is my stubbornness asserting itself. In any case, Zack hadn't seemed to notice.

"First, we have to establish whether Margaret Linney is alive or dead," he said now.

I love the *we*. I love the way he creases his forehead when he's serious, the way his gray-blue eyes darken, the way he listens intently to what I have to say.

"I think she's dead," I said. "From what everyone told me, she would never have abandoned her father."

Zack nodded. "Under normal circumstances. But the Golden Vista guy said she was desperate."

I'd traveled this mental path. "Because she was terrified someone would kill her."

"Right."

"Her husband."

"That's the only thing that would make sense, Molly. Because if she was afraid of someone else, she'd go to the police and tell her husband," Zack said, lapsing into the musical cadence of Talmudic disputation that I'd heard so often from my dad and brothers. "But she didn't do either. And if she's afraid of her *husband* . . ." He raised his palms. "Unfortunately, the police have a hard time protecting a woman from an abusive spouse or partner. They usually advise her to leave."

"No one I've talked to has suggested that Hank abused Maggie." I spread olive tapenade on a thick slice of warm, crusty bread.

"Maybe she didn't tell anyone. He's controlling, possessive, jealous, right? And there's reason to suspect he abused his father-in-law."

"Linney could have imagined that. He was probably paranoid from one of his meds. I have to check on that." I handed him the bread. Our fingers touched.

"Just because someone's paranoid—"

"Doesn't mean no one's after him," I finished.

Zack studied me. "But you don't buy it."

I slathered another slice and took a bite, savoring the meaty, salty taste of olives, capers, and peppers. "If Hank was abusing Linney," I said when I'd finished chewing, "all the more reason for Maggie not to skip. She would've worried that he'd take out his anger on her dad."

"Unless she feared for her life."

I pondered that. "Maybe."

"Okay, suppose he *wasn't* abusing Linney," Zack said reluctantly. "He's making Maggie's life miserable. He's cut her off from her friends. He's encouraged her to end her career. She wants out of the marriage, but she knows he'll never let her go, and if she leaves, he'll try to find her. So she fakes her kidnapping."

I'd come this far in my thinking, too. "And she leaves her father?" I said, not bothering to hide my skepticism.

"She'd planned to place him in a facility before she left. She was waiting for the right time. But something happened, and she had to move quickly."

"Like what?"

"Maybe Reston found out she was having an affair."

"We don't know that." I took another bite of the bread.

"Either that, or he accused her of it. In either case, she's afraid. That's why she was anxious for Golden Vista to take Linney right away. When they couldn't, she had no choice. Father or no father, she had to disappear."

"And she comes *back*?"

"She's feeling guilty. Her father has a debilitating disease—two, actually. Three, if he has MS. She doesn't want to wait until he's so far gone that he can't communicate or recognize her."

The waitress brought our orders—grilled halibut for Zack, Chilean sea bass for me. We ate for a while without speaking. I was aware of the clink of flatware against china and the conversation and laughter from the other diners. I doubted that any of them were talking about abuse and murder.

"So what do you think?" Zack asked.

"Great sea bass."

He smiled patiently. "I mean about my theory."

I speared a chunk of fish. "It works, until we get to the fire. Why hasn't Maggie come forward?"

"She's still afraid of Reston. Her father's dead, and her coming forward won't change that."

"So who killed him? And why now?"

"How do we know he was killed, Molly? It could have been an accidental consequence of the vandalism."

I rolled my eyes. "I *told* you. Linney was afraid of climbing stairs, but that's where he was. Upstairs."

"So he climbed carefully. He stayed after she left and decided to rest. Upstairs, in his old room."

I didn't answer.

"Why not?" Zack sounded annoyed, which is unusual for him. "It works."

"I don't buy the tape." I put down my fork. "What kind of daughter asks her feeble-bodied, feebleminded father to meet her at their old house when she knows damn well he has no way of getting there on his own?" The woman at the table next to us was staring at me. I leaned toward Zack and lowered my voice. "And how the hell was he supposed to get back to Muirfield? Especially when it was night."

Zack frowned. He chewed a few forkfuls of halibut, his jaw working the food hard. I ate my sea bass.

"So she's dead," he finally said.

"Even if she's alive, she didn't make that call, Zack. Whoever did used it to lure Linney to the house."

"I kind of figured that out," Zack said dryly. "So why the rush to place him in Golden Vista if she wasn't going to run away?"

"Maybe she *was,* but Hank found out. Ochs, the Golden Vista owner, left a phone message, telling her he had a bed for Linney. What if Hank checked the messages and figured out what Maggie was planning?" The thought had struck me after I'd left the facility.

"So you *do* think he killed her," Zack said. "Because she was having an affair?"

"Not necessarily."

He sighed. "Are we playing twenty questions?"

"There's this Robert Browning poem I studied in high school," I said. "'My Last Duchess.' Do you know it?"

He shook his head. "I wasn't the most motivated student."

"Except when it came to studying girls." I could smile about it now. "Anyway, it's a dramatic monologue narrated by a wealthy duke who's showing someone a portrait of his late duchess. From what the duke says, you get a picture of an arrogant, controlling SOB who treats people like objects and likes having them under his control."

"Creepy."

"Very. He was upset because the duchess didn't value him more than she valued everyone else. She smiled at everyone. She had a heart 'too soon made glad.'"

Zack raised a brow. "That's a crime?"

"Apparently to him. He killed her. Well, he doesn't come out and say so, because his visitor is an emissary for some other wealthy guy whose daughter he wants to marry."

"And you think Hank is like the duke."

"Even his best friend admitted that Hank warned Maggie about being too friendly with other guys. But would he *kill* her?" I sighed. "I really *like* Hank. I think he loved Maggie, and he seems genuinely heartbroken. But who knows what he's really like, or what went on in that house? Modine is another story."

"He's the contractor?"

"And Reston's partner." I repeated what I'd learned from Ned Vaughan. "I can see him panicking and killing Maggie if she threatened to tell Hank he'd propositioned her. He's a brute."

"According to Vaughan. Modine may be a nice guy."

"I doubt it. Call it gut feeling." Yes, I was prejudiced. I didn't fault Modine for protecting Reston's house against a trespasser, but had it been necessary to tie me up? I wasn't about to tell the truth to Zack—or to my family, who would all warn me to be careful. Which I am.

"What if Vaughan is trying to shift suspicion to Modine?" Zack said.

I frowned. "Why would he do that?"

"Because he was jealous of Hank and Maggie. After all, he knew her first. He *introduced* him to Maggie."

"He says no. He has a girlfriend."

"Well, *that* should convince a judge."

I had that coming. "And Fennel says no, and he knows everything." But Zack had planted a doubt. "He *was* edgy the entire time I was there. Smoked up a storm. I thought he was uncomfortable talking about his best friend."

"Maybe that's it, then. But what if Fennel is wrong?"

"Suppose Vaughan *was* jealous. Why would he kill Maggie?"

"Because he didn't want Hank to have her."

"And her father?"

Zack shrugged. "I have no clue."

"You're a big help." I picked at my fish and pictured

Vaughan, replayed our conversation. I shook my head. "I don't think he had feelings for Maggie, Zack. He's a dry kind of guy. The only thing he's passionate about, from what I could tell, is doorknobs and parquet floors. He *is* terrified of Modine. He looked like he was going to faint when he thought Modine would find out what he'd told me about the party. He wasn't faking that."

"So Modine's your man, huh?"

"He's leading the pack, for now."

"But if Modine killed her," Zack said a moment later, "why was Maggie anxious to place her father in a facility?"

He had me there. I twirled the base of my water goblet. "Maybe the Golden Vista thing isn't connected to her disappearance. Maybe Linney and Hank had a terrible quarrel and she knew she had to choose between her father and husband. And she chose her husband."

Zack nodded. "That's what Jewish law dictates, you know. We're commanded to honor a parent, but our first obligation— our loyalty—is to our spouse."

"Interesting."

"Michal, King David's wife, helped David escape from her father, King Saul, when Saul came to kill him. She fooled him into thinking David was sick in bed. Rachel and Leah chose their husband, Jacob, over their father, Lavan."

"Not a hard choice," I said. "As I recall, Lavan was manipulative and evil. Anyway, enough about this. It's depressing me. Tell me about your day."

His day had been busy: visiting two congregants in the hospital; leading a Talmud class for beginners, another for veterans; meeting with a future bride and groom; consoling a couple whose in vitro fertilization attempt had failed.

"So what happened last night?" I asked. "Of course, if it's confidential, I understand that you can't tell me."

"Actually, it turned out not to be a big deal." He cleared his throat. "I feel bad about the last-minute change in plans, Molly. It's something else that goes with the rabbi territory."

"I understand."

"Do you? You know, I've been giving a lot of thought to what you said the other night, Molly. I think—"

"Dessert?" the waitress asked, rolling over a cart.

We made our selections, and the waitress left.

"You were saying?" I prompted Zack. He seemed suddenly preoccupied, and I wondered what was bothering him. The thing that had bothered him when he'd picked me up?

"It's not important. It'll keep."

I felt another blast of cold air from the opened door. With it in blew my ex-husband Ron. He's hard to miss in a crowd. Tall, blond, and extremely handsome with chiseled features, like a young Robert Redford.

The nice thing about dining in kosher restaurants in your hometown is that you invariably know some of the people you see. The downside is that you may not always want to see them. Ron spotted us and waved. I watched him cross the room, stopping to chat at almost every table, smiling, laughing. I knew he was headed our way, and I felt the way I do when I'm in the dentist's chair, about to have a cavity filled—wishing I were somewhere else, tensing as I open my mouth for the prick of the needle, though at least the needle delivers Novocain and numbness.

"Hey, man. How're you doing?" he said when he was at our table. He punched Zack's arm playfully, a little too hard.

Zack smiled. "Fine. You?"

"Great. Couldn't be better. I'm meeting someone for dinner." That may sound like a non sequitur, but for Ron, dining or going to a movie alone, both of which I've done often, is a sign of social failure. "You didn't return my call, Molly," he said, with the petulance he thinks I still find boyishly cute.

"Sorry. I've had a busy day." Plus I'd been in no rush to talk to Ron, which is like taking cough medicine—mildly unpleasant on swallowing, with a bitter aftertaste.

"Can I talk to you a second? It's important."

"Now?" I repressed a sigh and looked at Zack. "I'll be right back."

"No problem."

"Don't worry," Ron said. "I won't steal her from you."

The last was a dig. Though he pretends otherwise, Ron has a problem with my dating Zack. It's not that he's pining for me, and I heard he's seeing someone new. Again. I think he's got a bad case of "finders, keepers" and a bruised ego, aggravated by the fact that he and Zack were high school pals, and that he was instrumental (or so he claims) in having Zack hired by the shul board (he's a member), which is basically how Edie came to fix us up. (Long story.) In Ron's head, he and Zack were best friends, and now he mourns that loss, too, and blames Zack and me for it. Mostly me, probably.

I followed him to a spot about ten feet away, next to a table a busboy was clearing.

"What's so important?" I asked.

"No 'hello'? No 'How are you?'"

I ignored his crooked smile, which I'll admit I'd found extremely charming, along with some other qualities. "Hello. How are you. What's up?"

He looked me up and down. "Sweater's a little low-cut and tight, Molly. Not exactly good for Zack's image, and people are already talking. Then again, you could wear a sack and you'd still look hot."

I gritted my teeth. "Ron—"

"Okay. I spotted Zack with another woman last night. Maybe you guys aren't seeing each other exclusively, so it doesn't matter, but if you are . . . I didn't want to be the one to tell you, but I thought you should know."

"Well, 'shul business' is five-seven, has long black hair, is in her mid-twenties, and a real looker. Listen, you know I love Zack like a brother. And he's a rabbi now. But once a player . . . I care about you, Molly. I don't want you getting hurt."

Strange as it may seem, I believed the last part. Ron isn't evil. He just doesn't have the monogamy or commitment gene. "I appreciate your concern, Ron. But I trust Zack." Given my history with men, it's taken me a while to be able to say that.

"And we all trust Saudi Arabia. I hope you're right, Molly. But if you're not, don't say I didn't warn you."

I returned to the table. The waitress had brought our cappuccinos along with you-can't-believe-it's-pareve (nondairy) cheesecake for me and a slice of lemon tart for Zack. I sat down and picked up my fork.

"What did Ron want?" Zack asked.

"Nothing important." I debated, then said, "He saw you on a date last night."

Zack shifted his eyes, avoiding mine. "I guess I should have told you, Molly."

It wasn't the reaction I'd expected. The forkful of cake I'd mouthed tasted like clay. The trust I'd just professed teetered.

"Hochman said he had to talk to me last night, that it couldn't wait," Zack said.

"Hochman?" I was barely listening. I was thinking about the seriousness in Zack's voice before the waitress had interrupted him with the dessert tray. He'd dumped me once before. Had he been about to tell me that we weren't going to work out just as I'd decided that we could? Were the lilies my consolation bouquet?

"The shul board vice president. He asked me to meet him at Rafi's."

So it *had* been business. I allowed myself a measure of relief, then wondered if I was the "business." "What did he want to talk about?"

"Chanukah."

"Chanukah?"

"His daughter Carole was with him when I got to the restaurant. She's starting a singles group at the shul and wants to launch it with a Chanukah bash. Hochman wants me to help. He thinks it'll be good for the shul."

I felt infinitely better and took another bite of the cake. "So the three of you talked. How is that a date?"

"The *two* of us." In the reflected glow of the hurricane lamp candle, Zack's face was a warm pink. "Hochman had to attend another meeting. So it was Carole and me. I couldn't just leave." He sounded uncomfortably earnest, as though he were being audited by an IRS agent.

"No," I agreed. "I take it she's single?"

"Apparently. I had to stay awhile. And I had to drive her home, because she came with her dad. It would've been rude not to."

"Unforgivably rude." Poor Zack, I thought. Ambushed. My trust restored, I was beginning to find this funny. "Did she ask you in for coffee?"

He nodded. "I thanked her and declined. I didn't want her to get the wrong idea."

"So why didn't you tell me?"

"There was nothing to tell. I'm not working on the event with her," he added. "I told Hochman."

"No Spin the Dreidel, huh?" I *tsk*ed. "Is that why you brought me the lilies? A guilt offering?" I teased.

"I brought you lilies because I felt bad about what happened."

"I thought you said nothing happened."

"I mean canceling our date. Are you upset?"

"About the lilies? I *love* lilies. Ron said she's a looker. Is she?"

He leaned back and gazed at me. "You're having fun with this, aren't you?" he said good-naturedly.

I smiled. "Kind of." I'm the one who usually overreacts and ends up apologizing and feels flustered. So I was enjoying the moment.

"Well, tell me when you're done." He slipped his fork into the tart.

I put my fork next to his, stopping him. "So what did you tell Hochman?"

"About what?"

"Come on." I clinked my fork against his.

"You *know* what I told him," Zack said, his voice suddenly low and intimate, as if we were the only two people in the room. "I told him that his daughter is lovely, but that I'm in a serious relationship." He leaned toward me so that his face was just inches from mine. "Molly," he said, so quietly that I had to lean in, too.

My heart thudded. "Yes?"

"You have cheesecake on your lip."

"Oh." Now *my* face was flushed. I ran my tongue across my lips. "Is that it?" Meaning the cheesecake.

"No."

That's when he said he loved me.

He said it again at my front door after we'd sat in his parked car talking for hours, the mist of rain fogging the windows and secluding us from the rest of the world. I told him I loved him, too, sure of my feelings, shy saying the words.

I went to sleep euphoric and woke up the same way. The day was glorious. The rain had stopped, the sun was out. The view of the mountains to the north was so sharp it hurt my eyes. God had washed the world.

I put on a robe and slippers and went outside to breathe in the crisp, cool air and get the *Times,* which the paperboy had tossed onto the driveway. I noticed that my Acura was listing to one side. *Two* flat tires?

Then I saw the red-lettered message on the front windshield:

BACK OFF, BITCH

CHAPTER THIRTY

Thursday, November 13. 8:12 A.M. 1000 block of South Stanley Avenue. A vandal smashed a car windshield and placed an aluminum container holding a fish with a rose in its mouth on the dashboard and taped a sign reading "Stop" on the car. (Wilshire)

"NICE MESSAGE," CONNORS SAID, UNSMILING, HIS HANDS tucked into the pockets of his tight jeans as he viewed my vandalized windshield. "Short and to the point."

"Plus it's got alliteration," I said, trying to make light of the whole thing because I didn't like the alternative. "It'll read well in next week's *Crime Sheet*."

Connors turned to me and frowned. "You think this is funny? 'Cause I don't."

"I don't think it's funny," I said.

The slashed tires and the message, plus the fact that the writer knew where I lived, had shaken me to the core. I don't know how long I'd stood there, staring at the writing, nauseated with fear, before I ran and knocked on Isaac's door. He's an early riser, but he hadn't heard anyone, seen anyone. For all I knew, the message could have been there all night.

"Did you call it in to Wilshire?" Connors asked.

"Not yet." My apartment is in Wilshire's jurisdiction, but I'd phoned Connors.

"Do it. They'll send out someone for prints, but with the rain they probably won't find anything usable. So who have you been pissing off lately, Molly?" he asked, part concern, part annoyance.

"I've been talking to a lot of people about Linney. His son-in-law, Hank Reston. His protégé, his neighbors, his doctor. The manager of an assisted living facility his daughter was checking out. Reston asked me to look into his wife's disappearance, by the way, so I can't see him doing this." I nodded toward my car.

"Maybe you should listen to the warning."

"I also had a little run-in with Reston's partner." I told him about Modine. "He's the one I told you about."

"The one whose name you didn't want to give me. Now you don't mind fingering him." Connors grunted. "What the hell were you doing trespassing in the house, Molly?"

"I was trying to find something that would prove Linney was killed. Maybe the windshield is a coincidence, Andy." Which I didn't believe for a minute. "You said Linney's death was probably unintentional, so why would anyone care if I talked to people who knew him? Unless you learned something that says otherwise?"

He didn't answer, and I could tell from the look in his eyes that he was deliberating.

"This is not for publication, okay? I'm only telling you be-cause I want you to back off." He scowled at me.

"You forgot the *bitch*."

"Cut it out. If I read about this in the papers—"

"It won't be from me. I promise."

"They didn't find any smoke in Linney's lungs, which means he was dead when the fire started. Cause of death was a broken neck incurred by his fall down the stairs. But," Connors said, his voice stern with warning, "that doesn't mean someone pushed him. He could have tripped."

Uh-huh. "The fact that someone doesn't like my poking around says otherwise, doesn't it? Anything else?"

"It's Hernandez's case. Talk to him."

"I spoke to him a few days ago. He wasn't very forthcoming."

"This may come as a surprise, Molly, but cops don't think it's their job to supply information to reporters."

"Which is why I rely on you." I smiled sweetly. "Did he tell you anything about the tape I found? The one with the phone call from Margaret Linney?"

Connors sighed. "You're not going to leave this alone, are you? You could get hurt, Molly. Or killed."

That made me shudder. "I don't have a death wish, Andy. Believe me, I'm taking that message very seriously and plan to be extremely careful. What about the tape?"

"You want me to jeopardize my relationship with my fellow detectives?" He shook his head. "I like you, and you've always played fair. But these are my people. Plus I could lose my job over something like this."

He was right, of course. I felt ashamed for having asked. "Can you phone Hernandez and vouch for me? Convince him to talk to me?"

"I can try. In the meantime—"

"I know. Be careful."

CHAPTER THIRTY-ONE

I SMELLED THE CHALLA EVEN BEFORE BUBBIE OPENED the door to her apartment.

"Five minutes, I'm ready," she told me when we were in the kitchen.

She removed her red-and-white checked apron, draped it over the back of a chair she groped for and found without much difficulty, and disappeared down the long hall to her bedroom. I remained in the kitchen, deeply inhaling the aroma of freshly baked bread. To me, it's headier than the most expensive perfume, and I've often thought someone could make a fortune bottling it. *Eau de Yeast.*

For as long as I can remember, Bubbie has been baking the braided loaves that are a part of every Sabbath meal and most holidays, and she hasn't let her failing eyesight stop her. We all use Bubbie's recipe, but for some reason her challas are the best—low, shapely hills with dense, cakelike insides and a thin crust evenly browned to a golden caramel.

The problem is that Bubbie doesn't use a real recipe—not for her challa, not for her potato or onion or noodle kugels or *kneidels* (matzoh balls). Her fingers are her measuring spoons; her curved palm, her cup. The month before Edie's wedding, Edie went to Bubbie's several times to learn her culinary secrets. The way Edie tells it, she stood at Bubbie's side, pencil and paper ready, and stopped Bubbie's cupped hand after she'd scooped sugar or flour or some other dry ingredient she was about to add to her battered stainless steel mixing bowl. Then Edie transferred the contents of Bubbie's hands into a measuring cup.

Still, Edie had only an approximation. There's no precise equivalent for a *bissele* (a little) potato starch or a *knip* (a pinch of) salt, or for Bubbie's basic instructions: *Shit arayn.* That's a regional pronunciation of Yiddish for *Pour it* (or *some*) *in.* As you can imagine, we Blume kids had great fun as adolescents repeating the phrase with feigned innocence that didn't fool anyone. My mom would sigh and shake her head. My dad would warn us to "knock it off." Bubbie would frown, and so would Zeidie Irving, but I could see he was having a hard time not laughing.

"Ready," Bubbie said now. She'd changed into a navy pleated skirt with a matching cardigan and had applied blusher to her lined, hollowed cheeks, and an uneven line of pale apricot to her thin lips. I helped her into her coat and made sure she took her cane, which she doesn't always do.

"Why are you looking around you every five seconds, Molly?" she asked as we walked to my car.

"Just habit," I lied.

The auto club had towed my Acura to my mechanic, who had replaced the ruined tires. Turpentine had removed the red ink from my windshield. But the threat was seared on my mind. And while I didn't really believe I was in danger, I was as jittery as if I'd had ten cups of coffee. Also, it was one thing to risk my well-being, another to risk Bubbie's.

I found a parking spot on Vista, a block away from Cyndi's on Melrose Avenue near Gardner, where they used to have a kosher Noah's Bagels. Bubbie usually goes to Supercuts, but she'd been more than willing to try a new place when I explained my ulterior motive. I think she got a kick knowing she'd be helping me.

She definitely got a kick out of Melrose. Bubbie lives on Spaulding off of Oakwood, only three blocks south, but she hadn't been here in twenty years. Melrose then, between Fairfax and La Brea, was a quiet street that went to sleep at five P.M. and was lined with colorless stores that sold antiques, hardware, uninspired low-end clothing, and cemetery monuments. You can still buy restaurant supplies and groceries in bulk at the Smart & Final across the street from Fairfax High, but most of the shops have been replaced by neon-lit establishments—some funky, some more hip—that offer eyewear, tattoos, body piercings, skateboard gear, tennis shoes, and vintage clothing, and by eateries that stay open late into the night. The pedestrian population, almost nonexistent twenty years ago, is eclectic: yuppies who walk to the Starbucks from their nearby apartments; tourists; natives in tank tops or dreadlocks. Auto traffic has become so bad that the city has implemented draconian rules to curtail the number of cars and their movement, but I'm not sure how successful they've been.

Cyndi's smelled of hair spray and dyes and other chemical products whose toxic properties I try not to think about when I'm having my hair highlighted. Cyndi herself, who was pointed out to Bubbie and me when we entered her long, narrow shop, was at her station, wrapping strands of hair around pieces of foil. She looked like a tall, thin mime—black Lycra top and pants, a white-white complexion with a slash of red for a mouth and kohl-lined eyes. Her chin-length hair was sectioned into thick spikes of purple, green, burgundy, orange, and blue. Crayola meets the Statue of Liberty. I thought Bubbie might have second thoughts, but she was as cool as the heavy metal blasting from the speakers that made it almost impossible for us to hear ourselves talk.

Ten minutes later Bubbie sat perched on Cyndi's chair, her thin legs encased in black Easy Spirit shoes that dangled several feet above the ground.

Cyndi ran her long, scarlet-tipped fingers through Bubbie's beautiful silver hair. "So what would you like?"

"Half a inch," Bubbie said firmly, her accent turning *half* into *heff* and *a* into *ah*. "The same style like I have now."

"Okay. You can have coffee while you wait," Cyndi told me, pointing to an urn on a stand at the back of the room.

"Thanks, but I like to watch."

With a look that said she'd added me to her list of weirdos accompanied by a suit-yourself shrug, she picked up her shears and a comb and got to work.

"I'm glad you were able to fit my grandmother in today," I told her after a minute or so.

"Next week it starts getting crazy, with Thanksgiving coming, and then the holidays." She studied me critically with teal eyes—probably tinted contact lenses. "Who does your hair?"

I told her.

"You could use a good conditioning, and I'd put in a few more low lights so it doesn't look brassy."

"Thanks for the advice." I waited another minute, watching a shower of hair speckle the white linoleum with gray. "Someone I know used to come here all the time."

"Oh, yeah? Who's that?"

"Margaret Linney. You may have known her as Maggie Reston."

Cyndi stopped midsnip and turned to me, a wary expression on her white face. "Who said I knew her?" she asked, her voice as sharp as her shears.

This was not going well. "Actually, I didn't know her. But I know her husband. He told me you did her hair."

"Is that right?" She sneered at me.

I threw Bubbie a quick look. She seemed to be taking everything in stride, but bringing her probably hadn't been the best idea.

"You're not here for a cut," Cyndi said. "You're here to pump me about Maggie. And you're using your grandmother as a shill. Shame on you!"

I was grateful for the loud music I'd found so annoying. "You're right, and I'm sorry. I *am* hoping to get information about Maggie."

"Why didn't you just ask me? Because you figured I wouldn't talk about her, that's why," she continued before I could answer. "You people," she said with disgust.

Bubbie G was rigid as a statue.

"Somebody killed Maggie," I said. "And last week somebody killed her father. I'm trying to find out who."

"I'm going to finish Grandma's cut. It's not her fault you dragged her here." Cyndi turned her back to me and bent to shape the hair along Bubbie's nape.

"Somebody warned me to back off." I met Bubbie's startled eyes in the mirror and winked. "They know I'm onto something."

Cyndi ignored me.

"The police haven't had any luck finding her," I continued. "Her husband's a wreck. He can't get on with his life until he knows what happened. Maybe Maggie told you something that could help him, or the police."

Still no answer.

"Excuse me," Bubbie said. "Who are the other people?" Bubbie pronounces *th*s as *d*s or *t*s.

Cyndi frowned. "What people?"

"You said, 'you people.' Somebody else bothered you?"

I stared at my grandmother. Way to go, Bubbie. I turned to Cyndi. "Right. What did you mean by that?" There was no way she could have known I was a reporter.

"I meant people who are nosy and pushy," she said. "A cop was here yesterday. He asked me a hundred questions."

At least someone had succeeded. "I hope you were able to help him."

"Who says I answered them?" She lifted a strand of Bubbie's hair with her comb, narrowed her eyes, and snipped an almost imperceptible amount. "All done. How do you like it?" she asked Bubbie, lowering the chair.

"Beautiful. Thank you." She scampered off the chair. "I'll wait by the front, Molly." Grabbing her cane, she walked to the bench we'd sat on earlier.

I returned my attention to Cyndi. "Why didn't you answer the detective?"

"I thought I was gonna puke from his breath, if you want to know, and I couldn't wait for him to leave. He smelled like a chimney."

"He smoked?"

"Am I *not* speaking English?"

I'd never seen Porter with a cigarette, and I didn't see Hernandez as the type to smoke. Then again, I wouldn't have pegged Ned Vaughan as a smoker, either.

"What did the cop look like?" I asked.

"Why? Are you planning to date him?"

"I know a few cops. I'm wondering which one talked to you."

"I don't remember his name. He looked like a bulldog. Thickset, beefy, red-faced. Red hair, too, what was left of it. Nothing on top," she said with vicious pleasure.

Roger Modine. I felt a prickling of unease at the base of my spine. "He wasn't a cop, Cyndi."

She smirked. "Uh-huh."

"I know the two detectives on this case. Porter and Hernandez." I described them to her. "You can phone them and ask them if they were here."

"Maybe I will."

I gave her the number to Wilshire. "I think you talked to Roger Modine. He's Maggie's husband's partner."

"Shit." Cyndi's hands were shaking. She dropped them to her sides. She licked her lips. "Did he kill Maggie?"

"I don't know. What did he ask you?"

"Why do you want to know?" She was throwing me one last challenge, but it was halfhearted, just for show, and we both knew it.

I told her how I'd met Linney, why I was interested.

She thought about that for a moment. "He wanted to know did Maggie say she was having trouble with anyone. Was she planning on meeting anyone that night. Stuff like that. But I didn't tell him anything." She ran a hand through a purple patch. "I should call the cops, huh?"

"Impersonating a police officer is a crime," I said. "*Did* Maggie tell you she was nervous about anything?"

"God, it's so long ago." Cyndi sagged onto the chair Bubbie had vacated. "Half a year, isn't it?"

"Five months this week."

Cyndi sighed. "She was a nice woman. Always smiling, always asking how I was, how's my daughter. They're still not sure she's dead, huh?"

"No," I said, speaking for "them." "Why?"

"'Cause she told me more than once that sometimes she felt like running away. Her husband and dad were always going at it. It was getting to her."

Nothing new there. "Did she ever mention Modine?"

Cyndi shook her head. None of the spikes moved.

"What was she like that last day?" I asked.

"Like I said, it's been a long time."

I tried another tack. "Did Maggie have the usual the last time she was here?"

"I can check."

She slid off the chair. I waited while she flipped through a large appointment book on the front counter.

"Cut and a shampoo, no manicure," she told me when she returned. She sat on the chair and frowned. "Which is strange because— Oh, *now* I remember. She had to get to an appointment. She said she'd come back the next day."

I waited, hoping there was more.

Cyndi pushed her foot against the scuffed wall and swiveled back and forth. "That's it," she said. "Sorry."

"Did she mention anything about a tiler?"

"Tiler." Cyndi tried out the word, and recognition flickered in her unnaturally green-blue eyes. "Tiler. Yeah." She nodded. "It's coming back to me. He was the appointment. She was on her cell phone and said something like, 'Tell Mr. Tiler I'll be a few minutes late.'"

That took me by surprise. "Tiler is a person?"

"As opposed to a duck? He was a lawyer." She seemed pleased with herself. "My cousin's first name is Tyler with a *y*. I told Maggie, and she said this was a lawyer's last name, with an *i*. And I said, 'Girl, as long as he gets you the money.'" She smiled.

An attorney. Not Linz. "Did she say what kind of lawyer?"

"No, but I remember thinking, 'divorce city.' She talked about it once, so I figured she was going to do it."

"Did she seem afraid that day?"

"Afraid?" Cyndi narrowed her eyes. "I don't think so. She was tense. I asked her was something wrong, and she said she'd almost made the biggest mistake of her life."

I wondered what Maggie had meant. Putting her father in Golden Vista? I checked the list of items I'd copied from the planner and asked Cyndi if Maggie had mentioned anyone whose name began with *V.*

Cyndi shrugged. "No clue. Sorry."

"Thanks a lot. You've been very helpful." I handed her a ten-dollar tip and my card. "If you think of anything."

Bubbie stood when I joined her at the front. She handed me her wallet and asked me to pay the cashier, but I insisted that the haircut was my treat.

"You were a big help," I told her.

She smiled. "A regular Dr. Watson." Bubbie is an avid mystery fan and is responsible for my love of the genre.

When we were on the sidewalk, she took my arm. "Very smart, Molly. Pretending like someone threatened you. I almost believed you myself." A few paces later, she asked, "So how much do they charge for a haircut?"

"Twenty dollars," I said, lopping off twenty-five. Almost four times what Supercuts charges.

"*A metziah,*" Bubbie said. A bargain.

Considering what I'd learned, it was.

CHAPTER THIRTY-TWO

THE MIRACLE MILE HARP BOARD RAN A TIGHT OPERA-
tion. The session had begun when I entered the small meeting
room at Councilman Bruce Harrington's Robertson Boulevard
headquarters two minutes after seven. Taking off my coat, I
slipped into the nearest seat and directed my attention to the
large table at the front and the eight people seated around it, including Jeremy Dorn, who chaired the board, and Linda
Cobern, who, given the dead bird, had probably come to mon-
itor the proceedings.

Linda looked startled to see me, then smiled stiffly, as though
she were making a plaster cast of her teeth. Earlier in the day I'd
returned her call, accepted her apology for being "a tiny bit tense
the other night," and explained that, while I was interested in

getting "a clearer picture of what HARP does," I didn't have the time to meet with her.

I *was* busy. My *Crime Sheet* column is due every Friday. I was interviewing people about Linney and Margaret. I was reviewing the galleys of my book. And I preferred getting the picture myself. Linney's death had overshadowed the vandalisms that had first interested me in HARP, and I hoped to learn something that might uncover the vandal's identity and, possibly, a lead to Linney's killer.

"Over here, Molly!"

Swiveling to my left, I saw a red-nosed Walter Fennel and, a few rows up, Tim Bolt. I should have figured the old guy would be here, but Bolt was a surprise. He hadn't expressed interest in HARP when we'd talked. Then again, I hadn't asked. I looked around but saw no sign of Winnie. Maybe she'd dropped Fennel off.

"Walter, we're in session," chided a woman with a helmet of short brown hair that made her round face look like a bowling ball.

"This is Molly Blume, everybody," Fennel announced in a high voice. He did his lip-sweeping thing. "She's a famous reporter and she writes terrific bestsellers."

All eyes turned to me and stayed on me as I changed seats. So much for anonymity. If my publisher decided to spring for a book tour, I might consider taking Fennel along to draw the crowds.

"The first item is the second story addition on Poinsettia," Dorn said. Tonight he was wearing a moss-green sweater and a smaller bandage, and he'd lost that glazed look. "Mr. Newman, do you want to show us your revised plans?"

A short, overweight man in suspenders stood and unrolled a set of drawings onto the table. "This is what we've done. . . ."

"That's Jeremy Dorn," Fennel whispered in my ear. "He's

the architect I told you about. You have to have an architect on the board. He became chair after me, but I don't think he has the balls for the job. Next to him is Brenda. She wanted to be chair and acts like she is. The blonde across from Jeremy is Nancy, and next to her is Roselle. She never says much. Adrian just had his gall bladder out, or he'd be here."

Brenda frowned at Fennel, then returned her attention to the petitioner.

"You're suggesting serious changes to the original structure," said Nancy with the long blond hair and a flat voice. "You're replacing an existing side window with a door."

"A French door instead of a French window," Newman said with strained patience. "So that we can walk out onto the patio. It won't change the appearance of the house."

"Still . . ." She looked to Jeremy for support.

"About this new *front* door." The architect pointed to the top drawing. "The original door isn't arched."

"Actually, we think the original *was* arched," Newman said. "We brought photos of several similar houses, and all the doors are arched. We're pretty sure this door isn't the original. The house has been remodeled several times, so I don't see how it's a contributing structure."

"But that was *before* HARP," Nancy said.

"Let's see the photos," Brenda said.

A woman next to Newman—I assumed she was his wife—handed him a stack of photos. Newman passed them around and crossed his arms—no small feat, considering his girth.

"Mr. Newman may be right," Jeremy said. "I'll try to take a look at the front door, maybe next week. Would that work for you, Mr. Newman?"

"The sooner, the better."

Nancy said, "The French door is a concern, Mr. Newman."

"It's a minor change. You won't see a difference."

"There's a big difference between a window and a door, Mr. Newman." She had a condescending half smile you wanted to smack off her face.

Newman clenched his fists. "I know the difference between a window and door."

"Well, then you can see that this poses a problem." She turned to Brenda. "Don't you think it's a problem?"

Brenda nodded. "Definitely a problem."

"*You* have a problem, you bitch," Newman said to Nancy.

The wife tugged on his shirtsleeve.

"Not smart," Fennel whispered to me.

"I won't be talked to like that," Nancy told Jeremy.

Linda Cobern had the helpless, frozen look of a mother whose children have turned on a porn video in front of guests.

Dorn said, "Mr. Newman, I understand that you're agitated, but you have to be civil."

"Civil?" With rising color in his neck and face, Newman exploded: This was his third time before the board in five months. His architect had redrawn the drawings twice to meet the board's conditions. He was beginning to think the board would never approve his plans.

"My wife and I and our five kids are living in a two-bedroom house with one bathroom because you don't want us to put in a French door!"

Nancy stood and held up a large, opened booklet as if it were the tablets containing the Ten Commandments. "These are the rules from the Department of the Interior for historical preservation zones," she said in that same monotone that made me want to scream. "Would you like me to read them to you, Mr. Newman? I don't make these up." She pressed the booklet to her bosom.

Fennel made a clicking sound. "She's a tough one," he said with admiration.

Dorn said, "Mr. Newman, can you make a copy of the drawings for us so that we can study them?"

"I've made copies. Twice. I think you people ate them."

He rolled up the drawings and twisted them into a tight rod that I'll bet he wanted to use on Nancy's head. He muttered "Fine" and returned to his seat.

Five months of living in cramped quarters could equal serious frustration with HARP, I thought as I watched him leave with his wife. I wrote his name in my notepad, shielding the paper from Fennel's eagle eyes.

The next petitioner wanted to paint his house pale yellow instead of its present white. That took about ten minutes of discussion regarding the definition of *pale* and *yellow,* after which he won approval, pending his submission of paint chips.

A homeowner who wanted to install security bars on his second-floor windows met stiff opposition until he threatened to hold the board liable if one of his young children fell out a window.

Another homeowner received permission to redo his driveway with the stipulation that he use the same material.

"Our last item is the roof on Vista. Mr. Lowenthal." Dorn nodded at a heavily freckled, red-haired man sitting next to Tim Bolt.

"I want to get this resolved," Lowenthal began. "I'm paying two mortgages, which I can't afford."

"Mr. Lowenthal, we've been over this. If you restore the original Spanish tile roof, the city will remove the lien, and you'll sell your house."

"I told you. The ceiling joists were damaged by rain. The ceilings would have caved in from the weight of the tiles."

"He put on a composition roof," Fennel whispered to me, his lip curled in disgust.

"A structural engineer can help you solve the problem," Dorn said.

"I met with an engineer. He said I'm talking tens of thousands of dollars that I don't have. For a roof."

"We have an obligation to preserve the integrity of the architecture," Nancy said. "You don't put a composition roof on a Spanish Colonial."

"Damn straight." Fennel nodded.

Lowenthal ignored Nancy. "I'm going to lose the house, Mr. Dorn. You people have to help me out here."

Jeremy said, "The roof—"

"Listen." The man ran a hand across his forehead, which was beaded with perspiration. "I lost out on two prospective buyers. I can't afford to lose another. Tell them, Tim."

Bolt nodded. "I have a client who's ready to buy the Vista property. But with the lien . . ."

So Bolt had come here as a Realtor. I half listened to the continuing exchange (and a running commentary from Fennel) with mixed feelings, happy the decision wasn't mine to make. Fennel had no such problem. I'd developed a fondness for the old man but found his pro-HARP zealousness irritating and sad. I also wondered whether HARP rules had placed other homeowners in situations like Lowenthal's, or worse. According to Ned Vaughan, Reston and Modine were having problems with several properties. HARP problems?

Maybe Tim Bolt knew. When the meeting ended at eight-thirty, with no resolution for Lowenthal, I went up to Bolt and invited him for a cup of coffee.

"Wish I could." He slipped an arm into the sleeve of a navy wool jacket. "I'm giving someone a ride home."

"Walter Fennel?"

Bolt looked surprised. "Yes. How do you know Walter?"

"I talked to him about Professor Linney. You probably know they were good friends."

He glanced at Fennel, who was in conversation with Brenda. "Right. Of course."

"What about after you drop Mr. Fennel off? I have a few questions."

"Actually, tonight isn't a good idea, Molly."

"What about tomorrow?"

"Tomorrow?"

"I can come to your house, if you want."

"Why don't we meet at Starbucks at eleven. The one on Detroit and Beverly?"

"I'll be there." He seemed distracted, or maybe he was just eager to get home. I remembered that his wife had been ill. "I hope your wife is feeling better, Tim."

"A little better, thanks."

"Who's better? You're feeling sick?" Fennel had walked over, looking like a mummy with his red shawl covering part of his chin. "Don't breathe all over me if you are."

"I'm fine."

"I'll go with Molly. She doesn't have a cold."

"I'm waiting to talk to someone," I told him. Jeremy Dorn, who was having a conversation with the other board members. He didn't look happy.

"I'm in no rush."

"Your wife will be wondering where you are," Bolt said. He sounded annoyed. "And it's out of Molly's way to drive you home. I'm just around the block."

"Oh, all right," Fennel muttered.

A few minutes later Dorn was putting on his brown suede jacket. I was headed his way when Linda Cobern accosted me. I figured that, like Sony and Nikon, she was eager to give me that "clearer picture."

"You probably won't believe me," she began, "but tonight's meeting wasn't typical."

"I was just lucky, I guess." I smiled, but I could see that she didn't appreciate my humor. "You don't have to worry. I'm not doing a piece on the HARP process."

"Frankly, I wish you would. So does Councilman Harrington. You have to admit your article was slanted. I could show you statistics that—"

I looked at Dorn. He was halfway out the door. "Would you excuse me? I have to go." I hurried toward him.

"You're not interested in being fair, are you?" she called after me. "You write incendiary journalism and don't care about the ramifications."

I'll admit the *incendiary* made me wince, although I wasn't sure if she'd chosen the word for its irony or had pulled it out of her I-hate-all-reporters phrase book. I was tempted to defend myself, to tell her that I'd been scrupulously fair, that she was trying to blame me for the divisiveness HARP had caused and the anger that had pushed someone to multiple acts of vandalism.

I didn't say a word. I've learned that there is no dignity or purpose in arguing with the reviewer who has just trashed your work, even if he or she has misread, misrepresented, taken things out of context, etc. And there's certainly no winning. All you can do is write the next book, or article, and develop a thicker skin.

CHAPTER THIRTY-THREE

I CAUGHT UP WITH DORN AS HE WAS ENTERING THE ELE-
vator, and managed to get inside before the closing doors
slammed into me. I wasn't sure if he remembered me.

He acknowledged my presence with a nod and pressed B.

"I'm Molly Blume," I said as the elevator rumbled and began
its descent. "We met at the HARP meeting. I'm—"

"The reporter. I was wondering when it would be my
turn."

I smiled. "I'd like to talk to you about Margaret Linney, Mr.
Dorn. Do you have a few minutes?"

He sighed deeply. "We weren't having an affair," he said in a
bored tone that implied he was tired of defending himself. "Is
that what you wanted to ask me?"

Talk about direct. "Among other things. Can I buy you a cup of coffee?"

The elevator stopped and the doors slid open.

"No thanks," he told me after we'd exited into a parking garage that was still dank from yesterday's rain. "Tonight was the end to a long, tiring day, and I'm looking forward to going home, having a glass of wine, and taking my dog for a walk. He doesn't give me attitude. Don't quote me on that." He started walking.

I followed. "Fifteen minutes?"

"Ten."

He had a long stride and I had to hurry to keep up. When he reached a black Ford Explorer, he stopped and leaned against the driver door.

He crossed his arms. "So what are the other things you wanted to know?" His voice echoed in the garage.

"For starters, is it really such a big deal if someone puts in a French door instead of a window?"

"Off the record?"

"Off the record."

He eyed me, probably deciding whether he could trust me. "It's ridiculous. One of the reasons I got on the board was to end that kind of stuff, but as you could probably tell, I'm outnumbered."

"By Nancy."

A smile tugged at his lips. "No comment."

"And the guy with the roof problem?"

"Composition is ugly," Dorn said with finality. "Look, I sympathize with Mr. Lowenthal's situation. Restoring the roof will be expensive. But we have to maintain standards. At the same time, I don't like the whole Big Brother thing. I'm hoping to change that, but it won't happen overnight."

I applauded his goal but agreed with Fennel: I didn't think

Dorn had the *cojónes* for the job—or *beitzim,* if you want to use the Yiddish slang. (Literally, *eggs.*) In any language, he didn't have what it took.

"I heard that residents in a few HARP areas are so unhappy that they're trying to rescind their status," I said.

"Ladera Heights and Mar Vista." Dorn nodded. "If it *does* happen, it won't be soon. And that's exactly why I'm getting involved, to make the system more reasonable and keep the homeowners happy and build a community."

"Hancock Park homeowners don't seem all that happy about becoming a HARP area. Yours was one of the recently vandalized homes, right?"

His hand went to his bandage. "That was terrifying, I can tell you. One minute I'm reading in my living room. The next, there's glass all over me and I'm bleeding. A few inches lower and I could have lost an eye." He grimaced.

"Who do you think did it?"

Dorn shrugged. "The police asked me. You were at tonight's meeting. It's not always that contentious, but there are quite a few unhappy homeowners in Miracle Mile, and I imagine it's the same in the other HARP districts."

"Anyone stand out in your mind?"

He hesitated, then shook his head.

"Roger Modine?" I thought I saw a flicker in his eyes but wasn't sure. "You can tell me off the record."

"Thanks, but being shot at once is enough for me."

"What about Arnold Seltzer? The man who was yelling at you and Linda Cobern at the Hancock Park HARP meeting?"

"Arnie's a flake, but he's harmless." Dorn checked his watch. "You have four minutes."

"Why would I think you were having an affair with Margaret Reston?"

"Because according to Walter Fennel, I was. The old goat

dropped hints whenever he saw me. He introduced you tonight, so you've obviously talked to him. I figured he told you. Why not? He's told the rest of the world."

Dorn sounded bitter, and I couldn't blame him. "Including Hank Reston?"

He grimaced. "I assume you've talked to Reston. What did *he* say?"

"That there was nothing going on between you and his wife."

The architect grunted. "Well, that's not the tune he was singing five months ago. Five months ago he was ready to take my head off."

"What happened?" We were down to less than three minutes, but I sensed that Dorn wanted me to hear his version. And I was more than happy to listen.

"Linney phoned Hank in a panic. Maggie was supposedly at the Muirfield house, but she hadn't answered her cell phone all day. Hank couldn't reach her, either, so he drove to Muirfield and waited. By the time Maggie and I arrived, he was convinced that she hadn't answered her phone because we hadn't wanted to be *interrupted*."

"Why *didn't* she answer it?"

"She didn't have it. She'd misplaced it. She *told* Linney he wouldn't be able to contact her. She also told him she wouldn't be at the Muirfield house until late in the afternoon. The old guy forgot." Dorn sighed again. "Maggie tried to explain, but Hank was too busy raging."

"I'm surprised he didn't fire you."

"Actually, he did." Dorn flashed a wry smile. "He hadn't wanted to hire me in the first place. I'm sure he thought Maggie and I were too chummy. We've known each other for years. This gave him an out."

"He wanted to hire his friend Ned Vaughan?" I said.

Dorn nodded. "That was awkward, especially because I know Ned. But I was Maggie's choice and Hank wanted her to be happy. Anyway, after he finally stopped yelling and let Maggie explain, he apologized profusely and rehired me. But I'm not sure he believed her. It's a shame. They really had something special, and he was ruining it with his obsessive jealousy."

"Maggie loved him?"

"Are you kidding? She was crazy about him. The truth is they should never have moved into her father's house. That's when things started turning sour. You want to hear the kicker? Linney had the cell phone the whole time. He put it in his desk drawer and forgot all about it."

Or not, I thought.

CHAPTER THIRTY-FOUR

MINDY WAS HALF RECLINING ON THE DEN SOFA, NURSING the baby and watching *Will and Grace* when I showed up a little after nine. It's one of my favorite shows, so I had no problem waiting for the commercial before asking her about Tiler.

"Never heard of him, which doesn't mean anything." She adjusted the pillow under the arm that cradled the baby's head. "Do you know what kind of law he practices?"

"No."

"The State Bar of California has a Web site. I'll check it when I'm at the office. Why do you need to know?"

I explained. "So it was obviously important to Margaret Linney. Can you check one more thing? Oscar Linney invested forty thousand with a Denver company, Skoll Investment. I was going to ask Reston about it, but then I found the tape, and forgot about it. Anyway, I tried the phone number. It's been disconnected, and there's no new number. I couldn't find a Web site, either. I'm beginning to think Skoll Investment doesn't exist."

"I wouldn't be surprised. I can't tell you how many people invest in phantom companies, especially the elderly. They're such easy prey, you know?" Mindy stroked Yitz's hair. "Many of them live alone, and they're not as mentally sharp as they used to be. They invest their hard-earned life savings with strangers who promise them riches and leave them with worthless paper."

"Financial elder abuse," I said. "The gift of old age." I grimaced.

"One of my colleagues, Mark, is an estate planner. He's had clients whose kids have emptied their parents' savings and coerced them to sign over their assets. The house, the pension fund, Social Security payments. If mom or dad won't sign, it's off to a nursing home. Or a beating."

"Maybe a nursing home would be an improvement."

"They don't think so. And some facilities are awful, Molly. Norm heard about one where a resident died sitting in a chair in his room and no one knew about it for over four hours. And a few residents have been abused by someone on staff. Robbed or fondled or raped. But those are the exceptions. Most of the abuse takes place at home. A son or daughter or some other family member who's frustrated and resents having to take care of a parent whose physical and mental deterioration is making them a burden. Women are abused more often than men, by the way."

"The abuser could be an in-law," I said. "Margaret was anxious to put her dad in a facility. Maybe she wanted to get him away from her husband."

Mindy nodded. "Norm has residents who don't want to spend time with their families, not even the holidays. And when they *do* go, they come back depressed and noncommunicative, and sometimes with bruises the family member explains away. The residents won't say, but Norm suspects they're being abused, and maybe pressured to relinquish assets. Was Linney in charge of his own finances?"

"He signed over his house to Margaret about a month before she disappeared. I assume he gave her power of attorney, but I don't know that for a fact."

"When did he invest in Skoll?"

"April." Before he signed over the house. I wondered if that had been his idea, or if Margaret—or Hank—had pushed him to do it. "There was a notation in Margaret's planner about bank and help." I pulled the stapled pages out of my purse and found the entry. "Here." I held up the page and pointed to the word.

Mindy glanced at it. "The last letter is smudged. Maybe it's the photocopy. See that little curved mark at the bottom?"

I peered at the page. "Now that you mention it."

"The spine of the letter looks curved, too. I think it's a *C*, not a *P*. That would make sense."

"HELC makes sense to you?"

"Home Equity Line of Credit. Maybe Margaret planned to withdraw cash."

I put the pages back into my purse. "Hank Reston didn't mention anything about Maggie taking out money. He would have known about it."

Mindy shrugged. "Could be she didn't get around to it. You said she had an appointment with the attorney. Maybe she wrote the *P* by accident. A Freudian slip."

"Maybe." I picked up the *National Geographic* on the coffee table and fanned the pages. "Or maybe she was going over all of her father's financial papers and came across a discrepancy. So she needed *help* from the bank."

"Possible."

"No, you're probably right. All this time I've been thinking that her murder and Linney's were crimes of passion. Maybe it's about money."

"It often is." Mindy removed Yitz from her breast. "Okay, halftime."

"Can I burp him?"

She handed me the burp cloth, which I draped on my shoulder. I scooped Yitz from her arms, careful to support his head, and laid him against my chest. I patted his back tentatively.

"He won't break," Mindy said. "If that position doesn't work, lay him on your lap. That's what I do."

A few seconds later I was rewarded with an adult-volume belch. "Can you believe this little guy? He sounds like Howard Stern." I nuzzled his neck. He smelled of baby—deliciously sour.

"God forbid." Mindy made a face. I handed her the baby, and she put him to her other breast. "So how's the rest of the investigation going?" she asked when he was suckling. "Are you making progress?"

"If you call getting a threat 'progress.'" I told her about the windshield and tires. "Don't tell Mom or Dad or the rest of the family. They'll worry."

Mindy frowned. "And I won't?"

"You don't panic. And I needed to tell someone, Mindy. I can't stop thinking about it. I keep looking over my shoulder to see if someone is following me." I'd done that in the parking garage, had frozen for a second when I'd heard echoing footsteps, until I'd realized they were mine.

"Why don't you drop this, Molly?"

"I have to *know*, Mindy." I ignored her frown, which had deepened. "And I figure I'll be safer when I find out who did it. On the plus side, Zack told me he loves me."

"He did?" Her smile turned into a yawn. "That's wonderful, Molly. Did you tell Mom?"

"I haven't had a chance. I will, when I see her. But I'm not telling anyone else, especially Edie. She'll make something bigger out of it."

"It's pretty big, Molly. I think you should tell her. She'll be hurt. After all, she set this up."

"There's nothing to tell, yet."

Mindy looked at me. "Are you saying you're not sure how you feel?"

"I'm sure. But things don't always work out, Min. I don't want any pressure."

"But you're happy about this? It feels right?"

"It feels very right, and I'm very happy. And nervous. He wants me to have lunch at his parents' this *Shabbos.*"

I found another flyer on my windshield. Pink this time, with a different message:

> I WATCH, AND AM AS A SPARROW
> ALONE UPON THE HOUSE TOP.

I had no idea what that meant, or where the quote was from. But I was unnerved, especially after I checked up and down the block and didn't see flyers on any of the other cars.

The night seemed suddenly darker, more forbidding. Was someone watching me? The same someone who had vandalized my car? But the tone of the messages was so different.

I considered spending the night at Mindy's. Instead I got into my car and drove home, checking my rearview mirror every few seconds. I didn't spot anyone following me, but how could I be sure?

At home I parked in the driveway, and with my keys in my hand, I ran to the porch. Inside my apartment I slid the deadbolt and felt my heart knocking against my rib cage.

The phone was ringing. Zack, I thought as I hurried to the kitchen and picked up the receiver.

"The tape was spliced," Hank Reston said. "Detective Hernandez came by the house a while ago and told me. I left a couple of messages on your machine."

"I just got back. I'm so sorry, Hank." I felt a wave of sadness. Suspecting is one thing, knowing is altogether different. I learned that when Aggie disappeared.

"I kind of knew when I heard the tape the first time, but I didn't want to. So she's dead," he said dully. "All this time . . . It's like losing her all over again, you know?" He paused. "But if Maggie's dead . . ."

I stayed silent and let him think it through.

"Someone lured the Professor to the house," he finally said. "He killed him, just like he killed Maggie. Why?"

CHAPTER THIRTY-FIVE

Friday, November 14. 9:12 A.M. 8100 block of Raintree Circle. A married couple are concerned for their safety because of a neighbor. The couple and the suspect were attending a homeowners' association meeting and at the end of the meeting the suspect accused the husband of stalking him and said he was going to get a gun. He made the comment four times in front of 12 to 14 witnesses. The suspect, who has accused the husband of stalking him and making threats toward him, has made numerous sexual gestures and comments toward the wife, they said, and added that the suspect is mentally unstable. (Culver City)

THE RECEPTIONIST AT FIRST AID HOME HEALTH CARE, A nasally young woman, transferred me to Sonia in Central Intake.

Sonia must have been doing an awful lot of intaking, because she kept me on hold for over ten minutes, during which I listened to the company's taped music and put a top coat on the nails I'd just polished.

"It's been a *crazy* day," she told me when she returned to me, her cheerful tone implying that she thrived on "crazy." "Sorry. How can I help you?"

"I'm interested in hiring someone to take care of my aunt." I could have said "grandmother," but that would be tempting Satan, who doesn't need encouragement.

"Home health attendant or LVN? Licensed vocational nurse," she explained.

"I don't know."

"What are your aunt's needs?" she asked patiently.

"She has Parkinson's and Alzheimer's, and she needs assistance getting around. We're afraid she's going to fall and hurt herself. Sometimes she forgets to take her medications." The last was something I didn't know about Linney, but it seemed plausible.

"The family would have to pay for a nurse to administer the meds," Sonia said. "Medicare wouldn't cover that, but they might pay for an LVN, depending. Does she have a catheter? Does she need her blood pressure taken regularly? Does she need insulin shots?"

I was getting dizzy from the questions. "I'm not sure. I don't think so."

"Well, then you're looking at a home health attendant, and unfortunately, Medicare doesn't cover that. We charge eighteen dollars an hour with a four-hour minimum for an attendant. Does that sound like something your aunt would be interested in?"

"I think so." Seventy-two dollars for four hours. I wondered what people did who needed home health care but couldn't afford it. "Actually, I'd like to hire the attendant who worked for my friend. Hank Reston? Well, she didn't take care of *Mr.* Reston. She took care of his father-in-law. Oscar Linney. Her first name is Maria."

"How long ago was that?"

"Just last week."

"One minute. I'll check."

I listened to more taped music and fanned my fingers. I thought about Zack, something I'd been doing from the time I woke up, bleary-eyed because we'd talked late into the night. I felt guilty about not having mentioned my car vandalism, but what was the point in worrying him?

"Maria Louisa de la Cruz," Sonia said when she came back on the line. "Unfortunately, she's not available."

"Has she taken another position?"

"She's not available." There was a tightness in Sonia's voice that hadn't been there a moment before.

Maria had probably been suspended for not showing up Friday morning at Reston's. Not fired, or Intaker Sonia would have said Maria was no longer with First Aid.

"Do you know when she'll *be* available?"

"I really can't say. We have a number of excellent attendants. I'm certain your aunt would like one of them."

"I'm sure," I agreed. "The thing is, my aunt is nervous about having a stranger in the house, but she was visiting Professor Linney and met Maria, and she thought Maria was extremely nice. So you can see why it would make it so much easier if we could get Maria." I put a smile into my voice. "Would I be able to talk to Maria? So that when she becomes available, we'd have first dibs?"

"We don't give out our staff's phone numbers. If you leave your number, I can give it to Maria. But if your aunt needs a caregiver, I wouldn't wait."

I'd achieved my first goal—learning Maria's full name. I doubted I'd achieve the second—talking to the caregiver and finding out if Linney had said anything that would shed light on who had killed him.

"Can I speak to a supervisor, Sonia?"

Sonia sighed. "I'll connect you with a staffing coordinator, but she'll tell you the same thing, Miss . . . ?"

"Blume. Thank you. I'd appreciate that."

A minute later I was talking to Patty Aragon, whose tone made it clear that Sonia the Intaker had labeled me stubborn and difficult.

"I'm sure we'll find someone to meet your aunt's needs," she told me.

"I wanted to speak to Maria Louisa de la Cruz."

"She's not available."

They should put it on a tape. "I assume she's been suspended because she failed to show up at Mr. Reston's home on Friday morning."

There was a short silence, and when Patty Aragon spoke again it was with controlled anger. "Obviously you're not interested in finding a caregiver for your aunt, if in fact you have one. I'm not going to discuss Miss de la Cruz. If that's why you phoned—"

"Mr. Reston asked us to look into the circumstances leading to Professor Linney's death." The *us* was an embellishment, but the rest was true, which I hoped gave my voice authenticity.

"Are you Mr. Reston's attorney? If so, I can give you the number of our legal counsel."

"Mr. Reston hasn't decided on a course of action. A great deal depends on what Miss de la Cruz says, which is why he asked me to talk to her." Here the truth and I parted like the waters of the Red Sea.

"I can't discuss Miss de la Cruz."

"Of course. If you could have her phone me—"

"Our attorneys have advised Miss de la Cruz not to discuss this matter with anyone until it's resolved."

"I understand. But if I could talk to Miss de la Cruz, we might be able to avoid more formal proceedings. Mr. Reston isn't a vindictive person. He wants an explanation."

"I don't know what Mr. Reston told you, but there's nothing to explain." She was practically spitting the words.

"Mr. Reston was depending on Miss de la Cruz to take care of Professor Linney. He told her he'd be away overnight on a business trip. She didn't show."

"Because Mr. Reston told her *not* to."

"Maybe something came up and she couldn't make it. Maybe she's afraid to tell you the truth."

"That *is* the truth. We're a highly reputable health care agency, and we pride ourselves on our record. I won't say we've never had a case where a caregiver or licensed nurse hasn't shown. It happens. But it's rare, and it didn't happen this time. Mr. Reston phoned her and told her he wouldn't be needing her that day."

Linney, I thought. The old guy had wanted to make sure no one would stop him from leaving the house. "He phoned First Aid?"

"No, he left a message on Miss de la Cruz's pager. We have the pager, Miss Blume. We have the calls."

"Calls?"

"There were two callers. The first call was placed at seven-thirty on Thursday. The second at eleven P.M. You may want to advise Mr. Reston that if he slanders First Aid, we may be taking legal action ourselves."

CHAPTER THIRTY-SIX

"I CAN'T STAY LONG," TIM BOLT SAID, HIS TONE JUST short of a whine. "Anyway, I told you pretty much everything I know."

He'd arrived twenty minutes late, just as I'd decided he wasn't going to show and had been about to give up the small table I'd been guarding toward the back of the packed coffee shop. Waiting in line to order, he'd seemed skittish—putting his hands into his pockets, taking them out, rocking on the heels of his brown suede moccasins, looking over his shoulder several times a minute. I wondered if the scent of caffeine had made him wired.

"I have just a few questions. By the way, I felt so sorry for your client last night," I said, hoping to relax him. He'd barely touched his coffee and had turned down my offer to buy him a pastry. "This whole thing must be frustrating for you, too."

"I'd like to make the sale, of course." He nodded. "But if I don't, there'll be other sales. Mr. Lowenthal may lose his house. I see the board's point, but I wish there were some way that he didn't have to spend a fortune."

"What do you think Professor Linney would have said about the roof?"

"Restoration." Bolt actually smiled, just for a second. "He'd never compromise, not in a million years."

I took a sip of my Frappucino. It would have gone well with a nosh, but unlike the Coffee Beans, Starbucks doesn't have kosher pastries, which is just as well. "Has HARP affected your listings in other areas, Tim?"

He settled against his chair. "A few. People are hesitant to buy before they know exactly what they can or can't do to the property. That's understandable."

"Definitely. I imagine contractors are being impacted by HARP, too. They're probably doing fewer or more limited remodels. Like Roger Modine, Hank Reston's partner."

"I know Roger. He did work on the Fuller house when Margaret and Hank were getting it in shape for selling." He picked up his coffee cup and took a tentative sip.

"I understand they're having problems with some properties they own jointly. Are those HARP related, too?"

Bolt hesitated. "You can look this up in the county records, so it's no secret. They own properties all over the city. They buy teardowns, build inexpensive new homes, and sell them for a large profit. In areas where property values are lower, they rent out the houses, wait for the home prices to rise, then tear down or remodel and sell. Their problem is with their properties in Ladera Heights and Mar Vista. Both are HARP districts now but weren't when they bought the houses cheap a couple of years ago, planning to hold on until the housing market rose. The market rose, but now instead of knocking the houses down, they have to restore them."

"And that's considerably more expensive," I said, remembering the lecture that had accompanied my tour of Ned Vaughan's home.

"Three to five times as much. You can't begin to imagine the costs involved."

"I heard that some homeowners in those areas are trying to rescind the HARP status."

"Well, even if that happens, it won't be soon enough for Hank and Modine. They have a considerable amount of money tied up in those properties. And the Muirfield house set Hank back a bundle. He paid two million six for the lot and tore down the existing structure. The new house had to cost several million. I think that's why he's so eager to sell the Fuller house."

Money is round, Bubbie G says. Sometimes it's here, sometimes it's there. Sometimes it rolls away from you. The idea that money was rolling away from Hank was surprising. It also raised troubling questions.

"Speaking of the Fuller house," I said. "How was Reston able to put it on the market if it doesn't belong to him?"

"He and Margaret had reciprocal powers of attorney. When he listed the property with my company, he signed a contract representing that he had the authority and power to sell it, and that he would get the necessary documents when it came time to close. Actually, Margaret put it on the market in May, with the understanding that the buyer wouldn't take ownership until the new house was ready. We had a buyer, but Margaret decided not to sell. Too much pressure from the Professor, I think. He was furious when she put it up for sale. He told me Hank had put her up to it, that he should never have deeded it to her."

I thought about my conversation with Cyndi. Was selling the

Fuller house "the big mistake" Margaret had referred to? "When did Margaret change her mind?"

"It was just before she disappeared. So now the house is back on the market. But as I told you, people are leery of buying homes where a crime took place. And now with the Professor dying there, and they're saying it's arson . . ." Bolt shook his head. "Hank is having Modine assess the damage, and he's talking about tearing the house down and building a new one. It'll depend on what the insurance pays. If they *do* tear it down, I'm glad the Professor won't be around to see it. It would break his heart."

"You liked him very much," I said.

Bolt nodded. "He wasn't an easy person. We didn't always agree, and he wasn't diplomatic, but I respected him for being direct. If he didn't like something or someone, he let you know it."

"Like his son-in-law."

"I didn't say that." Bolt had stiffened.

"That's what everybody's been telling me."

"Well, I guess you don't have to hear it from me, then," he said quietly. "I don't believe in gossip. It's hurtful, and dangerous."

There was pain in his voice, and a touch of anger. I wondered if he was speaking from experience. In general, there was a solemnity about him that made him seem older than his years and a little . . . different.

"I'm not asking out of curiosity, Tim. I feel responsible in a way for Professor Linney's death, because of my article." It had run just last week, I'd realized this morning as I e-mailed my *Crime Sheet* column to my editor. It seemed like ages ago. "It's obvious that someone killed him. I think it was the same person who killed Margaret."

Tim pushed his glasses against the bridge of his nose. "Do the police know for a fact that she's dead?"

"I don't know." It wasn't my place to tell him about the tape. "Professor Linney had X rays taken four times in three months. Do you know anything about that?"

"I saw the ambulance at the house. Margaret told me her dad fell. He was lucky he didn't break anything. One time he stayed in the hospital for a few days."

"Professor Linney told people that Hank was abusing him. Did he tell you that, too?"

Bolt didn't reply, which was an answer in itself. He ran his thumbs over the rim of the coffee carton so hard that I thought the carton would ignite.

"I don't want this coming from me," he finally said. His voice shook with nervousness.

I nodded.

"Hank hit him," he said in a low, pained voice, as if the words themselves hurt. "He was angry because the Professor wouldn't give him a loan. He was angry in general, the Professor said. He showed me the bruises. On his arms, on his legs. Once, when Margaret wasn't home, Hank pushed him because he wasn't walking fast enough. He fell and sprained his ankle. He wanted to report him but Margaret begged him not to. Another time Hank pulled him so hard he dislocated the Professor's elbow." A vein twitched in Bolt's jaw. "I tried talking to Margaret. She told me the situation was complicated and she was taking care of it. I told her I hadn't meant to meddle. I didn't bring it up again." The heightened color in his face suggested that her dismissal had hurt.

I can't say I was shocked by what Tim Bolt had told me, but I felt let down. As I'd told Zack, I liked Hank and was reluctant to accept that I'd misread him. Ego, I suppose. As for Maggie . . . Love may be blind, but I couldn't understand how she'd allowed the abuse to continue, even for a day. I said that to Tim.

"I don't think she believed him at first," he told me. "Hank was careful never to do anything when she was home. But the day before she disappeared, the Professor told me she was going to see a divorce lawyer. So I guess she finally realized he was telling her the truth."

Tiler. I'd asked Hank, but he hadn't recognized the name. Maybe she'd gone to Elbogen to ask him about the abuse, abuse he'd overlooked, or ignored. No wonder he'd been anxious when I mentioned Maggie's coming to see him.

"You live next door, Tim. Did you hear something, see something or someone? . . ."

He caught his lower lip with his teeth. I had a fluttery feeling in my stomach.

"I should have told the police right away, but I was afraid of what Hank would do," he said. "And if I tell them now, I'll be in trouble for withholding information."

"What information?" My hands tingled.

He looked behind him for a second, so I did, too. Reflex. His anxiety was contagious. Then he leaned toward me. "The night she disappeared? I told you I didn't hear anything. But I did. I heard her scream."

"Did she say anything?" I held my breath.

"She screamed 'Stop! You're hurting me!' And then she yelled for her father. It was Hank. I know it."

"Did she say his name?"

Tim shook his head. "Who else could it be? He didn't deserve her. She was so beautiful, so kind. She was an angel. He didn't deserve her."

CHAPTER THIRTY-SEVEN

AN HOUR LATER I WAS IN MY APARTMENT, CLEANING UP after preparing the marble cake I'd just put in the oven (my sister Edie's recipe) and talking on the phone with Rico Hernandez. His nickel.

"You have a good friend in Detective Connors," he said. "He tells me you're discreet."

"Like a PriceWaterhouseCoopers accountant," I assured him. "I have a few questions I hope you'll answer."

"I hear you've interviewed several people about Professor Linney and his daughter."

So we were bartering again, but it was a friendlier marketplace. I told him much of what I'd learned, in no particular order: Reston and Modine were losing money on properties in

HARP areas. Modine had impersonated a cop and tried pumping the hairdresser about Margaret's last day. He'd made a pass at Margaret. Margaret had been anxious to place her father in a facility. She'd made a manicure appointment for the Saturday after she disappeared. Two people had phoned to cancel the First Aid caregiver.

Hernandez had known about Reston and Modine's financial problems and the two First Aid calls. One call was from Linney, he confirmed; the voice of the other caller had been muffled and distorted. The rest of my information he'd found interesting ("Is that so?") and helpful. I didn't tell him that Dr. Elbogen had seemed nervous or that Hank had been a possessive, jealous husband and abusive toward Linney and anxious to sell the house. Those were impressions—mine or someone else's—not facts. I didn't repeat what Tim had heard the night Maggie disappeared. Tim was certain the person who made her scream was Hank. I wasn't. And I didn't tell the detective what I suspected: that Oscar Linney had hidden his daughter's cell phone and lied to make his son-in-law suspicious. And if that was true, had he lied about everything else, including the abuse? But if that was so, why had Elbogen been so nervous?

Hernandez seemed particularly interested in the fact that Modine had come on to Margaret.

"Vaughan doesn't want Modine to find out he told me," I said. "I think he's afraid of the man."

"You had a run-in with him, too, I understand," Hernandez said without a trace of humor. "Mr. Vaughan needn't worry. Any of the guests at the party could have overheard Modine." He paused. "Well, all of this has been helpful. Thank you. Last time, you asked about the tape. I can tell you it was spliced together. Your instincts were right."

"I know. Hank Reston phoned me last night. I wish I were wrong." If this little gem was Hernandez's idea of bartering, I'd been suckered. "Did you happen to check Modine's alibi for the night of Margaret's death?"

Hernandez hesitated. "He was home alone, watching TV, as he was on the night Professor Linney died."

So Modine had no alibi. "Hank Reston told me he was in Vegas when his wife disappeared. Is that true?" I scraped the spatula against the mixing bowl.

"He checked into the hotel around seven. He phoned his wife from his room at a few minutes past ten P.M. She phoned his room at ten-thirty. Based on certain evidence, we assume that Mrs. Reston was assaulted just after one."

"The broken clock." I licked the chocolate off the spatula.

"Correct. That's a span of three hours. It's a five-hour drive from Vegas to Los Angeles, four and a half if you're in a hurry."

"Reston could have broken the clock to give himself an alibi." I did another swipe of the bowl. "He said he went to the casino after he called his wife. Are there records from the hotel garage that prove he did or didn't leave the premises?"

"He self-parked. A frugal man, Mr. Reston."

"Apparently." I licked the spatula and thought about that.

"Detective Connors told me you were sharp," Hernandez said. "I see he was right."

I have to admit I preened just a bit. "What about last Friday evening?"

"Mr. Reston drove to Irvine and stayed overnight. He had clients to see in the morning."

Irvine is in Orange County, a little over an hour away. I did a final scrape of the bowl, placed it in the sink, and filled it with hot, sudsy water. "Is he your prime suspect?"

"Everyone the victim knew or came in contact with is a suspect, Molly, until we can rule him or her out."

The only "her" I could think of was the housekeeper, and I couldn't see her killing Margaret and Linney. "Who else do you suspect?"

"Sorry."

I could tell that this particular shop was closed. "I understand that the accelerant used in the fire was paint thinner. Did you find out where it came from?"

"We found an empty can in a Dumpster in front of a nearby house that's being remodeled. The house isn't ready to be painted, and the workers claim none of them put the can there. So it may very well be the one we're looking for. Unfortunately, it's standard paint thinner that you can purchase in any home improvement store. We're having the container checked for fingerprints."

"The living room window was shattered—I assume by an object. Was that how the fire started? Do you think the HARP vandal was responsible and didn't know Linney was inside?" Everything I'd learned said no, but I needed to rule out the possibility.

"It's unlikely."

"Why not?"

Again, he hesitated. "This is not for public dissemination, Molly. Understood?"

"Understood." I leaned against the kitchen counter, tense with anticipation.

"Someone lit a rag-covered brick and threw it at the living room window. But that wasn't the cause and origin of the fire."

"How do you know?"

"The point of origin of a fire is the most heavily damaged area, the most burned. That was a wastebasket in the kitchen. We know that because fires burn upward and outward, and there was no damage under the wastebasket. There was extensive damage in the other downstairs rooms, including the living room, and less damage upstairs."

"So the arsonist started the fire inside the house. Were there any signs of forced entry?"

"None."

"Interesting."

"Very. The funeral is Sunday morning, by the way. I thought you'd want to know." He gave me the address of a chapel in Universal City.

I wrote down the information. "Getting back to Margaret Linney's disappearance. Did you find any fingerprints other than those belonging to family members?"

"Not in her bedroom, aside from the housekeeper's. We found nonfamily prints in the downstairs rooms and on the front and side doorknobs."

"Can you tell me whose?" I prompted when he didn't continue.

"Prints from people who often came to the house. Ned Vaughan, Roger Modine, Tim Bolt, Walter and Winnie Fennel. We have a number of as yet unidentified prints that may belong to guests at Linney's party."

"What about the prints on Margaret's planner?"

"Margaret Linney's, her husband's, her father's, Roger Modine's." Hernandez paused. "Yours."

I ignored the disapproval in his voice. "One more question? Did you use bloodhounds to try to find Margaret Linney?"

"We did. They picked up her scent and lost it within a few hundred yards of her house. And they found it at the neighbor's."

I frowned. "The neighbor's?"

"Mr. Bolt. Apparently, Margaret Reston was in his house several times, including the morning before she disappeared. They've known each other for many years."

"Right." I remembered Bolt saying something about Margaret borrowing a book and looking at a painting.

"You've talked to quite a few people," Hernandez said. "Have you formulated any ideas?"

I couldn't tell whether Hernandez was making fun of me or really interested. "Not yet. 'Truth is a slowpoke.' That's a Yiddish proverb my grandmother told me."

"'*La verdad ama la claridad.* Truth loves clarity.' That's what *my* grandmother always told me."

"Also nice."

"I prefer John Wycliffe. 'I believe that in the end the truth will conquer.' Let's hope he's right."

CHAPTER THIRTY-EIGHT

SABBATH CANDLE-LIGHTING THIS FRIDAY WAS AT FOUR thirty-one, but you have an extra eighteen minutes if you're in a crunch, which for me is almost all the time.

This Friday was no different. I'd spent the rest of the afternoon finishing the edits on my manuscript and FedExing the manuscript to my editor. Then I showered and packed, phoned my mom and Bubbie G to wish them a good *Shabbos,* and stopped by the magazine kiosk on Fairfax and Oakwood for a copy of *People* because mine hadn't arrived with the mail and I'm one of those "people who need *People*." So it was four thirty-six when I slowed over a speed bump, pulled into Mindy's driveway, and parked behind her blue Suburban.

Most of the Jewish world is more punctual. Driving to Martel I'd passed men and boys, and had seen more in the distance, all of them dressed in Sabbath suits and black hats or yarmulkes and walking toward Beverly Boulevard or along it, mini caravans heading to various neighborhood shuls. I wondered if one of those men up ahead was Zack.

My niece Aliza opened the side door for me. She's five years old, has Norm's blue eyes and Mindy's straight dark brown hair, wet now from her bath, and you can tell she's going to be as tall as her mom. Her three-year-old strawberry-blond-haired, blue-eyed sister, Isabel, was right behind her, a ratty-haired doll cradled in her arms, her thumb planted in her mouth.

"Can you please put this on the kitchen table, Aliza?" I placed the Saran-wrapped marble cake securely in her upturned small hands.

Isabel removed her thumb. "Can I have?"

"Later," said Aliza, a mom-in-training. "It's for *Shabbos*. Right, Aunt Molly?"

"Right. Don't run," I said as she started to.

I pulled my roll-aboard up the three steps into the service porch. Isabel trailed behind me as I hurried to the guest room and watched as I shut off my cell phone and stored my purse in the closet.

"Mommy lit candles," she told me.

"I'm going to do that right now."

"Mommy said I can watch."

Mindy had set two tea lights for me on a round silver tray on the cloth-covered dining room table, next to the sterling silver twin candelabra that Norm's parents, following tradition, had given her when they became engaged, and the matching smaller candlesticks they'd added when each of the children was born. I lit my tea lights, waved my hands around the flames three times before covering my eyes, and recited the blessing, followed by prayers for my family and a special one for Bubbie G.

Peace washed over me like a wave.

Mindy was upstairs changing Yitz. Norm kissed his daughters and hurried out the door, and I held them up, one little girl in each arm, so that they could wave at their daddy through the breakfast room window. I waved, too, and found myself looking at The Dungeon, which was disappearing against the darkening sky.

The girls helped me set the breakfast room table. After that we built a tower with Lego blocks (the large, hard-to-swallow size), and I read them *Corduroy*. They played in relative quiet as Mindy and I recited prayers and harmonized to welcome the Sabbath with "L'cha Dodi." Mindy had to warn Isabel only once not to pick up Yitz, who was reclining in his infant seat, his lids heavy with impending sleep.

Dinner was delicious—sweet and sour meatballs, chicken soup, corn-crumb-topped chicken, and a potato kugel (Bubbie G's *Shit arayn* recipe). Dessert was my marble cake, which I thought was a little dry and not as good as Edie's, but I had two slices and a few Linzer cookies. We sang throughout the meal, and talked, and Norm posed questions to Aliza about the weekly Torah portion she'd studied in school, rewarding her with a jelly bean for every correct answer. It's what my dad used to do every week, and I wondered what it would be like to sit at a Sabbath table with Zack and our children. Mindy caught my faraway expression.

"What are you thinking?" she asked, and I said, "Nothing," but from her smile I suspected that she knew.

At seven we were done. The rinsed dishes were in the dishwasher, where they would wait until Saturday night. Mindy was upstairs putting the girls to bed. Norm had dozed off on the family room sofa while reading the *Times,* and I was trying not to do the same. During the week I usually stay up late, sometimes till two or three in the morning, but Friday nights are a soporific.

My sister-in-law Gitty, the nutritionist, says it's the wine or grape juice and the heavy meal. I think it's the candles, and the knowledge that the week has truly come to an end and that I can step off the carousel and stop spinning.

By the time Mindy came downstairs Norm was snoring lightly. She sat down next to me, put her feet on the coffee table, and yawned.

"Get some sleep before you have to feed Yitz again," I told her.

"He'll be up in half an hour. And Isabel has been coming into our bedroom lately around four every morning. I vaguely remember what sleep was like. It must be nice."

"Poor baby." I stroked her forehead. "A little sibling jealousy, huh?"

"Well, a few days ago she asked me how long Yitz would be staying with us. Mom says I was the same when you were born, so I guess it's payback time." Mindy smiled. "Tell me about your day."

"I found out Reston and his wife had reciprocal powers of attorney. That's how he was able to put the Fuller house on the market."

Mindy yawned again. "Right, but before he closes the deal, he has to get a declaratory judgment from a court saying he has full authority over the property. Or he has to convince a title company to insure that he has the title to the property."

"What's the difference?"

"Time, and money. Going the court route requires a motion. That can take two to three months. Going through a title company is faster, but it may involve a higher fee. The title company needs to be indemnified in case the other party says, 'Whoa, I didn't want to sell my house.'"

"I get it."

"One more thing. The title company will only recognize the

power of attorney for six months to a year. After that, it's a different ball game."

I wondered aloud when Reston and his wife had given each other powers of attorney.

"You can check County Records in Norwalk," Mindy said.

"Fun. That's completely out of my way."

"Or, if Reston went through the title company, you can ask them to run the property. They'll be able to tell you."

I nodded. Something was tickling my memory. . . .

"Did you find out if Linney opened a home equity line of credit? Molly? Are you there?"

I looked at her. "Sorry. I'm trying to—" I stopped. "Tim Bolt."

"What?"

"The other night at the HARP meeting? Walter asked me to take him home, and Bolt said, 'It's out of Molly's way.' How would he know that unless he knows where I live?"

"He probably meant because he lives around the corner from Walter. Did you ever mention what neighborhood you lived in?"

"I don't think so. I may have, when we were talking about HARP areas." I narrowed my eyes, trying to replay our conversations, but came up blank. "I can't remember."

"So now you're wondering if he vandalized your car, right?" Mindy removed her legs from the table and sat up. "Why would he do that?"

"Maybe he doesn't like my asking so many questions."

"Why would he care?"

"I don't know. He was close to the family. Maybe he doesn't want me digging up dirt about Maggie."

Mindy considered. "I think you're reading into this, Molly. You tend to do that."

"True. And 'Back off, bitch' isn't something Bolt would say,

I don't think. He's very quiet, a little intense. Maybe he left the flyers."

She wrinkled her forehead. "What flyers?"

I told her. "They don't have a threatening sound, Min. More like warning me to be careful. Maybe he's worried for me but is afraid to tell me 'cause he'd have to explain. Anyway." I shook my head to clear it. "What were you saying?"

"I asked if you checked into Linney and HELC."

"I didn't have time. It's like a credit card against the property, right? Suppose Linney had a line of credit. If he transferred the deed to the house to his daughter, what happens to the line of credit?"

"Depends how he did it. If the transfer went through escrow, then the line of credit would be closed and he'd have to pay off any outstanding loan. But he could have transferred ownership by filling out a Grant Deed form you can buy in any stationery store. He'd have to sign the form in front of a notary public, take it to County Records, pay a document fee, and file it. If he did that, the line of credit would stay open."

"And he could have withdrawn monies against the property."

"Right."

"For Skoll Investment, which as far as I can figure, doesn't exist. So where's the money?"

I was still thinking about that later as I was reading, yet again, about the royal family in my *People*. Norm had gone upstairs. Mindy had nursed and diapered a sleeping Yitz and was going to bed.

"Maybe I'll be lucky and get two hours," she said. In the doorway she turned around. "I almost forgot, Molly. I checked out your Mr. Tiler."

"A divorce attorney. I know. Thanks anyway."

"Intellectual properties."

I put down my magazine. "You're sure?"

"Only one with that name in the L.A. area. I have his address and phone number if you want to contact him. Gordon Tiler. Didn't you say Margaret Linney composed music? Maybe she wanted to protect her material."

"But why the exclamation points next to his name?"

Mindy covered her yawn with her hand. "Ask me tomorrow, when I have a functioning brain."

The problem with going to sleep early Friday nights is that I often wake up around one or two in the morning. Tonight I woke up a little after ten. I hadn't even slept three hours. Too much on my mind, including lunch tomorrow with Zack's parents.

Unlike weekdays, when I can watch an old movie or sit at my computer to write or play online mah jongg, on the Sabbath I can't do any activity that requires my turning on electricity. It sounds like an inconvenience, I know, and there was a time when that's how I regarded it, but I've come to appreciate it for what it is: a reminder that the day is special, a separation from the rest of the week, an opportunity to reconnect with the spiritual.

Still, I was the only one awake in a house that was dark except for nightlights in the bathrooms and halls, and the only sound was the *tick, tick, tick* of the clock on the nightstand. Lying on my back, I tried to trick myself back to sleep by sorting the bits of information floating around in my head. Modine and Reston and HARP. Linney and the cell phone. Grant Deeds and Home Equity Lines of Credits. Margaret's planner. All part of a pattern, like the winding ribbon in my computer's screen saver that changes color and size and has no discernible beginning or end.

The photocopied pages of Margaret's planner were in my purse. I left the warm comfort of the bed, slipped into my robe, and took the pages into the dining room.

The candles were still flickering, casting shadows on the walls. I placed the booklet on the table and read the pages for the fourth or fifth time. I don't know what I was expecting—some sort of epiphany, I suppose. But I was no wiser when I finished, just more frustrated.

At least two puzzles had been solved. Tiler and HELC. I hadn't noticed the little mark and the curve that had turned the *P* into a *C* until Mindy pointed it out. Reston hadn't either. "Banking is hell, everybody needs help," he'd said when I'd asked him about it. But wouldn't he have known there was a line of credit against the property?

A candle sputtered and died. I looked again at the entry. The little mark was faint, but there. Photocopies will sometimes pick up marks that aren't noticeable on the original.

It occurred to me that Hank could have erased the *C*, or part of it. Turned it into a *P* and rendered the entry meaningless.

I didn't recall seeing bank statements in the same folder that held the correspondence from Skoll Investment, but at the time I hadn't thought to look.

If Hank had altered one entry, had he altered others? I thought about the page that wasn't there, the one he claimed Maggie had ripped out.

I went through the planner, scrutinizing every letter of every entry and noticed little flecks between the letters of one: *Check out Sub-Zero.* I peered at the entry, then went into the dark kitchen and to the utility drawer where I groped around and found the magnifying glass Mindy keeps there.

With the magnifier, the flecks were larger, but they were still flecks. I was certain that Hank had erased the original entry and replaced it with *Check out Sub-Zero.*

Maybe not. Margaret may have erased it because she'd changed her plans. That's probably why she'd used pencil, not pen.

But Margaret wouldn't have changed the *C* into a *P.*

Even though I was wearing my velour robe, I felt cold. I returned the magnifying glass to its drawer, and myself to my bed, where I thought about Hank Reston.

A man I liked. A man who had asked me to find out what had happened to the wife he passionately loved.

A man who had probably tampered with her planner to keep me from finding out some truth, who told me he had "buckets of money" when he was having financial problems.

A man who had been reluctant to give me the name of the home health care agency that had received two calls instructing the caregiver not to show that Friday morning.

And the fact that he'd asked me to help him?

He could have done it to keep tabs on me and what I learned, and divert suspicion from himself. I'd told Connors that Reston had no reason to vandalize my car. After all, he'd asked me to investigate. But what if he'd slashed my tires and left a threat knowing I'd think exactly that?

I recalled being pleasantly surprised when Reston had left me alone to search through Linney's possessions. *Come to my house, look through anything you want, I have nothing to hide.* Saddam Hussein had said the same thing.

Maybe Reston had wanted me to find the tape.

He could have "found" it. It would be natural for him to go through his father-in-law's possessions. But unless I'd misread Hernandez, Reston was a prime suspect, and the police would have regarded his discovery more suspiciously.

But if someone else discovered the tape . . . a tape that the police would find to have been spliced, a tape that would give credence to the probability that Margaret Linney was dead, and allow the grieving widower to inherit her estate. And Linney's, now that he was dead, too. And be reimbursed by the insurance company for several million dollars' worth of stolen jewels.

CHAPTER THIRTY-NINE

Saturday, November 15. 12:30 P.M. Corner of La Brea Avenue and Venice Boulevard. A woman approached a man at a gas station and said, "You raped Saddam bin Laden." She then took out a knife and attempted to stab him before running off westbound on Venice. The suspect is described as a 40- to 49-year-old Caucasian woman standing 5 feet 6 inches tall and weighing 170 pounds, with brown hair and green eyes. (Wilshire)

HAVING LUNCH WITH ZACK'S PARENTS WAS LIKE GETTING six stitches under my chin, which I did one summer in camp: The anticipation was worse than the actuality, but I'd be lying if I told you the process was painless.

It wasn't that I didn't know his parents. Zack had introduced me to them three months ago at the shul's meet-the-new-rabbi dinner, and I say hello whenever I attend services at Zack's shul. (I'd first seen them at Zack's high school graduation reception, when I forced my friend Aggie to stroll with me past the Abrams family tableau. Several times. Seventeen-year-old girls with broken hearts do pathetic things, though come to think of it, there's no age limit on "pathetic.") Anyway, they're always warm and friendly. But now I would be in their home and, as Chef Emeril would say, Zack and I were "kicking it up a notch."

Since Wednesday night I'd built myself up to a state of nervousness that not even the strongest antiperspirant could have helped. Reason told me Zack's parents wanted to like me as much as I wanted to like them: He's an only child, thirty years old, and they're probably *chaleshing* for him to marry and provide them with grandchildren. My experience with Ron's parents, decent people understandably blind to their son's faults, told me the same thing. But reason and experience are powerless against my insecurity and tendency to overanalyze, insidious Merlins who turn truth into illusion and illusion into truth.

They'd probably checked me out with people in the community who knew my family or of them. (My parents had done the same with their prospective sons-in-law and daughter-in-law. It's the norm.) So they knew that I was divorced, that I'd left Orthodoxy for a few years. And if they'd vetted me with Rabbi Ingel, my high school Bible teacher, they'd no doubt come away with a less-than-flattering picture of "that Blume girl," which is how he'd refer to me. Then again, I had a few things to say about the rabbi.

"Larry and I think it's so sweet that you and Zack dated in high school, and now you're seeing each other again," his mother said when were seated around a table set with gold-rimmed cobalt dishes and crystal stemware on a white cut-lace cloth that I prayed I wouldn't be the first to stain.

His mother's name is Sandy. She's around five-four, a little chunky around the waist (or maybe it was the boxy cut of her brown bouclé suit jacket), and has brown eyes and short auburn hair that Zack told me she covers only in shul. Her hem, I noted, was just at the knee. She's fifty-seven, two years younger than Larry, who looks like an older version of Zack, with the same gray-blue eyes and more silver in his black hair and a crocheted yarmulke instead of Zack's black suede one. (The kind of yarmulke you wear—crocheted in any color or combination thereof, with or without the wearer's initials in Hebrew or English; black suede or black velvet; teeny, medium, large—is an indicator of where you belong in the world of Orthodox Judaism. But that's a chapter in itself.)

Sandy and Larry are both attorneys (she handles bankruptcies, he does insurance litigation), which is why they were disappointed when Zack turned down their alma mater, Harvard Law, and they have concerns about the pressures and politics that go with being a pulpit rabbi. I know this from Zack, not his parents. They joined the shul when he replaced the retiring rabbi, and I can see Sandy beaming when Zack delivers his weekly Torah *drash,* so I guess they've come to terms with his career choice. I hoped that boded well for accepting his romantic choice, too.

Zack had warned me that his parents were more formal than mine. They were more soft-spoken, too, which I suppose is natural when you're a family of three, not nine, and you don't have to yell to be heard or get your point across. Or maybe like me, they were on their best behavior.

They asked about my parents and siblings and what it was like growing up in such a large family. ("War and peace," I said, and was relieved when they laughed.) They were interested in how I'd decided to become a journalist and said they occasionally enjoyed my feature articles. (I gnawed on the *occasionally.*

Did they mean they didn't always have a chance to read them, or that they liked only *some* of the articles?)

Zack had bought them a copy of *Out of the Ashes,* and Sandy wanted to know whether I'm ever nervous interviewing convicted criminals or suspects.

"All the time," I told her. BACK OFF, BITCH flashed on and off in front of my eyes, neon red words on a giant marquee. "But I'm very cautious."

Zack's parents were probably assessing how safe he'd be around me, worrying that he'd hooked up with a Modern Orthodox La Femme Nikita. I wondered if they knew I'd almost been killed.

I'm giving you the highlights. Interspersed among the questions we talked about less personal subjects—movies, an exhibit they'd just seen at the Skirball museum, historic preservation around the country (Harvard Square, they told me, was on the endangered list), the crisis in Israel and the worrisome rise of anti-Semitism in Europe and around the world. Basically, though, it was an interview. They wanted to know as much as they could about the woman their only son had brought home. I didn't blame them, but I felt a little on edge. Had I been too flip? Had I talked too much? Revealed too much? I imagine it's like giving testimony in a deposition: You probably don't remember half of what you said, and regret the other half.

Sometime during the main course—cold roast beef, a cucumber salad, and linguini—the interview was over. Zack and his dad started discussing the Torah portion, *VaYerah,* the one where Abraham is asked to sacrifice his beloved son Isaac to prove his love for God. Sandy joined in. I enjoyed their animated discussion—it reminded me of the way my dad and my brother Judah go at it—and I found myself relaxing and actually tasting the food, which I'd been pushing around on my beautiful plate.

At some point, I'm embarrassed to say, my mind strayed to

Hank Reston and the adulterated entries in Maggie's planner. I hadn't resolved any of the questions that had plagued me last night, and when I awoke, I had a few more:

If Hank had killed Maggie and taken the planner, why had he returned it to the nightstand drawer? Did it contain something he wanted the police, or me, to learn so that we'd be led off the track?

If he *hadn't* taken the planner, who had? And why did that person return it?

And if—

"What do *you* think, Molly?" Larry asked.

I blinked and faced him. "Sorry?"

Sandy was looking at me. So was Zack.

"If Abraham believed God's promise," Larry said, "that He would make him into a mighty nation through Isaac, then how could he believe God really wanted him to *kill* Isaac?"

Fifteen years of Jewish studies, and my mind was a blank. I pictured Rabbi Ingel's smirk. "Faith," I said, because I had to say something, and because it's often the right answer.

Larry thought for a moment, then nodded. "Good answer."

Dessert was next. I'd offered to help before, but this time Sandy accepted. In the kitchen—a square, sunny room with white cabinets and a country French décor that matched the rest of what I'd seen in the single-story house—she handed me an ice cream scoop and brought up Ron.

"I know he and Zack were good friends," she said, slipping a slice of home-baked apple pie onto a plate. "It must be hard for you to see him when you come to shul."

"It's awkward, but we're managing." I placed a ball of nondairy vanilla ice cream next to the pie.

She was obviously fishing for The Reason. She wanted to assess responsibility. I wanted to alleviate her concern, but I rarely discuss Ron's infidelity. And I was pleased Zack hadn't betrayed my confidence.

"I'm glad." She put another slice of pie on a plate. "Can I be honest, Molly?"

Never a great opener. "Of course."

"Zack has been incredibly happy since he started seeing you, and we can certainly see why he's so taken with you. Everything he told us is true. You're lovely, Molly, and bright. And funny." She smiled.

If there was a *but,* I hoped she'd get to it and be done with it. I dug the scoop into the softening ice cream.

"He also told us you have reservations about being a rabbi's wife. I don't blame you. It's not an easy life, and it's not for everyone. People will always be watching you. What you say, what you do, how you dress. Zack said he told you he was engaged four years ago?"

I wondered where this was going. "Yes." Her name was Shani. They'd been introduced by a rabbi while Zack was studying for his ordination in New York, after he'd returned from Israel. He hadn't told me much else.

"She's a rabbi's daughter," Sandy said. "Larry and I met her, of course. She's beautiful, refined, intelligent. She would have made a perfect rabbi's wife. Did he tell you what happened?"

A rabbi's daughter. "He said she broke it off. He said it just didn't work out."

Sandy nodded. "I phoned her to see if I could help them patch things, although I had no idea what needed patching. Zack wouldn't tell us anything, but she did. Do you know why she broke off the engagement, Molly?"

I shook my head. She was going to give me the answer. I could think of two possibilities, neither of which I liked: (A) Even though Shani was a rabbi's daughter, she wasn't willing to be a pulpit rabbi's wife, in which case how could I possibly hope to do it? (B) Zack hadn't been religious enough for her, or his background prestigious enough, and he'd decided to set his sights lower, to compromise, but I wasn't really what he wanted.

"She realized he wasn't in love with her," Sandy said. "He'd been infatuated with the idea of marrying a rabbi's daughter and living the perfect life. She said he knew it, too. So she broke off the engagement because he would never have done it. He wouldn't have wanted to hurt her or cause her or her family embarrassment."

That was so like the Zack I'd come to know, I thought. But all I said was, "Oh."

"All those years he was away?" Sandy said. "He'd have me mail him everything you published. Every article, every column, every review. Your book. He didn't tell you?"

"No." My face tingled.

"When we told him B'nai Yeshurun was looking for a new rabbi, he didn't even ask about the salary." Sandy took the ice cream scoop from me and released the ice cream onto the plate. Then she took both my hands in hers. "He came home for you, Molly. He's been looking for you."

"How do you know?" I asked.

"Faith." Sandy smiled. "And he told me."

The house was quiet when Zack walked me back to Mindy's, and I figured that everyone was taking a Shabbat nap. I let myself in and did the same, and was surprised when Mindy woke me and told me it was time for havdalah.

"So how did it go?" she asked.

"They like me, they really like me."

She punched my shoulder. "Come on."

"It went great."

After havdalah I packed, kissed Mindy and the kids, and drove home. Inside my apartment I looked through my mail and checked my answering machine. Four messages—three from telemarketers, one from Ned Vaughan. He sounded stressed. I tried his number, but it was busy.

I showered and dressed and had my coat in my hand before Zack rang the front doorbell at a quarter to seven. We were headed for his car when Isaac came out and called my name. I turned around and smiled at his Big Bird parka.

"Next time you have a problem with the phone, you ought to tell me first," he said.

My smile disappeared. I walked back to the porch. "What are you talking about, Isaac?"

"This guy came around on Friday, after you left. He said you reported static on your line, from the rain. All I'm saying, Molly, is next time let me know."

I stood there for a moment, unable to speak. I swallowed hard. "Did you let him into my apartment, Isaac?"

"No way, José." Isaac pursed his lips. "Something's missing, you'll blame me. That's why I said, let me know."

"I didn't report a problem with the phone, Isaac."

Zack had walked over and was standing next to me. "What's going on, Molly?"

Isaac's jaw dropped open. "It's the guy who did that to your car, right? I knew it!"

"What car?" Zack said. "What guy?"

"Someone vandalized her Acura a couple days ago," Isaac said. "She didn't tell you? The cops were here and everything."

"I didn't want you to worry," I told Zack. I turned to Isaac. "What did this guy look like?"

"I couldn't tell. It was dark out, and he was wearing a jacket with a hood."

"Was he a big man?" I was thinking about Reston and Modine. And, yes, Tim Bolt and Ned Vaughan. Anyone I'd talked to in connection with Margaret Linney's disappearance. Fear has no logic.

Isaac narrowed his eyes. "Like I said, it was dark. He was tall, I think."

That didn't tell me much. Isaac is around five-six, so just about anyone would appear tall to him.

"I knew he was up to no good!" Isaac said with the surety of hindsight. "I saw him walking around the back, so I came out and asked what he was doing. He said you'd reported static, and all that, and he needed to check the wires inside the house. I did good, huh?"

CHAPTER FORTY

Sunday, November 16. 10:22 P.M. 6300 block of Green Valley Circle. When the results of an apartment complex's board elections were announced, a man complained, "The crooks are back on the board." When another resident told him he could always move, the loser stepped on his neighbor's feet and punched him in the temple. (Culver City)

NED VAUGHAN WAS THE LAST TO SPEAK AT THE FUNERAL. He followed several of Linney's colleagues from the University of Southern California, who talked about the Professor's directness and intelligence and sharp sense of humor, and a portly, gray-haired dean who went on and on about Linney's contribution to the field of architecture and to the university. Ned's eulogy was more personal, more eloquent. Tears streamed down his cheeks and he choked up a number of times as he narrated anecdotes about the man who had been his mentor and friend.

The room, overly air-conditioned and scented by sprays of flowers, was practically filled, mostly with people I didn't know. Colleagues and students, I assumed; the friends who'd attended all those parties. I did know some people. The board members I'd seen the other night—Brenda, Nancy, the woman whose name I couldn't remember and who'd barely said a word. Jeremy Dorn. Linda Cobern was sitting next to a distinguished man whom I finally recognized as Bruce Harrington. Elbogen was there, too. I saw the doctor when I entered the chapel. He looked startled when our eyes met and quickly averted his head.

I was sitting toward the back with Winnie and Walter. Winnie was composed and magnificent in black velour, like a giant cat. Walter's eyes were red and his nose was leaking. Every few seconds he blotted it with a balled handkerchief, although a few times I watched nervously as a drop clung to his nostril, and hoped the handkerchief would get there before the drop fell to his lips and he did his tongue sweep. Tim Bolt was across the aisle to my right. He'd been sniffling throughout the service, and at one point had bowed his head and sobbed. Having lived next door to Linney all these years, he probably felt the loss more than anyone else in the room.

"Tim's taking it real bad," Fennel said, looking at Bolt and echoing my thoughts. "His own dad wasn't around much, so maybe he saw Oscar like a replacement. Plus he takes things hard in general."

Roger Modine was a few rows up. He'd scowled at me as he'd passed my pew, looking stiff and uncomfortable in a navy sports jacket that strained across his barrel chest. Last night I'd speculated about the possibility that the contractor had tried to gain access to my apartment. He'd impersonated a police detective to obtain information about Margaret's last day. Maybe he was worried that I'd discovered something that would incriminate him. Like what? I wondered again now.

Hank Reston was sitting in the first pew, of course. He'd greeted me when I arrived and thanked me for coming, but I could tell he was distracted. He hadn't delivered a eulogy, but he'd introduced those who had. He'd probably arranged for the funeral, too. According to Walter, with Margaret gone there was no one else to do it.

"Oscar has a sister-in-law," Walter told me. "Vivian. But she and Oscar haven't talked in years, not since Roberta died. A shame, too, because Margaret loved her and it probably would've been good for her to have a woman around. I thought maybe she'd be here today, but I don't see her."

After the service, which was closed casket, I waited in the foyer to sign the guest book. There were five people ahead of me. Out of the corner of my eye I saw Ned Vaughan. He was a few feet away with an attractive blond woman who had her arm linked through his. The girlfriend, I thought. He had his eyes on Roger Modine, who was talking with Linda Cobern. Then Ned turned his head and saw me.

A moment later he was at my side, alone. "I left a message on your answering machine," he said, his voice tight with accusation.

"I tried phoning you Saturday night, but your line was busy. Was there something you forgot to tell me?"

"Detective Hernandez came to see me Friday afternoon about Modine. I asked you not to involve me. Aren't reporters supposed to protect their sources?" A vein pulsed in his forehead.

"You asked me not to tell Hank. I didn't. But you don't have to worry. Hernandez pointed out that there were a lot of people at the party who could have overheard Modine. He promised he wouldn't tell Modine how he knows. I think you can trust him."

Ned's smile was grim. "I don't have a choice, do I?"

"By the way, Margaret consulted an intellectual rights attorney. Do you know if that was related to her music?"

"I suppose so. I don't know." He reached into his jacket pocket, pulled out a pack of cigarettes, and put it back. "I'm going outside for a smoke."

I signed the guest book. I didn't see Winnie and Walter. They were probably walking to the burial site. I was heading to my car when I saw Porter with the USC dean. The dean was doing the talking. Porter was nodding and looked bored to death. I hoped he wouldn't notice me, but of course, he did.

A second or so later he was standing in front of me. The morning sun brought out the glints in his blond hair, the kind I pay good money for.

He planted his feet apart, the way he probably does in target practice or when he's about to take someone down. He oozed male authority. "Why am I not surprised that you're here, Blume?"

"Because you're psychic?" That annoyed him, but I didn't care. "You're here, too."

"Police business. Standard procedure."

"Well, you should thank me. I gave you an excuse to get away from the dean. He does go on, doesn't he?"

Porter scowled. "I hear you've been kissing up to Detective Hernandez."

"We exchanged information. I can kiss up to you, too, if you want. I wouldn't want you to feel left out."

He leaned toward me. "I don't like your attitude, Blume."

"If it makes you feel better, you're not the only one. Did you want to tell me something, Detective, or are you just determined to give me a hard time?"

"Your friend Hank Reston is offering a hundred thousand dollars for information that leads to the discovery of his wife's body."

"I heard the news on the way here." It had me thinking again that with Linney dead—and soon buried—it was an opportune time for someone to "find" Margaret's body. "He offered a reward before, right after his wife disappeared. And he's not my friend, by the way. He—"

"I'm surprised you haven't found the body yet. You've been digging around enough." Emphasis on the *digging*.

"And that bothers you?" I'd been about to tell him about the alterations in the planner, but now I was annoyed. Let him find them on his own.

"This is a lark for you, isn't it, showing up the cops? It'll make good material for one of your articles."

First Elbogen, then Linda Cobern. I was fed up with being maligned. "Have I published *one word* since the fire?"

"Oh, you will." He nodded and smiled a smug little smile.

"When I get the green light, not one minute before. I'm not trying to show anyone up. And this isn't a lark. You're probably aware that I've been threatened. I'd kinda like to know by whom."

"Why don't you let us find out?"

"Like you found out who killed Aggie Lasher?" That just slipped out. "I'm sorry. That wasn't fair."

He gazed at me as though I were a spider he was considering stomping on. "We don't need you interfering with this investigation, Blume."

"How have I interfered? I've interviewed people. That's my right. I've advised them to talk to the police and turn in evidence, like the tape of Margaret Reston's phone call, and her planner. I'd call that helping."

"And now your fingerprints are all over the planner *and* the tape. I'll ask the mayor to give you a medal."

"Which is why I had my prints rolled after I talked to Detective Hernandez, so that you could eliminate them."

"We did. But if you'd called us when you found the planner, instead of playing hot potato with it, we wouldn't be dealing with a dozen other fingerprints."

"Look, I had no idea that the planner had been missing or that you guys hadn't seen it. The whole place was fingerprinted. I found the planner in the nightstand. Roger Modine took it from me. He handed it to Hank Reston. That's three, by the way, plus Margaret makes it four, not a dozen." I shouldn't have added the last, but my mouth has a way of working independently of my brain.

"And the tape? When you found it you already suspected that Linney had been murdered. You must've figured no one else had seen it. But did you leave it for us to handle?" Porter snorted.

I had a retort all ready, but I swallowed it. Porter was right. I'd screwed up. "I'm sorry. I didn't know what was on it, but you're right."

"Sorry doesn't mean shit, Blume. What's done is done."

"I touched the plastic cassette, not the tape. Detective Hernandez said it was spliced. Did you find prints on the tape?"

"You two are such buddies, why don't you ask him?"

"I will. By the way, were Reston's prints on the cassette?"

"Like I said—"

"Come on, Porter. Tell me, and I'll give you something in return. Deal?"

"You already talked your heart out to Hernandez."

"This is new." I could see a flicker of indecision in his blue-blue eyes. "It's about Margaret's planner."

"What about it?"

"First tell me about the prints."

"I don't think so."

I could tell he wasn't bluffing. I deliberated for about a second, then told him about the changes.

"The lab boys downtown have equipment that can probably make out what was there," Porter said. "You can't remember what you read instead of the Sub-Zero thing?"

I shook my head. "I only saw it for a second. So about the cassette. Were Reston's prints on it?" For a moment I thought Porter wasn't going to answer.

Then he nodded. "He says Linney asked him to change the answering machine tape a few days before he died. So of course, his prints would be on it."

"Of course."

Porter's tone was bland, and I couldn't tell if he was being sarcastic. It was the answer I'd expected, but not the one I'd wanted.

CHAPTER FORTY-ONE

NOTHING HAD BEEN DONE TO THE FULLER HOUSE SINCE I'd been here a week ago. The plywood still covered the bottom half of the living room window. The front door was still ravaged, and the blackened stucco, more visible in the bright sunlight, made the house stiff competition for The Dungeon.

Oscar Linney would have cried.

The For Sale sign was gone, I noticed as I walked to the front door. Either Reston had removed it while the house underwent repairs, or he'd taken it off the market and planned to rebuild with the insurance money.

I slipped my hand through the gaping hole in the front door and turned the knob. This time I wasn't trespassing. I'd told Reston I planned to visit the house again, and he'd said, no problem.

The air still smelled of smoke, but I didn't feel as though I was choking. According to Hernandez, the fire had begun in the kitchen. I hadn't looked there before. I did now, but there wasn't much to see—just a black, sooty shell. I left quickly and headed for the stairs. Someone—probably one of Modine's men—had nailed plywood onto the two missing steps. With the bright light pouring in through the dining room windows and through the pane of glass above the front door, the steps looked less treacherous, but I had come directly from the funeral in two-inch Jimmy Choo heels and was careful with every tread.

I went directly to Linney's study, where a week's accumulation of ash had turned the dark wood furniture into a putty color. I searched through his desk drawers for anything I might have missed—letters, bank statements, correspondence about Skoll Investment. I hadn't really expected to find anything, but I felt a twinge of disappointment when I didn't. I had no better results in Linney's bedroom, and though I suspected I'd be equally unsuccessful in Margaret's room, I went there anyway.

The room smelled of lavender and jasmine. I sniffed the air. Perfume. The scent was strong.

Last week I'd assumed that the housekeeper had paid special attention to Margaret's room. Last week I'd believed that Reston was grieving for his missing wife, and speculated that he was keeping hope alive by preserving her room and her possessions.

But if Reston killed her? If he was contemplating razing the house, why would he send the housekeeper here?

I ran my finger across the top of Margaret's desk. There was only the faintest hint of ash.

Maybe it wasn't the housekeeper. Maybe Reston had been coming here. Every few days, daily. Dusting and perfuming, maintaining the room so that it looked as it had before Margaret disappeared.

Before she betrayed him?

I glanced at the bed. The white slippers were still there, waiting for Margaret to slip her feet into them.

Control, I thought, not love.

A husband who preserves the illusion of a perfect wife. A duke who veils the portrait of his late duchess, "looking as if she were alive," so that no one else can view her.

I went into the dressing room. The perfume bottles were dusted, the lipsticks circled around the vanity set. The comb, the brush with the mother-of-pearl handle.

A new mirror, exactly like the one Modine had broken. The contractor had offered to repair the mirror, or replace it. Reston had turned down the offer, but maybe Modine had done it anyway.

I didn't like thinking about Modine, particularly in this narrow dressing room where he'd trussed me like a chicken. I left the room and was heading for the stairs when I heard a shout from outside Linney's old office.

The French windows were open. I walked over and looked down at the garage where Margaret kept her studio and the garden where Tim Bolt had last seen her. No one was there. Another shout drew my attention to the neighboring yard to the left and the father and son who were playing ball.

"No fair!" the dark-haired boy yelled as he raced after the ball, which had sailed over his head.

I stood there awhile, smiling as I watched them. I don't know what made me look up. I can't say I felt someone watching me, but it was something like that. When I did, I saw a woman at the third-story window of the charcoal gray house kitty-corner to Linney's.

Our eyes met for a brief moment. Then a curtain covered the window and she was gone.

CHAPTER FORTY-TWO

I HALF WALKED, HALF RAN TO SECOND STREET, THEN TO Martel, where I rounded the corner and continued down the block until I was almost in front of The Dungeon.

I was out of breath, more from excitement than exertion. I slowed my pace, but my heart was pumping double-time as I stepped onto a narrow, cracked concrete aisle between two rows of junglelike shrubs. Vines grabbed at me and caught my hair, and for a moment I flashed to the man-eating plants in *Little Shop of Horrors,* a film that had truly terrified me. I pulled my hair free and pushed the vines away and finally arrived at the weathered black front door. I held my hand over the bell, and hesitated.

I knew I was being silly. It was daylight. People were nearby, some of whom had eyed me with curiosity as I'd galloped down

the block in my designer heels. I'm twenty-nine years old, I don't
believe in witches, but I felt as though I were seven again, whis-
pering with my friends about the bad guys inside the dark house.

I rang the bell.

Charlene Coulter. She was the woman I'd just seen in the
window of the three-story house on Martel, the only three-story
in the neighborhood. The last time I'd stood in front of the
French windows in Linney's office, night had been falling and I
hadn't seen anything. I hadn't been looking. I'd been concentrating on sucking in fresh air to dispel the smoke that had been
choking me.

I rang the bell again. I knew she was there. She couldn't
have disappeared.

She was the author of the flyers. I was certain of it. "I watch,
and am as a sparrow alone upon the house top." I'd looked that
one up in my *Bartlett's*. It's from Psalms 102:7. She had seen
something. She wanted to tell me about it, or why had she left
the flyers?

"She steals little boys like me and turns them into bats!" said
a young male voice.

I started and turned around too quickly, bending my right
ankle in the process. Pain shot up my leg.

"You're being silly, Kevin," a man said to a towheaded
youngster perched on a bright green bike.

"It's true!"

"It's not true." He turned to me and smiled. "Kids. She
doesn't like people bothering her, though."

I nodded. "I appreciate it. Thanks."

He shrugged and walked on.

I rang the bell again and again. I don't know why, but I
thought about poor, dead Oscar Linney, who had stood at the
door to his dream house, ringing the bell, rapping on the door
with his cane, begging his daughter to let him in.

Finally I gave up. I wrote my name and phone number on a piece of paper and slipped it under the black door.

According to the "Home" section in this morning's L.A. *Times,* Central Realty had numerous open houses this Sunday in Miracle Mile North. I'd jotted down the addresses before leaving for Linney's funeral. Now I drove to the nearest one, a two-story, red-tiled Spanish on Vista north of Beverly Boulevard.

The Realtor, a fortyish woman with blond hair and too-red lipstick, was in the dining room talking with a couple. I picked up a specs sheet, returned to the center hall, and walked up the stairs. A black couple was coming down the stairs. We exchanged smiles as we passed each other.

I love looking at houses, especially houses like this one that are well kept. I love taking in their character, imagining their secrets, exploring the nooks and crannies that make them special. I strolled through the rooms, sighed at the spacious closets, and walked down the stairs.

The Realtor was standing near the open front door with the first couple. "If you're interested, I'd make an offer. And I wouldn't wait. This is a beauty, and at the price, someone's going to grab it."

The price, I'd seen from the prospectus, was $759,000.

The Realtor turned to me and treated me to a wide smile. "My name is Dawn. Did you look around? Can I answer any questions?"

The couple I'd passed on the stairs had reappeared. They stood a few feet away, waiting their turn.

"You listed a two-story on Fuller between First and Second," I said. "I didn't see the sign when I drove by."

Dawn was immediately subdued. "There was a terrible fire, and someone died." Then, without a beat, "This house has an almost identical floor plan and several hundred more square feet. Did you see the bonus room upstairs?"

"It's lovely. Do you know whether that house will be for sale again?"

"Actually, the owner has taken it off the market permanently. He's rebuilding."

"I understand that it was taken off the market once before. When did it go on the market the second time?"

She looked puzzled. "Why?"

"Just curious."

"I don't know. I'd have to check at the office."

"It was the middle of June," said the woman who was waiting with her husband.

I turned to her.

"Jim and I loved that house," she told me. "We made an offer the first time it was on the market, but someone outbid us. Then that deal fell through, and we heard the house wasn't for sale. But I kept checking. When I heard it was available again, we were ready to buy."

"Why didn't you?"

She exchanged a glance with her husband. "He talked us out of it."

I frowned. "The owner?"

"The Realtor. Bolt. He told us the owner's wife was kidnapped, maybe killed. He said they found her blood in the house."

"That's the law," Dawn said. "We're obligated to reveal information about any crime that has taken place on the property."

The woman nodded. "We told him we didn't care. We figured that would lower the price. He kept telling us about other properties, how they were better for our needs. The fact that he lives next door had nothing to do with it, right?"

"Are you saying Mr. Bolt didn't want you to buy the house?" Dawn said. "Why would he do that?"

The black woman smiled. "Oh, I can't imagine." She turned to her husband. "Can you, Jim?"

Zack was preparing for a speech he had to deliver this evening at a bar mitzvah reception, so I was on my own. I spent the rest of the afternoon straightening up my apartment and doing laundry. Then I visited Gitty and Judah and played with Yechiel, who is almost a year old and is starting to walk and talk.

I was too lazy to cook and didn't feel like eating out alone, though I've done it many times and usually don't mind. I was feeling a little blue because of the day. Linney's funeral in the morning, my visit to the Fuller house. Tim Bolt turning out to be a bigot.

I went to my parents'. Noah was out with his girlfriend, and Joey with his. Liora was on a date with a young man from Baltimore. So it was just the three of us, and it was nice. We ate leftovers and watched *The Sopranos*. There was one explicit scene where Tony was really going at it with one of his girlfriends. I was a little embarrassed having my dad in the room, and I think he was embarrassed, too. Fathers and daughters . . .

Then I went home. Isaac popped out of his door to tell me he'd been on the lookout and everything was "hunky-dory." I checked the apartment anyway, my heart beating a little faster as I turned on the lights in every room and made sure nothing was out of place.

There were two messages on my answering machine. Zack had phoned from the bar mitzvah, "Just to say hi," and asked me to call him back on his cell. I knew he wanted to make sure I was all right, and though I pride myself on being independent, I have to say I liked being worried about. The second message was from a woman who didn't identify herself, but didn't need to:

"Tomorrow night, nine o'clock. Be careful. The night has a thousand eyes."

Whose eyes were watching me?

CHAPTER FORTY-THREE

Monday, November 17. 10:02 A.M. 400 block of Holt Avenue.
A woman received a phone call from a neighbor who threatened
to blow up her house if she continued to run her air conditioner
after 11:30 P.M. The suspect is described as a 30-year-old
woman standing 5 feet 6 inches tall. (Wilshire)

THE HOUSEKEEPER, A SHORT, THIN WOMAN WITH COAL-
black eyes and a long black braid with glints of indigo and strands
of silver, opened the door.

"Mr. Reston says to me you are coming at twelve," she told
me in a heavy Spanish accent when I was in the entry hall. "You
want to see *el profesor's* room, yes?"

Reston had suggested that I come at noon, when he would

meet me. The housekeeper's English wasn't great, he'd told me. I'd decided to come early.

"You're Louisa, right?" I smiled. "I'm Molly. Mr. Reston said it would be okay for me to talk to you about Professor Linney and his daughter."

"¡La pobrecita!" The woman sighed. "¿Ella esta muerta, verdad?"

I nodded. That much I understood: The poor woman. She is dead, true? Margaret's portrait, which I could see from where we were standing, seemed to belie that fact. I was taken again by the restless energy the artist had captured, the suggestion that Maggie wanted to leap off the mantel.

Louisa took me into the kitchen. We sat at the breakfast room table and I asked her what she remembered about the last days of Linney's life.

"No very much. He is no very different than always. Very sad, very angry. I no blame him. I feel sorry for him, you know?" She clucked.

"You knew him a long time? ¿Mucho tiempo?"

She nodded. "Sí. I am with the family twenty years, from when I am young girl. Very sad when Mrs. Roberta died. She is very nice lady."

"You said Professor Linney was angry. Was he angry with anyone in particular? ¿Específico?" I added, when Louisa seemed perplexed.

Her eyes slid sideways, toward the open doorway. "No, no one."

I'd assumed she wouldn't feel comfortable tattling on the man who paid her wages, but I had to try. "By the way, who was taking care of the old house, on Fuller?"

"Angelita, the daughter of my sister. She is going there every week before the fuego. The fire. But no more. Now she is looking for another job." Louisa sighed.

I wasn't sure whether she was sighing about the torched house or the fact that her niece was out of a job. Maybe both. "What about after the fire?"

Louisa shook her head. "Mr. Reston, he tells her there is no need."

I asked her about the day before Margaret disappeared.

"She is out of the house much of the day. When she comes back she is *muy triste*. Very sad. She is crying."

"Not nervous? *Nerviosa?*"

Louisa hesitated. *"Enojada."* Angry.

"¿Enojada?" I leaned toward her. "Why was she angry, Louisa? With whom? *¿Con quién?"*

"No sé." Louisa shrugged. "She goes into her room, and she is yelling. 'If you do not put it back by tomorrow, I am telling the *policía*. I do not care what you say.' "

I frowned. "Put *what* back?"

"No sé. She does not come out of her room." Louisa picked up a napkin and rubbed at an invisible spot on the table. "The *policía* ask me questions about *el profesor*. I do not tell them. They will think wrong things. But now he is dead, so it does not matter."

"What things?"

"He is yelling at Margarita to come out of her room. He is hitting the door." Louisa slammed the table hard with her palm several times. "He heard the phone call, he will not go to Goldavista."

So *Linney* had heard Ochs's message. "Then what happened?"

"Then Margarita comes out of her room and says I can go home early. And this is the last time I see her." The housekeeper sighed deeply. "I think all this time *el profesor's* heart is heavy because he is yelling at her this last day that she is living." She pressed her hand against her breast. "So many times he is crying. 'Margarita, I'm sorry. Margarita, don't hate me.' "

"But you didn't tell this to the police," I said.

"For what? *El profesor* is yelling all the time. He yells, and then he is sorry. They will not understand. A few weeks ago, before *el profesor* died, I tell *Señor* Reston. He says to me I am right not to tell."

CHAPTER FORTY-FOUR

A SECOND SEARCH OF LINNEY'S ROOM REVEALED LITTLE new. If there had been any bank statements from the home equity line of credit, they were no longer there. I did find statements for his checking account (he had a balance of $513.47) and a savings account with a little over $13,000. I jotted down the name and phone number of the bank and the account number.

The medicine cabinet was crammed with the usual assortment of vitamins, antacids, analgesics, cold medications, various ointments. There were vials of medications, including Mirapex. From my discussion with Elbogen, I knew that was for Parkinson's.

Louisa had told me she would be upstairs if I needed her. Leaving Linney's room, I heard the droning of a vacuum, a sound that grew louder as I neared the center staircase.

Reston's study was on the other side of the hall, to my right. On the phone this morning, when I'd told him I wanted to look through Linney's things again, he'd repeated what he'd said the other day: "Look anywhere you want." I doubted that his study or papers were included in that *anywhere,* and though technically he'd given me carte blanche, I had qualms about nosing through his property.

Yes or no.

I could wait and hope that the lab techs would decipher the original entry in Margaret's planner, and that Porter or Hernandez would share that information with me.

But I was here, and Reston wasn't.

The bookshelves were still empty. The rosewood desk, bare with the exception of a brass reading lamp, a combination phone and answering machine, and a black leather desk set, exuded the delicious fragrance of new wood. I sat on the edge of the studded leather chair, and with my ears straining for the reassuring hum of the vacuum, I opened the top right-hand drawer.

Mostly bills. Land phone, cell phone, utilities, cable company, Internet access, credit cards. I didn't examine any of them, or the itemized bill from the decorator. I was trying to adhere to a fine line between curiosity and research. I did check Reston's bank statement. He had $12,000 in his checking account, almost $70,000 in savings. But if he was hurting because of the HARP properties, $70,000 wouldn't cover many months of the mortgage on the Muirfield house.

I also found a statement from Linney's bank for his line of credit. The balance due was $456,821. A hefty debt. I looked at it again to make certain I hadn't missed a decimal point. The maximum line of credit, Mindy had told me, is usually 80 percent of the property's assessed value. Assuming that the Fuller house, before the fire, had been valued at around $650,000 to $700,000, the amount borrowed against it was close to the limit allowed.

The bottom drawer was a file cabinet. Many of the folders contained material related to Reston's carpet and flooring business. I thumbed through some of the other folders and found documents dealing with various properties that Reston owned, mostly in Los Angeles, some outside the state. I didn't find anything related to Skoll Investments.

A folder labeled INSURANCE contained an itemized list of all the jewelry that had been stolen the night Margaret had disappeared. There were also several letters from Reston, the most recent dated last Thursday, inquiring about the status of his claim.

I was reading the letter when the ringing of the phone startled me. After three rings the answering machine picked up, and I heard Reston's brief message. For a second I felt as though he were in the room, watching me snoop though his private papers.

The vacuum was still going. I checked my watch. Eleven-ten. Almost an hour before Reston was due home.

In a folder labeled FULLER HOUSE I found a certified copy of a Grant Deed, dated May 6 of this year, transferring ownership of the property on Fuller from Oscar Linney to Margaret Linney Reston. According to another notarized document, Linney had granted Margaret power of attorney on the same date. A busy day, apparently.

I wondered when Hank and Margaret had executed their reciprocal powers of attorney. I'd phoned Central Realty this morning, learned the name of the title company that had insured the property, and spoken to a title officer who promised he'd get back to me as soon as possible.

The home insurance policy was in the folder, too. Attached to the front was a page with handwritten figures and the words *Cash out? Approx. $500 G.*

I also found Linney's checkbook for his line of credit. There were numerous checks written in the past two months, all made out to HR Floor Covering. I did a mental calculation and came up with approximately $390,000. There were quite a few checks written before Margaret's disappearance. Two, totaling $43,400, were made out to Skoll Investment. Several were made out to cash. I added those up. Another $22,000.

No wonder Reston had changed *HELC* into *HELP.* I wondered how he planned to explain all this to Hernandez and Porter, who were certain to examine all of Linney's finances now that they viewed his death as a homicide. Of course, Reston could claim that the money was a loan, but if the police talked to Linney's friends, they'd learn what I had: that the old man would never have loaned his son-in-law a nickel, let alone over a third of a million dollars.

Well, that was Reston's problem, not mine.

I still didn't know what Margaret had written instead of *Check out Sub-Zero.* I found her burgundy leather planner in the bottom left-hand drawer, under a stack of folders. I paged backwards and there, on the left-hand side, was the entry I'd read on my photocopy: *Check out Sub-Zero.* The page for June 13–14 was gone. Either Reston was telling the truth and Maggie had ripped it out, or he had.

I'd brought a magnifying glass. I held it over the entry and moved it slowly left to right. There had definitely been an erasure. The good news, for me, was that Margaret had written with a heavy hand, and the author of the newer entry hadn't. So I could discern faint indentations of what could be letters. The bad news was that the indentations were covered by the newly penciled letters, light though they were.

I moved the lens back to the beginning of the entry and held it there. I wasn't sure, but it seemed to me that beneath the *Ch* was the indentation of part of what could be a capital letter *M.* Next to that was something that looked like a slash. I couldn't identify what was next to the slash, but I made out a capital *P* at the end of the line.

Wonderful. *M* and a slash and a *P.* I needed Vanna White and a few vowels.

The vacuum stopped, and so, for a second, did my heart. Then my heart pounded against my chest. I waited, prepared to shut the planner and return it to the drawer. The droning started again, and I let out my breath.

I looked at the left side of the previous page and found the line that corresponded to *Check out Sub-Zero*. It was blank. Using a pencil from my purse, I rubbed the edge lightly over the blank line, hoping to bring into white relief the indentations made by Margaret's writing. I peered at the line through my magnifying lens.

Nothing but gray striations.

I erased my pencil markings, brushed the residue into my purse, and checked my watch. Eleven-fifty. Ten more minutes before Reston came home, but what was the point? I was about to close the planner when I looked at the facing page and noticed the impressions of Margaret's heavy script. I switched on the desk lamp. Raising the page, I let the light reflect off of it. Then, putting my finger on *Check out Sub-Zero,* I found the corresponding impressions.

I felt a surge of excitement. The letters were there, sharp and legible. The problem was that they were backwards.

I moved my eyes from right to left, as though I were reading Hebrew. The first letter was definitely an *M.* Then a slash. Then a capital *D.* Then, an *R.* Then—

The vacuum stopped. I waited a second, but this time the droning didn't resume, which was a good thing, because if it had, I wouldn't have heard the thunk of the front door being shut.

I froze.

"Louisa?" Reston's voice boomed in the high-ceilinged entry. "There's a car in the driveway. Is Miss Blume here?"

"*La señora* is in *el profesor's* room, *Señor* Reston."

I held my breath until I heard his footsteps on the marble, heading to the right. Away from the study.

I had less than a minute. I looked at the planner and almost cried in frustration. I'd lost my place. My eyes flicked over the *M*, the slash, the *D*, the *R*. The next letter was *O*, then *P, DROP.* There was a space. Then *O, F, F, OFF.* Drop off.

"Molly? Miss Blume."

My hands were shaking and clammy. I made out the next word: *I, N, F, O.* Info.

Information about what?

"Louisa, she's not there," Reston called, back in the entry. "Do you know where she is?"

R, E. Re.

He was about fifty feet away. My stomach was in knots. Common sense told me to stop, but there was one more word. The first letter was *H.* Then *A, R, P.*

H, A, R, P. HARP. Of course.

M/Drop off info re HARP.

I slipped the planner back into the drawer, shut off the light, and was standing at the French windows looking out on the pool when Reston entered the study.

CHAPTER FORTY-FIVE

"THERE YOU ARE," HANK SAID. "LOUISA THOUGHT YOU were in Linney's room. Didn't you hear me calling you?"

My face felt sunburned. My heart was pounding. I put on a smile and turned around. "Sorry. I heard your voice, but not what you were saying." He was looking at me with curiosity, and I wondered if he could see the heaving of my chest. "I hope you don't mind that I'm in here. I was passing by and remembered that the room looks out on the pool. I was mesmerized by the view."

"Much prettier today than the last time you were here. It *is* beautiful, isn't it? Maggie would've loved the way everything turned out. I have to say Dorn did a great job."

"It's too bad Ned Vaughan couldn't do it."

"He felt bad about it. So did I." Hank shrugged. "But Maggie chose Dorn, and Oscar approved. And I have no complaints. Louisa said you talked to her, so that's done," he said, obviously changing the subject from Dorn. "And I guess you already looked in the Professor's room. Did you find everything you wanted?"

More than I wanted. I nodded. "By the way, I noticed that the Fuller house is no longer for sale."

"Too much damage. I'm going to rebuild with the insurance money."

"And list it again with Central Realty?"

Reston hesitated. "Actually, I plan to sell it on my own. I don't think Tim Bolt is the right person to handle it, but I don't want to insult him by going to another broker. Don't tell him I said that."

So Reston had learned of Bolt's bigotry, too. "I won't. Do you have time for a few questions?"

"That's why I'm here." He smiled.

In the kitchen I sat at the table while he filled two mugs with coffee. Just like last time, except that last time I'd been happily unaware of his financial problems and how he'd solved them. And the implications. I wondered about the altered entry. *M/Drop off info re HARP.* What info, and why had Reston erased it?

Hank brought the mugs to the table, placed one in front of me, and sat down across from me. "Thanks again for coming to the funeral, Molly," he said in his soft drawl. "That was real nice of you."

"I wanted to be there. It was an impressive turnout."

"Oscar had a lot friends. I just wasn't one of them. I wish things would've been different between us, but wishing doesn't make it so. Anyway." He cleared his throat. "Ned says you picked him cleaner than a corncob. So did he tell you all kinds of terrible things about me?" Reston treated me to one of his mischievous smiles.

"He's a loyal friend. He didn't want to talk about you."

"But he did, didn't he? So what did he say?"

"That you'd been waiting a long time to find someone like Maggie." I took a sip of the hot coffee. Hazelnut today, instead of cinnamon. "That you were possessive."

"He said that, huh?" Hank chewed on his lip. "Well, I guess that's true," he said quietly. "You find someone like Maggie, you don't want to let her out of your sight."

"To be honest, I'm surprised Ned and Maggie never got together. He was at the house all the time. And, well . . ."

"And he was educated. You can say it. You won't hurt my feelings. Actually, it was Ned's idea to introduce me to Maggie. He thought we'd hit it off. And he has a girlfriend. I told him if he ever *does* marry her, his wedding vows would probably be 'to love, preserve, and restore wherever possible.'" Hank laughed. "So what else did he tell you?"

"Not much." So Walter had been right about Ned. I couldn't wait to tell Zack, who had put the bug in my head. Still . . . "Actually, he seemed nervous and was happy to see me go."

"He's got a lot on his mind. USC, his other work. And he took Linney's death hard. So who else have you talked to?"

"Jeremy Dorn."

Hank stiffened. "And?"

"He said you fired him because you thought he and Maggie were having an affair."

"That was a dumb misunderstanding." Hank's face turned red. "Let me tell you, I felt like a jerk when Maggie explained everything. I felt like a bigger jerk when I had to beg Dorn to come back. And of course, he told the cops all about it, so I had to explain the whole thing to them, too." He grunted. "Your turn. Did you learn anything?"

"Number one, Tiler is the name of an intellectual properties attorney. Gordon Tiler. Your wife had an appointment with him that last day. Any idea why?" I'd phoned the attorney's Wilshire office this morning and had left a message, asking him to call.

"Beats the hell out of me." Hank was frowning. "You're sure?"

"Pretty sure. Was Maggie planning to do something with her musical compositions?"

"Not that I know. But she could've been. Anything else?"

"Professor Linney invested over forty thousand dollars with a Denver company called Skoll Investment."

Hank nodded. "I saw that in his check register when I was going over his papers after Maggie disappeared. Too long after, actually. I was focused on Maggie, and, well . . . Anyway, when I did ask him about it, he said it was none of my goddamn business. Pardon my French." He paused. "What was I going to do, fight with him? So I asked Ned to find out—Ned and Oscar were close—but Oscar wouldn't tell him, either. What kind of investments do they handle?"

"I don't think they exist." I told him about my attempts to contact the company.

"I dropped the ball on that one." Hank sighed. "Anyway, from what you're saying, that money was long gone. Bastards, preying on old people." He clamped his lips together.

In view of what I'd just discovered, I found his comment outrageous. Maybe that's why I asked him the next question. "Did Professor Linney write the checks from his personal checking account or another account?"

"Personal account. What other account would he use? Why?" He picked up his mug.

"Just curious." I'd caught him in a lie. I should have felt gratified, but I was angry, and sad. "I found a bank statement in his room for a home equity line of credit on the Fuller house. So I wondered if he used that account."

Reston took a sip of coffee. "Damn, this is hot," he said, but he held the mug to his lips. I think he knew I'd trapped him. I think he was replaying scenes in his head, trying to figure out if and how he'd left one of Linney's HELC statements in the old man's bedroom. And if he hadn't . . . And maybe he started wondering what I'd been doing in his study, why I hadn't heard him calling me, what I'd found.

He sighed again. For a moment I thought he was going to confess to embezzling the money from Linney's account.

"Come to think of it, Oscar *did* write those checks from his home equity account, Molly. I didn't have a good night's sleep, what with the funeral and all. I probably shouldn't be operating heavy machinery." The smile he gave me was a little strained.

There's a saying in Yiddish: "With lies you can go far, but you can't go back." Hank was stuck with his lie. I was curious to see where he went next. "Did Professor Linney write other large checks from that account?"

"To be honest, I haven't been on top of his finances. The interest on that account is paid automatically from his checking account, so I didn't worry about it. But I'll definitely look into it now. Thanks for bringing it up."

"The reason I'm asking is, maybe someone coerced Professor Linney to write the checks and killed him to keep him quiet."

There was a long silence. I listened to the hum of the Sub-Zero and thought about the planner. *M/Drop off info re HARP. M* as in Modine? Had he come to the house that night?

"Like who?" Hank finally asked.

"It would have to be someone who knew your wife. Someone who had a tape of her voice and spliced it to lure Professor Linney to the Fuller house." And saved the tape for that purpose? "Probably someone your wife called."

"I see what you mean."

"If you find funds missing from his account, you'll want to tell the police," I said.

He was staring at me. "Of course."

Maybe Modine had been searching for the planner in Maggie's dressing room. But I had found it first, and he'd had no choice but to give it to Reston. But he could have seen what was in it, I realized with a jolt. He'd taken it with him when he left Linney's room for a few minutes to check out a noise that turned out to be "the wind." A noise I hadn't heard. Had he erased the entry then? Or had he asked Reston to do it? *You have to help me, man. You know I didn't do it, but I don't need the cops on my back.*

"What about Roger Modine?" I asked, to see Hank's reaction. "He was around the house a lot. He could have helped himself to a few of Professor Linney's checks." In my mind I saw the contractor dangling the house keys in my face, smirking. "He showed me a key you gave him to the Fuller house. Has he had that a long time?"

Reston was looking at me as though I'd lost my mind. "Sure, he had a key. He was doing work in the house. But Roger wouldn't kill Oscar."

"His construction business has been suffering from the HARP restrictions. Maybe he was desperate."

Reston shook his head.

"He has a temper," I said. "He tied me up that night. That wasn't necessary. At the Hancock Park HARP meeting he looked like he was ready to strangle Ned Vaughan. By the way, what were they arguing about?"

Reston hesitated. "The survey results. He thought that as my friend, Ned should have supported us. We have some properties in Hancock Park and Windsor Square."

"He wanted Ned to *lie?*"

"Not *lie.*" Reston took another sip of coffee. "The survey was subjective. Basically what they did was take a bunch of photos and decide which house was contributory. The thing is, two architects could look at the same house and come up with two opinions. Roger thought some of Ned's calls were unfair. Anyway, it's over and done with."

Reston seemed uncomfortable, and I had the feeling there was more to the matter. "You also have properties in Ladera Heights and Mar Vista, right? Those are HARP areas, so I imagine they're giving you grief."

Was that the HARP "info" Modine had dropped off? Had he used the opportunity, and Hank's absence, to make a move on Maggie?

Reston had leaned back and tilted his chair. He studied me. "You really did your homework."

"You asked me to look into your wife's disappearance, Hank. That's what I did. And into Professor Linney's death."

"Are you saying our HARP properties are connected with Maggie's death or her father's?"

There was a warning in his question, and some anxiety. I reminded myself that I was sitting across the table from a man who may have murdered two people. I probably should have let it drop. But Louisa was in the house. "I know you're having problems with those properties, Hank. The police know it, too."

"Every business has cash flow problems. HARP is a pain in the butt, but we hope to move those properties soon." He sat upright, got to his feet, and pushed the chair back with an abrupt motion. It screeched across the high gloss of the new maple floor. "I think I made a mistake confiding in you, Molly. I thought you wanted to help me find out what happened to Maggie, and to her father. But it looks like you're just trying to make me out to be the villain. I didn't need your help for that."

"I told you when we first spoke that I was interested in finding the truth." I stood and picked up my purse.

"I loved my wife. I didn't kill her. I didn't like my father-in-law, but I didn't kill him, either. That *is* the truth."

I have to say he sounded sincere. "I understand that Professor Linney was taken to the ER several times by ambulance. You didn't mention that."

"Because it wasn't important," Reston said with a flash of impatience. "Like I told you, he had Alzheimer's and Parkinson's. His balance was off, he wasn't careful, so he'd trip and fall all the time. One time he dislocated his elbow. Another time he sprained his ankle."

The same injuries Tim Bolt had told me about, a different story. Which version was true? "Wasn't he hospitalized once for a few days?"

"He overdosed on Mirapex. That's the medication he was taking for the Parkinson's. He wanted to write a paper and was frustrated because his hand shook so much that he couldn't hold a pen. He thought if he took more of the Mirapex, he would eliminate the shaking. He ended up having a psychotic episode. Is that it?"

"He told several people that you abused him."

"Which people?" Reston demanded.

"I can't tell you that."

"I never laid a finger on him." Reston's face was flushed. He took a calming breath. "He was paranoid. He said people were out to get him and stealing his money."

"Well, it looks like they were," I said.

CHAPTER FORTY-SIX

AT NIGHT THE DUNGEON LOOKED LIKE A SET FOR "THE Cask of Amontillado," and I wondered again whether I was crazy to come here. ("You're going *where?*" Edie had said when I'd told her I couldn't play mah jongg tonight. And she's the level-headed one in the family.)

This time I was prepared for the attack of the vines and ducked my head a few times as I made my way to the front door. I wondered whether the interior of the house was junglelike, too.

Charlene Coulter must have been waiting in the entry, look-ing through her privacy window, because she opened the door as soon as I pressed my finger against the bell. All I could think of was the Big Bad Wolf eagerly welcoming Red Riding Hood.

Not that she looked like a wolf in Grandma's clothing. She

was younger than I'd expected—probably in her sixties, judging from the gray in the shoulder-length brown hair she wore brushed behind her ears. She was around five foot seven, neither heavy nor slim, in a pink sweater and charcoal pleated skirt that my sister Liora would wear.

"Contrary to public opinion, I don't eat humans," she said, a twinkle in her blue eyes. "Too much cholesterol and fat. Please, come in."

As you can imagine, my face was red. I stepped into a center hall that extended to the back of the house, and stared. The walls were painted with a trompe l'oeil of a garden beyond a mullioned window, and a skylight painted on the ceiling took my eye to a rose-streaked blue sky with feathery clouds.

"It's beautiful," I said.

"You were probably expecting a dark room lit with candles. I save them for the satanic rituals. Just kidding." Her smile, amused with a touch of bitterness, softened the sharpness of chin.

I didn't know how to respond. "Thank you for agreeing to see me, Mrs. Coulter."

Her smile disappeared. "I didn't really have a choice. I see that now. Let's talk in the parlor. Please call me Charlene. May I call you Molly?"

"I'd like that."

"You're writing about Oscar and Margaret, aren't you?"

"Yes. How did you know?" I asked as I walked with her along the hall, taking in the "view." A fountain, a bench. Mounds of blue and white hydrangeas, lilies, bushes of roses. Smoke curled out of the chimney of a small cottage in the distance.

"There's very little I don't know, Molly," she said solemnly. Then she winked. "I read your article about HARP, and I saw you talking to people in the neighborhood. You can see quite a bit when you live in the only three-story in the area. You can hear quite a bit, too."

I followed her into a cozy room with cream walls. She sat on a cerulean blue silk love seat and patted the cushion. "Come join me, dear. I've made us tea."

I sat next to her. On the glass table in front of us was a yellow-rose-patterned porcelain tea service that seemed to be floating on air above the bleached wood floor. Charlene poured tea into a cup.

"Sugar or artificial sweetener?" she asked.

"Artificial." I try to save calories where I can.

She placed a packet on the side of the saucer. "I used to take artificial sweeteners, but when most of your world is a substitute for reality, you try to indulge in the real thing whenever you can." She poured tea for herself and used tiny silver tongs to drop in two cubes of sugar. She looked up at me. "I'm sorry. I've made you uncomfortable."

"Not at all. I imagine you've been lonely since your husband died."

"Glen was my best friend. But I have other friends who visit, although people are so busy these days, don't you find? My son, Adrian, and his wife, Helene, come often with their little boy. They named him Glen. Isn't that lovely? Adrian placed the flyers on your windshield, by the way. I hope I didn't frighten you. I wanted you to be alert."

"I appreciate your concern." There was something I wasn't getting here. Something even Walter didn't know.

"You look troubled, Molly," Charlene said, misreading my furrowed brow. "Don't be. I don't have a sad life, just a different one. I have my groceries delivered, and a lovely young woman named Lucy comes every month to trim my hair and give me a pedicure. She's encouraging me to do something about the gray, but I like it." Charlene touched her hair. "What do you think, Molly? Be honest."

"I like the gray."

She nodded, pleased. "Glen would have liked it, too. And I buy everything from catalogs or on the Internet. I've learned that you don't have to leave your house if you don't want to. Or can't." She gazed at me. "I'm sure you've heard the stories. 'Charlene Coulter never leaves her house.' 'Charlene doesn't invite anyone over.' 'Something's wrong with Charlene.' In the beginning, every few months I used to try. For Glen and Adrian, more than me. The second I stepped outside, my heart would start racing and I found I couldn't breathe. So I stopped trying."

I tried to imagine never leaving my apartment, being confined to its few rooms. "Have you always been . . ."

"Agoraphobic. For me, it's not just fear of the marketplace. It's crowds, or open spaces where a crowd might form. It's elevators and stairwells or any place I'm not familiar with or that may not allow me a quick exit. Because you never know when somebody's going to pop up, do you? That's why there are two staircases in this house, and more than the usual number of doors to the outside. That's why I couldn't let you in yesterday, Molly. There were too many people on the block. I'm sorry."

My heart went out to her. She may have adjusted, but she was still trapped by her fears. "I understand."

"Do you? *I* don't, not really. Adrian and Helene had a small wedding ceremony here. I wanted so badly to attend their reception. I got dressed, but couldn't go. I just couldn't. And when their baby was born . . ." She looked wistful. "I've learned that acceptance is more important than understanding. But you asked me whether I was always like this. I suspect the seeds were there. I never did like crowds or parties. And then one day I was mugged and badly beaten, and my whole life changed overnight. Therapy didn't help. No one could convince me that I wasn't safest inside my own house. And now, with poor Margaret Linney gone, and Oscar, too, I see that's not so. A person should be safe in her own house, don't you think?"

Ordinarily I *do* feel safe. I suppose that's odd, given the data I collect about the frequent crimes that take place in homes. But reading about strangers being burglarized or assaulted or raped, or even murdered, isn't the same as knowing the victim. And certainly not the same as when it happens to you. I hadn't felt safe in my apartment in days. I wouldn't feel safe until Margaret and Oscar Linney's killer was behind bars.

"Were you living here when you were mugged?" I asked.

"We were in an apartment in Santa Monica with a glorious view of the Pacific. I used to walk on the beach every morning. Do you like the beach, Molly?"

"I love it."

"I love it, too. And then one day I was on the boardwalk in Venice, buying a pair of sunglasses at a kiosk. And the next day I woke up in the hospital. So we decided to move, and Glen built this house for us. For me, really. Three stories so that I could see around me without having to step outside my front door. I think now that we were wrong to do it. We should have considered the neighbors' feelings. But the city allowed it, and it didn't seem wrong at the time."

I wondered what Walter Fennel would say if he heard Charlene. Would her regret make a difference? "Do you miss the beach?"

"I *have* the beach. I have New Orleans and Lake Arrowhead and Sedona. I have many of the places that I've been to and loved."

"In your memory, you mean." I thought about Bubbie G, who has to rely on memory more and more to navigate through her darkening world.

Charlene smiled. "Well, that, too. But I have them here, Molly, in this house. Would you like to see?"

CHAPTER FORTY-SEVEN

"WELCOME TO PARIS," CHARLENE SAID, OPENING THE double doors to the living room.

It *was* Paris, or what I knew of the city from movies and books. Through the "shuttered window" painted on one of the walls, I saw people walking near the Arc de Triomphe; through another, traffic in front of the Eiffel Tower. On the wall to my right, people at sidewalk cafés were talking and laughing and drinking coffee. The sky painted on the arched ceiling was a darker blue that threatened rain.

"That's my favorite." Charlene pointed to the wall facing the street. "The Pont Neuf." The window I'd seen from the street had disappeared, covered by a shade that had been incorporated into the vista. "Glen and I spent most of our honeymoon near that bridge. He sketched, I watched and read novels and ate chocolate. It was the best time of my life."

"It's lovely. Did Glen do this?"

"It *is,* isn't it? Yes, this is Glen's. All of it is Glen's."

The dining room was a piazza in Florence. The family room provided a spectacular view of San Francisco from the Golden Gate Bridge. The bedroom Charlene had shared with Glen was conventional, but each of the four other rooms on the second floor took you to another locale. And then there was the third floor. With the exception of a small room at the back of the house, the room in which I'd seen her yesterday, the third story was a large panorama of the Pacific that Charlene had enjoyed from her Santa Monica apartment. I could practically taste the salt in the air and hear the seagulls squawking.

"I couldn't go out into the world, so Glen brought the world to me," she told me when we were back in the parlor. "I think he hoped that if I could get used to the people in these murals, that I'd eventually be able to face them outside. But that didn't happen."

"Can I ask you something, Charlene?"

"You want to know why we painted the house that gloomy dark gray." She smiled. "It was dove gray originally, a beautiful color. Some of the neighbors were giving Glen a hard time about the third story. 'If it's a dungeon, shouldn't you paint it black?' they said. And we found fresh graffiti on the walls almost daily. So we painted the house charcoal. We weren't going to leave it that way, but then we did. And the stories started. Of course, we heard them. So did Adrian. Thank God he was in high school, or he probably wouldn't have had *any* friends." Charlene smiled, but there was anger in her blue eyes. "And to tell you the truth, it suited me just fine that people kept their distance. I'd rather they think I'm crazy than pathetic. I didn't have to explain why I didn't leave the house, why I didn't invite guests. Except for Roberta."

"Roberta?"

"Roberta Linney. Maggie's mother. She showed up on my doorstep one Sunday morning twenty-five years ago with Maggie and we became close friends. She'd overheard Maggie talking with her friends about the bad people in The Dungeon, telling them she'd uprooted some of the flowers on our walkway. We used to have a beautiful walkway. Pansies and snapdragons in the fall. Petunias and lobelias in the summer. The gardener was tired of constantly replacing the flowers that were mysteriously decapitated or yanked out by the roots. He thought it was dogs. Glen and I knew better."

I didn't know how I would meet her eyes, but she wasn't looking at me. It occurred to me that Charlene didn't want to see in *my* eyes that I was one of those who had violated her garden or her walls. I wanted to tell her that none of my siblings or I had ever stepped onto The Dungeon's front lawn, that we'd never snipped a flower or lifted a marker. It was true. But we had whispered about the house. We had vandalized it with our silly tongues and childish laughter.

"After Glen died I told the gardener no more flowers. Because as I told you, Molly, acceptance is more important than understanding. And I could never understand, not really. So he planted those ugly shrubs, and they serve their purpose, don't they?" A smile flitted across her face. "But I was telling you about Maggie. Roberta and Maggie brought a box of pansies. Roberta made her apologize for what she'd done, and of course I forgave her. Then Maggie asked me to show her where to plant the new flowers. She was eight, I think, but mature for her age. I remember standing in the hall. I remember telling her to leave the flowers, that the gardener would plant them. All because I couldn't, absolutely couldn't walk out that door." She stopped.

"So what happened?" I asked, as though she were telling me a story.

"Roberta insisted. Maggie had to plant the flowers. So I

called instructions from the doorway, and that was when Roberta understood. The next day she came with photos she'd taken on a trip, and our friendship began. I found I could tell her things I couldn't tell Glen, because I didn't want to depress him. And she knew she could confide in me. After all, who would I tell?" There was humor in her smile now, and some irony, too. The smile faded quickly. "And then she died."

"She had cancer," I said.

Charlene nodded. "She was in tremendous pain. She wasn't afraid of dying, Molly. She was afraid of leaving Maggie with him."

I stared at her. "Are you saying he abused her?"

"Sexually? No." Charlene shuddered. "And not physically either. But he controlled her, Molly. He made her practice four hours every day. When other children were outside enjoying the sunshine, Maggie would be at the piano."

"I thought she loved it."

Charlene grimaced. "*He* loved it, so she convinced herself that she did, too. He wanted Maggie to become a concert pianist and a composer. So she did. She adored her father. She would do anything for him."

"And her mother?"

"She loved Roberta, but she picked up on the condescension Oscar showed her. To Oscar, Roberta was a breeder. He married to continue his impressive line. He was determined to make Maggie a star and bask in her glory."

"And then she gave it all up and married a man he disapproved of," I said.

"Yes. I can imagine how furious he must have been." Charlene seemed pleased by the prospect. "I never met Hank. Maggie stopped by to give me an invitation to the wedding. She was so obviously in love. It warmed my heart, because I knew Roberta was looking down, happy. I didn't go to the wedding, of course. And then Maggie went on her honeymoon, and I didn't see her until she and Hank moved back into Oscar's house." Charlene leaned toward me and clasped my hands. "She should never have moved back there. It's an evil house, Molly. You probably think I'm being melodramatic, but it's true."

I know it's silly, but I had goose bumps on my arms. "Do you know what happened to Maggie?" That was why I was here. That was why Charlene had left the notes, wasn't it? Because she had something to tell me? Or was she a lonely soul who needed company despite her insistence that she enjoyed her solitude?

Charlene released my hands. "If you mean, do I know who killed her?" She shook her head. "But I'm sure someone did. I wasn't at first, but after Oscar was killed, I knew. I saw Maggie gardening late on the afternoon before she disappeared. I was watching her from the room you saw me in. I was worried about her. She was attacking the plants and crying, wiping her eyes with her sleeve. And then she threw her little garden spade against the garage wall and sat down on the grass. She buried her head in her hands and sobbed. My heart broke for her. I wanted to comfort her, but all I could do was watch."

Had she cried because she'd decided she couldn't live with Hank and his jealousy? Because she'd had to face the fact that Hank was abusing her father? Because she'd been unable to place her father in Golden Vista?

"Why were you worried about her, Charlene?" I asked.

"She came to see me two days before she disappeared. She wanted to know what happened to her mother."

I frowned. "Her mother?"

"Someone had told her terrible things about Oscar. She didn't believe them, and she wanted to know if her mother had said anything to me so that she could tell this person he was a liar."

"Who?"

"She wouldn't say."

I licked my lips. "What did he tell her?"

"That Oscar killed Roberta by giving her an overdose of her medications." Charlene was watching me to see my reaction.

I took a moment to digest that. "What did you tell Maggie?"

"I told her I had no idea what had happened to her mother, and that her mother had trusted me not to reveal anything she told me. Maggie was furious. She demanded answers." Charlene sighed. "So I told her to talk to her aunt Vivian."

V for Vivian, not for Ned Vaughan. Linney's sister-in-law who didn't attend the funeral, who hadn't been in touch with him or Maggie since Roberta died.

"That night I heard her yelling at Oscar," Charlene said. "They were in his room, and his windows were open. Mine were open, too, so I could hear much of what they were saying. She told him she hated him. She told him that he was evil. She told him he'd tried to ruin her life but she wasn't going to let him do it, not anymore."

"Enojada," the housekeeper had said. Angry.

"What time was this?" I asked.

"Around nine o'clock."

"Tim Bolt didn't hear any of this," I said. "Or the other neighbors?"

"It was a warm June night. He probably had his air-conditioning running. Most of the neighbors do. I can hear the generators droning all night. I don't care for air-conditioning. It dries my skin and throat. Oscar didn't like it, either. And then if you have the television on, or the radio, you probably wouldn't hear a sonic boom."

I nodded. "What happened then?"

"Oscar told her that he'd die before he let her put him in a home, that he'd kill her if she tried. And the next day she was gone. But I didn't think he *killed* her. My first thought was that she ran away. 'Good for you!' I thought. 'Good for you!' But then I thought, why would she leave Hank? And then I started wondering. But Oscar is a frail man, Molly. How could he have disposed of the body? And then I thought, what if someone else helped him?"

My heart pounded. "Who?"

Charlene shook her head.

"Did you see anyone come to the house that night?"

"No. I went to sleep. I tried phoning Maggie first, but she didn't pick up the phone. I wanted to go over, but I couldn't. And when the police came and asked questions, I told them I didn't know anything. I can't leave the house, Molly. How could I possibly sit in a police station and tell my story? And then in a courtroom, with all those people? Day after day? I knew I wouldn't be able to do it. I told myself that if Maggie was dead, my telling wouldn't bring her back anyway. And just because I'd heard Oscar threaten to kill her didn't mean that he had. Some-one else could have killed her."

That was true, I thought. My head was reeling. "Why would Oscar kill Roberta, Charlene?"

She didn't answer.

"You said she was in terrible pain. Did he want to help her out of her misery?"

"Ask Vivian."

CHAPTER FORTY-EIGHT

Tuesday, November 18. 10:15 A.M. 9400 block of Culver Boulevard. After making a bank deposit, a woman discovered that $4,304.64 had been withdrawn from her account without her consent. She also discovered that a second account had been opened in her name and that five checks had been drawn on it. Also, an application for a credit card in her name had been denied. The woman told police and bank officials that she had not made any of these transactions or applied for a credit card. (Culver City)

CARTHAY CIRCLE IS ONE OF L.A.'S BEST-KEPT SECRETS, and from what I hear, the area's residents want to keep it that way. Adjacent to Miracle Mile and half a mile from my apartment, it's a small neighborhood bounded by Wilshire, Fairfax, Olympic, and Schumacher that was developed between 1922 and 1944 by J. Harvey McCarthy (hence the Carthay), who named the streets in honor of prominent figures of the California Gold Rush. Aside from a few Tudors, French Revivals, and American Colonials, most of the homes are Spanish Colonial Revival, so in all fairness, I can see why the residents wanted HARP status.

Carthay Circle isn't a circle. The *Circle* part came from the circular auditorium and dome of the Carthay Circle Theater that hosted the premiers of *Snow White* and *Gone with the Wind* before it was demolished in 1969. The streets, which are only one to three blocks long and don't connect to the major boulevards, have irregular patterns that would make a challenging geometry final. They form rectangles, triangles, trapezoids, and other shapes that don't have names. The idea was to create an enclosed community and encourage people to walk instead of drive. The unintended result is that if you're used to the typical grid pattern of L.A. streets, you can easily get lost and find yourself walking in rhomboids.

I discovered Carthay Circle when I was a teenager. Shabbat afternoons Aggie and I would sometimes walk across town to the Pico-Robertson area to visit friends or participate in a youth group. We'd meet at my house on Gardner and find our way to Wilshire and San Vicente, where Schumacher begins. Then we'd take Schumacher all the way to Olympic. It was a pleasant walk on a quiet, tree-lined street with beautifully landscaped lawns and little automobile traffic. And no telephone poles or electric wires—Carthay Circle was planned with underground utilities. And because Schumacher is angled, it cut off time and distance from our trek.

I drove up Schumacher slowly, looking for the house I'd read about in the police report, but the homeowner must have repaired the damage, because I saw no evidence of vandalism. On Santa Ynez I turned left and parked in front of the yellow Spanish Colonial one-story that belonged to Vivian Banning, Roberta Linney's sister and Maggie's aunt.

From what I remembered of Roberta from her wedding photo and a few other snapshots, I saw little resemblance between her and the tall, zaftig woman with Lucille Ball wavy red hair who opened the door. A wide purple headband, low on her forehead, kept the hair in check.

"Charlene is a sweetheart," Vivian told me when we were seated on a black leather sofa in her wood-paneled den. "I'm glad Roberta had her for a friend."

"She told me she advised Maggie to come talk to you," I said. "Did Maggie come?"

Vivian's blue eyes filled with tears. She blotted them with a tissue. "That poor thing. I hadn't seen her in twenty years. Can you believe it? We lived less than two miles apart, but it could have been two hundred. That son of a bitch didn't want me in my niece's life. He didn't even let her invite me to her wedding!" The tears started again.

There was no subtlety about Vivian. "Why?"

She thrust out her chin. "Because I told him I knew he killed Roberta. He said, 'Go ahead and prove it, you crazy bitch.' He knew I couldn't. She was taking so much pain medication, poor baby, and she told people she wanted out."

"Is it possible she *did* want to end it?" I asked, realizing I was risking the woman's wrath. "Maybe she asked him to end her pain."

Vivian snorted. "Did you ever meet my brother-in-law? He didn't have a compassionate bone in his scrawny body. Charlene phoned to tell me he'd died in a fire. I said, 'Well, it's a taste of what he'll be getting for eternity.' I was considering going to the funeral just so I could spit on his ugly face, but I figured it was closed casket. Were there a lot of people?"

I nodded. I'd been here minutes and felt drained. Her fury was like a tornado, leveling everything in its path.

"You should have seen him at Roberta's funeral. He played the grieving widower to the hilt. But he didn't fool me. I told him I hoped he never had a happy moment and rotted in hell for what he did to my sister."

"Why would he kill her?"

"She was a burden. He had plans for Maggie, and the cancer was interfering with them. He as much as said that to Roberta."

I don't know if I looked as shocked as I felt. "He said that?"

"Well, not exactly," Vivian admitted. "Maggie was fourteen. Oscar kept telling Roberta how the girl was on the verge of stardom, how sad it was she'd be missing out on all the music competitions across the country, blah, blah, blah. Then he'd say, 'Maggie wants to be here with you. She doesn't want you to feel guilty.' So of course, Roberta did. Between that and the god-awful pain and the little hints Oscar dropped about how much money he was spending on the caregiver, and how expensive Maggie's lessons were, and the trips—well, it's a wonder she didn't end things sooner. But she died just in time." Vivian clamped her lips together.

"What do you mean?"

"Maggie was practicing for a young concert artists competition. The winner was going to play at Carnegie. The competition was in March." Vivian paused dramatically. "Roberta died in January. Two weeks after that Oscar bought Maggie a grand piano."

"With Roberta's money?"

Vivian rolled her eyes. "Well, it wasn't his. Last I heard teachers aren't raking it in. And he wasn't chair then. He was an instructor. Roberta's money paid for their house, too."

Was this what Linney had meant when he'd said he'd done it for the best? "You said your sister ended it. So you think she killed herself?"

"Either she took the pills because he talked her into it, or he slipped them into a drink. I think he did it. I told all this to the police, Molly. I know they talked to Oscar. That's why he told me I could never see Maggie again. And they talked to Roberta's doctor."

"Elbogen." I saw the surprise in Vivian's eyes. "Maggie went to see him before she came to you," I explained. "What did he tell them?"

"That Roberta accidentally overdosed on the pain medication. He told me the same thing. He said that I was looking for trouble, that if I loved Maggie I'd leave it alone. So I did."

No wonder Elbogen panicked when I asked him about Maggie's appointment. He'd signed her mother's death certificate and may have covered up a suicide or murder. If that came out, he would be in serious trouble. He could lose his license. And if the police proved he suspected all along that Linney had killed his wife? Was that accessory after the fact? And where would that leave him?

Elbogen knew where I lived, I realized with some unease. My address and phone number were on the check I'd used to pay for the "consultation."

"Did Maggie say who raised her suspicions about her father?" I asked.

Vivian shook her magnificent head of hair. "I asked her if it was Hank, but she wouldn't say."

That had been my guess, too.

"My heart broke seeing her," Vivian said. "She couldn't stop crying about Roberta. And then she was furious. About what Oscar had done to her mother, to her marriage. She'd been planning to divorce Hank because she believed he was abusing Oscar and stealing his money."

So *that* was the "big mistake" she'd almost made. But I was confused. Hank *had* embezzled from Linney.

Vivian sighed. "The sad thing was, she'd already told him she was seeing a lawyer. He didn't take it well. Then she disappeared. So I don't know if she got a chance to tell him she wasn't leaving him after all."

I wondered if she had. "Did Maggie say anything else?"

"She was going to have it out with Oscar." Vivian looked troubled. "I guess Elbogen was right. I should have left things alone."

I stared at her. "You think Linney killed his own daughter?"

"I don't know." Vivian's eyes were filled with anguish. "I just don't know."

I spent a few hours collecting data at the police stations I'd missed yesterday. Wilshire was last. Hernandez wasn't in, but Porter was surprisingly pleasant, so I asked him if they'd found any prints on the actual tape.

"None," he said. "And we're still waiting to hear from downtown about the entry in the planner."

"I think I know what it is," I said, and told him.

Porter wrote that down. "You remembered, huh? See, it's all here." He tapped his head. "You just have to let it come to you."

I could have told him the truth, but why disappoint the man? "I think the *M* is for Roger Modine. He was there that night to drop off papers, but that doesn't mean he killed Margaret." Much as I disliked Modine, I had to play fair. "Maybe he didn't want to be grilled by the police."

"Steaks are grilled," Porter said.

On the way home I stopped at Linney's bank. At first the manager refused to acknowledge that Linney had banked with them, but when I assured him I hadn't come to inquire about the old man's accounts, he relented and after canvassing the tellers, he found one who had often dealt with Linney.

"He hasn't been here in months, but I don't remember seeing anyone with him," the young woman told me. "I guess he took a cab, 'cause he didn't look like he could drive. Although once or twice he said could I hurry 'cause someone was waiting for him outside."

So I really didn't learn anything I hadn't already known. And I still hadn't heard from Tiler. I left another message, and this time I said it was important.

Two exclamation points told me maybe it was.

CHAPTER FORTY-NINE

I DON'T KNOW WHAT WAS MORE CLUTTERED, MY HEAD OR my desk. I pushed stacks of papers aside, took a blank sheet, wrote down what I knew, what I didn't.

I knew from the housekeeper that Linney was enraged when he heard Ochs's message about Golden Vista. I knew that Vivian told Maggie he was responsible for her mother's death. I knew that Charlene heard Maggie confronting her father and heard Linney threaten to kill her.

The question was, *did* he? Elbogen had said that too much dopamine can create psychotic symptoms, including paranoia, and that Alzheimer's patients may become physically violent. According to Hank, Linney had overdosed on Mirapex once. Had Ochs's message, combined with Linney's mental and pharmacological condition, triggered a violent episode? Had he seen his own daughter as his enemy?

His fingerprints were on Maggie's phone receiver. Tim Bolt had heard Maggie scream, "Stop, you're hurting me!" and then, "Daddy!" Maybe he'd heard her scream, "Stop. You're hurting me, Daddy!"

I closed my eyes and pictured Linney coming into Maggie's room. He's yelling at her, out of control. She picks up the phone to call for help, but he wrestles it away and lets it drop. Maybe he puts his hands around her neck before he shoves her hard against the desk. She hits her head and slides down.

And then what? When he realizes that she's not moving, that she's dead, whom does he phone?

Who gets rid of the body?

But if Linney killed Margaret, where did Modine fit in, and the altered entry? And what about Reston, who withdrew almost $400,000 from Linney's account, who believed his wife was leaving him? Had he discovered that Linney killed Maggie? Had he exacted revenge and solved his cash flow problem at the same time?

There were other things I didn't know:

Who was behind all the HARP vandalisms?

Why was Ned Vaughan so nervous?

Who had taken Margaret's planner and returned it?

Who was behind Skoll Investment?

Who had told Maggie that Linney had killed her mother?

Most important, where was Margaret Linney Reston?

You hear about bodies being found all the time in ravines or in the mountains, in the ocean. Hernandez had told me they'd done a thorough search, but L.A. is a big city, and there's no shortage of places to hide a body. The Washington, D.C., police didn't find Chandra Levy until long after she disappeared. Laci Peterson and her fetus were recovered from a watery grave four months after she was seen walking her dog on Christmas Eve.

I remember watching a newscast not long ago about Ward Weaver, an Oregon City man who allegedly buried two young girls right on his property, and no one knew until he led police to them. The remains of one girl were found in a shed. The remains of the other girl were discovered days later in a barrel under a freshly poured cement slab. I couldn't begin to imagine the grief of those girls' parents, but I suppose they'd rather know than wonder.

Maybe I should go back to Adriana Caselotti's well, drop in a few coins, and wish for some answers.

I looked through my stacks of papers. *Crime Sheet* data. Notes on everyone I'd interviewed about Linney and Margaret. More notes for my L.A. *Times* article. All the HARP material, all the vandalisms that had intrigued me in the first place. Highland, Larchmont, Arden, McCadden, Hudson, Schumacher . . . Pumpkins, eggs, shattered windows, damaged driveways and gates. Lemons.

A damaged brick patio on an elevated concrete slab.

But the patio had been vandalized a few weeks ago, not five months ago.

I looked at my notes. "The homeowners cut down the tree and built the patio practically overnight."

I reached my dad on his cell.

"What's up, sweetie?" he asked. "Everything okay?"

"Everything's fine." I could hear sawing in the background. "Is there a way to find out when a job involving concrete was done?"

"The concrete batch plants keep computerized logs, Molly. The name of the driver, time loaded, time out on road, weight of load, volume of load, water added to mixture, type of concrete mix and any additives."

More than I needed to know, but my dad gives thorough answers. We tease him about it. "I'm surprised they need all those details."

"The information's critical depending on the usage. Also,

they need a record in case the test cylinder fails or in the event of a court case due to failure of the structure resulting in a lawsuit or loss of life. What's this for?"

"I'm just checking into something. Can you get a cement truck to pour the stuff at night?"

"*Concrete* truck. And you *place* concrete, Molly. You don't pour it. In L.A. you can get it delivered twenty-four/seven. Of course, it might cost you more, but if you're in a rush, the extra money might be worth it."

And maybe someone had been in a rush. "If you were building a patio, Dad, how deep would you dig a trench under the concrete?"

"Ground level or elevated?"

I pictured the yard at the back of the Arden house. The two men laying the bricks. "Elevated, about two feet."

"The heavier the load, the more support you want. If I were doing it, I'd dig about six to eight inches and put footings around the perimeter."

"If I give you an address, can you find out for me when a job was done, say five months ago?"

There was a beat of silence. "What's going on, Molly?"

I told him what I was thinking.

"I can check into it, but I won't have an answer today. Maybe tomorrow. Will that do?"

"Sure." I tried not to sound disappointed, but as I said, I'm not a good waiter. I thanked my dad and hung up.

The phone rang. I let the answering machine pick up and heard Hank Reston's drawl.

"I'm sorry about yesterday, Molly. I'd like to talk to you and explain a few things. Call me."

For my Larchmont tour guide, absence hadn't made the heart grow fonder.

"It's you," she said.

At least she'd opened the door. It was almost five o'clock, dark and chilly. I considered asking her if I could come in, but decided not to press my luck.

"I'm *really* sorry to bother you," I said. "I have a few questions about the patio that was vandalized on Arden. The property where they cut down the lemon tree?"

"I've told you everything I know." She closed the door an inch.

"I'm curious about a few details. When did they build the patio, do you remember?"

"When? I'd say about half a year ago. June or July."

There was a huge difference. "Is there a way you could find out exactly?"

She cocked her head. "Why do you need to know all this? Your article already ran in the paper. It was interesting," she added, throwing me a bone.

"Thank you." I take 'em where I get 'em. "I'm thinking of doing a follow-up."

"Well," she said after a moment, "it was the day after the police threatened to arrest those protestors. There was a story in the *Chronicle* with a picture of the tree."

"By any chance do you have a copy of that article?"

"No."

That would have been too easy. I would check the *Chronicle* archives online when I got home.

"But my friend might," she said. "She lives next door to the house with the tree."

"Would you mind asking her?"

"Now?"

This was like pulling splinters with a clothespin. "That would be great." I smiled.

She sighed to show me she was going out of her way. "Well, hold on."

Still no invitation to come in. I hugged my arms against the cold air while I waited. A few minutes later she was back in the doorway.

"The police came on June eleventh," she said. "The homeowners cut down the tree and built the patio the night of the twelfth. Well, except for the concrete. They did that the next morning. Does that help?"

That helped a great deal. What were the odds? I thought. My chest tightened, but I cautioned myself not to rush to conclusions. "You mentioned that they built the patio practically overnight." I'd noticed that when I reread my notes. "What did you mean by that?"

"Just what I said. The police threatened to arrest the protestors, and they finally left. But the homeowners worried that there would be *more* protests and more delays and the job would *never* get done. So they had the contractor cut down the tree the next night and dig the trench. The protestors heard about it. They were outside the house, holding a vigil. It was on local television."

"How deep was it? The trench, I mean."

"I don't know." The look she gave me said she doubted my sanity. "Anyway, around four-thirty in the morning they poured the concrete. Can you imagine waking up to the noise of a concrete mixer at four-thirty in the morning!"

"Not something I'd be happy about," I agreed.

"My friend told them to stop. She finally called the police. They showed up almost an hour later and ticketed the contractor and the driver of the concrete truck and made them wait until seven. That's when the *city* says you can start." Her sniff indicated what she thought about that city regulation.

"I think you said the contractor was very upset when the patio was vandalized a few weeks ago."

She nodded. "He pounded on my friend's door, wanted to

know if she saw who did it. His face was so red she thought he was having a heart attack. But in the end they didn't have to tear up the whole patio. They filled the cracks. They did lose all the brick, and brick's expensive. I don't blame the contractor for being upset, and the homeowners. But they never should have cut down that tree."

I phoned Hernandez and told him what I'd learned.

"So even though the police made Modine stop, by that time he'd already covered up anything that was there."

"Very interesting," Hernandez said. "Unfortunately, your hunch, strong as it is, doesn't give me enough to warrant demolishing the patio and digging under it."

I reined in my impatience. "It's more than a hunch, Detective. Maggie disappeared a little after one on June thirteenth. The concrete was poured hours later."

"It's not enough."

I was incredulous. "What if Margaret Linney's body is there? Don't you want to exhume it?"

"What if it's not? Do you have any idea how expensive it is to rip up a patio, and redo it, which is what the city would have to do after we were done? And I can guarantee you the homeowners wouldn't be happy with the results."

He was right about that. I've seen examples of the city's repair jobs. They aren't featured in *Architectural Digest*.

"And you're assuming that the homeowners would give us permission to do all this," Hernandez continued. "They don't have to, without a search warrant."

"Which you can get."

"Not with what you've told me. I'm sorry, Molly."

Sorry, as Porter had so eloquently told me on Sunday, doesn't mean anything. "So you're not going to do anything?"

"If you had a soil sample that would indicate the presence of human remains, that would be something conclusive that I could take to my captain."

"If I'm right, the body is under a concrete slab, so I can't very well get a soil sample. So you can't do *anything*?" I repeated.

"Not unless you can convince the homeowners to dig up their patio, or pay someone else to do it."

"Someone like who?"

"I have no idea. But it won't be the police or the city."

So I phoned Hank Reston.

CHAPTER FIFTY

*Wednesday, November 19. 9:12 A.M. 100 block of South Or-
lando Avenue. A man and a woman were arguing when he told
her, "The next time you call the police, you will be dead before
they get here." The suspect is described as a 50-year-old Asian
man standing 5 feet 7 inches tall and weighing 175 pounds, with
black hair and brown eyes. (Wilshire)*

I COULD HEAR THE JACKHAMMERS FROM HALFWAY DOWN
the block.

It was a beautiful November day with the weather in the low
seventies. Sprinklers shooting graceful arcs of water anointed me
as I walked to the Arden house. I recognized the dark maroon
Chevy Hernandez and Porter had parked in front of my apart-

ment, and Connors's gray Cutlass. There was a Dumpster in the driveway, and a truck. Sunrise Construction. I wondered if Reston had told Modine.

He'd been happy to hear from me. Or so he'd said.

"It's about Linney's home equity line of credit," he told me. "Roger and I were having problems with some of our properties in HARP areas, as you know. We needed cash to tide us over until we sold two of the properties. So I borrowed the money from Linney's account, fully intending to pay it back, of course. But it's not something I wanted to tell you or the police."

"I can imagine," I said.

"Technically, the house belonged to Maggie and me, Molly." He was defensive now. "Linney signed the Grant Deed to Maggie, and she and I had reciprocal powers of attorney. So there was nothing wrong in my borrowing the money. Anyway, I could tell you thought something wasn't kosher, and I didn't want you to get the wrong idea. That's why I'm telling you all this now."

And because the police will find out, if they haven't already. "What about Ned Vaughan? Why is he so nervous about Modine? And don't tell me it's about the survey."

Reston didn't answer right away. "It *is* about the survey."

I exaggerated a sigh. "If you don't want to—"

"Let me finish. But you can't tell anyone. Agreed?"

"Scout's honor." Since I've never been a scout, I figured it wasn't a real pledge.

"Roger wanted to make sure the survey was anti-HARP. So he asked Ned to help him out, and Ned said he'd try, but in the end the survey was pro-HARP. So Roger felt screwed."

I nodded. "And Ned would do it because . . . ?"

"Roger did him a few favors. You know Ned's been restoring his house, right? Roger got him material at cost, and a couple of times he had some of his guys do some basic stuff. Drywall, electrical wiring, plumbing."

"I still don't see why Ned is so nervous."

"Ned hasn't paid him for the material or the work. He told me he thought Roger was being generous, but Roger says Ned understood that it was . . . well, you know."

"A bribe."

Reston sighed. "So now Roger's threatening to tell the company Ned works for, and maybe the people at USC. I told him he'll make himself look bad, but he said he doesn't care. I've been talking to him, and I think he's calming down. Look, you really can't tell anyone about this. So have I cleared everything up?"

"All except one thing. Why did you change the entries in your wife's planner?"

"Why did I *what?*"

I have to say Reston played dumfounded well. "Erasing the fact that Modine was dropping off HARP papers at the house. Changing HELC into HELP."

There was a moment of silence. "Okay." Reston sighed again. "I didn't want all this stuff to distract you from what's important. Finding Maggie. I don't care about anything else. You can believe that or not."

"I think I may have found her."

You could have covered a football field with the silence.

"What do you mean?" Hank said, his voice choked.

I told him about the lemon tree and the patio and the homeowners' rush to build it. "I may be totally wrong, but I suspect that your wife's body is under that patio. The timing is too coincidental."

"You're saying she's been there all this time?"

I have to say he sounded anguished. "I could be wrong."

"Did you tell the police?" he asked.

"Five minutes ago. But they won't dig up the patio." I repeated what Hernandez had told me. "Maybe you can approach the homeowners and ask them for permission to do it. Of course, you'd have to pay for everything, including rebuilding the patio the way it was."

To be honest, I didn't see how Hank could say no. If he hadn't killed Maggie, he'd jump at the chance to find her and bring resolution to his life. That's what he'd told me he wanted more than anything. If he rejected my suggestion—well, he'd be looking awfully suspicious.

He said yes. Quickly, without a second's hesitation. Either he was innocent, or he was one step ahead of me.

"By the way," I said. "There's one thing I forgot to mention. Your partner, Roger, was the contractor."

I hung up and called Hernandez. I couldn't tell from his voice whether he was amused or annoyed or impressed. Maybe a little of each. I phoned him again early this morning after Reston informed me that the wrecking crew would start at seven. The Arden house owners had been angry when he'd approached them, then reluctant, and finally eager to exhume the body, if there was one.

"I figured you'd want to know," I'd told the detective.

And then I'd called Connors.

The wrought iron fence had been expertly repaired. The jackhammer's *rat-tat-tat-tat-tat* drummed in my ears and grew louder as I walked up the driveway and through the gate to the backyard. Reston was standing on the far side of the patio, which had been stripped of its brick layer. His hands were stuffed into his black Dockers, and his face was as rigid as the patio's concrete slab. Connors, Hernandez, and Porter were across from Reston and had their backs to me. They were all watching the man working the jackhammer and the two other men swinging sledgehammers in a syncopated rhythm that reminded me of figures in a music box.

The place looked like the aftermath of an earthquake. Piles of brick and chunks of concrete filled a wheelbarrow and littered the green lawn, though only a small section of the concrete had been removed.

I walked over to Connors. "Hey," I said.

"Hey." He nodded but didn't take his eyes off the man dancing with the jackhammer.

A half hour passed, then another. The three men took a break, during which they drank water from cups and splashed it over their grimy, sweaty faces. The demolition was going much more slowly than I'd expected. I was thinking how hard it is to break up concrete when there was another stop in the jackhammer's music. A sledgehammer clanked against the slab. The sound reverberated in the air. The man removed another chunk and tossed it onto the wheelbarrow. Then he crouched, his hands on his muscular thighs, and peered into the crack he'd created. He covered his nose with his hand and drew back so quickly he almost lost his balance.

"Jeez!" He stood and backed away.

I didn't think Reston could have been any stiffer, but he was.

Hernandez, dapper in a navy sports jacket and gray slacks, jumped onto the concrete slab. He walked over to where the man had been working the sledgehammer. With his hand cupped around his nose, he crouched and gazed into the crack.

A moment later he stood and brushed off his slacks.

"All right, we're stopping," he said.

A breeze came my way. And then I smelled it, too.

Connors told me it would take a few hours, maybe more, for the city to send equipment and men. I was hungry, so I drove to the Coffee Bean on Larchmont for a sandwich. While I was there I checked my home phone messages.

Gordon Tiler had returned my call and left his number.

I phoned him back, talked to his secretary, and a moment later I was actually on the line with the attorney.

"What's so important?" he asked.

I told him who I was and that I knew Maggie Reston had met with him the day before she'd disappeared. I told him I'd be grateful if he told me why. Of course, he wouldn't.

"Call Joan Eggers," he said. "Maybe she'll talk to you." He gave me a business number and hung up.

The 212 prefix told me she was in Manhattan. Her name sounded familiar and I wondered why. I tried the number and listened to her recording. Her voice sounded familiar, too.

I reached Connors on his cell phone. The equipment hadn't arrived yet. I asked him to let me know when I should return. Then I drove home and worked for a few hours on my *Crime Sheet* column. It was tedious, but it kept my mind off Arden and the smell coming from under the patio.

The title company officer phoned. Reston and Maggie had signed reciprocal powers of attorney on May 29. Two weeks before she disappeared. In less than two weeks from now the title company could have chosen not to honor the paper Maggie had signed. Not that it mattered, now that Reston had taken the house off the market.

It was after four when I returned to Arden. Two black-and-whites and a vehicle marked SID were parked in front. Scientific Investigation Division. No coroner's van, so they hadn't found anything yet.

A uniformed cop was guarding the gate. Most L.A. cops are cute and trim, and he was no exception.

"You can't go back there," he told me.

I said I was with Hernandez and Connors. He had me wait while he checked, then waved me on.

The stench in the yard was stronger. It was putrid, like the spoiled meat I'd found in my parents' freezer that we hadn't known had been broken for days, but worse. It's a smell I've never forgotten. I gagged but kept walking.

There were three more uniformed police. Reston was standing in the same spot, or close to it. His broad face was sunburned. Connors was off in a corner with Porter. Hernandez was talking to a man in a navy sports jacket and tie. From Hernandez's body language I assumed the man was his superior. A captain or lieutenant?

From where I stood I could see an opening six feet wide and eight feet long in what had been the patio. Two men with *SID* lettered on the backs of their jumpsuits were leaning over the cavity, their gloved hands carefully sifting the reddish brown earth as if searching for gold.

Connors saw me and walked over. "You don't look so great. Why don't you go home? I'll call you when we know."

"It's her, isn't it?"

"It's a body. Whose, we don't know. They're taking it real slow, real careful. They don't want to disturb the remains."

An ugly word, *remains.* It conjures up far worse images than *body,* especially if it's someone you know or know about.

I swallowed hard. "How much longer, do you think?"

"You're talking hours. After they remove the body, or what's left of it, SID is going to want to take soil samples for trace evidence. The M.E. will tell them how much and from where."

Night was falling. Someone set up lights that flooded the backyard. An hour later Hernandez made a phone call. All work stopped until a medical examiner and two assistants arrived with a stretcher and a plastic sheet. I asked Connors about the sheet, and he said that's what L.A. coroners use. Body bags are just on TV.

Reston had been sitting cross-legged in that same spot where he'd been standing. He got to his feet when the medical examiner arrived.

The medical examiner conferred with Hernandez and Porter. Photos were taken. There was more, careful sifting on the left side of the newly dug grave.

Another hour passed. I was getting used to the smell. Connors said the signals the olfactory nerve sends to the brain weaken after a while. The men from SID working at the grave had smeared Vicks VapoRub on their upper lips.

The outline of a shape was forming on the right side of the cavity. Next to it the cavity was about six inches lower. That's where they laid the plastic sheet.

Men with gloved hands crouched on all sides of the cavity. They started lifting the mound.

"Hold it, hold it!" the medical examiner called. He was a short, wiry man with jet-black hair and was waving his arms like a conductor. A minute or so later he said, "Ready? On my count of three. And very, very slowly. We're in no rush."

Connors had walked over to me. "You don't want to see this." He put his hands on my shoulders and turned me around, away from the cavity.

I felt like Lot's wife. She'd been transformed into a pillar of salt when she disobeyed God and turned her head to see what had happened to Sodom.

"Maaaaggieeeee!"

The howl curdled my soul. I turned my head, just for a second. But it was Hank Reston who had been turned into stone, not I.

CHAPTER FIFTY-ONE

RESTON HAD IDENTIFIED THE WEDDING RING THEY FOUND on the skeletal hand.

I learned this from Porter when I phoned the station at nine o'clock. I'd been sitting in my apartment, staring at my computer screen for hours, too numb to do anything, even think.

"Feeling pretty good about yourself, are you?" Porter said.

"No." I was too tired to come up with a witty rejoinder. "Did you arrest Modine?"

"We're holding him. We talked to him before his lawyer showed. He says the whole world knew about the late-night tree cutting and digging. It was on TV. Anyone who saw the news-cast could've taken the body to the site, dug a grave inside the trench, buried the body, and covered it. He says he started pouring cement at five the next morning, so he wouldn't have noticed anything unless it was staring him in the face."

I had to admit that was true. It also gave Modine an out, maybe one he'd counted on. "Do you believe him?"

"Verdict's still out. Here's a little something, because you've been such a big help. Not for publication yet. They found a match for a set of prints from the can of paint thinner. Guess who the proud owner is?"

"Roger Modine."

"Close, but no cigar. One of his workers. The guy had a rap sheet, so they had his prints on file. Sometimes you get a break."

I frowned. "You think Modine had a worker torch the Fuller house? Why would he be so stupid?"

"Not the worker. He has an airtight alibi. He was our guest that Friday, from around five till Saturday morning. DUI. Lucky, when you think about it."

Very. "So you think Modine torched the house?" Maybe he wanted to help out his partner and rid him of a house that wasn't selling. Maybe he didn't know Linney was inside. Maybe Reston did.

"Not necessarily," Porter said. "Anybody could have lifted a can of paint thinner from one of Modine's construction sites. His signs are up all over the area."

I wanted to take a long bath. Instead I drove to Vivian's. I didn't know if there had been anything on the news about the discovery of Maggie's body, but in case there hadn't, I wanted to tell her. She cried a little and hugged me and thanked me for coming.

I went back to The Dungeon. I was becoming an expert on ducking the vines, although I can't say I liked them any better.

Charlene looked somber when she opened the door, so I figured she'd heard. We sat in the parlor, and Charlene insisted on serving tea. I told her I'd just come from telling Vivian.

"Poor Vivian. Poor, poor Hank." Charlene sighed. "He must be devastated. And Tim. They just showed it on the television news, so I'm sure he's heard. This will be terribly hard on him. Someone should be with him."

"I know he was close to the family. He was sobbing at Professor Linney's funeral."

Charlene nodded. "He was closer to Oscar than to his own father, Roberta said." She frowned. "Come to think of it, I haven't seen him since Sunday. He's usually in his yard. He loves to garden." She paused. "His car is in the driveway, though. I hope he's all right."

"Why wouldn't he be all right?"

She hesitated. "He had a breakdown once. Maggie told me about it."

To be honest, I wasn't surprised. I'd sensed there was something off about Tim Bolt, but I hadn't been able to put my finger on it. I said that to Charlene.

She nodded. "He's a little intense and he tends to get emotional. That's why Maggie was worried about telling him she was getting married."

"Why would she be worried?" I took a sip of tea.

"They were childhood sweethearts. They even had a mock wedding ceremony when they were twelve. Tim wove two rings out of blades of grass." Charlene smiled.

I nodded. Tim had said something about having a childhood sweetheart.

"Roberta thought it was sweet," Charlene said. "She was happy that Maggie had a life away from the piano. Well, Maggie outgrew him, but Tim was jealous if she went out with other boys. He followed her around. He punched a boy once because he thought the boy was bothering Maggie, and he threatened to kill himself if Maggie didn't promise to marry him. That's when he went away for a while. When he came back, he was all better, thank goodness."

"Thank goodness." For a moment, I'd entertained some crazy thoughts. "And then he met Peggy, and they lived happily ever after." I smiled.

Charlene looked puzzled. "Who?"

"Peggy? His wife?"

Charlene frowned. "I don't think he's married, dear. In fact, I think he was hoping all these years that Maggie would come back to him. But Hank came into the picture."

"He has a wife." I stared at Charlene. I had a funny sensation in my chest. "He told me she hasn't been feeling well."

"Well, that's very, very odd. I don't know why he'd say that. I haven't left my house in years, but as I said, I can see into his yard, and sometimes into his windows. Not that I snoop." She blushed. "I've never seen a woman around there. Well, except Maggie."

CHAPTER FIFTY-TWO

"We have to stop meeting like this," Connors said.

I have his home number and had phoned him from my car when I couldn't reach Hernandez or Porter.

"So the guy's missing a few screws," Connors had said after I'd explained my concerns, but he'd told me to wait, don't do anything, he'd be right there.

"Did you check to see if he's in there?" Connors asked now. We were standing on the sidewalk, between Linney's house and Bolt's. Bolt's tan Volvo was in the driveway.

I shook my head. "You said not to. I've been trying his phone, but he's not answering. And his back window shades are all down." Charlene had taken me up to the third-story room and we'd looked out her window.

"Very suspicious. Remind me never to do that."

"He had a breakdown years ago, Andy," I said, impatient. "Maybe Linney's death sent him back down that dark road. And then when he heard that they found Maggie's body . . ." I'd heard it on the radio several times.

"So you think he killed himself?"

"He's obsessed with Maggie. He discouraged people from buying her house. He's the Realtor, by the way. I thought he was being particular since he lives next door. I thought he was a bigot. But I just talked to Reston. He followed up with several potential buyers. Tim talked every one of them out of making an offer. And 'Peggy' is just another variation of 'Margaret.' Peggy, Maggie."

Connors stared at Bolt's house. "Stephen King territory, huh? I'll go see if he's there. Don't even think about coming with me."

I sat in my car while Connors strode up the walk to the front door. I couldn't see what he was doing, but I assume he rang the bell.

A moment later the door opened, and I could see Tim Bolt in the doorway. He said something to Connors and shut the door.

I got out of my car and met Connors on the sidewalk.

"I'm really, really sorry," I said. "I was worried about him. What did you tell him?"

"That you thought he'd killed himself."

I stared at Connors. "You didn't."

"'Course not." He flashed a tired smile. "I told him somebody reported a mugging in the area and asked if he'd seen anything." Connors ran a hand through his hair. "Go home, Molly. Get some sleep. That's what I'm going to do."

I got back into my car and watched Connors drive off. I slid my key into the ignition and was about to turn it on when I heard the click of a gate. Looking up, I saw Tim walking along the side of his Volvo. He was holding a large white plastic bag in one hand.

It was dark and I didn't think he could see me, but I crouched down anyway.

He cut across the lawn and walked up to Linney's front door. The door opened, and he disappeared inside.

A few minutes later I saw the light go on in Maggie Linney's upstairs bedroom.

I left my car and walked up his driveway. I released the latch on the wrought iron gate and made sure it didn't click shut.

I told myself that if the side door was locked, I'd go back to my car and drive home.

It was unlocked.

Five minutes, I told myself. Maybe Charlene was wrong. Maybe Peggy Bolt was lying in her bed, resting from whatever ailed her.

The light was on in the kitchen. I walked through it to the center hall. From there I could see into the living room, dark except for the candles on the fireplace mantel, their ghostly shadows flickering on the cream walls.

I stepped inside the room and caught my breath.

The photos I'd seen of Bolt and "Peggy," his childhood sweetheart, had been edged in black ribbon. So had the colorful oil painting of the woman I now recognized as Margaret Linney.

Music was coming from above—no words, just a melody played on a piano. My heart pounded in my ears as I climbed the stairs to the landing and followed the music to a room at the back of the house.

The light was on and I stepped inside. I took in the mahogany four-poster queen-size bed covered with a scallop-edged, white matelassé spread. My mouth opened, but I couldn't make a sound.

It was Maggie's room. The pale mauve walls, the off-white trim and hardwood floors. It was her bed, her desk, her armoire. The needlepoint seat on the desk chair had the same forest motif.

Off the bedroom was a dressing room. It was identical to Maggie's, but reversed. A wardrobe on the right, a vanity table and mirror on the left. Lipsticks lined up like soldiers circled a mother-of-pearl comb and brush.

A mirror.

I sniffed the air. Lavender and jasmine.

I was shaking. I ran down the stairs and out the side door and slammed my thigh into the Volvo as I hurried to my car.

The light was still on in the Fuller house when I drove away.

CHAPTER FIFTY-THREE

Thursday, November 20. 10:24 A.M. 600 block of Masselin Avenue. A man called a woman on an apartment building's intercom, screaming her name and demanding she let him in, then hung up after she refused. (Wilshire)

I DON'T KNOW HOW CONNORS DOES IT, BUT I DON'T think I'll ever get used to seeing a dead body. I'd phoned Zack as soon as I came home, and even though it was late, he came right over and stayed until I lied and told him I'd be okay. I didn't tell him about Tim Bolt's room because I didn't want a lecture about what could have happened, and because I wanted to think things through.

I hadn't slept well, and I had no appetite. I wandered around the apartment, listless, then sat down at the computer. I was seriously behind in compiling my *Crime Sheet* data, which I had to e-mail to my editor Friday morning. Two hours later I had accomplished little and found myself staring at the screen saver, watching the ribbons twirl and change color.

Connors stopped by. I teased him and said I didn't know he was making house calls now. He said he was in the neighborhood, but his blush said otherwise. He's sweet that way.

Over a cup of coffee and chocolate chip cookies I'd filched from my mom, he told me the autopsy on Maggie Reston would take considerable time.

"We're lucky. She was buried under all that concrete, so the decomposition wasn't as advanced. That's why she smelled so bad. But at least the M.E. has tissue to work with, not just skeleton."

I grimaced. "Are there any preliminary findings?"

"You sure you want to hear this?"

I hesitated, then nodded.

"There's trauma to the back of the skull, where she could have hit her head against the desk. And the hyoid bone—that's the small bone in the neck—was broken."

I pictured hands around Maggie's neck, squeezing. I felt nauseated. "So she was strangled?" Though my brush with death is four months old, I have difficulty saying the word.

"The M.E. can't say for sure. You have to factor in the weight of the concrete. That could have caused the fractures. Modine claims he doesn't know anything about the body being under the patio, that the tree cutting and stuff was on TV, but they're holding him."

I nodded. "Porter told me. How long can they hold him?"

"Not a problem. They got him to cop to the vandalisms and the dead bird. They told him they had a witness."

That was a surprise. "Who?"

"No one. We're allowed to lie. It's why I took the job."

Connors smiled. "Modine says he was frustrated with HARP because he was losing jobs and having to redo work. The patio was the last straw. He wanted to discourage the Harpies from taking over Hancock Park. We may not have him for the murders yet, but Mr. Modine isn't going anywhere for a while."

At least that puzzle was solved. "What does he have to say about the fact that he was at Maggie's house the night she disappeared, and that he tried to hide it?"

"He was scared. He figured we'd think he killed her. He says Reston torched the Fuller house. Reston was complaining he'd never sell it because of its history, and there was going to be a problem with the title company. He claims Reston said he wished the place would burn down so he could collect the insurance money and rebuild. Reston says Modine is lying. Big surprise."

"Hernandez spoke to Reston?"

"They're talking to him now. My money's on Reston. So is Rico's. It seems he withdrew over a third of a million dollars from Linney's account." He cocked his head. "You don't seem surprised."

I told him what I'd learned. Then I brought up Tim Bolt. "I really think there's something off about him, Andy. I think you should persuade Hernandez to check him out."

"You thought he killed himself, Molly. He looked very much alive to me."

"I think he could be involved with Linney's murder."

"Based on what? That his wife's name is Peggy?"

"There *is* no wife."

Connors snorted. "According to this woman who hasn't stepped out of her house in twenty years or more. Have you considered that *she's* missing a *bolt?*"

"Very funny. And, yes, I did consider it." I hesitated. "That's why I went into Bolt's house last night, after you left. To check it out. There's no wife, Andy."

Connors stared at me. He opened his mouth, then closed it. "If you thought he was a murderer, Molly, why the hell would you *do* something dumb like that?"

"I didn't think so at the time." I leaned forward. "Andy, you have to *see* his place. He had about twenty candles on the fireplace mantel around pictures of him with Maggie. He trimmed them in black ribbon."

"So he's sad that she died."

"He duplicated Maggie's bedroom. Every detail." I described what I'd seen and watched the expression on Connors's face change from skepticism to concern.

For a while he just sat there, drinking his coffee, his long legs stretched under the table.

"So what are you thinking?" he finally said. "That Bolt killed Maggie and Linney?"

"Maybe not. Maybe Linney killed Maggie by accident, and called Tim to help him get rid of the body."

Connors's frown said he wasn't buying it.

"Linney was like a father to him, Andy. He was ill. Bolt probably didn't want to see him in jail for the rest of his life, or in an institution."

"Where he belonged. So why would Bolt kill Linney?"

The whys had been my last thought before I finally fell asleep, and my first on awaking. "Linney was always babbling about Margaret. He told Walter Fennel he dreamed he heard her scream. Maybe he was remembering more. Maybe Bolt was nervous that someone would start listening, and tell the police. I was snooping around. I think he knows where I live, by the way." I told Connors about Bolt's comment. "So maybe he's the one who vandalized my car and tried to get into my apartment to see what I knew."

Connors chewed a cookie while he thought that over. Then he shook his head. "The guy was obsessed with her, Molly. Why would he help the man who killed her?"

That was a good question. I broke a cookie into crumbs while I brooded about it.

"I'll run it by Rico," Connors said. He pushed himself away from the table. "You have more of those?" He pointed to the plate of cookies.

I put a handful in a bag and walked him to the door.

I worked for an hour on my column, then turned on the TV and switched channels until I found local news. The CEO of a major telecommunications company had been arrested for fraud. An AMBER alert had been issued for a seven-year-old girl who had disappeared with her nanny. I was about to switch to another channel when I heard the silver-haired male anchor say "Reston."

The screen showed the scene of the digging.

". . . update on the body that was discovered yesterday in Hancock Park. Although the police have not identified any suspects, they are talking to Roger Modine, the contractor who built the patio under which Margaret Reston was buried five months ago. Police are also talking to Margaret Reston's husband."

I listened another minute, then shut off the TV. Zack had phoned and asked me to join him for lunch. I was fishing through my purse for a lipstick when I came across the small piece of paper with Joan Eggers's phone number.

Where had I seen that name?

I checked my notes and ten minutes later I found it: She was one of the people who had phoned Oscar Linney the day before he died.

I was running late for lunch, but I placed the call.

"Joan Eggers's office," a woman said. "Megan Hanley speaking."

I introduced myself. "Ms. Eggers made a phone call a few weeks ago to an Oscar Linney. I wanted to talk to her about it."

"She's in a meeting right now. If you give me your number, I'll have her return your call when she's done."

I gave her my cell number. "What kind of—"

I was talking to a dial tone. I hung up, grabbed my purse, and drove to the restaurant on Pico and Beverwil.

Zack was there when I arrived, fifteen minutes late and breathless. He's more punctual than I am, but if he was annoyed, he didn't show it. We ordered soup and sandwiches, and though I told myself I wouldn't bring up the case, of course, I did. I repeated what Connors had told me, then told Zack what I'd seen in Tim Bolt's house. I was prepared for a lecture, but it didn't come.

"I'm still wondering whether Linney killed Maggie," I said, and explained. "Connors says Bolt wouldn't have helped him get rid of the body, but maybe he did."

Zack looked thoughtful. "There's a discussion in the Gemara about a thief who steals into a person's house." The Gemara is the collection of commentaries on the Mishna, the oral law. Together they form the Talmud. "The commentaries ask whether the homeowner can kill him. The answer is yes. The thief *knows* that the homeowner is allowed to kill him to protect his property, yet despite that, he sneaks in. So we assume he's prepared to kill the homeowner."

"Zack, this isn't about—"

"But if the thief is the homeowner's father? In *that* case the homeowner *can't* kill to protect his property. Because the earlier logic doesn't apply. The father may have sneaked into the house to steal, but a father has mercy on his child. He hasn't come prepared to kill him."

I thought about that. "So you're saying that as angry as Linney was, he wouldn't have killed Maggie."

Zack nodded. "Unless, of course, at that moment, he viewed her as his enemy, not his daughter."

362

CHAPTER FIFTY-FOUR

AT HOME I PHONED CONNORS AND LEARNED THAT HE'D relayed my suspicions about Bolt to Hernandez.

"So what did he *say,* Andy?"

"He's looking into it."

I was restless, edgy. I found myself walking from room to room. I kept seeing the demolished patio, the gloved hands about to slide Maggie Reston's remains from her grave to the plastic sheet. I kept seeing the room Tim Bolt had created. I heard the music. I smelled the lavender and jasmine.

I phoned Connors back.

"Maybe *Tim* killed Maggie," I said when he came on the line.

"The woman he loved?"

"He didn't mean to do it. Maggie and her father had a huge quarrel that day. The housekeeper heard it. So did Mrs. Coulter. What if Tim heard it, too? Suppose he went over to 'save' her from her father, or from her marriage."

"Come on, Molly."

"Charlene Coulter told me he punched a boy who was bothering Maggie. And he threatened to kill himself if she didn't marry him. Suppose that night Maggie told him to mind his own business and leave. Maybe he got angry. And Maggie got scared and picked up the phone to call the police. So he pushed her, and she hit her head."

Connors didn't say anything. I took that as a sign that he was thinking.

"How would he get in the house?" he finally asked. "Scratch that. He was the Realtor. He probably had a key. So why kill Linney?"

"Maybe Linney *did* hear things that night, but everyone thought it was his Alzheimer's. And then Bolt worried that someone would pay attention. So he lured Linney to the house with the spliced tape and canceled the caregiver."

"Where'd he get the tape?"

"He was obsessed with Maggie, Andy. He probably kept tapes just so he could hear her voice."

Connors sighed. "I'll phone Rico. Maybe he'll pay a visit to Bolt."

I hung up and turned on the TV. I was searching for a news channel when my cell phone rang. By the time I dug it out of my purse, the ringing had stopped.

The blinking envelope on my cell phone told me I had one new message. I accessed my voice mail and learned that Joan Eggers had returned my call.

I phoned her, and this time she answered herself. I told her what I'd told the assistant.

"To be honest, I'm disappointed," Joan Eggers said. "I assumed Professor Linney had decided to drop the matter."

So she didn't know that Linney was dead. "Actually, Gordon Tiler suggested that I talk to you. He's an intellectual properties attorney."

"I know Gordon. Look, Miss Blume." Her voice had taken on a steely edge. "I'll tell you what I told Professor Linney."

The anchor said, "Reston." I glanced at the screen and caught a glimpse of Hank opening the door to his black Mercedes. He was deluged by reporters.

"I'm listening," I told Joan Eggers.

"Professor Linney may have been planning to write a book about architecture in Los Angeles. But a title, two pages of notes, and a few photos isn't the same as a manuscript."

MS as in *manuscript,* I thought. Not multiple sclerosis. *Pb* was *publisher.* For a writer, I'd been incredibly dumb, but to be fair, I'd been looking at everything in Maggie's planner as though it were connected with the construction of the Muirfield house.

"That's what I told the daughter, too," the woman continued. "She said there was a partial manuscript, but she couldn't produce it."

My stomach knotted. "When did she tell you that?"

"When she phoned half a year ago. I thought you knew all this," Joan said, suddenly wary.

"I'm just trying to get all the facts straight."

"The facts are simple, Miss Blume. Our legal department says Professor Linney has no claim whatsoever. We're proceeding with Mr. Vaughan's book."

I was certain I hadn't heard correctly. I grabbed the edge of the table and found my voice. "You're publishing Mr. Vaughan's book? You're serious?"

"We've paid him a six-figure advance. I'd call that serious."

"And that was in June?"

"No, in *April*." She spoke with exaggerated patience, as if I had limited intelligence. "If Professor Linney continues to insist that he's entitled to some part of the advance we gave Mr. Vaughan, that's between him and Mr. Vaughan. I told *that* to the daughter, too."

My hand was shaking when I hung up.

Vaughan had received an advance months ago on a book he told me he'd recently agreed to take over—reluctantly. Vaughan, who was at the Fuller house all the time and could have used Linney's key to get inside. Vaughan, who was probably not making a mint teaching architecture but was spending thousands of dollars restoring his dream house in Angelino Heights and, come to think of it, had probably been pissed as hell that he hadn't been given the plum job of designing his *best friend's* dream house.

I reached for the receiver to call Hernandez when my phone rang. I jerked my hand back, then picked up the receiver.

"Molly?" It was Charlene. "I don't know if I should call someone. I'm really worried about Tim."

I had no time for Tim Bolt. "Charlene—"

"He has a gun, Molly. I saw him through the window. He was sitting in his yard, on a swing. I think he was crying. The gun was on his lap. I'm afraid for him, Molly."

My heart skipped a beat. "You're sure it was a gun?"

"Yes. I thought he was going to hurt himself, but then he got into his car with the gun and drove off. Where do you think he could have gone?"

My head was spinning. "I don't know. I'll call the police."

The TV anchor was still talking about Maggie Reston. "Authorities are declining to discuss the case, but they have confirmed that Mr. Reston is not a suspect at this time. In other news . . ."

Chapter Fifty-five

I PHONED RESTON, BUT HE WASN'T HOME. EITHER THAT, or he wasn't answering. I didn't want to think about that.

I contacted Wilshire. Neither Porter nor Hernandez was in. I told the dispatcher that Tim Bolt had a gun and that I feared he was going to kill Hank Reston, and why. I gave her the address to the Muirfield house.

"You need to calm down, ma'am," the woman said. "Are you inside the Muirfield residence, ma'am?"

"No, I'm not. Bolt is headed there right now. I'm sure of it. Please *hurry.*"

"Where are you now, ma'am?" she asked in a maddeningly soothing voice that told me she didn't know how much credence to place in what I was telling her.

"I'm at home. *Please,* send units to the address. If you don't believe me, find Detective Hernandez or Porter and tell them what I just told you. My name is Molly Blume," I repeated.

"I'll do that, ma'am. Give me a number where the detective can reach you."

I gave her my cell number. "Are you going to send the units?"

"We'll take care of it, ma'am."

I hung up and ran to my car.

Eleven minutes later I was on Third Street, waiting to turn onto Muirfeld. I twisted my head to the left and saw the Volvo parked just off Third. My heart thumped. I looked up the block. Reston's black Mercedes was in the driveway.

There was no black-and-white.

The queue of cars driving past me seemed endless. I looked up Muirfield again. The Mercedes's door opened and Reston stepped out. He headed toward his front door.

I moved my foot to the accelerator and, swerving sharply, cut in front of a black Land Cruiser twenty feet away. The driver braked to a sudden stop. The car behind him slammed into the Land Cruiser.

I heard the crash of metal on metal. The driver of the Land Cruiser was yelling an obscenity out his window, but I was barreling up Muirfield.

Reston was nearing his door.

Where the hell was the black-and-white?

I blared my horn. A gardener mowing the velvet lawn looked at me, but Reston paid no attention.

He opened the door.

I pulled up in front of the house and rolled down my window.

"Hank! Don't go in!"

My words were drowned out by the drone of the mower.

Reston stepped inside the house and shut the door behind him.

I phoned Wilshire and talked to the same dispatcher. "Tim Bolt's inside, and Reston just went in!" I told her after I identified myself. "Where's the black-and-white?"

"I spoke with Detective Porter, ma'am. Two units are on their way."

I hung up and punched in Reston's number.

After four rings, the answering machine picked up.

"Tim, this is Molly Blume. I know you're there, Tim. Pick up the phone. Hank didn't kill Maggie. Tim, do you hear me?

"Tim, I'm not lying to you. You would be killing the wrong person. Tim—" The tape cut off.

I pressed REDIAL. I ran out of the car and rang the bell. I pounded on the door.

I was still pounding, screaming Bolt's name, crying, when I heard the shot.

I froze for a few seconds. Then I ran past the handcrafted wrought iron gates to the backyard. I thought I heard a siren in the distance, but it could have been the ringing in my ears.

The entire back of the house was lined with French doors. I ran past the first two sets until I was in front of the living room.

Tim Bolt was standing in the center of the cavernous room.

Hank was slumped against the black marble fireplace. His face was pasty. Blood was streaming between the fingers he held against his chest. Maggie smiled down at him.

I twisted the brass handle and pushed the door open a crack.

"I swear. Didn't. Kill her," Hank said. He was wincing, and I could tell it took great effort for him to speak.

"Liar!" Bolt raised the gun. "She was an angel, and you killed her. You killed the Professor, too. I want you to say it."

"I didn't—"

"Say it!" Bolt's scream echoed in the high-ceilinged room.

He held the gun in his shaking hands and pointed it at Hank's chest.

My heart was racing. I opened the door wider and stepped inside, praying that the sound wouldn't startle Tim and cause him to fire.

"He didn't do it, Tim," I said, making my voice a soft caress. My chest felt as though someone were squeezing the air out of it.

Bolt started at the sound of my voice, but he kept his eyes on Reston. "Get out," he said quietly. "I don't want to have to hurt you."

The sirens were louder now.

"Tim, I know who did it," I said in that same, soft voice. "It was Ned Vaughan."

"You're lying."

"He stole Professor Linney's manuscript, Tim. He stole his money. Maggie found out."

Reston was staring at me, his mouth open.

Bolt kept the gun aimed at Reston's chest. "You're saying that because you don't want me to kill him. But why should he live? He killed Maggie!"

"If you kill him, you'll go to jail and Ned Vaughan will be free. Maggie's killer will be free. Is that what you want, Tim?"

"I don't know what to think!" His face was red, sweaty.

"You loved Maggie, didn't you, Tim? And you want the person who killed her to pay. Hank didn't do it. Ned Vaughan did."

"The Professor said Hank hit him! He said Hank stole his money!"

"Professor Linney was confused, Tim. Ned stole his money. I can show you. I can show you everything."

I heard a loud thump and looked past the living room into the entry. The beautiful front door crashed onto the marble floor. Two uniformed policemen stood in the doorway, their weapons drawn. I held up my hands and prayed they wouldn't think I was crazy.

"Tim, the police are here," I said, a little louder so they could hear me. My legs felt like Jell-O. "You need to put down the gun, okay? They'll shoot you if you don't."

Tim looked confused. "He has to pay. Doesn't he have to pay?"

"Someone will pay," I promised. "Will you put down the gun? Please, Tim. Put down the gun."

Chapter Fifty-six

Sunday, December 28. 12:35 P.M. Corner of Havenhurst Drive and Santa Monica Boulevard. A man who later was taken into custody allegedly forced his way into a woman's apartment through a bedroom patio door, choked her for about a minute, and then placed a knife against her throat. (Hollywood)

HALF AN INCH MORE AND HANK RESTON WOULD HAVE been dead. That's what the doctors told him, and what Connors told me.

Tim Bolt was taken into custody. I have to say the cops were gentle with him. He's under observation in the jail's psych ward. I went to see him a week ago but he isn't allowed visitors yet.

Ned Vaughan was home when Hernandez and Porter

showed up with a search warrant. Porter says Vaughan was more upset with the marks on his floors and the mess he and Hernandez made during their search than the fact that he was charged with two murders. He's probably having nightmares about what will happen to his house, with good reason. The D.A. is looking at the death penalty, and if they don't go for that, murder with arson attached will get Vaughan life.

I don't think Hernandez or Porter was as certain as I was that Vaughan was their man until they found Maggie's jewelry stashed around his house. Well, they found most of it. Vaughan had removed a few diamonds from the bracelet. Why on earth would he keep the stuff, I said to Connors. There's no way he could explain it. But as I said, criminals are often more greedy than intelligent, and I don't think Vaughan thought he'd be caught.

It wasn't just about money, though he was desperate for it. He was drowning in restoration costs, and his Victorian beauty was a mistress that seduced him with the promise of her charms and demanded proof of his love. Linney's canceled checks showed that the two he'd entered in his register for Skoll Investment had been made out to Vaughan, and Vaughan's bank statements showed deposits matching the amounts on those checks. I can hear him saying, "Oscar, we don't need Hank or Maggie involved. It's your money. You're a grown man, not a child. You signed away your house, not your life." I'm guessing the smaller checks, made out to cash, had been for Vaughan, too.

Vaughan claims he knows nothing about those and says Linney loaned him the $43,000 and liked Vaughan's idea of making up Skoll Investment. I said, yeah, sure. I was on the other side of the one-way mirror on the ground floor at Wilshire, listening to Porter and Hernandez take turns interrogating Vaughan, who was smoking up a storm. He hadn't asked for a lawyer yet, which was lucky, because even a rookie would have told him to shut up.

I knew Hernandez would be good. He'd had me squirming in my chair the other day. He had nothing but sympathy in his musical voice, saying he could understand how overwhelmed Vaughan must have felt by the bills, and got Vaughan to admit he'd been worried about losing his house.

Porter surprised me. I was sure he'd be playing bad cop, but he sat across the table from the architect. It must have been rough, he said, having all those money problems when your best friend was building a $6 million home he didn't even ask you to design. Some best friend, huh? It was probably Maggie's fault, Porter said. She was the one who said, honey, take Jeremy Dorn, not your friend Ned. If it hadn't been for her, you wouldn't be sitting here today, huh?

That's when Vaughan erupted. His face turned red, and he was like a volcano that had lain dormant for years and had begun to spew its lava and couldn't stop. Maggie was a self-centered bitch, he said, seething. If it hadn't been for him, she'd never have gotten away from Linney, never have married. And then she chose Dorn! And when Vaughan asked Linney—his mentor, his friend—to intercede, the old man said, "You know I don't lie, Ned, Dorn is a better architect."! So, yes, that's why Ned decided to write the book. Screw the old man. He'd show the world and Linney, who didn't even recommend Ned as acting chair when he retired!

So Maggie found out about the book, Porter said when Vaughan ran out of steam. She's got all that money, her dad's brain is scrambled, and she's harping about the book he can't even write. Go figure, huh?

Vaughan nodded. Maggie had phoned Linney's publisher to tell them she'd be working with her father on the book, and they told her Linney had canceled the project months ago, didn't she know? And anyway, someone else was writing a book about HARP in Los Angeles. She'd phoned around and finally talked to Joan Eggers, who had a signed letter from Linney relinquishing all his rights to the project.

That's when Maggie found out about Skoll Investment. She wanted that money back, and the advance. He mentored you, he treated you like a son, how could you *do* this to him? So that's when Vaughan told her about her wonderful father, how he'd cried about his wife and the nightmares that never stopped because of what he'd done. What nightmares? Ned had asked Linney. Tell me, maybe I can help you.

Maggie didn't believe Ned. And even when she found out it was all true, she said, Go ahead, tell the world, I want everyone to know what he did. But have a check by Friday. That's money he took against the house, my *mother's* house.

Vaughan stopped again. Porter said, So you really had no choice, huh, man? He clucked. She was going to ruin your reputation, you'd be in jail for money the old man lent you. Was that fair? So how did it go down? Where'd you get the key to the Fuller house?

Vaughan had a key, he told Porter. Linney was always losing his, so one time he made an extra and kept it. He tried talking to Maggie that day, but she wouldn't take his calls. He didn't know what to do. He couldn't sleep. So he drove to the house and saw her light on. He let himself in because he knew Maggie wouldn't. He begged her for more time, he couldn't get the money overnight. Use the publisher's advance, she said, but he'd already spent that.

She said she didn't care. She was going to phone the police, right now. He remembered grabbing her hand so she'd drop the receiver. She screamed for Linney, so he put his hand on her mouth, and she took a step backwards and lost her footing, and that's when she fell and hit her head against the desk. When he checked she wasn't breathing. He was terrified. It wasn't just the police. He could explain, he was sure they'd believe him. But Hank would kill him.

So Vaughan decided to make it look like a home invasion and kidnapping. That's why he took the jewelry. He hadn't planned to use it. He found a pair of gloves in the kitchen. He carried Maggie down the stairs and out the back door and put her in the trunk of her car, which he drove to the backyard of the empty house on Arden. He buried her in the newly dug trench and drove her car to a mall. He never meant to kill Maggie. He didn't want to kill Linney, either, but the old man heard her scream, and several times in the past few weeks he'd said, Weren't you there that night, Ned, didn't I hear your voice? So he had no choice, not really. And what kind of life did Linney have with his mind going, and his body, too? And the nightmares about his wife? Ned was doing him a favor, when you thought about it. At least he died with dignity. He was dead before the fire started, he didn't suffer. Ned wouldn't have let that happen.

Porter said, I figure you played a tape with Maggie's voice to get the old man upstairs, huh? Vaughan's smirk was an answer. I have to hand it to you, Ned, Porter said. The tape was clever. How'd you do that? Vaughan's smile deepened. Maggie called me a few times, he said. I kept the tapes and spliced them.

So you planned to lure Linney to the house? Porter asked. That's when Vaughan became still. Except for his eyes. They were darting right and left, searching for a way out. You could see in his eyes that he knew where Porter was going, that Ned had been thinking about killing Linney on the night he murdered Maggie. The jury would have a good time with that.

So how'd you get home if you left Maggie's car in the mall? Porter asked. And what about your car? We checked with all the cab companies, and there's no record of anyone dropping you off at the Fuller house that night.

Vaughan didn't answer.

I'll tell you what I think, Porter said. I think you used the bike we found in your garage. I think you biked to Maggie's, left your bike in the yard. After you killed her, you put it in the trunk, along with her body. And you biked home from the mall.

What do you want to bet we find some trace evidence from Maggie on your bike, huh?

That was when Vaughan asked for a lawyer.

You're probably wondering about the planner. Turns out Tim Bolt took it that morning when Linney had pounded on his door. He'd wanted something of Maggie's to remember her by. He knew he'd done wrong, and he couldn't give it back, not when the police were asking him questions, like what was Maggie doing in your house the day she disappeared? If he gave them the planner, they'd search his house and find the room. But when Linney died, he put it back.

Connors says Tim is convinced that Hank was abusing Linney. I don't think so. I think Hank did the best he could with a difficult man who made it clear he despised him. I think Linney did his best to break up that marriage and almost succeeded. I don't know if he helped his wife die or encouraged her to do it.

I have ambivalent feelings about Linney. He was crabby, egotistical, manipulative, and if you believe Vivian, a murderer. But as much as I detest what he did, I have pity for the old man whose failing mind made him easy prey for Vaughan. And he didn't deserve to be killed, though Vivian would argue otherwise. I told her Linney had been plagued by her sister's death, and I wonder if, now that he's dead, her hatred for him will burn less fiercely over time or burn itself out. Probably not.

I can see Linney hurrying on unsteady legs up those dreaded stairs toward the siren of Margaret's voice. One shaking, bony hand is gripping the banister; the other, his cane. Was Vaughan waiting for him in that bedroom? At what point did joy turn into bewilderment, bewilderment into fear? I'd like to think the Alzheimer's spared Linney the realization of Vaughan's double treachery, but I'm sure he knew. I imagine that in those last moments he was trying to escape not only his protégé turned enemy, but the truth.

A curse is not a telegram, Bubbie G says. It doesn't arrive so fast.

Hank was released from the hospital the Saturday after he was shot. When I visited him the day before that, he told me he wasn't sure what he planned to do with the Muirfield house. He insisted Maggie ripped out that page. She'd told him she loved him. In fact, she'd talked about having a baby, something he'd been wanting for some time. She didn't say a word about Vaughan. She probably didn't know how to tell him the truth about his best friend.

Hank wanted to pay me for my services, and for saving his life. I said no thanks, and anyway, you don't have the money. He had the grace to blush, but insisted the money was technically his. That's between him and the police, though so far they haven't filed charges.

They released Modine. He's going to have to pay for all the damage and put in a few hundred hours of community service. Hank thought Modine had torched the Fuller house, to do him a favor. And Modine suspected Hank, just as he'd told the cops. Modine had bitched about the damn patio to Hank and told him he was placing the concrete that morning.

Mr. Newman got his French door approved, by the way, but Lowenthal is still fighting about his roof. The Hancock Park Harpies got Harrington to push through a moratorium on tear-downs and remodeling, and by the time you read this, HARP will probably be there to stay.

I have mixed feelings about that and historical preservation in general. According to the National Trust, demolitions are reaching epidemic proportions in historic neighborhoods all over the country. In L.A. we've razed a lot of buildings: the Gilmore Bank that made way for The Grove. Rudy Vallee's Pink Palace. Irving Gill's Dodge House. The Peerless Hardware building with a mural painted by Ernesto de la Loza that paid homage to manual workers. The Carthay Circle Theater I told you about.

The verdict's still out on the Ambassador Hotel, but the Shubert Theater is facing the bulldozer. The Capitol Records building on Hollywood, the one that's circular and looks like a stack of records with a stylus on top, is a state historic resource, but other historic structures have been leveled.

There are buildings I want saved, some I don't care about as much. Who am I to judge? Who *should* judge what's historical? Is it fair to infringe on the rights of the individual so that you can pass by an old house and admire it? And what about those you hate?

Last week I baked chocolate chip cookies and took them to Charlene's. We had tea in the living room, and she cooed over the princess-cut diamond engagement ring Zack gave me last Saturday night. It was the second night of Chanukah, and he'd put it in a large yellow plastic dreidel along with Godiva chocolates, so how could I say no?

Charlene had the gardener tame the shrubs. She's thinking about painting the house a light gray, but I said, only if you want to. Come by again soon, she said, and kissed my cheek. I said of course I would. I love Paris.

The Bible talks about a house that has leprosy. It's a stain that comes from slander spoken inside the house, Zack told me, from the misuse of the power of speech. The priest would shut down the house, and after seven days, if the plague persisted and spread, he would order the afflicted stones to be hacked out and thrown outside the city, along with their dust. Sometimes the entire house is malignant. In that case, Zack says, you had to demolish the entire structure and take the debris outside the city.

I thought about that three days ago when I watched a bull-dozer tear down Oscar Linney's dream house.

Hank was on the lawn, looking on as the bulldozer crunched the top left corner of the house. His feet were spread apart, his large hands splayed on his hips. The December sun lit his broad face.

At one point he walked to a truck in the driveway and lifted out a sledgehammer. He took long, slow strides toward the living room and stood there a moment, holding the hammer in his hands, his face tight with concentration. Then he raised the hammer high and swung it into the wall.

Whenever I think of Hank, I see him as he looked that day, and I'm reminded of a poem by E. A. Robinson. "Reuben Bright."

> *Because he was a butcher and thereby*
> *Did earn an honest living (and did right)*
> *I would not have you think that Reuben Bright*
> *Was any more a brute than you or I;*
> *For when they told him that his wife must die,*
> *He stared at them, and shook with grief and fright,*
> *And cried like a great baby half that night,*
> *And made the women cry to see him cry.*
>
> *And after she was dead, and he had paid*
> *The singers and the sexton and the rest,*
> *He packed a lot of things that she had made*
> *Most mournfully away in an old chest*
> *Of hers, and put some chopped-up cedar boughs*
> *In with them, and tore down the slaughter-house.*

Some things you have to do yourself.

BUBBIE G'S CHALLA

2 ounces fresh yeast   1 tablespoon salt
  (4 squares)   ½ cup oil
2 cups warm water   2 eggs plus 1 egg, beaten
¾ cup plus 1 tablespoon   sesame or poppy seeds,
  sugar   optional
8 cups flour

In a medium metal or glass bowl, dissolve the yeast in ½ cup water. Stir in 1 tablespoon sugar. In an aluminum bowl mix the flour, sugar, and salt. Create a well in the center and slowly pour 1½ cups water into the well. Add the oil, 2 eggs, and yeast mixture. Mix wet and dry ingredients with a wooden spoon until you can no longer move the spoon.

Bubbie G kneads the dough by hand until it's smooth and elastic and doesn't stick to the sides of the bowl—about ten minutes. (You can use a mixer with a dough hook for 2–3 minutes, but don't tell.) If the dough is too sticky, knead in small amounts of flour until it's smooth.

Brush the top of the dough with oil, cover with plastic wrap and a towel, and let rise in a warm room for 1 to 1½ hours, until double in size. On a floured board divide the dough into two or three parts. Separate each part into four strands and roll each strand into a thick rope.

Place strands side by side and press tops together. Working from left to right, take the outside strand (#1) and weave over the next strand (#2), then under #3, then over the last (#4). To continue, take strand #2 (now on outside), weave over the next (#3), under #4, and over the last. Proceed until braid is completed. Pinch ends together and place the challa on a baking sheet sprayed with Pam. Brush the top of the challa with beaten egg. If you desire, sprinkle with sesame or poppy seeds.

Repeat braiding and egg glaze with the other dough. Let the loaves rise another hour. Preheat oven to 350 and bake challa for 25–35 minutes until the challa is golden brown and sounds hollow when tapped on the bottom. Cool on wire racks. Makes two to three challot.

If you're ambitious and want a taller challa, e-mail me at www.rochellekrich.com for instructions on making a six-braid version.

Glossary of Hebrew and Yiddish
words and phrases

Az es iz nisht vi ich vill, vill ich vi es iz If it's not as I
want it, I want it as it is. Yiddish proverb.

Baruch Hashem (ba-ruch´ ha-shem´). Thank God. Literally:
Blessed be God.

beitzim (noun, plural, bā´-tzim). Eggs; slang for "balls," meaning gumption. Use with caution!

Birkat hamazon (noun, bir-kat´ ha-ma-zon´). Grace after
meals.

bissele (noun, diminutive, bis´-se-le). A small amount (of), a
little.

bubbie (noun, bub´-bee). Grandmother; also, *bubbeh, babi,
babbi.*

bulvan (noun, bul-van´). An oxlike man; a boorish, coarse,
rude person.

chalesh (verb, cha´-lesh). To faint or swoon. Colloquially,
to crave. Also, *cha´-lesh-ing,* fainting. "I'm chaleshing
for . . ."

challa (noun, chal´-la or chal-la´). Braided loaf of bread. Plural
is *challot* (chal-lot´) or *challas* (chal´-las). See recipe on
page 381.

Chanukah (noun, cha´-nu-kah). Eight-day Festival of Lights in
the Jewish month of Kislev, which usually falls in
December.

chutzpah (noun, chutz´-pah). Audacity; gall.

Der emess iz a kricher (der e´-mess iz a krich´-er). Truth is
a slowpoke. Yiddish proverb.

drash (noun). Sermon.

dreidel (noun, drā´-del). A four-sided top used to play games on Chanukah.

emess (noun, e´-mess). Truth.

Gemara (noun, ge-ma´-ra). Collection of commentaries that, together with the Mishna, the oral law, forms the Talmud.

glezele (noun, diminutive, gle´-ze-le). A small glass.

gut (adjective). Good.

Gut voch A good week. A phrase uttered after the Sabbath ends to wish someone a good week, and the title of a song. In Hebrew, **Shavuah tov.**

HaMavdil (ha-mav´-dil). Literally, "He who separates." A song following the havdalah ceremony.

havdalah (noun, hav-dal´-lah). Separation. The blessing that marks the end of the Sabbath and separates it from the rest of the week.

kenehoreh (ke-ne-hor´-eh). Also, *kenayn-e-horeh* (ke-nain´-e-hor´-eh), a frequently used phrase that is an elision of *keyn ayin horeh* (kān a´-yin ho´-reh). Let there be no evil eye.

kiddush (noun, kid´-dush or kid-dush´). A prayer recited over wine at the beginning of a Sabbath or holiday meal. Also used to refer to refreshments served after synagogue services on the Sabbath or other Jewish holidays.

kneidel (knā´-del). Matzoh ball.

knip (noun or verb). A pinch, or to pinch.

kugel (noun, ku´-gel). A puddinglike dish, usually made of vegetables (like potatoes or onions) or noodles.

L'cha Dodi (l´-cha´ do-di´). Sabbath song, part of Friday night prayer service. Literally, "Come, My Beloved."

Lech lecha (lech le-cha´). Leave for yourself; go away. The opening verse of a portion in Genesis.

mazel (noun, ma´-zel). Luck; often used in a phrase, *mazel tov,* wishing one good luck at a celebration or happy occasion. Alternate spelling: *mazal* (ma–zal´) *tov.*

metziah (noun, me–tzee´–ah). Bargain; literally, "a find."

Mishna (noun, mish´–na). Jewish oral law; together with the Gemara, a collection of commentaries, it forms the Talmud.

mishpacha (noun, mish-pa´-cha or mish-pa-cha´). Family.

nahrishkeit (noun, nah´-rish-keit). Nonsense; silliness.

Nu (interjection). So.

pareve (adjective, pa´-reve). Nondairy.

Shabbat (noun, shab-bat´). Sabbath.

Shabbos (noun, shab´-bes). Sabbath. Also, *Shabbat.*

Shavuah tov (sha-vu´-ah tov). A good week. See **Gut voch,** above.

sheyfele (noun, diminutive, shā´-fele). Little lamb.

Shit arayn (shit a-rine´). A dialectical variation of *shis a'rayn.* Pour (it) in.

shul (noun). Synagogue.

Torah (noun, to´-rah or to-rah´). The Bible; also, the parchment scroll itself.

VaYerah (va-y´-rah). Opening verse of a chapter in Genesis. Literally, "And He appeared."

voch (noun). Week.

yarmulke (noun, yar´-mul-ke). Skullcap; synonym for *kippah.*

zeidie (noun, zā´-die). Grandfather; also, *zeidi, zeide, zeideh, zaydie.*

zemirot (noun, ze-mi-rot´; plural of ze´-mer). Songs usually sung during the Sabbath or holiday meals.